NIGHT
Embrace

NIGHT EMBRACE

Sherrilyn Kenyon

St. Martin's Press   New York

This is a work of fiction. All of the characters, organizations, and events portrayed in this novel are either products of the author's imagination or are used fictitiously.

www.stmartins.com

ISBN 978-0-312-65383-5

First Hardcover Edition: September 2010

10 9 8 7 6 5 4 3 2 1

For my fans who support me and who have given me untold smiles at conferences and booksignings and when I read my e-mails and letters.

To the RBL Romantica and DH posters whose presence is always a source of warmth.

For my family and friends who make my life worthwhile. And for my Kim and Nancy who believe in me and who are willing to give me the opportunity to introduce the world to the people who live in my heart and mind.

Thank you all! I hope each of you has all the blessings and riches you deserve. Hugs!

NIGHT
Embrace

Prologue

The roaring village fires burned high into the night, licking at the dark sky like serpents twining through black velvet. Smoke wafted through the misty darkness, pungent with the scent of death and vengeance.

The sight and smell should bring joy to Talon.

It didn't.

Nothing would ever bring joy to him again.

Nothing.

The bitter agony that welled inside him was crippling. Debilitating. It was more than even he could bear and that thought was almost enough to make him laugh . . .

Or curse.

Aye, he cursed from the excruciating weight of his pain.

One by one, he had lost every human being on earth who had ever meant anything to him.

All of them.

At age seven, he'd been orphaned and left the heavy responsibility of caring for his baby sister. With nowhere to go and unable to provide for the infant himself, he had returned to the clan that had once been led by his mother.

A clan that had banished both his parents before his birth.

His uncle had been in his first year as king when Talon

had forced his way into his hall. The king had grudgingly accepted him and Ceara, but his clan never had.

Not until Talon had forced them to.

They might not have respected his parentage, but Talon had made them respect his sword arm and temper. Respect his willingness to maim or slay any and all who insulted him.

By the time he'd entered manhood, no one dared to mock his birth or impugn his mother's memory or honor.

He had risen through the ranks of warriors and learned all he could about weapons, fighting, and leadership.

In the end, he had been unanimously voted his uncle's successor by the very people who had once mocked him.

As the heir, Talon had stood by his uncle's right side, protecting him relentlessly until an enemy ambush had caught them off guard.

Wounded and in physical agony, Talon had held his uncle in his arms while Idiag died from his injuries.

"Guard my wife and Ceara, boy," his uncle had whispered before his death. "Don't make me regret taking you in."

Talon had promised. But only a few months after that, he'd found his aunt raped and murdered by their enemies. Her body desecrated and left for the animals to prey upon.

Less than a full year later, he'd cradled his precious wife, Nynia, to his chest as she, too, drew her last breath and left him all alone, forever bereft of her gentle, soothing touch.

She had been his world.

His heart.

His soul.

Without her, he had no longer wished to live.

His spirit as broken as his heart, he had placed their stillborn son into her lifeless arms and buried the two of them together by the loch where he and Nynia had played as children.

Then, he'd done as he had been taught by his mother and uncle.

He had survived to lead his clan.

Laying aside his grief as best he could, he had lived only for the clan's welfare.

As a chieftain, he had spilled enough blood to fill the raging sea and had taken countless wounds on his own flesh for his people. He had led his clan to glory against all the mainlanders and northern clans who had sought to conquer them. With most of his family dead, he had given his clan everything he had. His loyalty. His love.

He had even offered them his own life to protect them from the gods.

And in one heartbeat, his clansmen had taken the last thing on this earth he had loved.

Ceara.

His cherished little sister whom he had sworn to his mother, father, and uncle he would protect at any cost. Ceara with her golden hair and laughing amber eyes. So young. So kind and giving.

To satisfy one man's selfish ambition, his clan had slain her before his eyes while he lay tied down, unable to stop them.

She'd died calling out for him to help her.

Her horrified screams still rang in his ears.

After her execution, the clan had turned on him and ended his life as well. But Talon's death had brought no relief to him. He had felt only guilt. Guilt and a need to right the wrongs done to his family.

That vengeful need had transcended everything, even death itself.

"May the gods damn you all!" Talon roared at the burning village.

"The gods don't damn us, we damn ourselves by our words and deeds."

Talon turned sharply at the voice behind him to see a man clothed all in black. Cresting the small rise, this man was unlike any he'd seen before.

The night wind swirled around the figure, billowing out his finely woven cloak as he walked with a large, twisted warrior's staff held in his left hand. The dark, ancient oak wood was carved with symbols, the top decorated with feathers fastened by a leather cord.

Moonlight danced upon hair that was an unearthly jet-black which the man wore in three long braids.

His silvery, shimmering eyes seemed to swirl like phantom mists.

Those glowing eyes were eerie and haunting.

Standing to the height of a giant, Talon had never before had to look up at anyone and yet this stranger seemed the size of a mountain. It wasn't until the man drew nearer that Talon realized he was only a few inches taller and not as ancient as he'd first seemed. Indeed, his face was that of a perfect youth who stood on the precious threshold between adolescence and maturity.

Until one looked closer. There in the stranger's eyes lay the wisdom of the ages. This was no lad, but a warrior who had battled hard and seen much.

"Who are you?" Talon asked.

"I am Acheron Parthenopaeus," he said in a strange accent that spoke Talon's native Celtic tongue flawlessly. "I was sent by Artemis to train you for your new life."

Talon had been told by the Greek goddess to expect this man who had roamed the earth since time immemorial. "And what will you teach me, Sorcerer?"

"I will teach you to slay the Daimons who prey upon hapless humans. I will teach you how to hide during the day so that the rays of the sun don't kill you. I will show you how to speak without revealing your fangs to the humans, and all else you need to know to survive."

Talon laughed bitterly as blinding pain swept through him once more. He ached and he hurt so much that he could scarcely breathe. All he wanted was peace.

His family.

And they were gone.

Without them, he no longer wished to survive at all. Nay, he couldn't live with this weight in his heart.

He looked to Acheron. "Tell me, Sorcerer, is there any

spell you have that can take this agony from me?"

Acheron gave him a hard stare. "Aye, Celt. I can show you how to bury that pain so deep inside you that it will prick you no more. But be warned that nothing is ever given freely and nothing lasts forever. One day something will come along to make you feel again, and with it, it will bring the pain of the ages upon you. All you have hidden will come out and it could destroy not only you, but anyone near you."

Talon ignored that last part. All he wanted for now was one day when his heart wasn't broken. One moment free of his torment. He was willing to pay any cost for it.

"Are you sure I will feel nothing?"

Acheron nodded. "I can teach it to you only if you listen."

"Then teach me well, Sorcerer. Teach me well."

Chapter 1

"You know, Talon, killing a soul-sucking Daimon without a good fight is like sex without foreplay. A total waste of time and completely un . . . satisfying."

Talon grunted at Wulf's words while he sat at a corner table at the Café Du Monde, waiting for his waitress to return with his black chicory coffee and beignets. He had an ancient Saxon coin in his left hand that he rolled between his fingers as he scanned the dark street in front of him and watched the tourists and locals drift by.

Having banished most of his emotions fifteen hundred years ago, there were only three things Talon allowed himself to enjoy anymore: loose women, hot chicory coffee, and phone calls with Wulf.

In that order.

Though to be fair, there were times when Wulf's friendship did mean more to him than a cup of coffee.

Tonight, however, wasn't one of them.

He'd awakened just after dusk to find himself pathetically low on caffeine, and though the theory went that immortals couldn't have addictions, he wouldn't wager on it.

He'd barely taken time to pull on a pair of pants and his leather jacket before he came seeking the goddess Caffeina.

The cold New Orleans night was uncommonly calm.

There weren't even many tourists on the street, which was unusual this close to Mardi Gras.

Still, it was prime Daimon season in New Orleans. Soon the vampires would be stalking the tourists and preying on them like an open banquet.

For the moment, though, Talon was glad it was quiet, since it allowed him to deal with Wulf's crisis and feed the one craving that wouldn't wait.

"Spoken like a true Norseman," Talon said into his cell phone. "What you need, my brother, is a mead hall filled with serving wenches and Vikings ready to battle their way into Valhalla."

"Tell me about it," Wulf agreed. "I miss the good old days when Daimons were warriors and combat trained. The ones I found tonight knew nothing about fighting, and I'm sick of the whole 'my gun will solve all' mentality."

"You get shot again?"

"Four times. I swear . . . I wish I could get a Daimon up here like Desiderius. I'd love a good down-and-dirty fight for once."

"Careful what you wish for, you just might get it."

"Yeah, I know. But damn. Just once, can't they stop running from us and learn to fight like their ancestors did? I miss the way things used to be."

Talon adjusted his black Ray-Ban Predator sunglasses as he watched a group of women walk past on the street nearby.

Now there was one challenge he could sink his fangs into . . .

Under his closed lips, he ran his tongue over his long left canine tooth while he watched a beautiful blond woman dressed in blue. She had a slow, seductive walk that could make even a fifteen-hundred-year-old man feel underage.

He *so* wanted a piece of that.

Damn Mardi Gras.

If not for the season, he'd be hanging up on Wulf and running after her to fulfill his first comfort.

Duty. How it reeked.

Sighing, he turned his thoughts back to their conversation. "I tell you, what I miss most are the Talpinas."

"What are those?"

Talon cast a wistful look at the women who were quickly drifting out of his line of sight. "That's right, they were before your time. Back in the better part of the Dark Ages, we used to have a clan of Squires whose sole purpose was to take care of our carnal needs."

Talon sucked his breath in appreciatively as he remembered the Talpinas and the comfort they had once provided to him and his Dark-Hunter brethren. "Man, they were great. They knew what we were and they were more than happy to bed us. Hell, the Squires even trained them how to pleasure you."

"What happened to them?"

"About a hundred or so years before you were born, a Dark-Hunter made the mistake of falling in love with his Talpina. Unfortunately for the rest of us, she didn't pass Artemis's test. Artemis was so angry, she stepped in and banished the Talpinas from us, and implemented the oh so wonderful you're-only-supposed-to-sleep-with-them-once rule. As further backlash, Acheron came up with the never-touch-your-Squire law. I tell you, you haven't lived until you've tried to find a decent one-night stand in seventh-century Britain."

Wulf snorted. "That's *never* been my problem."

"Yeah, I know. I envy you that. While the rest of us have to pull ourselves back from our lovers lest we betray our existence, you get to cut loose without fear."

"Believe me, Talon, it's not all it's cracked up to be. You live alone by choice. Do you have any idea how frustrating it is to have no one remember you five minutes after you leave them?"

Wulf expelled a long, tired breath. "Christopher's mother has come over here three times in the last week alone just so she can meet the person he works for. I've known her for what? Thirty years? And let's not forget that time sixteen years ago when I came home and she called the cops on me because she thought I had broken into my own house."

Talon grimaced at the pain in Wulf's voice. It reminded him why he no longer allowed himself to feel anything except physical pleasure.

Emotions served no purpose in life and he was much better off without them.

"I'm sorry, little brother," he said to Wulf. "At least you have us, and your Squire, who can remember you."

"Yeah, I know. Thank the gods for modern technology. Otherwise I'd go insane."

Talon shifted in his fold-up chair. "Not to change the subject, but did you see who Artemis relocated to New Orleans to take Kyrian's place?"

"I heard it was Valerius," Wulf said in disbelief. "What was Artemis thinking?"

"I have no idea."

"Does Kyrian know?" Wulf asked.

"For an obvious reason, Acheron and I decided not to tell him that the grandson and spitting image of the man who crucified him and destroyed his family was being moved into the city just down the street from his house. Unfortunately, though, I'm sure he'll find out sooner or later."

"Man, human or not, Kyrian will kill him if they ever cross paths—not something you need to cope with this time of year."

"Tell me about it."

"So, who got Mardi Gras duty this year?" Wulf asked.

Talon dropped the coin in his hand as he thought about the ancient Greco-Roman slave who would be temporarily moved into the city tomorrow to help combat the Daimon explosion that occurred every year at this time. Zarek was a known Feeder who preyed on human blood. He was unstable at best, psychotic at worst. No one trusted him.

And it was just Talon's luck to have Zarek here, especially since he'd been hoping for a Dark-Huntress to come visit. It might drain his powers to be in the presence of another Dark-Hunter, but he would still rather have an attractive woman to look at than deal with Zarek's psychosis.

Besides, for what he had in mind, he and a Huntress didn't need their Dark-Hunter powers anyway . . .

"They're importing Zarek."

Wulf cursed. "I didn't think Acheron would ever let him leave Alaska."

"Yeah, I know, but word came from Artemis herself that she wanted him here. Looks like we're having a psycho reunion this week . . . Oh wait, it's Mardi Gras. Duh."

Wulf laughed again.

At last the waitress brought his coffee and a small plate of three beignets that were heavily covered with powdered sugar. Talon sighed appreciatively.

"Coffee arrived?" Wulf asked.

"Oh, yeah."

Talon took a whiff of his coffee, set it aside, and reached for a beignet. He'd barely touched the pastry when he saw something across the street, on the right side of Jackson Square down the Pedestrian Mall. "Ah, man."

"What?"

"Friggin' Fabio alert."

"Hey, you're not too far from the mark either, *blondie*."

"Bite me, Viking."

Peeved by the timing, Talon watched the group of four Daimons stalking the night. Tall and golden blonde Daimons who possessed the godlike beauty of their race. They strutted around like punkish peacocks, drunk on their own power as they scoped out tourists to kill.

By nature, Daimons were cowards. They only stood their ground and fought against Dark-Hunters when they were in groups and only then as a last resort. Because they were so much stronger than humans, they preyed openly on them, but let a Dark-Hunter near them and they ran for cover.

There had been a time once when it wasn't like that. But the younger generations were more careful than their ancestors. They weren't as well trained or as resourceful.

However, they were ten times cockier.

Talon narrowed his eyes. "You know, if I were a negative person, I would be seriously annoyed right now."

"You sound annoyed to me."

"No, this isn't annoyed. This is mild perturbance. Besides, you should see these guys." Talon dropped his Celtic accent as he invented a conversation for the Daimons. He raised his voice to an unnaturally high level. "Hey, Gorgeous George, I think I smell a Dark-Hunter."

"Oh no, Dick," he said, dropping his voice two octaves, "don't be a dick. There's no Dark-Hunter here."

Talon returned to his falsetto. "I dunno . . ."

"Wait," Talon said, again in the deep voice. "I smell tourist. Tourist with big . . . strong soul."

"Would you stop?"

"Talk about inkblots," Talon said, using the derogatory term Dark-Hunters had for Daimons. It stemmed from the strange black mark that all Daimons developed on their chests when they crossed over from being simple Apollites to human slayers. "Damn, all I wanted was a drink of coffee and one little beignet."

Talon glanced wistfully at his drink as he debated what should take priority. "Coffee . . . Daimons . . . Coffee . . . Daimons . . ."

"I think in this case the Daimons better win."

"Yeah, but it's *chicory* coffee."

Wulf clucked his tongue. "Talon wanting to be toasted by Acheron for failure to protect humans."

"I know," he said with a disgusted sigh. "Let me go expire them. Talk to you later."

Talon stood up, zipped his phone into the pocket of his motorcycle jacket, and stared longingly at his beignets.

Oh, the Daimons would pay for this.

Taking a quick drink of coffee that scalded his tongue, he skirted through the tables and made his way toward the vampires, who were stalking toward the Presbytere building.

His Dark-Hunter senses alert, Talon headed to the opposite side of the square. He would head them off and make sure they paid for their soul-stealing ways.

And for his uneaten beignets.

Chapter 2

It was one of *those* nights. The kind that made Sunshine Runningwolf wonder why she bothered leaving her loft.

"How many times can a person get lost in a city where she's lived the whole of her life?"

The number seemed to be infinite.

Of course, it would help if she could stay focused, but she had the attention span of a sick flea.

No, actually she had the attention span of an artist who seldom stayed focused on the here and now. Like an out-of-control slingshot, her thoughts drifted from one topic to the next and then back again. Her mind was constantly wandering and sifting through new ideas and techniques—the novelty of the world around her and how best to capture it.

To her there was beauty everywhere and in every little thing. It was her job to show that beauty to others.

And that neat building they were constructing, two or three, maybe four streets over, had distracted her and got her thinking up new designs for her pottery as she wandered through the French Quarter toward her favorite coffeehouse on St. Anne.

Not that she drank that noxious stuff. She hated it. But the retro-beatnik Coffee Stain had nice artwork on the walls and her friends seemed partial to drinking gallons of the tar-liquid.

Tonight she and Trina were going to go over . . .

Her mind flashed back to the building.

Pulling out her sketchbook, she made a few more notes and turned to her right, down a small alley.

She took two steps, and ran into a wall.

Only it wasn't a wall, she realized, as two arms wrapped around her to keep her from stumbling.

Looking up, she froze.

Ay, Caramba! She stared into a face so well formed that she doubted even a Greek sculptor could do justice to it.

His wheat-colored hair seemed to glow in the night and the planes of his face . . .

Perfect. Simply perfect. Totally symmetrical. Wow.

Without thinking, she reached up, grabbed his chin and turned his face to see it from different angles.

No, not an optical illusion. No matter the angle, his features were perfection incarnate.

Wow, again. Absolutely flawless.

She needed to sketch this.

No. Oils. Oils would be better.

Pastels!

"Are you all right?" he asked.

"I'm fine," she said. "I'm sorry. I didn't see you standing there. But do you know your face is pure eurythmy?"

He gave her a tight-lipped smile as he patted the shoulder of her red cape. "Yes, I do. And do you know, Little Red Riding Hood, the Big Bad Wolf is out tonight and he's hungry?"

What was that?

She was talking about art and he . . .

The thought faded as she realized the man wasn't alone.

There were four more men and one woman. All insanely beautiful. And all six eyed her as if she were a tasty morsel.

Uh-oh.

Her throat went dry.

Sunshine took a step back as every sense in her body told her to run.

They moved in even closer, penning her between them.

"Now, now, Little Red Riding Hood," the first one said. "You don't want to be leaving so soon, do you?"

"Um, yes," she said, preparing to fight. Little did they know, a woman who made it her habit to date mean biker types was more than able to deliver a swift kick when she needed it. "I think it would be a really *good* idea."

He reached for her.

Out of nowhere a circular something whizzed past her face, grazing his outstretched arm. The man cursed as he pulled his bleeding arm to his chest. The thing ricocheted like Xena's chakram, and returned to the opening of the alley where a shadow caught it.

Sunshine gaped at the outline of a man. Dressed all in black, he stood with his legs apart in a warrior's stance while his weapon gleamed wickedly in the dim light.

Even though she could see nothing of his face, his ever-changing aura was mammoth, giving him a presence that was as startling as it was powerful.

This new stranger was dangerous.

Deadly.

A lethal shadow just waiting to strike.

He stood in silence, looking at her attackers, the weapon held nonchalantly, yet somehow threateningly, in his left hand.

Then, total chaos broke out as the men who surrounded her rushed the newcomer . . .

Talon fingered the release for his srad and folded its three blades into a single dagger. He tried to get to the woman, but the Daimons attacked him en masse. Normally, he'd have no trouble whatsoever obliterating them, but Dark-Hunter Code forbade him to reveal his powers to an uninitiated human.

Damn.

For a second, he considered summoning a fog to conceal them, but that would make fighting the Daimons more difficult.

No, he couldn't give them any advantage. So long as the woman was here, he was fighting with his hands tied behind his back, and given the superhuman strength and power of the Daimons, that wasn't a good thing at all. No doubt that was why they'd attacked.

For once they actually stood a chance against him.

"Run," he ordered the human woman.

She started to obey him when one of the Daimons grabbed her. With a kick to the groin and a whack across his back after he doubled over, she dropped the Daimon and ran.

Talon arched a brow at her move. Smooth, very smooth. He'd always appreciated a woman who could watch out for herself.

Using his Dark-Hunter powers, he summoned a fog wall behind her to help shield her from the Daimons, who were now more focused on him.

"Finally," he said to the group. "We're all alone."

The one who appeared to be the leader rushed him. Talon used his telekinesis to lift the Daimon up, spin him head over heels, and slam him into a wall.

Two more came at him.

Talon caught one with his srad dagger, the other he kneed.

He tore through the two of them easily enough and was reaching for another one when he noticed the tallest of them running after the woman.

That momentary distraction cost him as another Daimon attacked and caught him in the solar plexus. The force of the blow knocked him back, off his feet.

Talon rolled with the punch, and shot upright.

"Now!" the female Daimon shouted.

Before Talon could catch his balance completely, another Daimon grabbed him by the waist and shoved him backward, into the street.

Straight into the path of a mammoth vehicle that was going so fast he couldn't even identify it.

Something he assumed was the grill of it hit his right leg, shattering it instantly.

It pitched him forward, onto the pavement.

Talon rolled for about fifty yards, then came to rest under a streetlight on his stomach while the dark vehicle went careening down the street, out of sight. He lay with his left cheek against the pungent asphalt, his hands spread out beside him.

His entire body ached and throbbed and he could barely move from the pain. Worse, his head pulsed as he struggled to stay conscious.

But it was hard.

An unconscious Dark-Hunter is a dead one. The fifth rule of Acheron's handbook came to mind. He had to stay awake.

With his powers waning from the pain of his injuries, the fog shield began to dissipate.

Talon cursed. Any time he felt any sort of negative emotion, his powers diminished. It was yet another reason he kept such a stranglehold on them.

Emotions were deadly to him in more ways than one.

Slowly, carefully, Talon pushed himself to his feet at the same time he saw the Daimons fleeing down another alley. There was nothing to be done about it. He'd never catch them in his current condition, and even if he did, the worst thing he could do to them was bleed on them.

Of course, Dark-Hunter blood was poisonous to Daimons . . .

Shit. He'd never failed before.

Grinding his teeth, Talon fought the wave of dizziness that consumed him.

The woman he'd saved ran to him. By the confused look on her face, he could tell she wasn't sure how to help him.

Now that he could see her up close, he was taken by her pixielike face. Fire and intelligence burned deep in her large, dark brown eyes. She reminded him of the Morrígán, the raven goddess he had sworn his sword and loyalty to all those centuries before when he had been human.

Her long, straight black hair fell in braids of all sizes around her head. And she had a smear of charcoal across one cheek. Impulsively, he brushed his hand over it and wiped it from her face.

Her skin was so soft, so warm, and it smelled strangely like patchouli and turpentine.

What an odd combination . . .

"Oh my God, are you okay?" the woman asked.

"Yeah," Talon said quietly.

"I'll call an ambulance," she said.

"Nae!" Talon said in his own language, his body protesting the gesture. "No ambulance," he added in English.

The woman frowned. "But you're hurt . . ."

He met her gaze sternly. "No ambulance."

She scowled at him until a light appeared in her intelligent eyes, as if she had had an epiphany. "Are you an illegal alien?" she whispered.

Talon seized on the only excuse he could give her. With his heavy, ancient Celt accent it would be a natural assumption. He nodded.

"Okay," she whispered to him as she patted him gently on the arm. "I'll take care of you without an ambulance."

Talon forced himself to move away from the glaring lamplight that hurt his light-sensitive eyes. His broken leg protested, but he ignored it.

He limped over to lean against a brick building where he could take the pressure off his damaged leg. Again the world tilted.

Damn. He needed to get to safety. It was still early evening, but the last thing he needed was to be trapped in the city after sunup. Whenever a Dark-Hunter was injured, he or she felt an unnatural urge to sleep. It was a need that would make him dangerously vulnerable if he didn't get home soon.

He pulled his cell phone out to notify Nick Gautier he was hurt, and quickly learned that his phone, unlike him, wasn't immortal. It was in pieces.

"Here," the woman said, moving to stand beside him. "Let me help you."

Talon stared at her. No stranger had ever helped him

like this. He was used to fighting his own battles and then cleaning up after them alone.

"I'm all right," he said. "You go do—"

"I'm not going to leave you," she said. "You got hurt because of me."

He wanted to argue, but his body throbbed too badly to bother.

Talon tried to move away from the woman. He took two steps and the world started to shift again.

The next thing he knew, everything went black.

Sunshine barely caught the man before he hit the ground. She staggered from the sheer size and weight of him but somehow kept him from falling over.

As gently as she could, she lowered him to the sidewalk.

Note, she said *as gently as* she could.

As it was, he slammed into the pavement rather forcefully, making her hurt for him all over again as his head practically made a dent in the sidewalk.

"I'm sorry," she said, straightening up to look down at him. "Please tell me that didn't just give you a concussion."

She hoped she hadn't hurt him even worse by trying to help.

Whatever was she going to do now?

The illegal biker-looking alien dressed all in black was huge. She didn't dare leave him on the street unattended. What if their attackers came back? Or some street punk rolled him?

This was New Orleans where most anything could happen to a person while conscious.

Unconscious . . .

Well, there was no telling what the unsavory ones might do to him, so leaving him alone was not an option.

Just as her panic was getting the better of her, she heard someone call her name.

She looked around until she saw Wayne Santana's beat-up blue Dodge Ram pulling up to the curb. At thirty-three, Wayne had a ruggedly handsome face that looked a lot older. His black hair was laced liberally with gray.

She breathed a sigh of relief at seeing him there.

He rolled his window the rest of the way down and leaned out. "Hey, Sunshine, what's going on?"

"Wayne, could you help me get this guy into your truck?"

He looked really skeptical about that. "Is he drunk?"

"No, he's hurt."

"Then you should call an ambulance."

"I can't." She gave him a pleading look. "Please, Wayne? I need to get him back to my place."

"Is he a friend of yours?" he asked even more skeptically.

"Well, no. We just kind of collided out here."

"Then leave him. The last thing you need is to get involved with another biker. It's none of our business what happens to him."

"Wayne!"

"He could be a criminal, Sunshine."

"How could you say such a thing?"

Wayne had been convicted of involuntary manslaughter seventeen years ago. After he'd served his time, he'd spent several months trying to find a job. With no money, no place to live, and no one willing to hire an ex-con to do anything, he was on the brink of committing another crime to return to jail when he'd applied for a job at her father's club.

Against her father's protests, Sunshine had hired him.

Five years later, Wayne had never missed a day of work or been late. He was her father's best employee.

"Please, Wayne?" she asked, giving him the puppy-dog look that never failed to bend the men in her life to her will.

As he left the truck to help her, Wayne made a series of irritated noises. "One day, that big heart of yours is going to get you into trouble. Do you know *anything* about this man?"

"No." All she knew was that he had saved her life when

no one else would have bothered. Surely such a man wouldn't hurt her.

She and Wayne struggled to get the unknown man upright, but it wasn't easy.

"Jeez," Wayne muttered as they staggered with him between them. "He's huge and he weighs a friggin' ton."

Sunshine concurred. The man was at least six feet five inches of lean, solid muscle. Even with the thick leather motorcycle jacket concealing his upper torso, there was no doubt just how well toned and muscular he was.

She'd never felt such a hard, steely body in her life.

After some doing, they finally got him into the truck.

As they headed toward her father's club, Sunshine held the stranger's head on her shoulder and brushed his wavy blond hair back from the chiseled features of his face.

There was a wild, untamed look about him that reminded her of some ancient warrior. His golden hair brushed against his shoulders in a loose style that said he was attentive to his appearance, but not obsessive about it.

Dark brown eyebrows arched over his closed eyes. His face was ruggedly scrumptious with a full day's growth of beard. Even unconscious, he was compelling and drop-dead gorgeous, and his nearness stirred something needful deep inside her.

But what she liked most about this stranger was the warm masculine and leather scent of him. It made her want to nuzzle his neck and inhale the heady mixture until she was drunk with it.

"So," Wayne said as he drove. "What happened to him? Do you know?"

"He got hit by a Mardi Gras float."

Even in the dim light of the truck's cab, she could tell Wayne was giving her the are-you-nuts? stare. "There's no parade tonight. Where did it come from?"

"I don't know. I guess he must have ticked off the gods or something."

"Huh?"

She brushed her hand through the man's tousled blond

hair and toyed with the two thin braids that hung from his left temple as she answered Wayne's question. "It was a big Bacchus float. I was just thinking this poor guy must have offended our patron god of excess to have been run over by him."

Wayne muttered under his breath. "Must be another frat-boy prank. Seems like every year one of them is stealing a float and taking a joy ride in it. I wonder where they'll leave it parked this time?"

"Well, they tried to park it on my friend here. I'm just glad they didn't kill him."

"I'm sure he will be too, when he wakes up."

No doubt. Sunshine leaned her cheek against the stranger's head and listened to his slow, deep breaths.

What was it about him that she found so irresistible?

"Man," Wayne said after a brief silence. "Your father is going to be pissed about this. He'll have my balls for dinner when he finds out I took an unknown guy up to your place."

"Then don't tell him."

Wayne gave her a mean and nasty glare. "I cannot not tell him. If something happened to you, it would be my fault."

She sighed irritably as she traced the sharp line of the stranger's arched brows. Why did he seem so familiar to her? She'd never seen him before and yet she had a strange sense of déjà vu. As if she knew him somehow.

Weird. Very, very weird.

But then she was used to weirdness. Her mother had written the book on the subject, and Sunshine had redefined it.

"I'm a big girl, Wayne, I can take care of myself."

"Yeah and I lived for twelve years with a bunch of big hairy men who made meals off little girls like you who thought they could take care of themselves."

"Fine," she said. "We'll put him in my bed and I'll sleep at my parents'. Then in the morning, I'll check on him with my mother or one of my brothers."

"What if he wakes up before you get home and steals you blind?"

"Steals what?" she asked. "My clothes won't fit him and I have nothing of any value. Not unless he likes my Peter, Paul and Mary collection anyway."

Wayne rolled his eyes. "All right, but you better swear to me you won't give him a chance to hurt you."

"I promise."

Wayne looked less than pleased, but he remained technically quiet as he drove them toward her loft on Canal Street. However, he cursed underneath his breath the entire way.

Luckily Sunshine was used to ignoring men who did that around her.

Once they reached her loft, which was located directly over her father's bar, it took them a good fifteen minutes to get the stranger out of the truck and inside her home.

Sunshine led Wayne through her loft to the area where she'd strung tie-dyed pink cotton fabric along a wire to seal her bedroom area off from the rest of the large room.

Carefully, they placed her unknown guest on her bed.

"Well, let's go," Wayne said, taking her by the arm.

Sunshine gently shrugged his touch away. "We can't leave him like that."

"Why not?"

"He's covered in blood."

Wayne's face showed his exasperation. It was a look everyone had around her sooner or later—okay, it was most often sooner. "Go sit on the couch and let me undress him."

"Sunshine . . ."

"Wayne, I'm twenty-nine years old, a divorced artist who took nude drawing in college, and I was raised with two older brothers. I know what men look like naked. Okay?"

Growling low in his throat, he stepped out of her bedroom and went to sit on her sofa.

Sunshine took a deep breath as she turned back to her hero dressed all in black. He looked humongous on her bed.

He was also a total mess.

Tentatively, so as not to hurt him, she reached to unzip his motorcycle jacket, which was the neatest thing she'd ever seen. Someone had painted gold and red Celtic scroll-work all over it. It was simply beautiful. A true study in ancient artistry, and she should know. All her life, she had been drawn to Celtic things. She'd cut her teeth on their art and culture.

As soon as she unzipped the jacket, she paused in shock as she saw he wore nothing underneath it. Nothing except lush, tawny skin that made her mouth water and her body instantly throb. Never in real life had she beheld a man with a body so hard and so well toned. Every muscle was defined, and even while relaxed, his strength was evident.

The man was a god!

She ached to draw those perfect proportions and immortalize them. A body this fine definitely needed preserving. She pulled the jacket off and carefully laid it on the bed.

Turning on the lamp that rested on her scarf-covered nightstand, she took a good look at him and was floored by what she saw.

Ca-ram-ba!

He was even more gorgeous than the people who had attacked her. His wavy blond hair curled becomingly around the nape of his neck, and two long, thin braids hung down to his bare chest. His eyes were closed, but his dark eyelashes were sinfully long. His face was perfectly sculpted with high, arching brows and he had a very dignified, yet untamed look to him.

Again, she had a strange sense of déjà vu as her mind flashed on an image of him awake and poised above her. Of him smiling down at her while he slid himself slowly in and out of her body . . .

Sunshine licked her lips at the thought as she throbbed in painful need.

It had been a long time since she had been this attracted

to a stranger. But something about this man really made her ache for a taste of him.

Girl, you have been too long without a man.

Unfortunately, she really had.

Sunshine frowned as she moved closer and got a better look at the torc he wore around his neck. Thick and gold, it had Celtic dragon heads facing each other.

What was so odd was that she'd sketched that very same design years ago in art school and had even tried to cast it into a torc for herself, but the piece had ended up a big mess. It took a lot of metalworking talent to make something that intricate.

Even more impressive was the tribal body tattoo that covered the entire left side of his torso, including his left arm. It was a glorious maze of Celtic artwork that reminded her of the Book of Kells. And unless she missed her guess, it was designed as a tribute to the Celtic war goddess, the Morrígan.

Without thought, she ran her hand over his tattoo, tracing the intricate design.

His right arm had a matching three-inch band of scrollwork around the biceps.

Incredible. Whoever had drawn his tattoos certainly knew their Celtic history.

And as her finger brushed against his nipple, she was jarred from her artist's appreciation of the design.

The woman in her snapped to the forefront as her gaze darted over his lean muscular ribs and abs so tight and well formed they should be part of a body-builder show.

Oh yeah, this was one fine-looking man.

Even though there was a lot of blood on his pants, there didn't appear to be any injury to have caused it. Come to think of it, there weren't even many bruises. Not even where the Bacchus truck had slammed into him.

How weird was that?

Her throat dry, Sunshine reached for his fly.

Part of her couldn't wait to see what was underneath those black pants.

Boxers or briefs?

If he was this studly fine so far, it could only get better . . .

Sunshine!

It was just an artist's appreciation for his body, she told herself.

Yeah, right.

Ignoring that thought, she unzipped his pants and discovered that he wore *nothing* underneath them.

Commando!

Her face flamed at the sight of his extremely endowed maleness nestled against dark blond curls.

Oh come on, Sunshine, it's not the first time you've seen a guy naked. Jeez! Six years of art school, you saw naked men galore. And you've had plenty of them to date, not to mention that Jerry the ex-ogre wasn't exactly small.

Yeah, but none of them had looked *this* good.

Biting her lip, she pulled his heavy, black Harley boots off, then slid his pants down his long, muscular legs. She hissed as her hands came in contact with his skin, which was liberally laced with short blond hairs.

Oh yeah, he was definitely hot and fine.

As she folded the pants, she paused and ran her hand over the fabric. They were made of the softest material she'd ever touched. Almost like chamois, only different. It was a strange texture. They couldn't possibly be real leather. They were so thin and—

Her thoughts stopped as she caught sight of him on her bed.

Oh yeah, baby. Now that was every woman's fantasy. A gorgeous naked guy at her mercy.

He lay across the pink comforter with one tanned arm draped over his stomach and his legs slightly apart, as if waiting for her to join him there and run her hands up and down that lean, hard body.

He was a luscious one to stare at.

She sucked her breath between her teeth as she ached to climb up that strong, magnificent body and lay herself over him like a blanket. To feel his large, strong hands on her skin as she took him into her body and made wild monkey love to him for the rest of the night.

Umm-hmmm!

Her lips burned for a taste of that marvelous golden skin. And he was *all* golden skin. There wasn't a tan line on him.

Gimme!

Sunshine shook her head to clear it. Goodness, she was acting like a total goober over him.

And yet . . .

There was something very special about this man. Something that called out to her like a siren's song.

"Sunshine?"

She jumped at Wayne's impatient call. She'd completely forgotten his presence. "Just a minute," she said.

I just want one more peek. A woman needed a good ogle every now and again, and how often did a woman get a chance to ogle an unconscious handsome god?

Resisting the urge to fondle her guest, she covered him with a blanket, picked his jacket up from the bed, then left the room.

As she walked to the sofa, she studied his bloodied pants. Where had the blood come from?

Before she could investigate the pants, Wayne pulled them from her hands and grabbed the wallet out of the back pocket.

"What are you doing?" she asked.

"Checking him out. I want to see who this guy is." Wayne opened the wallet and scowled.

"What?"

"Let's see, seven hundred and thirty-three dollars in cash and not a bit of ID. Not even a license or credit or debit card." Wayne pulled a huge dagger out of the other pocket and flicked a release that spread the dagger out into a circle of three lethal-looking blades. Wayne cursed even louder. "Shit, Sunshine, I think you found yourself a drug dealer."

"He's not a drug dealer."

"Oh yeah, how do you know?"

Because drug dealers don't rescue women from rapists.
But she didn't dare tell Wayne that. It would only get her
lectured and give him indigestion.

"I just do, now put that back."

"Well?" Camulus asked Dionysus as Dionysus entered the
hotel room.

Styxx looked up from his magazine at the sound of his
voice. The Celtic god, Camulus, had been sitting on the
couch across from him in the hotel suite while they had
waited for news.

Dressed in black leather jeans and a gray sweater, the
ancient deity had been flipping channels incessantly since
Dionysus left, making Styxx want to snatch the remote
from his hand and slam it down on the iron-and-glass coffee table.

But only a fool took a remote from a god.

Styxx might have a death wish, but he had no desire to
be ruthlessly tortured before he died.

So Styxx had gnashed his teeth and done his best to
ignore Camulus and wait for Dionysus's return.

Camulus wore his long black hair pulled back in a po-
nytail. There was something devilish and evil about him,
but then, given the fact he was a god of war, that was
understandable.

Dionysus paused just inside the door. He shrugged out
of his long cashmere coat, then pulled his brown leather
gloves from his hands.

At six ten, the god of wine and excess would be an
intimidating sight to most people. But then, Styxx was only
two inches shorter, and being the son of a king and a man
who longed for death, he found very little intimidating.

What was Dionysus going to do? Send him back to his
hellish isolation?

He'd been there, done that, and had the Ozzy T-shirt to
prove it.

Dionysus was dressed in a tweed jacket, navy turtleneck, and pleated brown slacks. His short dark brown hair was perfectly streaked with blond highlights and he had an immaculate goatee. He looked like a successful billionaire magnate, and did, in fact, run a major international corporation where the god got his jollies by crippling his competitors and taking over other businesses.

Forced against his will into retirement centuries ago, Dionysus spent his time between Olympus and the mortal world, which he hated almost as much as Styxx did.

"Answer my question, Bacchus," Camulus said. "I'm not one of your dickless Greeks to be kept waiting for an answer."

Rage flared in Dionysus's eyes. "You better take a more civil tone with me, Cam. I'm not one of your flaccid Celts to shake in terror of your wrath. You want to fight, boy, bring it on."

Camulus shot to his feet.

"Whoa, hang on a second," Styxx said, trying to calm them down. "Let's save the fighting for when you two take over the world, okay?"

They both looked at him as if he were insane to come between them.

No doubt, he was. But if they killed each other, he'd never die.

Cam glared at Dionysus. "Your pet is right," he said. "But when I have my godhood back, you and I are going to talk."

The gleam in Dionysus's eyes said he was looking forward to it.

Styxx took a deep breath. "So, is the woman with Talon?" he asked Dionysus.

Dionysus smiled coldly. "Just like clockwork." He looked at Camulus. "Are you sure this will immobilize him?"

"I never said it would immobilize him. I said it would neutralize him."

"What's the difference?" Styxx asked.

"The difference is he's about to become an even bigger distraction and concern for Acheron. Yet another way to weaken the Atlantean in the end."

Styxx liked the sound of that.

Now they would just have to ensure that the Dark-Hunter and the woman remained together. At least until Mardi Gras, when the threshold between this world and Kolasis would be thin enough to breach so that they could release the Atlantean Destroyer from captivity.

It had been six hundred years since the last time this had occurred and it would be over eight hundred years more before it occurred again.

Styxx cringed at the thought of living another eight hundred years. Another eight centuries of lonely, never-ending monotony and pain. Of watching his keepers come and go, grow old and die, as they lived out their mortal lives surrounded by family and friends.

They didn't know how lucky they were.

As a human, he had once feared death. But that was ancient aeons ago.

Now the only thing Styxx feared was that he would never escape the horror of his existence. That he would keep on living, century after century, until the universe itself exploded.

He wanted out, and up until thirty years ago he hadn't had a hope of it.

Now he did.

Dionysus and Camulus wanted to reclaim their godhoods and they needed the Destroyer and Acheron's blood to do it. It was a pity Styxx didn't have Atlantean blood in him or he would gladly offer himself up as sacrifice.

As it was, Acheron alone held the key to the Destroyer's release.

Styxx was the only creature alive who could deliver Acheron to them.

Just a few days more and everything would be set right. The old powers would return to dominate the earth and he . . .

He would finally be free.

Styxx sighed in sweet expectation. All he had to do was keep the Dark-Hunters at each other's throats and keep them distracted while he prevented the gods from killing each other.

If either Talon or Acheron ever realized what was happening, they would stop it. They alone had the power to do so.

It was him against them and this time, this time, he would finish what he had started eleven thousand years ago.

When he was through here, the Dark-Hunters would be without leadership.

He would be free and the earth as all knew it would be a whole new place entirely.

Styxx smiled.

Just a few days more . . .

Chapter 3

Talon woke up to find his arm on fire.

Hissing, he jerked his hand away from the sunlight that was streaming in through the window, across an extremely pink bed. He pushed himself back against the white wicker headboard to avoid any more of his body from coming into contact with the deadly rays.

He blew cool air across his hand, but still it burned and ached.

Where the hell was he?

For the first time in centuries, he felt a wave of uncertainty run through him.

Talon was never out of his element. Never out of control. His entire life was one of extreme balance and moderation.

Never in his Dark-Hunter existence had he found himself unsure or confounded.

But right now, he had no idea where he was, the time of day, or who the women were he heard on the other side of the pink drapes.

Squinting against the bright sunlight that painfully pierced his eyes, he looked around the odd room and realized he was trapped between two open windows. His heart hammered. There was no safe way off the bed. The only direction he could go was to his left and into the corner that was occupied by a frothy pink nightstand.

Damn.

Through the pounding pain in his head, the night before came flooding back to him with stunning clarity. The attack.

The woman . . .

The great big whatever slamming into him.

Though his body ached and was sore, his Dark-Hunter powers had allowed him to heal while he slept. In a few hours, even the soreness would be gone.

Until then, he needed out of this death trap of sunlight. Closing his eyes, Talon willed a dark cloud to cover the sun so that the bright daylight would no longer play havoc with his eyesight.

If he wanted to, he could summon enough clouds to turn the day sky as dark as night. But it wouldn't do him any good.

Daylight was still daylight.

His unique Dark-Hunter powers gave him a great deal of control over the elements, weather and healing, but not control over Apollo's domain. Light or dark, the daytime still belonged to Apollo, and even though Apollo was technically retired, the Greek god would never tolerate a Dark-Hunter walking about on his shift.

If Apollo caught sight of him outside or near a window during the light of day, Talon would be nothing more than a strip of fried bacon on the sidewalk.

Extra-crispy Celt didn't appeal to him in the least.

His eyes no longer burning, Talon started to leave the bed, then paused. There was nothing between him and the patchouli- and turpentine-scented sheets.

What's happened to my clothes? He was quite sure he hadn't undressed himself last night.

Had they . . . ?

He frowned as he searched his memory. No, it wasn't possible. If he'd been awake enough to have sex with her, he would have been awake enough to leave this place long before sunup.

"Where is it?"

He looked up at hearing the unfamiliar voice on the other side of the pink tie-dyed fabric, which was hung to form a wall around the bed.

Two seconds later, the fabric slid open to reveal an attractive woman who appeared to be in her late thirties. Her long black hair was pulled into a thick braid and she wore a long flowing black skirt and tunic.

She looked remarkably similar to the woman he'd met last night. And at first glance, she would be easy to mistake for her younger counterpart.

"Hey, Sunshine, your friend's awake. What's his name?"

"I don't know, Starla. I didn't ask."

Oh, but this is getting stranger and stranger.

Unperturbed by his presence, the woman walked into the room to the side of the bed where the nightstand stood. "You look like a Steve," she said as she bent down, lifted up the pink scarves, and started digging through a stack of magazines that was hidden beneath it. "Are you hungry, Steve?"

Before he could answer, she raised her voice. "It's not here."

"It's under the old copies of *Art Papers.*"

"It's not here."

Sunshine entered the room. Walking with the grace of a fairy princess, she wore a long-sleeved purple dress so bright, he had to squint from the hue. As she crossed in front of the window, he realized the material was rather sheer, gifting him with a pleasant view of her lush, ample curves and the fact that she wore nothing beneath that dress.

Nothing except her tanned skin.

His throat went dry.

She was wiping paint from her hands with a towel as she moved to the nightstand without even glancing his way.

"It's right here," she said, pulling out a magazine and handing it to the older woman.

Finally, Sunshine looked to the bed and met his gaze. "Are you hungry?"

"Where are my clothes?"

She cast a sheepish look at Starla. "Did you ask his name?"

"It's Steve."

"It's not Steve."

Sunshine paid him no attention as she turned Starla to face him. Both women stared at him lying there on the bed as if he were some inanimate curiosity.

Talon moved the pink sheet up higher over his waist. Then, suddenly self-conscious, he moved his bare leg under the cover as well, and bent his knee so that the center part of his body wasn't quite so obvious underneath the thin cotton.

Still the two women stared at him.

"You see what I was telling you?" Sunshine asked. "Does he not have the most incredible aura you've ever seen?"

"He's definitely an old soul. With Druid blood. I'm sure of it."

"You think?" Sunshine asked.

"Oh, yeah. We need to talk him into letting us do a past-life regression and see what we come up with."

Okay, they were both nuts.

"Women," he said sharply. "I need my clothes, and I need them *now*."

"See," Sunshine said. "See the way his aura changes. It's absolutely living."

"You know, I've never seen that before. It's really different." Then Starla drifted out of the room as she flipped through the magazine.

Sunshine was still wiping paint off her hands. "Hungry?"

How did she do that? How could she shift from one topic to the other and then back again?

"No," he said, trying to keep her on the main point. "I want my clothes."

She actually cringed. "What happened to the tags in your pants?"

Talon frowned at the odd question. He was keeping a

rein on his irritation and temper, but something about being around this woman made it difficult. "I beg your pardon?"

"Well, you know they were covered in blood . . ."

A bad feeling settled into his stomach. "And?"

"I was going to clean them, and—"

"Oh shit, you washed them?"

"It wasn't the washing that damaged them so much as the drying."

"You dried my *leather* pants?"

"Well, I didn't know they were leather," she said softly. "They felt really soft and strange so I thought they were pleather or something. I wash my pleather dress all the time without it disintegrating and shrinking like your pants did."

Talon rubbed his forehead with his hand. This was so not good. How on earth could he get out of her apartment in the middle of the day with no clothes on?

"You know," she continued, "you really shouldn't cut the tags out of your clothes."

It had been a long time since he had felt real, deep aggravation, but he was starting to feel it now. "Those were *custom,* handmade leather pants. They never have tags."

"Oh," she said, looking even more sheepish. "I would have bought you some more, but since they didn't have tags in them, I didn't know what size to buy."

"Great. I live to be stuck in strange places, naked."

She started to smile at him, then pressed her lips together as if thinking better of it. "I have some pink sweatpants that really wouldn't fit you, and even if they did, I'm sure you wouldn't want to wear them anyway, would you?"

"No. Did you wash my wallet too?"

"Oh, no. I took it out of your pants."

"Good. Where is it?"

She became quiet again and a feeling of doomed dread consumed him.

"Do I want to know?" he asked.

"Well . . ." He was beginning to hate that word since it seemed to portend doom for him and his belongings. "I put it on the washing machine at the Laundromat with your keys, and then I realized that I didn't have change for the washer, so I went to the change machine. I was only gone a second, but when I got back your wallet was gone."

Talon grimaced. "And my keys?"

"Well, you know when you wash just one thing it unbalances the machine? Your keys ended up getting jarred off the top of it and they went down a small drain."

"Didn't you get them back?"

"I tried, but I couldn't reach them. I had three other people try, but they're gone too."

Talon sat in stunned disbelief. Worse, he couldn't even get mad at her since she'd only been trying to help him. But he really, really wanted to be mad.

"I have no money, no pants, no keys. Do I still have my jacket?"

"Yes, it's safe. And I saved your Snoopy Pez dispenser from the washer too. And your boots and knife thing are right here," she said, holding them up from the floor by the bed.

Talon nodded, feeling strangely relieved by the knowledge that she hadn't destroyed everything he'd had on him last night. Thank the gods his motorcycle had been left by the Brewery. He shuddered to think what she might have done to it. "Is there a phone I can use?"

"In the kitchen."

"Could you please bring it to me?"

"It's not cordless. I always lose those things or I drop them someplace and break them. The last one I had ended up drowning in the toilet."

Talon looked uneasily at the woman and the faint sunlight in the room. He wondered which one of them was the most lethal to him.

"Would you mind pulling down the shades?" he asked.

She frowned. "Does the sunlight bother you?"

"I'm allergic to it," he said, falling into the lie Dark-Hunters used when caught in similar situations.

Although he doubted if *any* Dark-Hunter had ever found himself in a situation similar to this one.

"Really? I've never known anyone allergic to sunlight before."

"Well, I am."

"So you're like a vampire?"

The word hit just a little too close to home. "Not exactly."

She moved to the window, but when she pulled the shade down, it fell.

Gray sunlight spilled across the bed.

With a curse, Talon shot into the corner, narrowly missing the pale sunbeams.

"Sunshine, I . . ." Starla's voice broke off as she entered the room and caught sight of him standing naked in the corner. She eyed him in an odd, detached way, as if he were an interesting piece of furniture.

Talon and modesty were strangers, but the way she stared at him made him damned uncomfortable.

In spite of the sunlight, Talon grabbed the pink blanket off the bed and clutched it to his middle.

"You know, Sunshine, you need to find a man like that to marry. Someone so well hung that even after three or four kids, he'd still be wall to wall."

Talon gaped.

Sunshine laughed. "Starla, you're embarrassing him."

"Oh, believe me, that's nothing to be embarrassed over. You ought to be proud. Strut it. Trust me, young man, women your age would love to have some of that."

Talon snapped his gaping jaw shut. These were the strangest women he'd ever had the misfortune of being near.

Gods, get him out of here.

Starla looked up at Sunshine in the window. "What are you doing?"

"He's allergic to the sun."

"It's so cloudy outside, it's almost dark."

"I know, but he says he can't be in it."

"Really? So you brought home a vampire? Cool."

"I'm not a vampire," he reiterated.

" 'Not exactly,' he said earlier," Sunshine said. "What's not exactly a vampire?"

"A werewolf," Starla said. "With his aura, it makes sense. Wow, Sunny, you found yourself a werewolf."

"I'm not a werewolf."

Starla looked really disappointed by the news. "What a pity. You know, when you live in New Orleans, you expect to meet the undead or damned at least once in a while." She looked back to Sunshine. "You think we should move? Maybe if we lived over by Anne Rice we might catch sight of a vampire or werewolf."

Sunshine replaced the shade. "I'd be happy to see a zombie."

"Oh, yeah," the older woman concurred. "You know, your dad said he saw one out on the bayou right before we got married."

"That was probably the peyote, Mom."

"Oh. Good point."

Talon's jaw went slack again as he looked back and forth between them. Mother and daughter? They certainly didn't act that way, and Starla didn't look that much older than Sunshine, but there was no denying the similarities of their features. Or the oddity of them both.

Oh yeah, insanity ran deep in the roots of that family tree.

Sunshine lowered the shade for the other window.

Wrapping the blanket around him, Talon carefully stepped through the room and was relieved to find a rather bare, open loft on the other side of the drapes.

There was another row of windows on his left where Sunshine had sectioned off a small drawing studio. But the rest of the loft was blissfully dark and devoid of sunlight. Keeping the blanket wrapped around his hips, he made his way toward the phone in the kitchen.

"Well, Sunshine, now that he's awake and I agree he's not threatening—"

Talon arched a brow at that comment. There had never been a time in his life he hadn't been threatening! He was a Dark-Hunter. That term alone inspired terror in the things that gave evil a bad name.

"—I'm going to go down to the club and pay some bills, make some orders, and do real work."

"Okay, Starla, I'll see you later."

He had to get out of this place. These women not only lacked sense, but they were too weird for words.

Starla kissed Sunshine's cheek and left.

After several minutes of looking, Talon found the phone cord in the wall and trailed it to the old-fashioned dial phone, which was hiding in a kitchen drawer that also contained a wide assortment of dry paintbrushes and tubes of acrylics.

He pulled the phone, painted with wild fluorescent colors, out of the drawer and placed it on the counter next to a pink pig-shaped cookie jar that held small cinnamon-scented rice cakes.

Picking up the receiver, he dialed Nick Gautier, who had once been the Squire, or human helper, for Kyrian of Thrace. Since Kyrian had married Amanda Devereaux a few months ago and had left behind his official Dark-Hunter status, Nick had become Talon's unofficial, part-time Squire. Not that Talon wanted a Squire. Humans had a nasty way of dying around him, and Nick had a mouth on him that was guaranteed to get the boy killed one day.

Still, there were times when a Squire came in handy. Now was definitely one of them.

The phone rang until the message came on that the cellular customer was unavailable.

Damn. That meant making the one call he'd rather be killed again than make. If the other Dark-Hunters ever found out about this, he'd never hear the end of it. Squires were sworn to an oath of secrecy. They were forbidden to ever reveal anything that was embarrassing about a Dark-Hunter or anything that could endanger them.

Unfortunately, other non-Squired human helpers didn't make such an oath.

Oh yeah, Nick Gautier was a dead man when he got his hands on him.

Preparing himself mentally for what was to come, he called Kyrian of Thrace who answered on the first ring.

"Talon?" Kyrian said as soon as he recognized his voice. "It's noon, what's wrong?"

Talon slid a glance to Sunshine, who was singing "Puff the Magic Dragon" as she passed him to enter the kitchen. "I . . . uh . . . I need a favor."

"Anything."

"I need you to go to my place and get my spare keys, another cell phone and some money."

"Yeah, okay. Did you have to ditch your bike?"

"Yeah, she's in the Brewery parking lot so I need you to bring her to me for tonight."

"Okay, where do I bring her?"

"Hang on." Talon pulled the phone away from his ear. "Sunshine?"

She turned to look at him.

"Where the hell am I?" Even with the phone on his shoulder, he heard Kyrian's mocking laughter.

"You know the nightclub Runningwolf's that's on Canal Street?"

He nodded.

"We're directly over it."

"Thanks." He relayed the information to Kyrian.

"Talon, I swear, your hormones are going to get you killed someday."

He didn't bother to correct Kyrian. They'd known each other for over a thousand years and Talon had never before been caught out like this. Kyrian wouldn't believe the truth of how he came to be in this loft. Hell, he barely believed it himself. "I also need you to bring me some clothes."

The silence in his ear was deafening.

Oh yeah, Nick was such a dead man when Talon got his hands on him.

"What?" Kyrian asked hesitantly.

"I lost my clothes."

Kyrian laughed. Hard.

"Shut up, Kyrian, it's not funny."

"Hey, from where I'm standing it's funny as hell."

Yeah, well, from where Talon was standing, with a pink blanket wrapped around his hips, it wasn't.

"Okay," Kyrian said, sobering. "We'll be over there as soon as we can."

"We?"

"Me and Julian."

Talon cringed again. An ex-Dark-Hunter and an Oracle. Great. Just great. They would never let him live this down and by nightfall one of them would be guaranteed to post this on the Dark-Hunter.com Web site for everyone to laugh about.

"All right," Talon said, tamping down his ire. "See you in a little while."

"You know," Sunshine said as soon as he hung up. "I could just go buy you some clothes. I do owe you."

Talon glanced around the loft. It looked as if a bottle of Pepto-Bismol had exploded, or the Cat in the Hat had come for a visit. There was pink everywhere. But what struck him most was the dilapidated condition of her furniture and her piecemeal decorations. Definitely a starving artist, the last thing this woman could afford was a pair of two-thousand-dollar pants, and the earth would stand still and shatter before Talon ever put denim on his body.

"It's all right," he told her. "My friends will take care of it."

She brought him a plate of muffins and what appeared to be grass. "What's this?"

"Breakfast . . . or lunch." When he didn't take it, she added, "You need to eat. It's good for you. It's a cranberry bran muffin with flaxseed and alfalfa sprouts."

There was nothing on that plate that came close to re-sembling food. Especially to a man who was born and bred to be a Celtic chieftain.

Okay, Talon, you can cope with this. "Do you have any coffee?"

"Ew! No, that stuff will kill you. I have herbal teas, though."

"Herbal teas? That's mulch, not a beverage."

"Oooo, Mr. Picky woke up on the wrong side of the bed."

No human had ever been so flippant with him. Even Nick knew better. Feeling totally out of his element, Talon gave up.

"Fine. Where's your bathroom?"

Then right behind that came the thought, *Please tell me you have one inside this loft and not out back in a parking lot.*

She pointed to a dark corner of the loft. "Right there."

It was another area sectioned off by a hanging curtain. How wonderful was this?

And he'd mistakenly thought the Middle Ages were over.

Oh, what fond memories . . . not.

Talon walked over to it and had just pulled the curtain closed and dropped the blanket to the floor when Sunshine joined him. She held a pink towel and washcloth in her hands and stopped dead in her tracks when she caught sight of him standing there naked.

She put the towel on the sink and moved around him, looking him up and down. "You are just simply male perfection, you know that?"

He would have felt flattered had she not looked like someone sizing up a car. It wasn't desire for him that made her say that. Her tone was detached, the way her mother's had been.

She ran her warm, smooth hand down his back, over his tattoo. "Whoever gave you this tattoo was a very talented artist."

Chills spread over him as her hand glided down his spine to his hip. "My uncle did it," he said before he could stop himself. He hadn't spoken of his uncle with anyone in centuries.

"Really? Wow." She slid her hand up across his shoulders to the Dark-Hunter bow-and-arrow brand on his right shoulder blade. "Where did this come from?"

Talon shrugged her touch away. That was one mark he would never talk about to an uninitiated human. "It's nothing."

It was then her gaze fell to his erection. Her face turned as pink as the towel. "Sorry," she said quickly. "I tend to not think before I act."

"I noticed." But what made it so bad was that she continued to stare at his erection. She had yet to look anywhere else.

"You really are a *big* man."

For the first time in over a thousand years, he felt his cheeks warm. Grabbing the towel, Talon covered himself.

Only then did she look away. "Here, let me get you a razor." She dropped to her knees, giving him a nice view of her bottom as she rummaged around in a makeshift pink wicker cabinet next to the pedestal sink. Her hips moved provocatively as she searched, only adding to his desire.

He clenched his teeth. That woman had the sexiest bottom he'd ever seen. One that made his groin burn even more as he thought about lifting that gauzy skirt and burying himself deep inside her. Of sliding himself in and out of her moist heat until they were both sweaty and spent.

Oh yeah, she was definitely a woman who could satisfy a man. He'd always been partial to women with lush curves and . . .

She emerged with a pink razor and toothbrush.

Talon curled his lip at the thought of using such girly items. "Do you own anything not pink?"

"I have a purple razor if you'd rather."

"Please."

She pulled out a darker pink one.

"That's not purple," Talon said. "It's pink too."

She rolled her eyes at him. "Well, that's all I have unless you want my X-Acto blade."

Extremely tempted, he took the razor from her.

Sunshine didn't move until he got into the claw-footed

tub and pulled the shower curtain closed. Only then did she allow herself to bite her knuckles at the luscious view of his naked backside. She was definitely going to have to sketch him.

That man was *hot*. Burning. And every time he spoke with that wildly exotic accent of his, she melted. It sounded like some unique combination of English and Scottish.

Fanning her face, she forced herself to leave the bathroom and head back to her kitchen. But what she really wanted to do was peel her clothes off, climb into the shower behind him, and lather that lush, tall, lean body of his until he begged her for mercy.

The feel of all that supple, hard skin under her hands . . . Heaven. Pure heaven.

And he hadn't even gotten mad about his pants! She still couldn't believe how well he took it all. Normally, guys would be shouting at her by now and she'd be giving them the heave-ho out the door.

But he had merely shrugged it off. Oooo, she liked that.

Now that she thought about it, he really didn't have a whole range of emotions that he showed. He was patience incarnate, which was a very nice change of pace.

"Hey, Steve?" she called.

"My name isn't Steve," he said from the shower. "It's Talon."

"Talon what?"

"Just Talon."

She smiled. Talon. It suited him.

"What did you want?" he called.

"What?" she asked.

"You called me like you had a question. What do you need?"

Sunshine bit her lip as she tried to remember. Oops. "I forgot."

She actually heard him laugh. Wow. That was a first. By now most guys would be flaming mad at her.

Sunshine spent the next five minutes trying to find her sketchbook, which she had somehow placed in the refrigerator. Again. She took a seat at her breakfast counter and started sketching her newest find.

Talon.

She took her time drawing the well-sculpted planes of his face, the intricate tattoo on his body. She'd never seen any man with proportions more perfect. And before she knew it, she was lost in those lines. Lost in her mind as she let her creativity flow and reproduce the things she found so incredibly fascinating about the man in her shower.

Before she realized how much time had passed, he turned the shower off and came out from behind the curtain with a damp towel draped around his lean hips.

Oh, mama.

Sunshine once again felt the urge to bite her hand in appreciation. With the exception of the two thin braids that swung with his movements, his golden-blond hair was slicked back and his jet-black eyes flashed with intelligence and arcane power. She'd never seen eyes so dark, especially on a blond man.

He had such a powerful presence that it made her breathless just to look at him. It was as if the very air around him were rife with energy and strength, and she wished most of all that she could capture that with her art.

But no one would ever be able to duplicate or create an aura so intense. It was something that could only be experienced in the flesh.

With every step he took closer to her, her heart pounded harder. The man was so overwhelmingly masculine. So very choice.

His intensity, his raw animal magnetism . . . set fire to her blood.

He'd been handsome last night in her bed, but upright and conscious, he was totally devastating.

"You know, Talon," she said, tracing the lines of his perfect muscles with her gaze. "Towels look really good on you. You go outside like that and you'll start a whole new fashion craze."

An amused smile hovered at the edges of his lips. "Do you always say everything that comes to your mind?"

"Mostly. I do have some thoughts I keep to myself. I used to not care and would say anything at all, but then one time my college roommate called the psycho unit on me. You know, they really do have white coats."

Talon arched a brow at the sincerity he sensed from her. That was a true story. The woman was eccentric, no doubt, but far from a crackpot.

Well, maybe not *that* far.

She reached over to his untouched "breakfast" and picked up the so-called muffin that had shiny little particles in it he couldn't even begin to identify. "You still haven't eaten your muffin."

Yeah, right. He still hadn't eaten his boots either, and he'd rather feast on one of them than that thing in her hand.

"I'm not hungry."

At least not for food.

She dropped the muffin to the counter and he swore it thunked. Her brow furrowing, she reached out and touched his torc. Her fingers brushed against the skin of his neck, raising chills and other things on his body.

"This is so beautiful. I've always wanted a torc, but never could find one that seemed like me." She ran her thumb over the right dragon head. "Are you from Scotland?"

"Not exactly," he said, watching the way she studied the piece, which had been a gift from his aunt on his wedding day. Both he and Nynia had received matching torcs from her. He didn't know why he still wore it, other than the fact that taking it off would cause him more pain than he was willing to deal with. In some odd way, removing the torc would be like losing Nynia all over again.

Against his will, his mind drifted back to the moment when Nynia had placed the torc around his neck. Her smile had been blinding and her face filled with love as she kissed him on his lips.

Gods, how he missed her. Even after all these centuries.

There were times when he swore he could still smell the warmth of her hair. Feel her touch. It was like the ghost itch of a missing limb that, even years later, you swore you could still feel.

There was something about Sunshine that reminded him of his wife. And it wasn't just the fact that both women possessed the ability to drive him crazy.

Sunshine was strangely fascinating. Much like him, she saw things on another level, things that were hidden from this plane of existence.

Her mind flashed from one thing to another like bursts of lightning, which was as intriguing as it was confusing. Nynia was the only other person he'd ever met with that trait.

As a mortal man, he had often been confounded by Nynia's unique logic.

"You know," Sunshine said, "you say 'not exactly' a lot. You're not exactly a vampire. You're not exactly from Scotland, and you're allergic to daylight. What else?"

"I hate bran muffins and grass."

She laughed at that, a rich, throaty sound that warmed him. He watched in fascination as she used a stained rag to clean the charcoal from her long, elegant fingers. "So how long until your friends get here?"

"A couple of hours, no doubt. I live way outside of town."

Sunshine looked down at the towel around his hips. If she kept him here like that, there was no telling what might happen.

Actually there was, which meant she really needed to get some clothes on him . . . fast.

He took a deep breath, the gesture accentuating the muscled indentations of his hard, defined abs.

Oh yeah, she needed to cover up that temptation.

"I tell you what, Mr. Talon No-Last-Name. Why don't I go out and get you something to put on until your friends get here?"

Because I don't want you to leave. Talon blinked at the bizarre, uncharacteristic thought.

Where had that come from?

There was something compelling about this woman. Something strong and at the same time vulnerable. He felt in her a need to make amends for what she'd done to him. Why, he couldn't imagine. Especially since she had saved his life.

Had she left him out on the street, he would be dead now. A fried stain on the sidewalk.

"You don't have to, you know."

"I know. But I insist. It's the least I could do since I destroyed your pants."

As he looked at her kind, compelling face, which was framed by straight, jet-black hair, he became fascinated by the way her lips curved. The way they held a hint of a smile even while she was relaxed. Sunshine was more than just her name, it was also her attitude. Happy, warm.

She was totally irresistible and he wanted a taste of her so badly that he wasn't sure why he hadn't already sampled her.

He needed to taste her. To *feel* her.

Sunshine watched while Talon studied her lips. There was enough heat in his obsidian gaze to set fire to a glacier. He had yet to touch her and still she swore she could feel him surrounding her with heat, with need.

The air around her seemed sexually charged. It practically sizzled with eroticism and longing. She'd never felt anything like this in her life.

Talon oozed an inhuman sexual attraction. She was drawn to him in a way she'd never been drawn to any man.

His eyes narrowing, he dipped his head and took possession of her lips with a masterful kiss that made her head literally spin. Her body melted.

She moaned at the taste of his lips against hers as his tongue swept passionately into her mouth. He pulled her up from her bar stool, into his strong arms, and ran his hands over her back, clenching the fabric of her dress in his fists.

The raw, manly scent of him invaded her as she felt his muscles flex around her. His virile potency was almost more than she could take.

This was an earthy man who knew his way around a woman's body. She could feel it in his masterful kiss, in the way he knew just where and how to caress her.

Her body burning with desire, she clutched at his bare shoulders as she felt him harden even more against her stomach.

She'd never experienced anything like this. It was as if he were starving for her.

Only her.

When he finally pulled back, she realized she had surrendered her weight to him and he had supported all of her without even tightening his muscles. Jeez, the man was strong.

He brushed his thumb over her swollen lips, his eyes so warm and tender that it made her even more breathless than his kiss. "I'm a thirty-three waist and a thirty-eight inseam."

"Um-hmm," she breathed without hearing him. She swayed toward him for another kiss.

Talon felt a strange stirring inside him at the dazed and adoring look on her face.

"Kiss me again," she whispered an instant before she claimed his lips with hers.

He cupped her head in his hands as he explored her mouth, being careful not to let her accidentally brush her tongue against his fangs and learn the truth about him.

But it was hard to pull back when the taste of her drove him so close to madness. Her patchouli-and-turpentine scent intoxicated him and he ached to pull the hem of her dress up and slide his hand over her lush thighs to her . . .

Her tongue came dangerously close to his fangs.

Pulling back, he released her.

That had been just a bit too close for comfort, but not nearly as close as he wanted to get to her. He dropped his gaze to her body, outlined by her dress. She was a full-bodied woman, not tiny or petite. And she had large, lush breasts—something he'd always been partial to.

Clenching his teeth, he fought the vicious need to take her into his arms and sample those breasts with his mouth. His hands.

His tongue.

Better still, his fangs . . .

"Okay," she said in an odd, high-pitched voice. "That was nice." She clapped her hands together and took a step back. It wasn't until her gaze fell to the towel that the light came back into her dark brown eyes. "Clothes. You need clothes before I do something I might *not* regret. What was your size again, Steve?"

"Talon."

"Talon. Size. Clothes. Cover him up."

Talon smiled as he watched her trying to keep her mind focused while her eyes continued to drift over him with desire.

He liked this woman. In spite of her peculiarities, there was something very refreshing and pure about her.

"I'm going to go get *Talon* clothes." She left, then came back a few seconds later. "Keys," she said, heading to a pink canister on the kitchen counter. "Need keys for car." She left only to return again. "Purse. Money for clothes."

Talon raked his hand through his wet hair as she left one more time and wondered if she'd forgotten anything else.

She had.

"Shoes," she said the next time. "Must have shoes to shop and keep feet warm." She slid her feet into a pair of mules by the door.

"What about a coat?" Talon asked as he noticed she was heading out again. "It is wintertime."

"Coats are good in the winter," she said, going to a rack by the door he assumed was her closet. She pulled on an old brown overcoat that seemed completely not her style. "Be back shortly."

"Wait."

She paused to look at him.

Talon quirked his lips as he crossed the room and undid her misbuttoned coat. Straightening it, he buttoned it correctly.

"Thank you," she said, smiling a smile that did the oddest things to his groin and stomach.

All Talon could do was nod, especially since what he really wanted to do was pick her up in his arms and carry her to the bed and make love to her for the rest of the afternoon.

"I'll be back," she said, heading out.

After she was gone, he finally allowed himself to smile broadly. She was definitely something else.

Something that reminded him of a warm spring day after a harsh winter. It had been a long time since anyone had touched him the way she did. A long time since someone had stayed in his thoughts.

"You like her."

He turned his head to look over his shoulder at the spirit that flickered there. "She's interesting," he said to Ceara.

Ceara moved forward to stand by his side. Her pale cheeks held an ethereal blush as she shimmered between this plane of existence and the next.

She should have crossed completely over to her eternal rest or rebirth centuries before, but she had refused to leave him alone.

And though it was terribly selfish, Talon had been grateful for her company. Especially back in the days when he'd been unable to stay in touch with his Dark-Hunter brethren via modern technology.

Back then, his isolation had been hellish. He'd spent days alone, never daring to let any human near him for fear of his curse. Never daring to reach out to anyone for anything.

The only relief he'd known was his sister's infrequent visits.

But every time he looked at Ceara, he was painfully reminded of how badly he had failed her. He should have been able to help her the day she died. Had he not been a fool, she would have lived out the life she deserved. A life filled with a husband and children.

Instead, she'd been sacrificed because he had been a stupid, arrogant ass.

The first time she'd come to him after their deaths had shattered him. There had been no accusations from her, no hatred, even though he deserved it.

She had shown him only compassion and love.

"I promised you I would never leave you alone, my bràthair. *And I won't. I will always be here for you."*

Over the centuries, her presence had been the only thing that kept him grounded and allowed him to function. Her friendship and love had always meant everything in the world to him.

Ceara brushed a sisterly hand over the bruise on his right thigh. He couldn't feel it like a real touch, but the gesture caused his skin to tingle. "It no longer bothers you?"

"No. I'm fine."

"Speirr," she said, speaking his name in their native Celt. "You know to be honest with me, *bràthair*."

He reached to brush a tendril of blond hair from her cheek, only to remember he couldn't touch her.

He closed his eyes as he remembered the past.

Their clan had slain her just days before her sixteenth birthday.

"She will be our sacrifice to the gods and they shall forgive us for the transgressions of our leader . . ."

Talon clenched his teeth against the grief and guilt that swelled inside him. Her death had been his fault. He had killed her as surely as if he'd been the one holding the knife.

But he pushed those thoughts away and found the numbness he needed to function.

I'm no longer human and there is no past. Acheron's litany ran through his mind, allowing him to suppress everything.

There was only now and the future. His human life far

behind him, he was a Dark-Hunter whose entire existence was to seek out and destroy the evil that preyed on the humans who had no knowledge of what lay in the darkness waiting for them.

"My leg"—unlike his heart—"only hurts a little."

She shook her head at him. "This is not a safe place for you, Speirr. There is too much light. I don't like for you to be here."

"I know. I'm leaving as soon as I can."

"Very well, then I shall leave until you need me."

She faded away and left him alone. Again.

Talon's gaze fell to the counter where Sunshine had been sitting when he joined her. He frowned as he caught sight of the sketch she'd been working on.

Picking it up, he was impressed by how well she had captured his likeness.

The woman was a brilliant artist. She was able to put emotions and meaning into even the simplest of lines. He'd never seen anything like it.

Unfortunately, he couldn't leave it here.

He tore the page out and used his powers to burn it. Dark-Hunters were forbidden to allow their likenesses to be captured in any medium or form. No one needed proof of their immortality. Such evidence would only lead to questions and complications none of them wanted.

He just hoped she didn't reproduce it after he left.

Talon glanced around the loft and noted that the entire area was littered with framed and unframed art. The floor, a long drawing table, and three easels were scattered with half-finished projects.

Crossing the room, he went to examine them closer. He lost track of time as he looked them over, then found more paintings leaning against the wall by the bedroom. Sunshine liked vivid colors in her work, and her brushstrokes on canvas were as light and gentle as the lady herself.

But it was her pottery that fascinated him most. The pieces were a fiery mixture of color, and the designs of them were far from modern. She must have studied Greek and Celtic cultures extensively to reproduce such authentic copies. It was remarkable how true to the past they were. If he didn't know better, he would swear a Were-Hunter had brought them forward in time.

A knock sounded on the door.

Talon set the bowl he was looking at back with the others on the shelf by the door. He stepped to the door and opened it to see Kyrian and Julian standing on the other side.

They both gaped as they caught sight of him standing virtually naked in the loft.

Talon quickly slammed the door shut.

Kyrian roared with laughter. Talon cringed.

"C'mon, Tally," Kyrian teased from the other side. "Don't you want your clothes, your keys? Oh wait, how about some dignity?"

Talon opened the door, grabbed Kyrian by the shirt and hauled him inside. "You are such an asshole."

Kyrian laughed even harder as Julian Alexander walked in.

By his expression, Talon could tell that Julian wanted to laugh too, but he was trying hard not to. Talon appreciated it.

Kyrian, on the other hand, wasn't so kind. "Nice knees, bud, but the hairy legs could use a Bush Hog."

"Shut up." Talon grabbed the bag of clothes from Kyrian's hand and pulled his leather pants out. "Julian, I just want to thank you for being a grown-up and not laughing at my expense."

His hands in his pants pockets, Julian nodded. "Well, having been in your shoes, I can relate. Of course, in my defense, my towel was at least dark green and not pink."

The two of them roared with laughter while Talon groaned.

Kyrian flicked at the edge of the towel. "What is this? Lace?"

"No," Julian said, "I think it's called crochet."

Talon bared his fangs at the two of them. "Better be

careful, *humans,* or I might decide to feed off you."

"Uh, half-human," Julian reminded him. "Feed off me and I'll give you a bellyache from hell."

Growling at them, Talon quickly exchanged his towel for his pants.

"So," Kyrian said. "Have you become Ravyn now? Do I need to forewarn Nick you'll be shedding your clothes on a daily basis or what?"

Talon rolled his eyes at the mention of the Katagari Dark-Hunter. Ravyn was a shapeshifter who often got caught naked after sunup. "No, it's a one-time thing." *I hope.* "Speaking of Nick, where is he? I tried to call him for this chore."

"He's in class."

"Yeah, well, he's still on Dark-Hunter payroll, so tell him to keep his phone turned on."

"Ooo," Kyrian said. "Getting testy in your fierce naked-ness."

Talon ignored him as he pulled his black T-shirt on.

Sunshine paused beside Selena Laurens's tarot-card stand in Jackson Square. Selena's brown frizzy hair was tied back with a leopard-print scarf, and her thin body was covered with a black-and-white houndstooth coat.

"Hey, Sunny," Selena greeted her. "I was wondering if you were sick or something since you're not out here with your art."

"Oh no, someone came up."

Selena arched a brow at her. "Someone old or someone new?"

"New."

Selena looked a bit skeptical. "I hope this one is nicer than that last bozo you dated."

Sunshine wrinkled her nose as she remembered Greg. A rough biker, he'd been less than desirable and he'd kept confusing her with his ex-girlfriend Sara—nothing like being called the wrong name while having sex with someone.

Not to mention, he'd borrowed three hundred dollars from her the day before she'd kicked him out. Although, all things considered, it was worth the three hundred dollars to be rid of him.

"He seems to be." She patted her bag with Talon's clothes. "Well, I need to be getting back to him—"

"Sunshine!" Selena snapped. "Tell me you didn't."

"Didn't what?"

"Leave him in your loft unattended."

"It's okay. He's safe."

Selena groaned. "Woman, that generous heart of yours gets you into more trouble. Do you know this guy at all?"

Sunshine took a deep breath. She was so tired of everyone lecturing her. "I'll see you later, Madame Selene." She rushed back down the street toward her car with Selena fussing at her the whole way.

Ugh! Why couldn't anyone ever trust her? She wasn't a two-year-old. And being absentminded didn't equate to stupidity. If her kindness killed her, then she was better off dead than living a cold, unfeeling life where she misered up all her feelings and possessions.

Besides, Talon wasn't like other men. She knew it. He seemed to have a lot more heart than most men she'd known.

He was electrifying. Dangerous. Mysterious.

Best of all, he was waiting naked in her loft.

Getting into her car, she headed home.

It didn't take long to reach her father's club and pull around to the back where she always parked. Sunshine frowned as she saw a huge black Harley motorcycle parked beside a black Lamborghini.

Talon's friends?

Hmm, maybe Wayne was right. Maybe Talon *was* a drug dealer.

Not quite so sure of him, she got out of her car and used the back door that opened into the empty club.

She rushed up the steel-and-concrete stairs to her loft.

Pushing open the door, she froze as she caught sight of

three men, all of whose testosterone levels were off the Richter scale. They were absolutely devastating.

Whoa, she needed a sketchbook. Pronto.

Talon was dressed in black leather pants and a tight T-shirt that hugged every crevice of his deadly male perfection.

He stood talking to the two men in her kitchen—two incredibly handsome men. Men who were dressed like professionals and not out-of-work bikers.

How wonderfully refreshing.

"Hi, Sunshine," Talon greeted her. "These are my friends."

The one who was Talon's height held his hand out to her. "Kyrian Hunter," he said in an enchanting accent that was nothing like Talon's.

Sunshine shook his strong, callused hand as she recognized the name. "So you're Selena's brother-in-law. She talks about you and Amanda all the time."

Kyrian was slightly leaner than Talon, with laughing green eyes and an easy smile. His blond hair was a shade darker than Talon's and cut in a very hip style. "I think I should be afraid of what she says about me. Knowing her, there's no telling."

Sunshine smiled. "It's all good, I promise you."

"This is Dr. Julian Alexander," Talon said, introducing the other man, who wore a navy sweater and khakis.

"Nice meeting you," Julian said, extending his hand.

Sunshine responded in kind. Julian was about two inches shorter than the other two and yet his aura was every bit as strong and powerful. His eyes were a gorgeous blue and his hair the same shade as Kyrian's. He was also the most subdued of the three of them, but his eyes were no less friendly.

"Doctor?" she asked.

"I teach Classics at Loyola."

"Oh. Do you know Selena Laurens too?"

Julian nodded. "Very well. She's best friends with my wife."

"Grace?" Sunshine said. "You're married to Gracie?"

Recognition hit them at the same time.

"That was you?" she asked, stepping around to view him from behind. Oh yeah, now *that* she remembered. "You're Mr. Hot Bottom!"

His face went flush with embarrassment.

"Hot Bottom?" Talon asked. "This I've got to hear."

"Oh yeah," Kyrian added.

"We need to be going," Julian said, pushing Kyrian toward the door.

"Oh, like hell," Kyrian said. "Not until I hear this."

"Nice seeing you again, Sunshine," Julian said, shoving Kyrian out the door.

"Don't worry, Kyrian," Talon called. "I'll be sure to give you the *full* details."

Sunshine set the bag of clothes on her counter as the door slammed shut. "I guess you won't be needing these after all."

"Sorry." He leaned against the counter and watched her. "So, tell me how you met Julian."

She shrugged. "I sell my artwork at Jackson Square and I have a booth space next to Selena. A couple of years ago, she brought this bodacious guy to work with her wearing a tight tank top and shorts. Julian had really long hair back then. Anyway, there was this huge crowd of women who had gathered around to watch him. Selena thought it was a disaster, but I made so much money selling sketches of him that I didn't care."

Talon frowned as a very peculiar wave of jealousy went through him. And before he could stop himself, he asked, "Did you keep any of the sketches?"

"I only had one left, and I gave it to Grace about a year ago."

More relieved than he cared to admit, Talon watched her watch him. Her gaze traced the curve of his lips, the line of his jaw, and it made him ache to possess her, to kiss her lips one more time.

"You know, you are really handsome when you smile."

"Am I?" he asked, taking a strange amount of satisfaction from that.

"Yes, you are."

Sunshine swallowed as she realized there was no more reason for him to stay. Not that she should care; she needed to get back to her work. And yet at the same time she didn't want him to leave. "I guess you'll be going now that you're all dressed."

He looked askance at the sunlight. "I'm afraid I can't leave until the sun goes down."

"Oh." Sunshine tried to stifle the giddiness inside her.

He cleared his throat. "If you have things you need to do . . ."

"Oh no," she said quickly, then paused. "I mean, I . . . um . . . it would be rude, *very* rude, to leave you here alone. Especially since I don't have a TV or anything else for you to do." She licked her lips. "Well, since you can't leave, what would you like to do for the rest of the afternoon?"

"Honestly?"

"Yes."

"I'd like nothing better than to make love to you."

Chapter 4

Sunshine pulled back, startled by Talon's frankness. But more than that, she was stunned by how much she she wanted the same thing from him, a man she barely knew at all. And yet there was no denying how much she wanted to make love to him.

How much she ached to caress every inch of that divinely powerful masculine body.

Her lust didn't seem wrong to her. It seemed oddly right and only natural. In a strange way it felt as if she did know him. As if they were supposed to be much more intimate than just strangers who had collided by happenstance out on a dark street.

She wanted him on a level she didn't comprehend.

"You don't beat around the bush, do you?" she asked flippantly.

"No," he said, his jet-black eyes burning her with their heated potency. "I don't."

The power of his desire rolled over her, captivating her. He was so intense, so mesmerizing. And she found herself inexplicably drawn to him.

He reached out and touched a lock of her hair. Desire coiled through her veins, making her throb.

Nowhere else did their bodies touch and yet she swore she could feel him with every single cell of her body.

She quivered with need.

With heat.

With desire.

He bent down and whispered in her ear, his breath tickling her skin. "I've always been a firm believer in seizing the moment. In taking what I want when I want it. And right now, Sunshine, I want *you*. I want to taste every inch of your body. To feel your breath on my neck while I make love to you. To take my tongue and explore every part of you until you beg me to stop."

She shivered at the way he said that. "Life is short, I suppose."

He gave a short laugh at that as he nuzzled her cheek with his lips. His whiskered skin teased hers and she shivered at the manly feel of him. "More so for some than for others."

Sunshine drew in a deep breath as seriousness settled back over them both. The mood of the room wasn't just serious, the air between them was rife with salacity.

With sexual electricity.

Talon moved his mouth dangerously close to hers.

Slowly.

Seductively.

Time was suspended as she waited for his lips to claim hers. As she waited to taste his passion again.

Then, he took her into his arms and kissed her so possessively that it made her breathless.

Sunshine moaned as she tasted him with her lips and with her heart. He invaded every sense she possessed. His muscles bunched and flexed under her hands as his tongue swept against hers. She heard him growl low and deep in his throat like some uncaged beast.

She shivered again.

She brushed her fingertips against the warm nape of his neck, playing with the soft, tender skin there before she ran her fingers upward, through the golden strands of his hair, letting them wrap around her flesh.

How she liked the way this man felt in her arms. The scent of leather and Talon invaded her head and made it reel. He surrounded her with the strong hardness of his body.

She felt his desire for her as his erection pressed against her stomach, and it ignited her own, making her ache for his body, his touch. She wanted him inside her so desperately it stunned her. Never in her life had she wanted a man like this.

He lifted her up in his arms, supporting her weight as he deepened his kiss. Effortlessly, his strong hands held her bottom against his hips so that his bulge pressed against her core. She moaned at the intimate contact with leather and man.

Kissing him back as hard as she could, she wrapped her legs around his waist.

She felt his satisfied laugh rumble out of his body. It made his stomach caress her between her legs, his chest brush against hers, enflaming her even more.

Oh, hon, what are you doing?

Sunshine heard her reasonable voice in her head. She hadn't had a one-night, or in this case one-day, stand since college. The one time she'd done it, she'd felt so sleazy afterward that she had sworn she'd never do it again.

And here she was on the verge of repeating that fiasco.

Good grief, she knew nothing about this man.

Not even his last name.

But for some reason, none of that mattered. The only thing she could focus on was how good he felt as she held him. How wonderful he'd looked in her bed, and the fact that she really liked him. More than she should. More than what made sense.

Right or wrong, she wanted to share her body with him.

No, she *needed* this. It was what she wanted deep down in her heart. And she'd always followed her heart—wherever it led her.

There would be no regrets about this. No second-guessing.

He slid the hem of her dress back, over her thighs. She shivered at the feel of the cool material crawling up her skin, followed by the heat of his hands. He glided his palms up the backs of her thighs until he cupped her bare bottom. He growled in pleasure, the sound deep and primal.

Needful.

"I like the way you feel, little Sunshine," he breathed against her lips.

Sunshine couldn't think straight with his large, strong hands on her naked skin. He dipped his head to her neck where his lips burned her. His teeth scraped her skin as he nipped it tenderly.

She was about to comment on how sharp his teeth were when he delivered a hot, shivery lick to her skin.

Her thoughts scattered.

The man was simply too delectable; she couldn't let him leave without sampling that lean, hard body. She pulled his T-shirt over his head and ran her hands over his chest and tattoo. Oh yeah, she wanted this!

She wanted *him*.

Talon gave her a tight-lipped smile as he saw the raw hunger in her dark brown eyes. He was going to savor this woman.

Every last tiny inch of her.

What with her passion and zest for living, he could only imagine how good a lover she would prove.

It had been a long time since he had found a woman who fascinated him. As a Dark-Hunter, he had chosen his lovers randomly, knowing he'd never see them again.

For centuries, he'd contented himself with one-night stands. With wanton women who wanted nothing more from him than the few hours of pleasure he could give them.

He had met them all in the dark of night.

Never in the light of day.

After minimal conversation to placate them, he had screwed them wildly, and in the end, they had gone their separate ways. Most of the time, he hadn't even bothered asking their names.

But in the back of his mind, he knew something was different today.

Something was different about Sunshine.

He couldn't count how many centuries had passed since he had last shared a real laugh with a lover.

And this woman made him laugh. She made him crazy.

Best of all, she made him burn.

Sunshine had stumbled into his world and turned it upside down. She'd touched the emotions he'd buried long ago. Made him feel strangely alive again, which for a man who had died fifteen hundred years ago was quite a feat.

She gave him feelings he didn't understand. He felt like a kid on Christmas morning, overloaded with sights and smells. His senses were overwhelming him with need.

With desire for her.

Licking his lips in anticipation, he ran his hand over her silken thigh, up to her hips. This woman had the finest ass he'd ever caressed. He pushed her dress up to her waist while she locked her ankles behind his back.

His head spun at the feel of her wrapped around him like this. The heat of her inner thighs burned his waist as he felt her wetness against his stomach.

Returning to her lips, he carried her to the bed and laid her down on the mattress. Without breaking his hold, he lay down on top of her and kissed her fully, deeply, as he ground his swollen groin against the part of her he couldn't wait to bury himself into. He sampled the warmth of her mouth and listened to her moans of pleasure.

Closing his eyes, he inhaled her unique scent and let it wash over him.

Sunshine wanted to weep at how good he felt on top of her. The leather of his pants caressed her intimately as his lips tormented hers. His braids tickled her neck with every movement he made. And his hands felt wickedly wonderful as he ran them over her body, seeking out every part of her.

She almost whimpered in protest when he moved away.

He pulled her dress from her and tossed it to the floor.

She felt more than just physically naked in front of him. For some reason she felt spiritually bare as well. It was as if he could see deep inside her somehow, as if he knew things about her no one else knew.

As if they were connected on a level that transcended their physical bonding.

At least she thought so until he returned to lie on top of her. Then her thoughts scattered again and she became one with the moment. It was strange, really, this sensation of him.

Sunshine hissed at how wonderful he tasted. All that lush, tawny skin made prickly by his masculine whiskers. She so loved the taste of a man's jaw.

No man had ever tasted more perfect.

She brought her hands around his waist, to his fly. His bulge was huge. Pulling back slightly, she watched his face as she opened his pants and touched him for the first time.

He closed his eyes and growled deep in his throat as he rocked himself gently against her hands. Oh, she liked the feel of him there. He was so hard and ready for her.

She laced her fingers through his short curls, moving her hand lower until she could cup the soft heat of him in her palm.

Talon moaned in pleasure. It felt so incredibly good to have her holding him like that. He'd had sex more times than he could count and yet there was something new about this experience.

Something fresh.

She pulled his pants down lower so that she could tuck her toes into them and pull them off. It wasn't until she frowned that they both remembered he still wore his boots.

"Oops," she said with a smile.

Talon chuckled, kissed her deeply, then rolled over to remove his boots. She rose up on her knees and leaned her naked body against his bare back, making him tremble from the feel of her breasts against his spine.

"I just love this tattoo," she said as she slowly traced it down his back with her tongue.

"I love when you do that," he said, tossing his boots and pants into the corner. He gripped the edge of the bed as she explored his back with her mouth.

"Does it have any special meaning?"

He closed his eyes as she returned to tracing the marks with her tongue. "They're Celtic symbols for protection, power, and longevity." Talon clenched his teeth at the irony. His uncle had had no idea what was awaiting his nephew when he had placed those markings on his skin. Just how long his life would be.

She gave one long, warm lick, then pulled back. "I can't believe your uncle did this. My father had a cow when he saw mine."

Talon looked at her over his shoulder. "You have a tattoo?"

She wrapped her left leg around his waist and showed him her inner ankle. It was a very small, stylized Celtic sun with the jagged symbol for creativity.

Smiling, he ran his hand over it. "Very nice."

"Yes, but it hurt for days. I can't imagine how much worse yours must have been."

She had no idea. Especially since his had been performed long before the days of sterilized needles and machinery. His uncle had meticulously tapped the design into his body over a three-month period. Some of it had gotten infected and only Nynia's herbal abilities had spared his life.

"It wasn't so bad."

"Ooo," she said teasingly, wrinkling her nose. "Mr. Tough Guy."

"Would you rather I say it hurt?"

"It never hurts to admit that you feel pain."

"Baby," he said gently. "I don't feel pain. Ever."

She looked at him in surprise. "Really? Not even a little?"

He shook his head as he clamped his emotions down. He didn't dare allow himself to feel the pain of all he'd lost. Even after all these centuries, it would destroy him.

"It's a waste of time and energy. It also drains the mind and makes it weary."

"But without pain, you can't have joy. It's the balance that makes us appreciate the extremes."

Now that was a deep concept. Very deep, considering they were sitting bare-assed on her bed. "Do you always philosophize while you're naked with a man?"

She nipped his shoulder impishly with her teeth. "It's rather hard to find a man who's willing to do that."

He dropped his gaze down to her breasts. "I imagine it would be a lot easier if you didn't look so damned good without your clothes on."

She moaned as he dipped his head and took one of her breasts into his mouth. She lay back on the bed, drawing him with her.

Talon sighed at the feel of her puckered areola under his tongue. He brushed his hand down the curve of her hip, over her soft thigh, and through the moist tangle of curls until he could touch the part of her he craved the most.

She groaned and shivered as he carefully separated the tender folds until he could tease her cleft.

Oh yeah, he wanted this part of her. Wanted to see her head thrown back against the pillows and hear her scream out loud while she came for him.

Sunshine clutched his head to her breast as she opened her legs wider, giving him access to her body. She ached and throbbed at the feel of his hand stroking her. And when he plunged his fingers inside, she cried out.

Her body burned for his in a most unbelievable way. It was hot and fierce and made her tremble with need. She'd never wanted a man as much as she wanted this one. She wanted to pull him close to her. Closer and closer until they truly melted into one being.

Unable to wait any longer, she reached down between their bodies so that she could guide him deep inside her.

They groaned in unison.

Sunshine arched her back, drawing him in even deeper.

He was so hard and hot, so full. She'd never felt anything better than him filling her.

He sat back on his legs and pulled her hips so that he could slide into her, slowly, deeply. It was a rolling rhythm that made her writhe from the intense pleasure of his intimate strokes.

She stared at him as he watched her with a tender look on his face.

"You are beautiful," he breathed, rolling his hips against hers and thrusting himself even deeper and harder inside her.

"You too," she said as she clutched at his knees.

His eyes darkened as he watched her and he gave himself over to their union. She'd never had a man make love to her like this. It was as if he were nothing but sex. As if he could feel nothing but her body.

He had such a way with his hips as he slid himself in and out, hard and deep. He teased her with his hands, his fingers stroking her in time to his thrusts. The pleasure of his touch permeated every fiber of her being.

And when she came, the orgasm was so intense that she screamed.

Talon growled at the sound of her ecstasy as her body clutched his. Crying out, she reached up and pulled him down on top of her.

Then, she did the strangest thing of all . . . she nuzzled his neck and face, raining kisses all over his cheek and shoulder.

Talon froze.

Her arms held him tight against her as she wrapped her entire body around his. The tenderness of her touch and actions pricked him, breaking through the chokehold he kept on his emotions.

It was as if she really cared for him. As if he meant something to her. As if she were making love *with* him.

Only one woman had ever held him like this . . .

He could barely breathe. For the first time in fifteen hundred years he actually felt as if he were making love to a woman, not just satisfying a primitive urge.

No, this wasn't meaningless sex.

He *felt* her. Felt connected to her. Felt as if they were something more than strangers with no ties to each other.

Her lips scorched his skin as she continued to nuzzle his neck and thrust herself against him. He held her tight and closed his eyes. His senses and emotions reeled from the pleasure of the moment.

When he came in her arms, he shivered to the core of his battered and weary heart.

He lay there, vulnerable and panicked.

No, he couldn't have felt that. He couldn't have felt *her.* It wasn't possible.

He was mistaken. What they had was sex. Incredibly great sex, but nothing more than that.

Sex.

Simple.

Basic.

Uncomplicated.

And he was going to prove it to himself one way or another . . .

Sunshine lay in complete satisfied bliss, breathing raggedly, drifting slowly back into herself. That was the most incredible orgasm she'd ever experienced. She couldn't believe the way he'd felt, the way he'd touched her.

She held his head close to her heart and felt his ragged breath falling against her breast. She cradled him with her entire body and just soaked up the warm masculine weight of him.

Used to men who quickly dosed off after they came, she was completely unprepared when he rolled over onto his back and pulled her to lie across his chest.

"You didn't think I was through with you, did you?" he asked in her ear.

"Well, yeah."

He laughed. "Lady Sunshine, I've only just started."

To her delight and awe, he proved those words well over the course of the next few hours.

They made love on her bed, on the floor, on her sofa. He took her in so many different positions that she felt as if he were reenacting the entire *Kama Sutra.*

Finally, they ended up in the kitchen where he set her up on the counter and then made slow, tender love to her.

Oh heaven, the man felt incredible! He had more stamina than an entire team of athletes and was completely shameless when it came to making love to her. She'd never been with a man and felt so at ease with her body and his expectations.

A man like this was all too hard to come by.

After they had finished with the counter, which she would never be able to look at again without blushing, Talon stood naked, looking into her refrigerator with his two braids tucked behind his ear as he searched for food.

He was still breathing heavily from their last go-round and Sunshine wondered idly if she'd gone bow-legged at some point from this afternoon's marathon.

Still, he looked scrumptious as he moved containers around in his quest for nourishment. His bare backside was a feast for the eyes and when he bent over to look into her bottom drawer, she couldn't resist running her hand up his muscular thigh, between his legs, to cup and fondle him.

He sucked his breath in sharply between his teeth and straightened.

Sunshine gave him a mischievous grin that garnered her a quick kiss before he returned to searching her fridge.

"My lady, do you own anything made of meat?"

Sunshine ran her hand across his back, smoothing down the red marks where she'd sunk her nails in during her last orgasm. "I have soy burgers, and I did pick up some granola bars, wheat germ, and oatmeal while I was out."

He actually whimpered.

"Sorry. I'm a strict vegetarian."

He sighed. "And I'm a strict carnivore."

She licked her lips and smiled as she remembered his

playful nips and bites on her flesh. "I noticed."

He turned toward her and gathered her naked body against his. He kissed her lips as if he were still able to savor her even after all they had done this afternoon. Then, he pulled back. "As much as I want you again, I have got to have something more to nourish me than your hot, lush body."

He grabbed her soy cheese from the top shelf and the whole wheat crackers she had on the counter.

Sunshine started to warn him about the cheese, but thought better of it. He did need something other than her to nibble on, though to be honest, she liked being his chew toy.

The man was insatiable, and best of all, he was the champion at what he did.

She watched curiously as he grabbed his Snoopy Pez dispenser from her counter, then went back to the living room.

Sunshine picked up their glasses of water and followed him to the Art Deco coffee table.

Talon sat down before it and sliced the cheese, then placed it on the crackers. He fed her one. "So tell me, if I wasn't here, what would you be doing today?"

She laughed. "I'm sure I would probably be sitting more comfortably, for one thing."

His face amused, he dipped his head to nuzzle at her neck. "Can I rub anything to make it feel better?"

She hissed at his deep, sensuous voice. "Your rubbing it is what got me into trouble."

He ran his tongue over her collarbone, then he pulled back and ate a cracker.

He choked.

Sunshine handed him the water.

Talon drank it down fast and scowled at her. "How old is this stuff?" He checked the expiration date on the cheese and his scowl deepened. "Soy?" he said as he finally recognized the package. "You let me eat *soy* cheese?"

"It's good for you."

"It's nasty."

"Oh," she said, as if she were talking to a child. "You poor baby. I'm so sorry."

"No you're not."

"Not true. I *am* sorry I don't have anything a big he-man like you can stand."

Talon sat back and shook his head at her. He should have had Kyrian bring him a burger along with his clothes. Even so, he had thoroughly enjoyed the day with her.

Even if it did mean eating things that should be classified as toxic waste products.

Cringing, he reached for another cracker, more prepared this time for the disgusting taste of it. By sheer force of will, he downed six crackers with cheese, though they barely took the edge off his hunger.

Thank the gods he had his Pez. Grabbing Snoopy, he quickly popped three Pez cubes into his mouth to kill the taste.

"How can you eat that?" she asked. "It's nothing but flavored sugar."

"Yes, but it's *good* sugar."

She wrinkled her nose at him.

Talon gave her a wicked grin. "You know the best way to eat these, don't you?"

She shook her head.

He pulled Snoopy's head back and took the small square out with his fingers. He held it up to her lips. "Bite down gently on it and hold it between your teeth."

She hesitated, then obeyed.

For a full second, Talon watched her sitting there naked with the cube between her teeth. Then, he leaned forward and used his tongue to pry it loose.

Sunshine moaned at the taste of him combined with the sugar. Opening her mouth, she gave him a long, hot kiss. "Now, that was nice."

"Worth polluting your system for?"

"Umm-hmm," she breathed, running her fingertip along his jaw.

Once all the Pez were gone, she picked up the Snoopy dispenser and looked at it. "This seems so out of character for you, Mr. Tough Man. I find it hard to believe a guy who can fight off six criminals single-handedly would haul around a Peanuts Pez."

He brushed her black hair back from her shoulder and let his hand linger in the strands. "Actually, I collect the dispensers. This one is a vintage 1969 one."

"Really?"

He nodded.

She looked at it again. "Is it worth much?"

"A couple hundred dollars."

"No kidding?"

"No kidding."

"Wow. And I almost fed it to the washing machine."

He laughed at that. "I'm glad you didn't. Me and Snoopy go way back."

He took Snoopy from her hands and set it on the coffee table. When he turned back to face her, the gleam in his eye was one she'd become quite familiar with.

"Are you really sore?" he asked.

All things considered, she should be, but his touch was so gentle that she wasn't. "I'm not. You?"

"Never better."

He leaned back on the floor and pulled her across him. Sunshine straddled him and moaned at how good his steely abs felt against her.

To her amazement, he was already hard again. "You don't ever wear out, do you?"

He cupped her face in his hands and gave her a dark, serious stare. "It's you, love. Definitely you. With anyone else, I would have been curled up and sleeping hours ago."

"You mean that?"

He led her hand to his swollen shaft. "What do you think?"

"I think I should have taken more vitamins this morning."

"And I'm thinking there are still several positions we haven't tried."

Talon woke up in Sunshine's bed just as the sun set. He smiled in sleepy pleasure as he smelled the scent of turpentine and patchouli on his skin.

Sunshine.

She was still nestled in his arms, sound asleep. To his amazement, he felt his body starting to harden again.

After this afternoon, he should be sated for at least a day or two, if not for a full week.

For that matter, he shouldn't be able to move.

Yet he wanted to take her again. Right now. He wanted to feel her arms and legs wrapped around him, holding him close as he lost himself to the sensation of her flesh sliding against his.

Only Nynia had ever made him feel like this. He had been completely insatiable with her. To look at her was to burn for her.

He'd never thought to find another woman so appealing. And yet all he wanted to do was spend the rest of the night inside Sunshine. To feel her breath against his neck as he buried himself in her moist heat over and over again.

But he couldn't. He was supposed to meet Acheron at Jackson Square.

Not to mention that there were Daimons on the street ready to kill, and he had innocent people to protect.

"Talon?"

Inwardly, he cringed at the sound of her sleepy voice. He'd hoped to make a quiet exit while she slept.

How he hated messy exits.

"Evening, love," he murmured, kissing her brow.

She smiled a smile that dazzled him. "Are you leaving?"

"Yeah, I have to go meet someone."

"Okay," she said.

She got up from the bed, and wrapped a sheet around

herself. "It was really great meeting you, Talon. Thanks for a wonderful day."

She left him alone then.

Talon frowned. This was normally the part where his lovers begged him to stay, at least for a little while longer. Where they told him he was the best lover they had ever known and then cried at the thought of never having him again.

But Sunshine seemed completely fine with his leaving. She didn't seem to be the tiniest bit sad.

What was this?

He scooted out of bed and left the room to find her in the kitchen, holding a rice cake between her teeth while she poured herself a cup of pink juice.

"Sunshine, are you okay?"

She took the rice cake out of her mouth and looked at him. "I'm fine."

Her face paled a degree. "Oh Lord, you're not going to get possessive or weird on me now, are you? Please tell me you're not one of those guys Trina told me about who gets a little sex from a woman and then thinks he owns her."

A *little* sex?

A little sex!

Talon was dumbstruck. He was used to leaving his lovers, but this had to be the easiest time he'd ever experienced, and he found it strangely disconcerting.

Unsettling.

Humbling.

Especially given the way the two of them had carried on. This had been the best marathon of sex he'd ever had. She had met his passion and stamina in a way that was unbelievable.

Now she was fine with him just walking out the door?

"Are you sure you're okay?" he asked again.

"Look, it's cool, okay? I knew when I agreed to this that you wouldn't be hanging around afterward. I'm not stupid, you know. I'm a big girl. You're a really big guy and I'm sure you have a life to get back to." Panic drifted through her eyes. "Oh God, you're not married, are you?"

"No, I'm not married."

She let out a relieved breath. "Then, no harm, no foul."

She crossed the short distance to her fridge to return the juice jug.

"Sunshine?"

She paused to give him a peeved stare. "What, Talon? You're not having separation anxiety, are you? Today was fun and it was worth it, but I've got to get back to work. I have a ton of stuff that I need to do tonight."

"Yeah, but . . ." He didn't finish the sentence. He refused to.

"But?"

He clamped his jaw shut. Fine, if she wanted him gone, he was gone.

He shouldn't have spent the day with her anyway.

This close to Mardi Gras, he couldn't afford *any* distractions. Never mind one that came in the form of a dark-haired temptress.

"Nothing," he said.

She looked relieved. "Since you have to meet someone, you go ahead and shower and I'll make us some dinner."

Talon took her up on the shower, but when he was finished, he declined eating her tofu salad and soy steaks.

"Thanks again, Sunshine," he said as he shrugged his leather jacket on over his T-shirt. "I had a really good day."

"Me too," she said with a smile while she nibbled her salad and flipped through an art magazine.

He still couldn't believe how well she was taking his leaving her. Damn.

A part of him continued to expect her to at least beg him to call her.

Ask for his e-mail.

Something.

But she didn't.

Man, how he hated the twenty-first century.

She looked up as he headed for the door. "You take care of yourself, Talon. And in the future, please try and stay out of the way of runaway Mardi Gras floats, okay?"

Talon lifted both brows in stunned shock. "Excuse me?"

"Don't you remember last night when you got mowed down?"

Talon nodded hesitantly, unable to believe that that was what had slammed into him. "I was hit by a Mardi Gras float?"

"Yeah, it was Bacchus."

Now that was adding insult to injury. Jeez. He only hoped Nick didn't find out about it. Ever.

Nicholas Ambrosius Gautier had come into this world with not a lot of prospects. Born the bastard son of a career felon and a teenage Bourbon Street stripper, he wasn't exactly the most law-abiding of folks. In fact, his junior high guidance counselor had once voted him Most Likely to Get the Death Penalty.

But one night when Nick had made a stand against the gang he ran with, fate had changed his life and sent in a Dark-Hunter guardian angel who had taken a smart-mouthed kid, cleaned him up, and given him a real future.

Now, nine years later, he was a pre-law student, and instead of playing penal roulette like his father, he was almost a respectable citizen. *Almost* being the operative word.

All thanks to Kyrian of Thrace and Acheron Partheno-paeus.

There was nothing he wouldn't do for them and that was why he was sitting in his car, parked in a vacant field just after sunset, instead of being off with his latest girlfriend, putting a really big smile on her face.

Even with the car running, it was cold out here. That damp, frigid cold that could go deep into the bones and make them ache. His thermos of coffee all gone, Nick just wanted to get back home and thaw out.

Instead, he was waiting for Talon's Mardi Gras re-inforcement to be delivered, because Zarek, having spent the last nine hundred years in Alaska, had no idea how to drive a car. Apparently, cars weren't the transportation of choice for snowbound Dark-Hunters.

Yee-freakin'-haw. This was one event he could have waited his lifetime for.

"Nick, you there?"

"Yeah," he said into the portable radio he had in the passenger seat of his Jaguar that kept him in touch with the incoming helicopter. "What's your ETA?"

"About two minutes," Mike said.

Nick started scanning the dark sky for the black H-53E Sea Dragon Sikorsky helicopter. It was a long-range, custom-built military-class chopper that the Squires often used to transport Dark-Hunters. The helicopter was fast and versatile, and could be refueled while in flight.

Its back section was equipped with a steel passenger area that kept sunlight from touching the Dark-Hunters. The windows in the passenger compartment could be lightened with a flip of the switch to allow a Dark-Hunter to see outside after dark should he desire it.

A few Dark-Hunters such as Acheron owned their own helicopters and flew them when needed.

Tonight, though, Mike Callahan, who was a Dorean Squire (meaning he didn't have a particular Dark-Hunter he served) was bringing in Zarek from Alaska.

Nick had heard a lot of rumors through the on-line Squire bulletin boards about Zarek of Moesia being psychotic. He wasn't sure how accurate that information was, but in a few minutes he'd find out firsthand.

"Hey, Mike," he said, radioing the pilot. "How bad is he?"

Mike snorted. "Let me put it to you this way. If you have a gun, unload it."

"Why?"

"Because if you don't, you're going to shoot this asshole which will only piss him off more. For once, I actually pity the Daimons."

That didn't sound encouraging.

"What? He's worse than Acheron?"

"Nick, take my word for it. You ain't never seen anything like this one. I now know why Artemis and Ash
locked him in Alaska. What I can't figure out is why on
earth Artemis wanted him moved into a large population.
My opinion, it's like tossing a grenade on a gas station."

Oh yeah, his gut was knotted now.

Nick waited as the helicopter landed on the private airstrip Acheron used when he visited. At one end of the field
stood a building that appeared to be a dilapidated barn. In
actuality, it was a modified modern hangar equipped with
an alarm system and doors so thick it could double as a
bomb shelter. That barn currently housed the twenty-eight-
million-dollar MH-60K Sikorsky helicopter that Acheron
used to transport himself and his custom-built Buell motorcycle.

Ash had arrived in style the day before.

Now Zarek.

Yup, Mardi Gras was starting to look scary.

Nick got out of the car and locked his radio in the trunk,
then stood to the side of the field until Mike cut the motor
and the blades stopped spinning.

When everything quit moving, the lean, middle-aged
Squire got out of the helicopter and removed his helmet.
Mike had never been overly friendly, but tonight he looked
thoroughly disgusted and extremely irritable.

"I don't envy you this," Mike said as he tossed his helmet back into his seat.

"C'mon, stop messing with me, Mike. He can't be that
bad."

Nick changed his mind as soon as Mike slid open the
passenger door and he caught his first look at Zarek of
Moesia.

Zarek emerged from the opening like Lucifer from his
deepest pit, with a chip on his shoulder so large, Nick was
amazed they had managed to get the helicopter off the
ground.

Dressed all in black, Zarek wore jeans, Harley biker

boots, and a long-sleeved T-shirt. He seemed completely oblivious to the cold damp air that made up a New Orleans winter night. He had a long silver sword earring in his left ear, with a hilt made of a skull and crossbones.

Zarek stepped out with a sneer that was made more sinister by his black goatee. His straight black hair brushed his shoulders and his jet-black eyes were filled with contempt and hatred. Nick was used to bad attitude; hell, he'd been weaned on it. But he'd never met a man who had one worse than Zarek.

He reminded Nick of the murderers his father had brought home. Cold. Unfeeling. Lethal. Whenever Zarek looked at you, you got the feeling he was measuring you for your coffin size.

Zarek braced his left hand against the side of the chopper, and leaned back in long enough to grab a large black duffel bag. Nick stared at Zarek's huge hand in awe. Each finger, including his thumb, was covered with a long, articulated silver claw and tipped with a point so sharp that Nick knew it must be Zarek's weapon of choice.

This man liked to get down and dirty with his kills.

Shit, for Zarek, being called psychotic would be a step up.

As he walked away from the chopper, Zarek hissed at Mike, baring his fangs.

For once, Mike didn't comment. That told Nick more than anything else just how vicious Zarek was. He'd never known Mike to take something like that and not make a smart-mouth comment.

"Well, if you're through taunting poor Mike, are you ready to go?"

Nick regretted those words as soon as Zarek looked at him. The glacial, hostile glare chilled him even more than the frigid winds. "You give me any lip, little boy, and there won't be enough left of you to run through a sieve."

Nick didn't scare easily, but those words were said with such growling sincerity that he actually took a step back, and for once kept his big mouth shut.

Without another word, Zarek walked with a predator's deadly grace toward the car, with his lips curled into a permanent snarl. He pitched his duffel bag onto the floorboard, then got in and slammed the car door shut.

In that moment, Nick seriously regretted buying a car with no backseat.

Then again, given Zarek's vicious, unpredictable nature, Nick would much rather have him beside him than *behind* him.

Mike let out a relieved breath and clapped him on the back. "May God take a liking to you, kid. I damn sure wouldn't want to be in your shoes tonight."

Nick had never been overly religious. But as he walked to his anthracite Jag, he found his religion all over again.

He got in and started the car, then headed toward the city. They were supposed to meet up with Talon, Valerius, and Acheron in about half an hour at Jackson Square. Damn, this was going to be the longest drive of his life.

He pushed the accelerator down even more—warp speed would suit him just fine.

As he drove, Nick couldn't keep his gaze from repeatedly wandering over to Zarek's left hand, covered with the silver claws, which was splayed out over his left knee.

The silence was deafening and stagnant, and was relieved only by Zarek flexing his claws against the black denim. After a time, the metallic scratching sound started to get on Nick's nerves. He turned on the radio.

"You like rock?" he asked.

The radio shut off immediately.

Nick swallowed as he realized one of Zarek's Dark-Hunter powers was telekinesis.

"Little boy, I'm not your friend. I'm not your Dark-Hunter and I'm not your friggin' date. You only speak to me when I ask you a question. Otherwise you keep your mouth shut, your eyes off me, and you might live long enough to get me to the French Quarter."

Nick gripped the wheel. Okay, now that pissed him off,

but not to the point it made him suicidal. Only an absolute fool would tangle with a man this lethal.

Zarek flipped open his duffel bag and pulled out a credit-card-sized MP3 player and a pair of dark sunglasses. He put on his headphones and sunglasses, then leaned his head back against the seat. Nick heard Nazareth's *Hair of the Dog* playing in a whisper from the headphones. The true antisocial anthem. How incredibly apropos.

When the car radio unexpectedly flipped back on, Nick actually jumped.

Oh yeah, Zarek was one psychotic SOB and the sooner he got him out of his car and to Acheron, the happier Nick would be.

Talon was still thinking of Sunshine when he crossed the Pedestrian Mall to meet with Acheron. He glanced down the street to where he had met Sunshine the night before, and his gut wrenched.

How he missed her. And that was the craziest part of all. He barely knew her. She had swept into his life like a hurricane, wreaking total destruction and chaos, and still . . .

He sighed. She'd been a nice diversion. But he had business to attend to.

His excursion with her was over. He would never see her again.

That was that.

As of this moment, she no longer existed.

Yeah, right.

Talon ignored the derisive voice in his head. He had no choice but to forget her. He'd made a pact centuries ago and it was a pact he would honor for the rest of eternity. For him there would never be a home, a family, and most definitely not a girlfriend or a wife. Even if he hadn't taken Artemis's oath, those things would be forbidden to him.

Besides, he liked his life as it was. He had a lot of

freedom. Time to do what he wanted and enough money
to purchase anything that appealed to him.

Life as a Dark-Hunter was good.

Very good.

Entering the square, he caught sight of Acheron Parthenopaeus standing against the wall of a building with his
arms folded over his chest. The tall Atlantean warrior stood
apart from a crowd that was listening to a street performer
sing his rendition of the Scooby-Doo theme.

Standing six feet eight with long metallic purple hair and
wearing black wraparound sunglasses long after sundown,
Acheron was a hard man to miss.

Talon usually referred to Acheron as T-Rex. The nickname stemmed more from the man's intimidating, carniv-
orous presence than from his ancient age.

There was something truly eerie about Acheron's lethal
aura. It flowed out of him like a dangerous tsunami. The
very air around the man seemed charged with mystical energy so powerful that it could make the skin on your arms
or back of your neck crawl if you stood too close to him.

And judging by the berth the crowd had given T-Rex,
Talon would say he wasn't the only one to feel it.

Then again, Talon amended, as he noted Acheron's
black motorcycle jacket with silver chain mail draped over
one sleeve and his leather pants that had laces instead of
seams, maybe it was Acheron's eccentric, unorthodox looks
that made people leave him alone.

Whatever it was, no one wanted to get in that man's
way.

Acheron turned his head.

Even with the black wraparound sunglasses covering his
eyes, Talon knew T-Rex was staring straight at him. Talon
gave a short laugh as he noticed Acheron's new facial ad-
dition. A silver nose stud.

T-Rex had two very strange penchants: he was always
finding new places to pierce his body, and his hair color
changed faster than the unpredictable Louisiana weather.

T-Rex also had a strange scar of a hand print that came

and went on his neck. No one was sure if the scar was real or if it was some weird trick to throw them off guard that Acheron used. His accent was the same way. There were times when Acheron's voice was heavy with an odd melodic accent Talon assumed to be his native one from Atlantis, and other times T-Rex sounded just like any other television-programmed American.

The ancient warrior seemed to take a great deal of pleasure in keeping people guessing about him. He was even more private than Talon and that was saying something.

Acheron retrieved his black suede backpack, which was decorated with an anarchy logo from the street. He slung it over his shoulder, then tossed a few bills into the musician's guitar case and headed over.

Several members of the crowd visibly tensed and recoiled as Acheron moved through them with the fluid long-legged gait of a dangerous predator. Those who dared to look at him quickly averted their gazes.

It was ironic, really, since Acheron was the last person on earth who would ever harm a mortal. He was the oldest protector mankind had.

For centuries he had fought the Daimons single-handedly.

Alone.

Without friend or Squire.

Talon had heard rumors that Acheron had been trained to fight by Ares himself. Other rumors claimed Acheron was the son of a god and a legendary Atlantean hero.

But basically no one knew anything about Acheron other than he was tall, private, intimidating, and very, very strange.

As Acheron drew near, Talon inclined his head toward Acheron's purple hair with its four small braids that framed his face. "You know, I think I need to drop the T-Rex and start calling you Barney."

One corner of Acheron's mouth quirked up. "Don't start on me, Celt." He raked an amused look over Talon's leather pants, T-shirt, and jacket. "Nice to see you *fully* dressed for the occasion."

Talon winced at the underlying meaning of that comment. "Kyrian told on me, huh?"

"Oh, yeah. The pink towel bit was my favorite part."

Kyrian would pay for this. Even if Talon had to hunt him down. "I swear . . . Does Nick know?"

Acheron smiled a real smile that flashed a tiny bit of fang.

Damn, he was screwed now.

Oh, what the hell, it'd been worth it. Spending the afternoon with Sunshine had more than made up for any embarrassment.

T-Rex looked over his shoulder as if sensing something, and a corner of his leather jacket fell away from his throat to show the hand print was gone again.

Talon followed his line of vision to see Valerius approaching them. He'd only met the Roman general one other time when Valerius had first arrived to assume Kyrian's Dark-Hunter duties.

Valerius had taken one look at Talon's jacket and torc, and sneered the word *Celt*, thus letting Talon know friendship with this Dark-Hunter was about as likely as finding a parking space for a tank on Bourbon Street during Mardi Gras.

And just think, he was doomed to spend eternity in New Orleans with this prick. As Nick would say, yee-freakin'-haw.

The Roman's black hair was pulled back into an impeccable queue. He wore black pleated pants, loafers, turtleneck, and a long cashmere coat. If one didn't know better, he would appear to be an affluent attorney, not a Daimon executioner.

And it was all Talon could do not to laugh at how out of place Valerius looked standing next to him, and most especially Acheron, who was a poster boy for the goth movement. Right down to the silver stud in Acheron's nose and the silver buckles that decorated the side of his pointy-toed boots.

"How very punctual you are," Acheron said to Valerius as he looked at the cracked pocket watch he'd pulled out of his jacket pocket. The watch had suffered a mishap about a hundred years ago during a major Daimon uprising. The watch had survived, the Daimons hadn't.

Valerius's black eyes smoldered with resentment as he looked up at Acheron. "I might not like the fact that you are my commander, Greek, but as a soldier I will obey you regardless of my personal distaste for your company."

Talon smirked. "Gee, T-Rex, doesn't it make you all warm and fuzzy just to be near him?"

"Show respect to your betters, Celt," Valerius snarled, curling his upper lip. "Or I'll show you how we Romans dealt with your barbaric kind."

The words didn't elicit any emotion other than bored amusement, but Talon had never been the kind of man to let an insult pass without comment.

He was certainly too old now to change his ways.

"Ah, respect this," he said, flipping Valerius off.

Acheron barely caught Valerius as he lunged for Talon. He placed himself physically between them; not that Talon needed it, but judging by the fury in Valerius's eyes, the Roman certainly did.

"Children, don't make me separate you again." Acheron glared at Valerius and forced the Roman to take a step back. "Believe me, Val, I don't need you to fight my battles and I take no offense to Talon."

"My name is Valerius." Valerius straightened his coat with a regal, arrogant jerk. "And I do take offense to him."

Yeah, well, what was new? The man seemed to take offense at everything.

As usual, whenever two or more Dark-Hunters came together, Talon felt his powers weakening. It was a safeguard Artemis used to ensure her Dark-Hunters couldn't combine strengths and go after the gods or prey on mankind. The only exception to that was Acheron. As the designated trainer and the eldest of their breed, his presence didn't drain their powers, but everyone else's did.

They wouldn't be able to stay together much longer or they would be depleted for the night.

Talon glanced past Valerius's shoulder to see Nick and Zarek walking past the bakery on the corner and heading toward them. "Look unalive, men," he said to Acheron and Valerius, "here comes our reinforcement."

Valerius turned around and let out a vulgar curse that seemed at odds with his regal Roman air of refinement and good breeding.

"Back at you," Zarek snarled as he paused beside Acheron.

Disgust was evident on Valerius's face. "Not another friggin' Greek."

"What's the matter, Roman?" Talon asked. "Greeks bother you?"

His nostrils flared, Valerius raked a sneer over Zarek. "Trust me, had I been at Troy when they left the horse behind, there would have been roasted Greek on the beach that day."

Talon hissed in mock sympathy. "Damn, T-Rex, he really hates your ancestors."

Acheron gave him a droll stare. "No offense, Talon, I was around before they were."

"Oh yeah, sorry." Talon exchanged glances with Nick, who was much quieter than normal. The Squire looked a bit strained.

Hmm, that was interesting. He'd have to keep Zarek around if the man had that kind of suppression power. It was nice to know Nick had an off switch.

"Any problems with your flight?" Acheron asked Zarek.

"I didn't eat my pilot if that's what you mean. And little Nicky here is still breathing and not bleeding."

"Well," Acheron said, his tone flat. "I suppose that's an improvement over last time."

Talon wasn't sure if Acheron was joking or not, but knowing Zarek's reputation, he didn't really doubt it was true. Rumor had it that Zarek had cut up and eaten the last Squire Acheron had sent for him.

Talon swept a glance around the five of them.

Were they a motley bunch or what? The only thing they had in common was height. Collectively, they must look like refugees from the NBA since they ranged in height from Nick's six feet four to Acheron's six feet eight.

Nick was dressed in jeans, a dark green sweater, and bomber jacket—the perfect image of a rich college student. Talon looked like a biker who had just left Sanctuary, New Orleans's premier biker bar. Acheron looked like a refugee from the Dungeon—the local underground goth hangout. Valerius was the professional contingent, and Zarek . . .

Zarek just looked like he was ready to kill something.

"So why are we congregating?" Zarek asked.

The repugnant hatred in Valerius's eyes was searing. "Did anyone speak to you, *slave*?"

Acheron barely caught Zarek's hand before his claw sliced Valerius's vulnerable throat. Never before had Talon seen Acheron struggle so hard to hold someone back. It spoke a lot for Zarek's power.

And his temper.

"Cease!" Acheron ordered Zarek. "I know it's been a long time since you were around another Dark-Hunter, Z, but remember, whatever you do to him, *you* will feel it tenfold."

Zarek's face hardened. "Pain I can take, it's him I can't."

Valerius still had his lips curled. "I don't see why we need a whipping boy for the Daimons to play with. You know, he was so worthless in his lifetime that my father had to pay a slaver to take him off our hands."

Zarek let out the snarl of a wild beast. An instant later, Acheron was thrown clear of him and Zarek bolted at Valerius. He caught the Roman around the waist and the two of them hit the street. Hard.

Before Talon could pull him off Valerius, Zarek got in a number of solid punches and one last kick to the Roman's ribs as Talon hauled him up.

Just as Acheron had said, Zarek's face showed every blow he had given to Valerius. His nose and lips were bleeding profusely. Zarek didn't seem to notice and if he did, the satisfied gleam in his black eyes said the ex-Roman slave thought it well worth the cost.

Valerius was only slightly more subdued as he regained his feet. "You should be beaten for that."

Talon tightened his hold on Zarek.

Angrily, Zarek shoved him away. "Get your fucking hands off me, Celt." Then he turned back to Valerius. "Try beating me, you sorry piece of shit, and I'll force-feed you that black heart of yours."

"Enough!" Acheron roared. "Another word from either one of you, and I swear I'll rip both your hearts out."

Valerius wiped the blood from his lips.

Zarek raked his hand across his face, removing the blood, while he glared murderously at Valerius.

Acheron was a man of infinite patience and Talon had never seen Acheron exasperated before. But he saw it now.

Acheron glared at the Dark-Hunters. "Next time I'll just send the three of you e-mails. What was I thinking when I decided to have this meeting?"

Nick spoke up. "Oh, I know. That men who are a couple of thousand years old could actually behave like grown-ups?"

Zarek elbowed Nick in the stomach.

"Oops," Zarek said to Acheron. "Involuntary arm spasm."

Acheron cursed under his breath. "I swear, Daimons or not, if you don't behave, Z, I'm going to send you to Antarctica and leave you there to rot."

"Ooo," Zarek breathed in a bored tone. "I'm terrified. Those killer penguins and hairy seals are *really* scary."

Acheron growled a low warning at Zarek.

Talon felt for his frustrated leader. He knew why Acheron had set up this meeting. The Atlantean had wanted to know what would happen when the three of them crossed paths. Better to see how much hostility there was up front and be here to control it than to chance a random meeting where Zarek could beat the snot out of Valerius without someone there to break them up.

Now Acheron knew exactly what he was dealing with and how much space to put between them. Talon had to salute the Atlantean's wisdom. Acheron might be young in appearance, but he was truly ancient in his powers, knowledge, and ability to handle the rogue Dark-Hunters who answered to him.

Acheron passed a look to each of them. "If you can control yourselves for five minutes, we need to divide up the city. Since I'm the only one able to take the cemeteries, I'll grab those. Valerius, I want you in the garden and business districts, Zarek and Talon can take the Quarter. On Mardi Gras itself, we all need to be in the Vieux Carré no later than nine."

He turned to Nick. "You are on standby. In the event one of us goes down, I need you to mobilize quickly."

"Just one little problem."

"And that is?"

Nick indicated Valerius with his head. "If he goes down, he's on his own."

Zarek smiled. "I knew I liked this kid for a reason."

Nick shot him a disbelieving stare.

"Nick," Acheron said, his voice laced with warning, "your duty is to all of us. Valerius is a Dark-Hunter same as me, Talon, and Zarek."

"I know I swore my oath, but I swore it to protect Kyrian of Thrace and hell will freeze colder than Santa's iceberg before I ever lift even an eyebrow to help the man who tortured and crucified him."

Valerius's eyes blazed.

"That was his grandfather, not him."

Nick pointed a finger at Valerius. "He was there, too, watching it happen, and he did nothing to stop it. I refuse to render aid to someone who could do that." He looked back at Ash. "You, psycho-ass, and Talon, I'll cover, but not him."

"Psycho-ass?" Zarek repeated. "Hmm, I like that."

Acheron ignored Zarek. "Nick—"

"It's all right, Greek," Valerius interrupted. "I would rather die than have his plebeian help anyway."

"Make that three votes, then," Zarek said. "I would rather he died too. Now all together, let's vote this asshole off the island."

Talon hid his amusement and wondered how much longer it would be before Acheron splintered Zarek and Valerius into itty-bitty Dark-Hunter pieces.

Maybe he should tell Nick to get a dustpan ready. The look on Acheron's face said the wait wouldn't be much longer.

"Fine, then," Acheron said to Nick. "Call Eric St. James and have him resume Barnacle Squire status for Valerius should Valerius need anything."

Nick nodded. "Can I have him cover Zarek too? I still have school to worry about."

Before Acheron could answer, Valerius sneered, "I will not work with a slave as an equal nor will I share a servant with him."

Zarek's nostrils flared. "Trust me, boy, we're not equal. You're so far beneath me that I would sooner sit in shit than let you wipe my ass."

Talon caught Valerius before he reached Zarek.

He exchanged looks with Acheron. "This is going to be fun, isn't it? Constantly separating the two of them while fighting off the Daimons. Should we just forget the whole thing and hole up in our homes until it's over?"

But even more discouraging was the knowledge that if Kyrian found out Valerius was in the city, he would make Zarek's attack look like a loving embrace. And since Kyrian was no longer a Dark-Hunter, his powers wouldn't be dampened by Artemis's restriction. He would have free rein to kill the Roman.

Acheron sighed irritably. "I'm almost ready to agree with you." He turned to Valerius. "Go patrol your districts."

Valerius gave him a rather sarcastic Roman salute, then turned on his heel and left them.

The air between them warmed up considerably. Hell, Zarek even looked almost . . . tolerable. A noticeable amount of tension left the man's body.

"Am I staying with you and Kyrian or Nick?" Zarek asked.

Acheron fell quiet while he fished a key out of his jacket pocket. "We thought it best that you have your own place. I had Nick rent a townhouse for you over on Dauphin Street. He painted the windows black and made sure they were all blocked from daylight."

Zarek's face returned to stone and his black eyes blazed. For some reason, the man was furious as he snatched the key from Acheron's hand and turned to leave.

"I'll have Nick show you where it is," Acheron said.

"I don't need anyone to show me a damn thing," Zarek snarled. "I'll find it on my own."

After Zarek stalked off, Nick grimaced. "I know," he said to Acheron. " 'Nick, go after psycho-ass and show him where he lives.' But might I point out that in doing this, I should qualify for hazard pay?"

Acheron arched a brow. "Might I point out that staying here with me is far more hazardous to your health?"

Nick feigned surprise. "What? Am I still here? Oh no, sorry, thought I'd left ten minutes ago."

He sprinted off after Zarek.

Once they were alone, Talon raked a hand through his hair. "Some nights it's not worth getting up, is it?"

"You've no idea." Acheron let out a long, deep breath as if he were expelling all the tension in his body.

"So tell me, T-Rex, what did you do to Artemis to make her dump this on you?"

As expected, Acheron said nothing. To Talon's knowledge, he had never divulged anything personal about himself or the exact nature of his relationship with the goddess.

"Walk with me, Talon."

That didn't sound good, but Talon followed him.

Acheron remained silent as they left the Pedestrian Mall and headed down Pirate's Alley in the direction of Royal Street.

Just beside the St. Louis Cathedral, near the small garden behind it, Acheron stopped. Talon glanced about uneasily. Dark-Hunters didn't do well around holy places. Since they were men who had lost their souls, souls that had lost their bodies tended to want to take up residence with them. A strong Dark-Hunter could fight the souls off, but only Acheron was completely immune to possession.

It was the main reason Dark-Hunters lived only in new houses and why Nick had taken a psychic into Zarek's townhouse to ensure no ghosts were hanging out. A possessed Dark-Hunter was a scary thing.

"Tell me about the woman you spent the day with."

He started at Acheron's words. The man's powers had never ceased to amaze him. "Nothing to tell, really."

"Don't lie to me, Talon. Sunshine is still within you. I can feel her there. She's in your thoughts and your blood."

The man was truly eerie. "Look, I know where my duties lie. I made an oath to Artemis and I'm not trying to find a way to break it."

"That's not what concerns me."

"Then what is?" Talon asked.

"Do you remember what I told you the night you took vengeance against your clan?"

"Nothing comes without a price."

"Exactly. This woman is inside you, little brother. If you don't get her out, she will unlock those emotions I taught you to bury."

"Would that be so bad?"

Acheron removed his sunglasses and gave him a hard, serious stare with those ageless, timeless glowing eyes. "Yes, it would. You are the one Dark-Hunter I can depend on to have a clear, level head. I need you to stay focused, especially since we have Daimon Fest coming up and two Dark-Hunters in town who hate each other.

"Your emotions are the key to your powers, Talon.

When you lose your control, you lose your Dark-Hunter immortality with it, and I don't want to see you dead because you can't control your libido."

"Don't worry. I'm under control."

"Good. Just make sure you stay that way because if you don't, you *will* get yourself killed."

Chapter 5

"Oh, thank God you're there," Selena said in Sunshine's ear as soon as Sunshine answered the phone. "Where have you been? I've been ringing the phone off the hook all day long trying to reach you. I know you can never find the damn thing, but dang, girl . . . I've been so worried that I was about to head over there and see if you were okay or if this unknown guy had murdered you in your loft." Selena finally took a breath in the midst of her tirade. "Please tell me he's not still there."

Wiping off her paint-stained hands while she cradled the phone between her ear and shoulder, Sunshine smiled at Selena's concerned voice and her motherlike lecture. "No, Selena, Mr. Bodacious is gone. He had to go meet some friends."

"Well, what time did he leave?"

"A few minutes ago."

"Sunshine!"

"What?" she asked in feigned innocence.

"Oh, honey," Selena gasped, "don't tell me you spent the whole day with him playing Parcheesi or something."

Sunshine bit her lip as she remembered exactly what they had spent the day doing. It made her warm and tingly all over again. "We didn't get to the Parcheesi, but we did it on the backgammon table a couple of times. And on the couch, the kitchen counter, the floor, the coffee table, and—"

"Oh, my God, TMI—way too much information. Tell me you're joking about this."

"Nope, not a bit. I'm telling you, Selena, forget the Energizer Bunny, this guy had it all."

Selena groaned. "What were you thinking? You just met him."

"I know," Sunshine said, agreeing completely with her friend that she was a lunatic for doing something so stupid. "It's so not like me, but I couldn't help myself. It was just like that weird magnetic force that grabs me when I'm walking past the Frostbyte Cafe and makes me swerve in to get a triple scoop of Ben and Jerry's Chunky Monkey."

That was her one major vice. Sunshine had never been able pass up Chunky Monkey.

"The power of temptation was just too much, Selena. I couldn't resist it. He was a Chunky Monkey container and all I could think was, 'Someone give me a spoon.' "

"Oh, good grief," Selena said.

"Yeah. It was weird. I was here, he was here, and then he said, 'Let's do it,' and the next thing I knew, the spoon was in my hand and I was going for it."

Selena made a disgusted noise. "Please tell me no one was using a spoon."

Sunshine smiled devilishly. "No, no spoon, but there was a whole lot of licking going on."

"Oh, oh, oh! You're killing me. Don't go there."

Sunshine laughed. "I can't stop myself. He was so hot that I feel this deep need to share his spectacular hotness with you."

Selena snorted at her. "Are you at least going to see him again?"

"No, unfortunately not. I didn't even get his last name."

"Sunshine! Girl, you are nuts."

"Yeah, I know. It was just a once-in-a-lifetime kind of thing."

"Sheez, are you okay, though? He didn't hurt you or anything?"

"Oh no, not at all. It was the best day of my life. Freaky, ain't it?"

"Ah jeez, Sunny. I can't believe you did this. You've been hanging around all those weird friends of yours so much that you're picking up their bad habits. Bringing home stray men you don't even know. Next thing you know, you'll be dancing naked on tabletops . . . Oh wait, that was me."

Sunshine laughed. "Don't worry. It'll never happen again. You know me, I do date occasionally, but I usually spend at least a few normal, boring days with a guy before we rock the house down. Of course, no one ever rocked my house down the way this guy did. He leveled the mother to its foundations."

Selena shrieked. "I can't believe you keep telling me this."

Sunshine laughed at the tortured angst in Selena's voice as she continued to tease her. "I can't believe I spent the day in bed with this guy, but I'd do it again in a heartbeat. I'm telling you, these were the best eighteen hours of my life."

"Jeez, you didn't even know him a whole day?"

"Well, I know him now. Every last yummy inch of him. By the way, he had a lot of inches."

"Stop it, Sunny," Selena begged, her voice cracking with laughter. "I can't take any more. I don't need to know the sexual athlete of all time is running around New Orleans and I'm married to the lawyer. This is so cruel."

Sunshine laughed again. "Well, Bill is nice, in a very Bill sort of way."

"Oh gee, thanks, now you're ripping on my Bill."

"I'm sorry. You know I love Bill, but this guy was really, really great." Sunshine, dragging the heavy, psychedelic phone in her wake, crossed the kitchen toward her fridge to get some guava juice. Teasing Selena was fun, but oddly enough there was a part of her that was extremely sad Talon had left.

He really had been a lot of fun and not just in the bed, or on the floor, or on the other five thousand places where they'd had sex. He'd been fun to talk to too.

Best of all, he hadn't lost his patience with her.

She opened the fridge, then laughed again.

"What?" Selena asked.

Sunshine saw Talon's prized Snoopy Pez dispenser standing up, looking straight at her. She couldn't believe it.

So that was what he'd been doing in the fridge while she was in the shower. No wonder he had looked uncomfortable when she caught him.

How adorable.

"Awww, he left me his Snoopy Pez dispenser on top of the soy cheese."

"What?" Selena asked.

"Nothing," Sunshine said, taking the cold plastic toy into her hand. "It's an inside joke."

"Oh, don't tell me you did something with the cheese."

"No, we just ate it. Jeez, Selena, get your mind out of the gutter. Not everything has to do with sex."

"Well, with the two of you it does. The basis of your whole entire relationship seems to be nothing but sex . . . Oh wait, it's only been eighteen hours since you met him. Does that qualify as a relationship?"

"Believe me, the way he does sex, it counts. Besides, he did leave me his Pez dispenser."

"Ooo," Selena teased, "he's bodacious and generous. What a guy."

"Hey now, be fair to my bodacious biker. It's a valuable Pez dispenser. A 1960-something collector's item."

"Yeah, but did he leave you his phone number?"

"Well no, but he did put Snoopy on the top shelf so I would find it."

"Enough said. Case closed. You're still riding the loser train when Snoopy becomes something valuable."

"Okay, fine, Selena, you're bringing me down from my love fest and I'm losing my afterglow. It's been ten months since I last slept with a guy and it'll probably be forever and a day before another one who's not gay darkens my doorstep, so let me go back to work where I can bask in the after-greatness of my afternoon."

"Okay, sweetie. I'll call you later. I was just concerned. You go back to work and I'll see you tomorrow."

"Okay, thanks. Bye."

Sunshine hung up the phone and looked down at the Snoopy in her hand. She laughed.

Talon might not be perfect, he might even occasionally screw up and get run down by a Mardi Gras float, but he had been a great guy, and great guys were hard to come by in this day and age.

It was a pity she'd never see him again. But then, she wasn't the kind of woman to mope over what could have been. She was an artist with a good career that she had worked very hard for.

A serious relationship with someone wasn't something she was looking for right now.

She liked living alone. Loved having the freedom to just pick up and go whenever and wherever she wanted to. Her brief marriage in her early twenties had schooled her well on what a man expected from a wife.

She had no intention of *ever* revisiting that fiasco.

Talon had been a fun afternoon diversion, but that was all he was. Her life would now go on just as it always had.

Her heart lighter at the thought of him, she took Snoopy into her bedroom and set him on the nightstand by the bed.

Sunshine smiled. She'd never had a memento before. But that's what Snoopy was to her. A token reminder of a wonderful day.

"Have a nice life, Talon," she said, turning off the light by the bed before she headed back to her work. "Maybe someday we might meet again."

.   .   .

It was just after one A.M. when Talon found himself outside the club Runningwolf's on Canal Street. He'd tried to tell himself that he was here because Daimons were often found hanging in and around clubs where drunken humans made easy pickings.

He'd tried to tell himself that he was just doing his job.

But as he looked up at the dark windows above the club and wondered if Sunshine was up there in her bed or if she was at her easel painting, he knew better.

He was here because of her.

Talon cursed under his breath. Acheron was right. She was inside him in a way no one had been inside of him in centuries.

No matter what he tried, he couldn't get her out of his mind.

Over and over, he could feel her. Feel her body under his, her breath on his skin. Hear the sound of her soft Southern drawl whispering in his ear.

And when she had touched him . . .

It was like a song from heaven.

The physical comfort and companionship she'd given him this afternoon had touched him profoundly.

He'd felt welcomed in a way that wasn't sexual.

What had she done to him? Why after all these centuries had a woman crept inside his feelings?

His thoughts?

Even more frustrating, he knew if he were human, he'd be with her now.

You're not human.

He didn't need the reminder. All too well, he knew what he was. He liked what he was. There was a special kind of satisfaction that came with his job.

And yet . . .

"Speirr? What are you doing?"

He tensed at Ceara's voice coming out of the darkness and at the fact that someone had caught him doing something he shouldn't be doing.

"Nothing."

She appeared beside him. Her shimmering face smiled knowingly.

He let out a disgusted breath. Why did he bother trying to hide anything from the ones who could see straight into his thoughts?

"Yeah, okay," he admitted reluctantly, "so I wanted to check up on her and see how she's doing."

"She's fine."

"And that *really* irritates me." The words were out before he realized it.

Ceara laughed at that. "You were expecting her to be sad?"

"Of course. She should at least have had a moment or two of regret or something."

Ceara clucked her tongue. "Poor Speirr. You found the only woman alive who doesn't think you hung the moon and the stars."

He rolled his eyes at her. "So maybe I'm being a little arrogant . . ." She arched a brow and he corrected himself. "So I'm being a lot arrogant, but damn, I can't get her out of my thoughts. How can she feel nothing?"

"I didn't say she felt nothing, I only said she's not sad."

"So she did feel something for me?"

"If you like, I could do more investigating."

"*Nae,*" Talon said quickly. The last thing he wanted was for Ceara to find out what he and Sunshine had been doing all afternoon.

Ceara was naive and he wanted to keep her that way.

His sister walked a small circle around his body. For some reason she'd always liked to do that. As a little girl, she'd made him dizzy as she raced around him at a dead run, giggling as she went.

Even though she was a young woman before him now, in his heart he always saw her as that chubby little toddler who used to sit on his lap for hours, playing with his braids as she gibbered her baby speech at him.

Just like Dere . . .

His stomach clenched at the memory.

Ceara hadn't been his only sister. Three more had been born between them. Fia had died her first year of life. Tress had lived to age five when she perished of the same illness that had claimed their mother.

And Dere . . .

She had died at age four.

She'd gone out at sunrise, wanting to see the fey folk Talon had teased her with. He'd told her how he often saw them out the window at daybreak while she slept.

Only five years old himself, he had heard someone leave their hut. At first he had thought it was his father. But as he snuggled back down to sleep, he'd realized Dere wasn't in their bed.

He'd gotten up immediately and rushed out to find her.

She had slipped on the rocks along the edge of the cliff that looked out onto the sea where he'd told her the fey frolicked in the early dawn's light.

He heard her scream and had run as fast as he could.

By the time he reached her, it was too late. Her young arms had been unable to hold on until he got there.

She lay below on the rocks with the waves rushing over her.

Even now, he could see her lying there. Could see the looks on his parents' faces when he had awakened them with the news.

Worst of all, he could see the accusation in his father's eyes.

Neither of his parents had ever uttered the words aloud, but in his heart he knew they had blamed him for it.

Not that it mattered. He blamed himself. He always had.

It was why he had been so protective of Ceara and Tress. Why he had been so determined that nothing bad would ever happen to his youngest sister.

Tonight, he saw a hesitancy in Ceara's steps.

"So, what's the news from the Daimon world?" he asked her.

Ceara paused. "How did you know?"

"You've been strangely quiet tonight. It's not like you

to stay hidden while I hunt unless you're conferring with the others."

Her eyes glowed warmly. "I never could hide from you." She wrapped her arms around herself. "There was talk. There is a force here. One not Daimon born."

"Goblin, ghoul, demonic? What?"

"No one seems to be sure. There are Daimons surrounding the source of it, but it is not one of them. It's something else."

"A god?"

She looked up, exasperated. "I'm trying to find someone who knows, but as yet . . ." She paused and wrung her hands. "I want you to be careful, Speirr. Whatever this thing is, it holds a great deal of malice. Hatred."

"Can you locate it?"

"I have tried, but it moves whenever I draw near. It is as if the source knows to avoid me."

This wasn't good, especially with Mardi Gras right around the corner. When Bacchus came to town, even the most moderate of things went wild. To Talon it sounded like something or someone was counting on the excesses of the celebration to propel whatever plan it had.

Talon's thoughts were distracted as a car drove down the street in front of him. It was an old VW Beetle. Someone had painted the top of it dark blue with glow-in-the-dark stars and the lower half was bright sunshine yellow with red peace symbols.

He smiled at the sight. It had been parked outside the club earlier when he had left. Instinct told him it had to belong to Sunshine. No one else would be caught dead in such a monstrosity.

True to his suspicions, the car turned into the alley behind Runningwolf's.

With his honed Dark-Hunter sight, he watched her leave her car and pause to pull a sealed box out of the backseat. His body hardened instantly.

Tonight, she wore her black hair in two braids down the side of her face. She was dressed in a long fuchsia sweater coat that displayed her lush curves to perfection.

In his mind, he could imagine walking up to her, pulling her back against his front, and just inhaling her warm patchouli scent. Letting his hand trail down the front of her, to her tight black sweater held closed by small buttons. Of working those buttons through the cloth until she was exposed to him.

His body burned with aching want.

"Speirr?"

Ceara's voice jarred him from his reverie. "I'm sorry, I was distracted."

"I said I will go and investigate further. Or do you need me to stay here and keep you grounded?"

"No, thanks. I'm grounded."

"I'm sensing conflict inside you. Are you sure you want me to leave?"

About as sure that the world would end in fifteen minutes. No, he wasn't sure. Because every time he looked at Sunshine, he had a nasty tendency to forget everything else.

To want nothing more than to stare at her. To touch her.

"I'm sure."

"Very well, then. I shall listen out for you. If you need me, call."

"I will."

Ceara vanished and left him alone in the darkness.

Sunshine slammed her car door closed and entered the rear door of the club.

He took a step toward her before he even realized what he'd done.

Talon ran his hands over his face. He had to get her out of his thoughts. There was no point in this. Dark-Hunters didn't date and they damn sure didn't have girlfriends. Well, no one except Kell, but he was weird anyway and Kell's girlfriend was a constant source of irritation for Acheron.

Not that Talon minded being an irritation to Acheron. It

was actually enjoyable to nettle the Atlantean, but he couldn't screw up Sunshine's life that way.

Dark-Hunters didn't date and most especially not this one. He'd already learned his lesson and he'd learned it hard.

Unlike the others, he was cursed by his own gods. It was why he refused to have a Squire. Why he refused to have *anyone* near him.

"For what you have taken from me, Speirr of the Morrigantes, you will never again know the peace or happiness of a loved one. I curse you to walk eternity alone. Curse you to lose everyone you care for.

"One by one, they will suffer and die, and you will be powerless to stop it. Your agony will be knowing they are doomed because of your actions and wondering when, where, and how I will strike them down. I will claim them all and live only to watch you suffer."

Even after all these centuries the angry god's words rang in his ears.

Talon groaned at the pain of the memory of his wife dying in his arms. *"I'm afraid to die, Speirr . . ."*

It had been all his fault.

Every death.

Every tragedy.

How could so many lives have been shattered by one stupid mistake? He had let his emotions lead him and, in the end, he had destroyed not only his own life but those of the ones he loved.

He winced at the truth of it.

Agony seared him so deeply that he cursed aloud from the force of it.

"You were born cursed," Gara's gnarled old voice whispered in his head. *"Born bastard to a union that should never have been. Now get out and take the babe with you before the wrath of the gods falls to my head."*

At age seven, he had stared in helpless disbelief at the old crone his mother had worked for. When his mother and

Tress had taken sick, Gara had allowed him to do his mother's tasks.

After his mother's death, the old woman had turned on him.

"But Ceara will die if I leave. I don't know how to care for an infant."

"We all die, boy. It's no concern of mine what becomes of the child of a whore. Now get out and remember how quickly our fates change. Your mother was a queen. The most beloved of the Morrigantes. Now she is a dead peasant, like the rest of us. Not even worth the dirt that covers her."

The cruel words had torn through his child's heart. His mother had never been a whore. Her only mistake had been to love his father.

Feara of the Morrigantes had been worth all the treasures of the earth to him. Her value was beyond measure . . .

"Push it away," he said, taking deep breaths to calm himself.

Acheron was right, he had to keep his emotions buried. They were what had led him astray to begin with. The only way he could function was to not remember. Not feel.

And yet he couldn't help feeling. He couldn't seem to repress the memories that he had buried fifteen hundred years ago . . .

"So the son of the whore has returned to beg you, my king, for his shelter. Tell me, King Idiag, should I cut off his head, or just slit his nostrils and then turn this pitiful wretch out into the storm to die like the worthless dung he is?"

Talon could still hear the laughter of his mother's people. Feel the fear in his young heart that his uncle, like everyone else, would forsake him and Ceara. He had clutched his sister close to his chest while she squalled, wanting the food and warmth he had been unable to provide her.

Barely two months in age, Ceara had refused to suckle the bladder he had tried to feed her with.

For three days as they traveled without stopping, she'd done nothing but scream and cry.

No matter what he tried, Ceara would not be placated.

Idiag had stared at him for so long that he was sure his uncle would send them to their deaths. The fire in the hall had crackled while the people held their collective breath, waiting for their king to pronounce judgment.

Talon had hated his mother then. Hated her for making him beg for his sister's life. Making him suffer like this when he was just an untried lad who wanted only to run away and hide from his humiliation.

Hide from the screaming baby who never took pity on him.

But he had made a promise and he never broke his word. Without his uncle's help, another sister would die.

When Idiag finally spoke, his eyes were blank. Unfeeling. *"No, Parth,"* he'd said to his guard. *"He has suffered much to travail the winter's harshness to reach us, especially with nothing more than rags on his feet. We will give them shelter. Summon a wet nurse for the babe."*

Talon had wanted to collapse in relief.

"And the boy?"

"If he survives the punishment his mother ran away from, then he will be allowed to stay here as well."

Grinding his teeth, Talon remembered the grueling torture they had meted out. The days of beatings and starvation.

The only thing that kept him alive was the fear that should he die, Ceara would be turned out after all.

He had lived solely for her.

Now he lived for nothing at all.

Talon forced his feet to carry him down the street away from Sunshine's club and her comfort. Away from these memories that had somehow been set loose.

He had to find his peace.

He had to forget the past. To bury it.

But as he walked, repressed thoughts and memories tumbled through his mind.

Against his will, he remembered the day he had discovered his wife . . .

Nynia.

Even now, the mere mention of her name was enough to bring him to his knees. She had been everything to him. His best friend. His heart. His soul.

She, alone, had given him solace.

In her arms, he hadn't cared what the others thought of him. Only the two of them had existed in the world.

As a mortal man, he had taken her as his first and only lover.

"How could I ever lay hands to another woman, Nyn, when I have you?"

Those words haunted him now along with the memory of how many women he'd slept with since his death. Women who had never meant anything to him. They had merely been passing flings designed to ease a physical craving.

He had never wanted to know anything about them.

Never really wanted to know any woman except his wife.

Nynia and the perfect love she had given him had touched something inside him and given it wings. She'd shown him things in the world that he'd never seen before.

Kindness.

Comfort.

Acceptance.

She had confused him, aggravated him, and made him deliriously happy.

When she had died, she had taken him with her. He had survived physically, but not his heart.

It had died that day too.

And he'd never thought to desire a woman that way again. Not until he had felt the warmth of a graceful artist's hand on his skin.

The mere thought of Sunshine was enough to make him feel sucker-punched.

"Get her out of my head," he said between clenched

teeth. He would never again let himself be open to so much excruciating pain. He would never again hold someone he cared for in his arms and watch her die.

Never.

He had been hurt enough in his life. He couldn't stand any more.

Sunshine was a stranger to him and she would remain that way. He didn't need anyone.

He never had.

Talon froze as an odd noise on the wind intruded on his thoughts. It sounded vaguely like a Daimon feeding . . .

He pulled his Palm Pilot out of his jacket pocket and opened up his tracking program. Designed to pick up traces of the Daimons' elevated neuron activity that came from their psychic abilities, the tracking program allowed Dark-Hunters to pinpoint any concentration of Daimons after dark. During the daylight hours while the Daimons rested, their brain activity was too human for the trackers to be of any use.

But once the sun set . . .

Those little brains of theirs started snapping and humming.

Talon frowned at his findings.

It showed nothing and his Dark-Hunter senses didn't pick up a Daimon either, but his gut instinct was off the radar.

He headed toward a dark alley. A woman stumbled out, falling against him. Her eyes were glazed as she glanced up at him. There was a small bite wound on her neck that was healing even as he looked at it and the collar of her blouse held traces of blood.

"Are you okay?" he asked as he righted her.

She smiled a smile that was delirious and vague. "I'm fine. Never better." She stumbled away from him and headed into the building to his right.

In that instant, he knew what had happened.

Unmitigated rage descended on him as he stalked farther

into the alley where she'd been. He saw the dark shadow and knew it in a heartbeat.

"Damn you, Zarek. You better lay off the feeding crap while you're in this city."

Zarek wiped the blood away from his lips with his hand. "Or what, Celt? You going to hit me?"

"I'll rip your throat out."

He laughed at that. "And kill yourself in the process? You don't have it in you."

"You have no idea what I'm capable of. And you better pray to whatever god you worship that you never find out."

His expression pure evil, Zarek smacked his lips in a way Talon knew was designed to piss him off thoroughly.

It worked.

"I didn't hurt her. She won't even remember it in three minutes. They never do."

Talon moved to grab him, but Zarek caught his hand. "I warned you not to touch me, Celt. No one touches me. *Ever.*"

Talon shrugged off his hold. "You swore an oath, just like the rest of us. I won't have you preying on innocents in my town."

"Oooo," Zarek breathed. "How cliché, little partner. Wanna tell me to be out by sunup, or better yet, this town ain't big enough for the two of us?"

"What is your problem?"

Zarek started past him.

Unwilling to let him prey on someone else, Talon shoved him against the wall. His own back throbbed viciously as if he'd been slammed against the wall too, but he didn't care.

He wasn't about to let Zarek have free rein over the lives of innocent people.

Zarek's eyes flared with hatred. "Let go of me, Celt, or I'll rip your arm off. And you know what? I don't care if I lose both of mine in the process. That's the difference between us. Pain is my friend and ally. You fear it."

"Like hell I do."

He shoved Talon away from him. "Then where is it? Hmmm? You buried your pain the night you left your village in flames."

Talon paused at the words, wondering how Zarek knew that, but his anger overrode it as he thought about Zarek judging him. "At least I don't wallow in it."

Zarek laughed at that. "Do I look like I'm wallowing? I was having fun with her until you showed up." He licked his lips again as if resavoring the feeding.

"You should try it sometime, Celt. There's nothing like tasting human blood. Haven't you ever wondered why the Daimons feed before they take human souls? Why they don't just kill the human quick? It's because it's better than sex. Did you know you can see straight into their minds when you do it? Feel their emotions? For one instant, you actually bond with their life force. It's one hell of a high."

Talon glared at him. "Nick's right, you are psychotic."

"The correct term is *sociopathic* and yes, I am. But at least I have no delusions about myself."

"Meaning?"

He shrugged. "Take your meaning wherever you can find it."

The man was disgusting. Insufferable. "Why do you have to make everyone hate you?"

Zarek snorted at that. "What? You want to be my friend now, Celt? If I clean up my act, will you be my buddy?"

"You're such an asshole."

"Yeah, but at least I know what I am. I have no pretensions. You don't know if you're a Druid, a Dark-Hunter, or a playboy. You lost yourself a long time ago in the dark hole where you buried the parts of you that once made you human."

Talon was aghast at such a low, self-serving life-form trying to play sage with him. "*You* are lecturing *me* on humanity?"

"Ironic as hell, isn't it?"

Talon's jaw ticced. "You don't know anything about me."

With his silver claws flashing, Zarek slowly pulled a cigarette out of his jacket pocket and lit it with an old-fashioned gold lighter.

Putting the lighter back in his pocket, he took a long drag on the cigarette, exhaled the smoke, then cast Talon a sardonic, lopsided sneer. "Ditto."

With one last, parting grimace, Zarek walked slowly away from him, out of the alley and back toward the street.

"Lay off the feeding, Zarek, or I will kill you myself. I swear it."

Zarek raised his clawed hand and flipped him off without breaking stride or looking back.

Talon growled low in his throat as Zarek vanished into the night. How could Acheron stand dealing with him? That man could try the patience of a tree.

One day, Artemis was going to have to put Zarek down. In truth, Talon was astounded the order for Zarek's execution hadn't already been handed out. But then maybe that was why Artemis had sent him here. In Alaska, Zarek was on his home turf where he knew the terrain better than anyone and he would be able to avoid an executioner.

Down here, Zarek was at the mercy of Acheron, who knew these streets like the back of his hand. If the order came down, Zarek would have nowhere to hide.

It was definitely a thought.

Talon shook his head to clear it of Zarek. The ex-slave was the last person he wanted on his mind tonight.

His cell phone rang. Talon answered it to find Acheron's thick Atlantean accent.

"Hey, I'm down on Commerce Street in the Warehouse District. There's a murder scene here that I would like to confer with you about."

"I'm on my way." Talon hung up and headed to where he'd left his motorcycle.

It didn't take long to grab his bike and make his way over to the scene. Cops were everywhere, questioning witnesses, marking off the area, and taking notes and pictures.

A large crowd of locals and tourists had gathered to watch the spectacle.

His eyes aching from all the bright police lights, Talon parked his bike and made his way over to Acheron, whose hair was now blond.

Jeez, the man changed hair colors more often than most people changed socks.

"What's up, T-Rex?"

Acheron grimaced at the nickname, but didn't comment. He inclined his head toward the body that had been draped with a body bag, but not yet sealed up. "That woman died barely an hour ago. Tell me what you feel."

"Nothing." As soon as the word left his lips, Talon understood. Whenever someone died, their soul lingered for a brief time before it moved on. There was only one exception to that—when the soul was captured and trapped by someone else. "It was a Daimon kill?"

Acheron shook his head no.

"Is she a new Dark-Hunter?"

Again the *no* shake. "Someone fed on her until they drained the life out of her and could steal her departing soul. Then they ripped her apart with something like a claw. The police are trying to convince themselves that it's an animal, but the depth and precision of her wounds are too precise."

Talon went cold. "Claws like the ones Zarek wears?"

Acheron turned his head to stare straight at him. All Talon could see was himself in the dark lenses. "What do you think?"

Talon ran his hand along the edge of his jaw as he watched the police work over the area. This was disturbing.

"Look, T-Rex, I know you have a soft spot for Zarek, but I have to tell you that I found him having lunch a few minutes ago outside of a club. It looked like he was enjoying himself a little too much, if you know what I mean."

"So you think he killed this woman?"

Talon hesitated as he remembered what Zarek had said when he had caught him with the woman in the alley. *I didn't hurt her.* Was that an admission he had hurt someone else or was it a statement that he never hurt the women he fed on?

"I don't know," Talon answered honestly. "If you're asking me if he's capable, I'd definitely say yes. But I sure would hate to consign a man to Shadedom without more evidence."

Shadedom was the hellish existence that came to any Dark-Hunter who died without a soul. Since they no longer had a real body or a soul, their essence suffered eternity trapped between this plane of existence and the next. It was said to be the most grueling torture imaginable.

"So what do you think?" Talon asked. "Do you believe he did it?"

A slow smile slid across Acheron's face, but he didn't answer the question. The hair on the back of Talon's neck rose. Something about all this just didn't seem right.

For that matter, something about Acheron didn't seem quite right either.

Acheron took a step away from him. "I'll go talk to my good buddy Zarek, and see what he says."

Talon frowned. This definitely wasn't right. Acheron never referred to anyone as his "buddy."

"By the way," Acheron said. "How are you doing? You seem tense. Uneasy."

He was. It was like someone had opened a floodgate on his hormones and emotions, and he wasn't sure how to close it again.

But he didn't intend to burden Acheron with that. He could control himself.

"I'm fine."

Talon glanced away from Acheron for a second to watch the arrival of the coroner. "By the way, T-Rex, what happened to your nose stud and . . ." His voice trailed off as he turned back and saw nothing but empty space.

Talon looked about.

Acheron was gone. The only trace of his presence was

two bloody shoe prints that marked the concrete where he'd stood a second ago.

What the hell?

Acheron had never done that before. Man, this night was getting stranger by the hour.

". . . there's a disturbance on Canal Street. At Club Runningwolf's . . ."

Talon's heart stopped at the words he overheard from a police scanner.

Sunshine.

Every instinct he possessed told him it involved her. He ran for his bike and quickly headed back toward the club.

Chapter 6

By the time Talon reached Sunshine's club again, it was complete chaos on the street outside the club's entrance and in the alley behind it.

A large crowd of people stood around outside where two ambulances were parked while medics tended three wounded officers. Someone had beaten them to a pulp.

He paused near one ambulance as he heard the officer giving his report to a detective.

"He was at least six feet six. Lean, muscular build. Caucasian male dressed in black, with long black hair and a goatee. Mid- to late twenties with this huge silver claw thing on his hand. He looked like the devil himself when we came up on him. Man, he tore through us like we was nothing. I got at least two bullets into him and he didn't even flinch when I shot him. He just kept on coming at us. He must be on PCP or something."

Talon froze.

Zarek. There was no one else who could fit that description.

Damn. He shouldn't have left the area while Zarek was here. Zarek must have attacked them just a few minutes after he left.

"So what happened?" the detective asked.

"Me and Gabe had a disturbance call about a fight in the alley. We got here in time to see the claw guy fighting two men. We yelled for them to stop, but the guy ignored us. He ripped their hearts right out of them. Right in front of us."

Talon groaned. They had seen Zarek take out a pair of Daimons. Great. Just great. He closed his eyes and cursed. This night was starting to rate right up there with abscessed teeth.

"Johnny got here right as I pulled my weapon and ordered the claw guy to stop. He turned on us like a wild beast. Next thing I know, I'm on the ground bleeding, you guys are here, and he's gone."

"And the bodies?"

"He must have taken them with him while we were trying to get to the cars for safety. I'm telling you, Bob, the man was insane."

Talon raked his hands through his hair. Not even in town one night and now Zarek had the entire police force looking for him.

How had the man managed to last so long?

His phone rang again, but the caller ID didn't display the caller's identity. Expecting it to be Acheron since Acheron's phone almost never registered a number, he was surprised to hear Zarek's thick Greek accent on the other end. "The Daimons wanted to party with your girlfriend, Celt. Don't leave her unprotected."

The phone went dead.

An eerie chill went up Talon's spine. How could Zarek have known about him and Sunshine?

The man's powers were rating right up there with Acheron's.

His instincts on alert, Talon looked up to the roof above his head—to the old abandoned drugstore next door to the club. Silhouetted against the dark sky was a figure. To a human's eyes, the man standing on the rooftop would be invisible, but Talon's honed Dark-Hunter vision saw him clearly.

It was Zarek.

Zarek inclined his head to him, put the phone in his

pocket, then stepped back and vanished into the darkness.

Talon frowned. Psycho Zarek had been watching over Sunshine all this time? Even while the cops were looking for him?

How unlike Zarek was that?

Talon immediately hit the automatic call-back feature on his phone.

"What?" Zarek asked, his voice surly. "Can't you see I'm trying to get out of here before the cops find me?"

"What were you doing at Runningwolf's?"

"Picking my nose, Celt. What do you think? I saw the Daimons on the street and I tracked them inside."

That explained that, but Talon had a bigger concern. "How did you know about me and Sunshine?"

"I overheard the Daimons talking about the two of you. You should be more careful, Celt. A mistake like that one could be costly."

"Costly how, Zarek? I've just seen the body of a woman who'd been drained of her blood and her soul."

"Ooo," Zarek breathed. "Here's a news flash. It was a Daimon attack. Ever notice that tends to be their MO?"

"Yeah, but I've never known a Daimon to *claw* a woman up while killing her. Have you?"

There was a brief pause. "What are you saying?"

"I think you know, Zarek."

"Yeah, and you can kiss my ass, Celt. Maybe I should have left your bitch to them after all."

The phone went dead again.

Talon ground his teeth, torn between the deep need to find Zarek, beat the crap out of him, and wash his mouth out, and a deeper need to make sure Sunshine was okay.

Putting his phone in his pocket, he decided to leave Zarek to Acheron, who'd already said he was going to talk to him. Acheron was much better at handling Zarek anyway.

At least Ash could kill the bastard and not die in the process.

Talon expelled a long breath as he thought over Zarek's

warning that the Daimons were after Sunshine. It didn't
make a bit of sense.

Why would the Daimons be after her? And how could
the Daimons know about the two of them?

This made the second attack on her in as many nights.
Daimons took their victims where they found them. They
didn't stalk someone who got away. They just moved on
to the next handy meal.

He didn't know what they wanted with her, but until he
found out, he wasn't going to leave her in danger.

Scanning the crowd, Talon found Sunshine standing just
under a light outside the club, next to a large, muscular
man with black hair who was speaking to a uniformed police officer. She wore only her thin black sweater without
the fuchsia one she'd had on earlier. Her arms were crossed
over her chest as if she were cold.

Talon made his way through the crowd to her side.

Her face lit up the moment she saw him. "Talon? What
are you doing here?"

He was more relieved than he would have thought possible. Just seeing her here, unharmed, and hearing his name
on her lips . . .

He shouldn't feel anything for her and yet there was no
denying the raw emotions he felt every time she met his
gaze.

"Are you okay?" he asked, shrugging off his jacket and
holding it up for her.

She nodded as she allowed him to help her into his
jacket. "Did you hear what happened? Some guy went nuts
in the alley where I park my car and killed two men. Then,
he attacked the police. It's terrible!"

Before he could think, Talon pulled her into his arms
and held her close. She was shaking and cold, but she still
felt so wonderful that he didn't want to let go of her. "I'm
glad you weren't hurt."

The man who'd been talking to the police officer looked
at them with a stern scowl. "You know, bud, I don't know
you from Adam, but that's my baby sister you're hanging
on to. So I'm thinking the wisest course of action for you

is to let her go and introduce yourself. Pronto."

Talon bit back a smile. He knew exactly what the man meant. Some things were very sacred and little sisters were one of them.

Reluctantly, he withdrew from her.

Sunshine punched her brother gently on his arm. "Talon, this is my brother Rain. Rain, meet Talon."

Her brother snorted. "God, with a name like Talon your parents must have been holdover hippies too."

"Something like that."

"That's his pet phrase," Sunshine told her brother. "That and *not exactly.*"

Rain sized him up, then offered him his hand. "Nice meeting you, Talon. I better get back to work. Sunny, yell if you need one of us."

The implied threat wasn't lost on Talon, who bit back a smile. If the man only knew how much power a Dark-Hunter wielded . . .

"Us?" Talon repeated.

Her brother indicated two men over Talon's shoulder who were also talking to the police. The older man was a Native American whose shamanic powers were easily discernible, and her other brother was almost a facial clone of Sunshine. "Our father and older brother, Storm, work in the club too."

Talon gave a tight-lipped smile as he turned back to face Rain. "Storm, Rain, and Sunshine, huh?"

She grimaced. "My mother's doing. I'm just glad she stopped at three. I was told the next one would have been named Cloudy Day."

He laughed at that. Gods, how he'd missed her. All he wanted to do right now was take her into his arms and run her up to her bed and inspect every inch of her to make sure she was unhurt.

Yeah, okay, so he had another, less pure, motive for that thought too. But still he felt an insane need to prove to himself that no one had touched her.

That she was completely whole and safe.

He darted his gaze all over her body, assuring himself that she was fine. His concern for her was so unlike anything he'd experienced in such a long time that he wasn't really sure how to cope with it.

Rain excused himself and drifted back into the club, leaving them alone.

An awkwardness fell between them as he tried to think of something to say to her.

Finally, she cleared her throat. "I didn't think I'd see you again."

He didn't know what to respond to that, especially since that had been his intention. "I . . . um . . ."

"Oh, you want Snoopy back."

"No," he said quickly. "I came back for you."

A slow, seductive smile spread over her face. "Really?" she asked.

"Yeah. I heard about the attack and was worried," he said before he could stop himself.

"Really?" she repeated.

He nodded.

Smiling wider, she walked herself into his arms. "That was very sweet of you."

Not really, Talon thought as he held her and inhaled her warm patchouli scent. But he had to admit she felt good in his arms. Her breasts were flattened against him and all he could think about was how delicious they had tasted, how soft and good they had felt in his hands.

He groaned inwardly at the thought.

Walk away from her . . .

I have to protect her.

He was sworn to protect humans. Especially those the Daimons would prey upon. It was his duty to keep her with him. To watch over her.

Hey, how stupid do you think I am, Talon? This is yourself you're talking to and all the lies in the world aren't going to convince me that you have a moral or noble reason for this. You want in her bed again. Admit it.

Oh, come on, I can control myself for a few days. She

has to be protected and who else could do it?

Zarek was out of the question. He'd end up feeding off her and Talon would kill him if the psycho dared to touch her. Valerius would sooner die than watch over a "plebeian." Nick would make a move on her, and he'd have to kill the horny toad. Kyrian had a new baby and was too exhausted to think, and Acheron . . .

He had too many responsibilities pulling at him to worry about baby-sitting.

That left him and him alone.

"You know, Sunshine, I don't think you should stay in your loft alone."

She stepped away from him. "Believe me, I'm not. I'm going home with Storm tonight."

Talon paused. That wasn't an option either. Her brother was a big man, but no match for a Daimon.

"I don't know, Sunshine. I'm thinking . . ." Well, he couldn't really say what he was thinking, especially the part that bordered on salaciousness.

But then he didn't have to. She smiled a wicked smile. "You know, if you want me to go home with *you,* all you have to do is ask."

"I didn't think it would be that easy."

She rose up on her tiptoes and gave him a devilish look. "For anyone other than you, it wouldn't be."

Those words made his heart soar. He really liked this woman. She was bold, quirky, and sassy.

Sunshine took his hand and led him into, and through, the club to a door in the far right rear corner. It opened into the back hallway that Talon recognized from earlier in the evening. On the right was the door to the outside where her car was parked and on the left was the steel staircase that led up to her loft. She headed for the stairs.

Sunshine held tight to Talon's hand as she mentally castigated herself. She probably shouldn't be doing this, especially since two murders had been committed tonight. But instinctively she knew Talon would never hurt her.

He'd saved her life and he'd done nothing even remotely harmful to her.

Besides, she liked being with him. She could take her art supplies with her and get back on schedule tomorrow.

Tonight, she just wanted a few more minutes with him. One more evening to bask in his warmth before she went back to the rigors of her life.

It had been so considerate of him to offer her his jacket. His warmth and scent clung to it, making her want to snuggle in deep.

She entered her loft, gave him back his jacket, and left him by her white and pink striped couch while she went to pack an overnight bag. In all honesty, she'd rather stay with him than Storm anyway.

Storm snored.

Loudly.

Not to mention that the last time she had gone to her brother's place, she'd had to spend two hours cleaning it before she was able to touch anything in the apartment without cringing. He was an absolute pig and he didn't care about making her feel welcome. Rather, he treated her as a live-in servant who should be happy to do for ole big brother.

And ole big brother stunk. Not literally, but in the figurative sense.

She grabbed a change of clothes, shoes, and hair ties and shoved them into her wicker tote bag along with her toothbrush and moisturizer—a woman always needed her moisturizer—then she rejoined Talon.

He stood at the rear of the loft, near the windows, looking through the landscape paintings she'd done of Jackson Square. Her breath caught in her throat.

What was it about this man that was so powerful? His wavy blond hair fell around his face while his two thin braids hung down to his shoulder. His black leather pants cupped a butt so fine that it should be stamped with *Grade A Prime* on each cheek. And his back . . . Even with his jacket on, she knew how perfect and well sculpted it was.

She stared at his large, tawny hands that held her work. They were so strong and at the same time tender. She loved the way they had felt on her body, the way his fingers had tasted when she nibbled them.

The man was simply scrumptious from the top of his blond head to the bottom of his black biker boots.

He turned slightly as she joined him. "I like the way you painted the sun coming in over the cathedral. I can almost feel the sun when I look at it."

His compliment warmed her. An artist never heard enough compliments on her work. "Thank you. My favorite is the sunset over it. I love to watch the light fading around the buildings. When it hits some of the signs and glass, it makes them glow and sparkle like fire."

He reached out and cupped her face in his warm palm. "You have such an incredible way of capturing things."

She bit her lip and gave him an impish smile. "Yes, I do." And little did he know it, but she fully intended to capture him as well. At least for a little while.

He was like some wild, untamed creature that you could keep and feed for a time, but in the end you knew you'd have to let it go for its own sake as well as yours.

"So, tell me, where do you live?" she asked.

He cleared his throat and dropped his hand from her cheek.

The uncomfortable look on his face made her stomach sink. "Oh Lord, you do have your own place, don't you? You don't happen to live with your mom or some creepy old aunt?"

He looked offended by that. "Of course I have my own place. It's just . . ." His voice trailed off and he looked away.

Oh sheez, here it comes . . . "You have a live-in girl-friend?"

"No."

Ugh! It was even worse than she thought. "Live-in boy-friend?"

He gaped at her while his midnight eyes flashed with

indignation. "Jeez, Sunshine, what do you think I am?"

"I don't know, Talon. I asked a simple question and you got all weird on me. What am I supposed to think?" She swept her gaze down the expensive biker's outfit he wore. The man had a body to beat the band and was too bodacious to be real. That tended to make a woman go, hmmm . . .

"And you do wear a lot of leather."

"What's that supposed to mean?"

She gave him a *duh* stare. "I am an artist, you know. I tend to hang out with an awful lot of homosexual and bisexual guys."

If he had looked offended before, it was nothing compared to the look on his face now. "Now there's a stereotype I hadn't even considered. Thank you very much. For your information, I happen to like leather since it tends to protect *my* hide on the occasions when I wreck my motorcycle and go skidding down asphalt."

"Well, that's true too. So why did you get all weird on me when I asked you where you live?"

"Because I figured if I told you where I lived, you'd get *all weird* on me."

She hesitated as a million scary locations came to her mind. He lived in a cemetery or crypt. A run-down shack. A cardboard box. A dock house. A broken-down camper or bus. Good Lord, in this city there was no telling where he might make his home. "Okay, you live somewhere freaky, don't you?"

"I live out in the bayou."

Relieved, she scoffed at his evasiveness over something so silly. "Oh please, I know several people who live out by the bayou."

"Not *by* the bayou, Sunshine. I live *in* the bayou."

Was he serious? Who in their right mind lived in the bayou with the snakes and gators and other things she didn't want to even think about? Things that carried guns and did lots of illegal activities like feeding murdered bodies to gators.

"You live *in* the bayou?"

He nodded. "It's really peaceful out there. No modern sounds to intrude on you. No neighbors. No traffic. You can almost feel like you're living centuries ago."

There was a wistful look to him as he said that. "That means a lot to you, doesn't it?"

"Yes. It does."

She smiled. Yeah, she could see Talon out in the bayou all alone. He reminded her a lot of her father, who loved to spend hours outside just soaking up nature. They both shared that quiet kind of peace-with-the-universe attitude.

"How long have you lived there?"

He avoided looking at her. "A really *long* time."

Sunshine nodded.

As they started for the door, she dropped her wicker tote and retrieved her Studiopack French Easel Backpack from the corner. She always kept it well stocked in case she decided on a whim to go some place else and paint.

"What is that?" he asked.

She winked at him. "An artist on the go, that's me. I never go anywhere without supplies."

He smiled as he took the backpack from her. "So, you're still feeling adventurous, huh?"

"Always. Just bring the gator-be-gone spray and I'm all yours."

Talon stared at her as he felt another stupid urge to grin. His face was starting to ache from the effort it took to not expose his fangs to her. She was extremely funny and amusing.

If not, to an extent, insulting.

He was still chafing over her assumptions about his clothes. The things this woman got into her head . . .

But he liked that about her. She didn't play games with him, but spoke whatever thought, no matter how outrageous, was on her mind.

Sunshine locked the door, got halfway down the stairs, then stopped. "Oh man, I forgot my overnight bag." She made a disgusted sound before sprinting up the stairs and rushing back inside her loft.

She came out a few minutes later with her wicker bag, reached the top of the stairs, then remembered she had no coat.

One more time, she went back inside before she rejoined him. "I swear I'd be wearing a pumpkin on my shoulders."

It took a second for her words to sink in—she'd lose her head if it ever came off her body.

Laughing, he paused on the stairs as she walked past him. "By the way, I don't look gay in leather."

Sunshine turned to look up at him. She passed a hot, lustful glance over his body that made him harden instantly. "No, baby, you don't. I honestly have to say you wear that outfit like nobody's business."

A slow smile spread across his face as he followed her the rest of the way out of the club.

Oh yeah, the two of them had some unfinished business to take care of once he got her home.

Business he shouldn't even be contemplating, but he had his reputation to uphold. Besides which, he owed her a payback. When she left his cabin, she'd never again doubt his sexual orientation or his attraction to her.

As they reached the outside doors, Sunshine led Talon away from the club.

"Are you going to tell your brother where you're going?"

She shook her head. "I'll call him in a little bit and tell him. Believe me, it's not something I want to do face to face."

"Stern, is he?"

"You've no idea."

Talon led her to his bike and pulled out a spare helmet from the saddlebags. "You want to put your backpack in here?"

She shook her head as she took the backpack from him and shrugged it on. "It's designed for motorcycles and hiking. I'm fine wearing it. It's really not that heavy."

"Ride many bikes, do you?"

"Yup, I do."

Talon watched her pull her helmet on and fasten it. Man, the woman was beautiful to him. Her long, graceful fingers tucked her braids in easily and her dark brown eyes glowed.

He removed the small sunglasses that he wore at night and pulled his own helmet on, then got on the bike and kick-started it. Sunshine joined him on the bike. Her arms came around his waist as she slid her body closer to his.

Talon almost moaned. He could feel every inch of her pressed intimately, erotically against him. Her breasts on his back, her inner thighs against his hips.

And the way her arms held him . . .

He could just imagine her sliding her hand down from his waist to the hard bulge in his pants where she could cup and stroke him through the leather. Of her unzipping his pants and kneading him gently with her hand as he hardened and strained to possess her.

Better yet, he could see her down on her knees in front of him, taking him into her mouth . . .

Unknown feelings swirled inside him, turning him inside out. All he wanted was to keep her here like this for eternity. To stop the bike and sample every inch of her lush, full figure with his mouth and fangs.

He wanted to devour her.

To taste and tease her until she called out his name while her body shook from ultimate pleasure.

Unbidden, he mentally felt her body arch against his as she clutched at his back in the midst of an orgasm.

He'd learned today that she always tensed her body until the last orgasmic shudder had subsided, and then she relaxed and rained kisses on his skin.

It was a sweet sensation that had no equal.

Talon clenched his teeth in an effort to control himself from yielding to the craving he felt for her body. He drove them through town, out toward the bayou where he lived.

As they rode, Sunshine leaned her head to rest between his shoulder blades and tightened her hold around Talon's lean, muscular abs. She remembered how he'd looked standing naked in her loft. The way he'd looked leaning over her as they made love. Slow. Easy. Then fast and furious.

This man had an indefinable way with his body. He knew every way and then some to give a woman pleasure.

Sunshine could feel his chest rise and fall under her arms as they rode through the dark night. What she was doing with him was insane and yet she couldn't seem to stop herself.

Talon was compelling. Dangerous. Dark and mysterious. Something about him made her just want to crawl inside him and stay there forever.

Crazy, huh?

Yet there was no denying what he did to her. What she felt every time she thought about him. The way she wanted to yell at him to stop the bike so that she could tear off his jacket and lick every inch of his tattoo.

Every inch of his powerful, masculine body.

Oh, how she wanted this man.

"Are you okay?"

She tensed at the sound of Talon's deeply accented voice in her ears. "Hey, your helmets are microphoned."

"Yeah, I know. But are you okay?"

She smiled at his concern. "I'm fine."

"You sure? You kind of jumped a second ago like something startled you."

"No, really. I'm fine."

Talon wasn't so sure and at the moment he wished one of his Dark-Hunter powers included mind-reading. Unfortunately, his powers ran more along the lines of commanding the elements, healing, projection, and telekinesis. He was better able to shield himself and others, which was why, unlike Zarek, he never had to worry about cops or anyone else seeing him slay a Daimon.

He could summon the elements to shield him from people's sight or to confuse them. If need be, he could even project new thoughts to someone to alter their perceptions of reality.

But he preferred not to do that. The human mind was frail and such tactics had been known to leave lasting damage.

With his arcane powers came a great deal of responsibility. Acheron had taught him that.

Having been abused as a child by those who had more strength and power than he did, Talon had no wish to victimize anyone else. There was nothing he wanted or needed so badly that he would violate someone else to get it.

They didn't speak again until he reached his garage at the end of a long, winding dirt road. There were no lights out here, no pavement. Nothing but Louisiana wildlife.

Sunshine frowned as their headlight illuminated a strange mailbox out in the middle of nowhere. It was a black box that appeared to be pierced by two long silver nails. One was going horizontally through the box, the other diagonally.

She cringed at the sight of the dilapidated shack they neared and she hoped this wasn't his house. It looked like it was ready to cave in.

If not for the clean, crisp mailbox, she wouldn't have believed anyone had been out here in a hundred or more years.

Talon stopped the bike and held it upright between his muscular thighs. He pulled a small remote from his pocket and used it to open the dilapidated shack door. It lifted up slowly.

Sunshine gaped as the lights came on and she saw inside the "shack."

There was nothing run-down about the inside of the building. It was high tech and sparkling, and filled with a fortune in motorcycles and one sleek black Viper.

Oh God, he *was* a drug dealer!

Her stomach knotted in fear of what she had let herself in for. She should never have come out here with him!

He parked the motorcycle next to the car, then helped her off the seat.

"Um . . . Talon?" she asked, looking around his collection of vintage Harleys. "What do you do for a living? You said you were an illegal alien, right?"

He gave that familiar tight-lipped smile as he placed his helmet on a rack that contained twelve helmets she was sure cost a minimum of a thousand dollars each. "Yes, and to answer your first question, I'm independently wealthy."

"And you got that way how?"

"I was born into it."

Sunshine felt a little better, but she still had to ask the one question that was nagging her most. "So you don't do anything illegal like run drugs, right?"

Once again, he looked offended. "Good Lord no, woman. Why would you think that?"

Her eyes wide, she looked around the expensive garage and high-tech male toys. "I have *no* idea."

He pressed a button and closed the main door, sealing them in.

She followed after him while he led her to the back of the garage where he had two very nice, expensive catamarans docked. Everything in this building was truly state-of-the-art. "If you have all this money, why are you an illegal alien?"

Talon snorted. He could tell her that he was in this bayou before America was even a country, and that he didn't need any stinking piece of paper to make him legal, but as a Dark-Hunter he was forbidden to tell her anything about their lifestyle or existence. So he opted for an easy and true excuse. "You have go to the courthouse during daylight hours to fill out the paperwork. Since I can't go out into sunlight . . ."

She looked at him skeptically. "Are you sure you're not a vampire?"

"I wasn't until the moment I saw you."

"Meaning?"

He moved to stand next to her so that she had to crane

her neck to look up at him. His jaw flexed as he stared down at her while his body craved hers in a way most desperate. "Meaning I would love nothing more than to sink my teeth into your skin and devour you."

She bit her lower lip and gave him an impish, heated once-over. "Mmm, I like it when you talk like that."

She stepped into his arms.

Talon's body burned as he dipped his head down to kiss her.

Sunshine moaned at the taste of him. What was it about this man that attracted her so and made her want to gobble him up?

He pulled back suddenly and she pouted in protest.

"We'd best hurry," he said. "It'll be dawn before much longer and it's still a ride to my cabin."

"Your cabin? Is it anything like this shack?"

"You'll see." He moved away from her to start the catamaran.

Sunshine took a seat and strapped herself in. Once she was secured, they left the comfort of the garage and headed out into the eerie darkness of the swamp. The engine's motor was so loud, it made her ears ache as they sped toward his cabin.

It was so dark out here that she couldn't focus her eyes on anything at all.

How could Talon see to drive the boat? Any minute, she half expected them to plow into a tree or stump.

And yet Talon maneuvered them effortlessly without any hesitation or slowing of speed.

After a few minutes, her eyes adjusted to the blackness and she was able to see outlines and swamp gas. Mostly, she just saw fog and a few things that looked vaguely like animals falling into the water.

Maybe she was better off blind after all.

At long last, they reached a small isolated cabin set deep in the swamp. Alone. Isolated. Spanish moss hung down from the top of the porch and the wood of the place had lightened to a faint gray that stood out even in the darkness of the night.

Talon parked the catamaran beside a small dock and got out. He helped her onto the dock and as she followed him up the narrow plank toward the dark porch, she realized there were two alligators in front of the door.

She screamed.

"Shh," Talon said with a laugh. "There's nothing to fear."

To her extreme astonishment, he bent down and patted the biggest gator on the head. "Hey Beth, how's it going tonight?"

The gator snapped its jaw and hissed at him as if it had understood his question.

"I know, girl. I'm sorry, I forgot."

"What are you? Dr. Dolittle?"

He laughed again. "No. I found these two when they were small hatchlings and raised them. We're family. I've known them so long that I can almost read their minds."

Well, she had reptiles in her family tree too. Only hers walked on two legs.

The big one came up to her and eyeballed her like she was the daily special at the Crocodile Cafe. "I don't think she likes me."

"Be nice, Beth," Talon said.

The gator swished its tail, then ambled off the porch, into the swamp water. The other one looked at her, snapped its jaws, then joined its friend.

Talon opened the door to his cabin and turned on a dim desk lamp. Sunshine stepped inside hesitantly, half afraid he'd have the housekeeping abilities of her brother.

Or that there would be something worse than gators inside. Something like a monster anaconda he intended to feed her to.

She hesitated in the doorway.

The place was bigger inside than it appeared from the outside, but it was still basically only one room. There was a small kitchen off to her left and a door to her right she assumed was the bathroom.

He had three big tables set up with computers and other electronic equipment. And there was a large black futon on the floor to the rear of the cabin.

She was thankful everything was clean and sanitary. How wonderfully refreshing to know that all men weren't the pigs her brothers were.

"Interesting place you have here, Talon. Have to say I love the blank, black walls."

He snorted at her tone. "This from a woman who lives inside a pink cloud?"

"True, but everything here is so dark. Don't you find it depressing?"

He shrugged. "Not really. I no longer think about it at all."

"Not to be rude, but it seems to me that you do that a lot."

"Do what?"

"Not think about things. You're one of those guys who just exists, aren't you? No thought about the past or tomorrow. Just what you plan on doing in the next hour or so."

Talon dropped his keys on the table next to his primary computer. She was very astute. One of the drawbacks of immortality was the fact that you weren't really goal-oriented. His world existed of getting up, tracking and slaying Daimons, and then returning home.

A Dark-Hunter never thought about the future. It just kept on coming regardless.

As for the past . . .

There was no need to go there. All that would do was dredge up memories he was much better off not remembering.

He looked at her and the passionate gleam in her dark brown eyes. She had a love of life that glowed and it captivated him. What would it be like to live that way again? To actually look forward to the future and plan for it?

"You probably think about the future all the time," he said quietly.

"Of course."

"And what do you see in your future?"

She shrugged her backpack off and placed it by his desk. "It depends. Sometimes I dream of having my art hung in the Guggenheim or the Met."

"Do you ever dream of having a family?"

"Everyone has those dreams."

"No, not everyone."

She frowned. "You really don't?"

Talon fell quiet as he recalled his wife's face and remembered the nights he'd lain awake while she slept by his side with his hand on her belly so that he could feel their son moving inside her.

The dreams he'd had then.

When he had looked into Nynia's eyes, he had seen into forever. Had imagined the two of them old and happy and surrounded by their children and grandchildren.

And with one overwrought emotional act, he had damned both of them and ruined every dream the two of them had shared.

Every hope they'd had.

He winced as pain lacerated his chest.

"No," he whispered past the sudden lump in his throat. "I don't think about having a family at all."

Sunshine frowned at the thickness she heard in his voice. He cleared his throat.

What about her question could have possibly hurt him?

As he showed her where to store her bag and backpack, the phone rang.

Talon moved to answer it while she set about unpacking a few essentials and laying them about the cabin.

"Hey Nick . . . yeah, I heard about Zarek." He gave her a sheepish look as he listened. "Nah, man. I . . . um. I'm not alone right now, okay?"

He moved away from her, but still she could hear him

plainly. He was acting kind of nervous and she wondered why.

"I spoke with Zarek earlier, and he had definitely been sucking on the red mojo juice right before that happened. I don't know what got into him, but he was in a foul mood." He paused for several minutes. "Yeah, and listen, I have a woman here, her name is Sunshine. If she calls you for anything, get it for her without shooting off your mouth . . . Yeah, back at you." He hung up the phone.

"Who's Nick?" she asked.

"He's my personal assistant. He's on payroll, so anything you need, you just push four and the pound sign and it'll ring his cell phone."

Ooo that was neat. "Really? You have a personal assistant?"

"Unbelievable, isn't it?"

"Well, I have to say you are the first biker I've ever met who has a stock portfolio and an assistant."

He laughed.

"So, what's 'red mojo juice'?" she asked. "Some kind of wine?"

He looked *very* uncomfortable. "Something like that."

There he went again with his secrets. Ugh! The man needed to loosen up a bit. Be more trusting.

She'd definitely have to work on him.

Talon headed for the small kitchen. "I don't know about you, but I'm kind of wired. I don't normally go to sleep until a couple of hours after dawn. You hungry?"

She watched him search through his cabinets and pull out a couple of pans. "Not really, but I can make you something if you like."

He looked up, his face startled by her offer. "Thanks. That'd be nice."

She took the pan from his hand and set it on the stove. "So what are you in the mood for?"

He licked his lips sinfully as his gaze roamed over her body, making her instantly hot. Needful.

"How about naked Sunshine al dente covered in

whipped cream and chocolate?" He brushed the hair back from her neck. "We could even put a cherry on top."

She laughed at that. "That could be arranged."

Sunshine moaned as he dipped his head down and nuzzled her neck while he cupped her breasts in his hands.

Her breasts tingled and swelled as desire swept through her, making her instantly wet and throbbing for him.

"Are you always this insatiable?" she asked.

"Only when I see something I want," he said, moving his hand to cup her between her legs. "And you I want most of all."

She hissed at how good his fingers felt stroking her through the denim.

Her heart pounding, she looked down to watch his hands as he unfastened her jeans. His long, finely shaped fingers opened her fly, pushing the flaps aside until her lacy white panties showed. He teased her ear with his tongue, his breath hot against her skin, as he dipped his hand under the elastic band and found the center of her body.

Sunshine reeled at the sight of his hand there, of his fingers gently caressing her nether lips. His tanned skin stood out darkly against the white as he slid his fingers inside her.

Groaning, she rubbed herself against him, needing to feel him deep inside her again.

He growled like a ferocious beast before he knelt down behind her and pulled her jeans and panties free.

At his bidding, Sunshine allowed him to remove her shoes and jeans.

He was on his knees and still completely dressed as he turned her to face him and stared at the dark triangle between her legs.

His obsidian gaze met hers and she saw the fire inside him. "Open yourself for me, Sunshine. I want you to invite me in."

She blushed at what he was asking. She'd never in her life done anything like this and yet she wanted to please him.

Swallowing her inhibitions, she parted her legs and

reached down to open her nether lips for him. "I'm all yours, baby."

He was like a wild, hungry beast as he buried his face between her legs and took her into his mouth.

Sunshine cried out in pleasure. She leaned back against the counter for support. His tongue swirled, then he gently sucked and nibbled. She buried her hands in his soft hair, her body burning at his touch.

Her nipples were so tight they hurt. "Oh yes, Talon, yes," she breathed, pressing him closer to her.

Talon growled deep and low in his throat as he tasted her. Her feminine scent invaded his head as her graceful hand tugged at his hair.

He ran his tongue over the hard edge of her cleft, sampling and tasting the woman before him. It had been so long since anyone or anything had given him this much pleasure.

But please him she did.

Her passion, her creativity, her quirkiness. All of it was a magnet that drew him against his will.

He licked and teased her. Tasted her. Let her murmurs of pleasure become his and when she came, calling out his name, he swore that he saw stars from it.

Sunshine's breath came in short, sharp gasps as she looked down to see Talon rising up from the floor. He towered over her, his eyes dark, his face still hungry.

"What is it about you that I can't resist?" he asked. "Every time I get near you, all I can think of is tasting you."

He led her hand to his groin where she felt him hard and throbbing for her.

"I don't know," she said, her voice ragged as she dipped her hand below his waistband and trailed her fingers through his short, crisp hairs until she could wrap her fingers around his swollen manhood.

He drew his breath in sharply.

"But I feel the same for you," she said, sinking her hand lower, seeking out his soft sac.

He closed his eyes, his jaw flexing, as she caressed him. She knew she gave him pleasure and yet he acted as if her touch pained him.

She felt strangely vulnerable as she stood there with her lower body exposed while she wore her sweater and bra. Talon was still fully clothed.

It was erotic and disconcerting.

As if sensing her thoughts, Talon removed the rest of her clothes. She was completely naked now.

He was not.

He ran his hands over her, masterfully, tenderly. "Tell me your fantasies, Sunshine. Tell me what you dream about late at night when you're lying in bed alone."

She'd never in her life shared such an intimacy and yet before she realized what she was doing, she found herself confiding in him. "I dream of a handsome stranger approaching me."

He circled behind her. "And?"

"It's dark and hot. I imagine him standing behind me and pulling me against him. Feeling him take me from behind while I can't see him at all, I can only feel him."

Talon moved away from her and turned out the light.

Sunshine shivered in the darkness. "Talon?"

"Shh." His deep, accented voice seemed to engulf her.

Then she felt his hands on her. Completely blind, she was all sensation as he pulled her back to his front and she realized he'd removed his jacket and shirt. He ran his hands over her breasts, cupping them while he nibbled the back of her neck.

She'd had this fantasy for years, but never before had it been real. Never had she seen her dream man's face. Tonight, she envisioned Talon. She imagined what his hand looked like as he resumed stroking her between her legs.

She heard him unzip his pants. The heat of his body warmed hers as he whispered to her in a language she didn't understand. It deepened his voice, made it even more enticing.

Erotic.

Then, he was inside her, hot and hard. She moaned, arching her back, as he sank himself deep into her over and over again.

He buried his hands in her hair while nibbling her shoulders. Her neck.

His touch was hot, scorching.

He bent her forward.

Sunshine gasped as he penetrated her even deeper than before. He thrust himself against her, pounding pleasure into her body with such intensity that she found herself moaning and gasping in time to his movements.

Talon clenched his teeth as he felt her body clutching his. She was so wet and hot, so silky. It was crazy but when he was inside her, he could almost feel his missing soul.

"Come for me, Sunshine," he whispered in Gaelic, then he remembered that she couldn't understand him so he offered her the translation.

"Talon." Her voice was a mixture of pain and pleasure. Of hot, demanding need. She was on the edge of climax.

Seeking to help her reach it, he reached his hand down to her cleft and stroked her in time to his thrusts.

She screamed out almost immediately as she came in his arms. Talon quickly joined her in that place of divine pleasure.

They were both sweaty and panting as he pulled her naked body back against his. He laughed in her ear, grateful that for once he didn't have to hide his fangs when he smiled.

In the dark, she couldn't see him.

But he could see her plainly. Her long, black braids were hanging down, trapped between her back and his chest. The scent of them hung thick in the air and she was wet and hot against him.

He carried her to a chair and sat down with her in his lap. They were both still panting and weak.

She leaned back against him, then reached her arm up

around his neck to hold him close. He ran his mouth and tongue over her cheek, nibbling her gently.

Sunshine had never before been like this with a man.

Sure, she'd had sex and her ex-husband had been a horny toad, but she'd never wanted anyone the way she wanted Talon.

His body was so warm and hard beneath her, so innately masculine, that she had no desire to ever move again from his lap.

She sighed contentedly.

"Talon, do you do this with every woman you meet?"

"No," he whispered in her ear. "I don't, and I've never brought a woman out to my cabin before. You're definitely a special case."

"You sure?"

"Positive. What about you? Do you go home with every guy you meet?"

She leaned back, wishing she could see his face. "No. I promise you, you're a special case too."

He kissed her gently.

They sat like that for a long time, just holding each other, lost in the quiet stillness of the dawn.

Sunshine wasn't sure what she felt for Talon. There was a part of her that wanted to hold on to him like this forever and another part of her that told her she was an idiot for thinking any such thing about a guy she had just met.

Yeah, he looked great in leather pants and could rock every piece of her body, but at the end of the day would he bother hanging around, or would he be just like every other guy she'd known? Selfish. Possessive.

Judgmental.

She didn't know for sure.

She wasn't sure if she wanted to wait around and find out.

Sunshine yawned. It had been a long night, emotionally and physically draining.

Now all she wanted to do was cuddle up to that warm masculine body and sleep.

Talon felt suddenly awkward. Bringing her here had seemed like a good idea at the time, but now that he thought about actually going to bed with her to sleep . . .

It was an intimacy that he hadn't experienced since the death of his wife. There were plenty of times he'd had sex with women and afterward they had both drifted off to sleep for a little while, but this was entirely different.

They would actually spend the day together. Sleeping. Their bodies touching . . .

She yawned again. "I'll be right back."

Turning on the light for her, Talon didn't say anything as she grabbed a T-shirt from her bag and headed to his bathroom.

While she was gone, he listened to her in the other room. He could hear the water running as she washed her face and brushed her teeth.

This felt so strange.

Memories drifted through his head. Memories of a life he'd purposely forgotten.

Memories of a man he'd buried.

He remembered countless nights when he had climbed into bed to wait for his wife as she readied herself for sleep. Nights when he had watched her brush her hair until it gleamed in the firelight and then braided it before she joined him.

Nights of listening to her hum while she sewed before the fire . . .

He gazed over to his dresser where Sunshine had placed a small cosmetics bag, a pink hairbrush, and a small bottle that probably contained her patchouli oil.

He stared at the dainty items that looked so out of place among his belongings. Items that were feminine and foreign, and that wrung his gut.

How he'd missed sharing his life with someone. Having someone to care for, someone who cared for him.

It was something he hadn't thought about in a long, long time. Something he hadn't dared think about.

Now that he thought about it, he had to admit life as a

Dark-Hunter did have moments of profound loneliness.

Sunshine came out with her black hair still braided and her legs peeking out from the hem of the shirt. The smile on her face tugged at his warrior's heart.

Centuries ago, he'd looked forward to battle, knowing that if he survived, he would return to the warm embrace of loving arms. The comfort of a friend.

As a Dark-Hunter the best he could hope for after battle was curling up to the computer or phone and sharing the fight with someone who lived hundreds, if not thousands, of miles away.

That had never bothered him before.

Tonight for some reason, it did.

"You okay?" she asked.

He nodded.

Sunshine wasn't so sure of his answer. There was a haunted look to his face. "Have you changed your mind about me staying over?"

"No," he said quickly. "It's just been a long night."

She nodded. "Tell me about it."

She climbed into his bed and pulled the black comforter over her body, then turned out the lamp by the bed.

Talon turned to look at her. She lay on her side, facing the wall. Her head looked small against his king-sized pillow and she looked so tiny and womanly against the blackness of his bed.

Most of all, she looked delectable.

He lay down beside her. Before he could stop himself, he pulled her into his arms, spooning up behind her.

"Mmm," she breathed sleepily. "I really like it when you do that."

Pain ripped through him as he closed his eyes and inhaled her unique scent. She felt so incredibly good in his arms.

Nae! his mind roared. He couldn't do it. He couldn't let himself care for her that way.

There could never be anything between them. Tomorrow

he would have to let her go back to her life while he returned to his.

That was the way of things.

Kissing her gently on the back of her head, he sighed and forced himself to sleep. He could never have her; she could never be more than a passing whim for him.

Never.

Sunshine lay there for quite some time listening to Talon breathe. There were no words to convey exactly what she felt lying beside this man. It was as if they fit. As if they were meant to be together.

Why was that?

She wasn't sure how long she lay there before sleep overtook her, but when she finally slept, she found herself having the strangest dream . . .

She saw Talon as a young man, probably no older than twenty. His long golden-blond hair was braided down his back while the two shorter, thinner braids dangled from his left temple. His youthful face was covered in a thick dark blond beard, but still she recognized him.

Recognized him as a young man who meant the entire world to her.

He held himself above her, his hard, masculine body naked and pressed against her own as he slid himself in and out of her with such tenderness that it made her heart soar and ache at the same time.

"Oh, precious Nyn," he breathed in her ear. He drove himself deep and hard into her, punctuating each word he spoke. "How can I leave you?"

She cupped his face in her hands and kissed him, then forced him back so that she could look into his amber eyes as he made love to her. "You've no choice, Speirr. You've fought too hard and suffered too much to be heir not to do this. This will ensure that the clan will take you as their king when your uncle dies."

She saw the anguish in his eyes and felt his body grow rigid around hers. "I know."

They loved each other so much. They always had. Ever

since the day when she was six and he eight, and he had nobly saved her from a flogging by a rooster.

He had been the hero of her heart.

They'd grown up apart and yet never parted.

Even as children, they had known their friendship would be stopped or ridiculed, and Speirr had suffered enough ridicule to last ten thousand lifetimes.

She would never hurt him more.

So they had never told anyone of the times when they would sneak away from their families and duties to be together.

For years their meetings had been innocent. Meeting to play a game or to fish. Sometimes to swim, or to share the heartbreaks they felt.

It had only been during this last year that they had dared touch each other's bodies.

She was the daughter of a fishmonger—the lowest of the low. Even so, Speirr had never treated her as the others did. He never mentioned that she smelled of fish oil or wore clothes that were threadbare and patched.

He'd respected her and treasured her friendship as much as she treasured his.

She had given him her virginity gladly, knowing there could never be anything between them. Knowing the day would come when he would have to marry another.

And though it broke her heart, she knew she had no choice except to let him go now. He needed to marry another to erase the taint his mother had left with him. To prove to everyone that he was noble in blood as well as in spirit.

"You will make a fine husband, Speirr. She is lucky to have you."

"Don't," he said, holding her tighter. "I don't want to think of anyone else while I'm with you. Just hold me, Nyn. Let me pretend for one moment that I'm not my mother's son. Let me pretend that there's only you and I in the world and no one and nothing to ever separate us."

She clenched her eyes shut as pain assailed her.

How she wished it were true.

He pulled back to look down at her. He cupped her face tenderly. "You are the only warmth in my heart. The only sunshine my winter has ever known."

Oh, how she loved him like this. When he, the fierce, bold warrior-prince, dared to be the bard who lived in his heart. Only she knew this side of him. Only she had ever known he had the talent of a poet.

To the rest of the world he must always be fierce and strong. A fighter of unquestionable prowess and skill.

But it was his poet's heart she loved best.

"And you are my fire," she breathed. "And if you don't go off and meet with your uncle now, he'll extinguish you."

He cursed as he pulled away from her.

She watched him dress and helped lace him back into his armor. He was a prince. Not just in title, but in bearing and form. There had never been a more noble man.

After she was dressed, he pulled her into his arms and gave her one last scorching kiss. "Meet me tonight?"

She looked away. "If you wish it, Speirr. I will do anything you ask, but I don't think it will be fair to your new wife to meet you on your wedding night."

He flinched as if she'd slapped him. "You're right, Nyn. Most of all, it wouldn't be fair to you."

Sunshine moaned as she felt herself leaving Nynia and moving toward Speirr. They were still by the loch, only now it was him she felt. His emotions.

It was through his eyes she saw them.

Speirr was heartbroken as he watched Nynia step out of his embrace. The pain inside him was so intense that he feared it would cripple him.

He reached his hand out for her, knowing she was gone.

Lost.

Lost to him forever.

Just as his mother had been.

Just as his sisters and father were.

Gods, it was so unfair.

But then, life was never fair. Especially not to a man

who had duties and responsibilities. A man who had to force respect for himself and his sister at the point of his sword.

His life had never been his own.

Turning away from her, he mounted his horse and rode to meet his aunt and uncle so that they could finalize the marriage between their clan and the Gaulish-Celt tribe that bordered them to the north.

This marriage would finally silence the tongues of the gossips and doomsayers who wanted someone else to be named heir.

Sunshine thrashed in her sleep as her dream shifted. She saw Talon later that day, standing between a beautiful woman in her early thirties and a man only a few years older. The woman had the same blond hair and blue eyes as Talon while the man was black haired and black eyed.

They stood in the middle of an old wood hall. The room was crowded with people who were strangers to the three of them. Everyone was dressed in fine plaids and wore gold jewelry.

Speirr's uncle was dressed in black leather armor and his aunt in gold armor with a long, plaid skirt.

To the people gathered there, Talon looked strong and proud. Fierce and princely.

The Gauls' whispered voices echoed in the room as they retold stories of his prowess in battle, told each other that he was the Morrigán's favored warrior.

It was said the goddess herself walked beside him in battle and dared anyone to mar his beauty or dull his sword.

What no one knew was that Speirr was ready to bolt as he waited to meet his bride.

"I swear, lad, you're as skittish as a colt," his aunt whispered with a laugh.

"You were too, Ora," his uncle teased her. "I remember your father threatened to tie you to his side if you didn't stop fidgeting while our parents bound us together."

"Aye, but I was much younger than he is."

His aunt placed a comforting hand on his shoulder.

Speirr took a deep breath as a young woman was brought forward to stand before him.

"My daughter Deirdre," King Llewd said.

She was beautiful. That was Speirr's first thought. With hair as golden fair as any he'd ever seen and blue eyes that were kind and gentle.

But she was no match for his Nynia. No other woman could ever come close to her.

Speirr stepped back instinctively.

His uncle pushed him forward.

Deirdre smiled invitingly. Her eyes warm and accepting.

He stepped back again.

This time, his aunt nudged him toward his bride. "What have you to say to her, lad?"

"I . . ." Speirr knew the words that would bind them together. He'd rehearsed them incessantly.

But now they lodged in his throat.

He couldn't breathe.

He stepped back again, and again his aunt and uncle moved him forward, toward her and a destiny that seemed suddenly bleak. Cold.

"Speirr," his uncle said with a warning note in his voice. "Say the words."

Do it, or you will lose everything.

Do it, and I will lose the only *thing.*

In his mind, he saw the hurt in Nynia's eyes. Saw the tears she'd tried to hide.

Speirr clenched his teeth, flexing his jaw with determination. "I willna do this." He whirled around and left the hall, hearing the shocked gasps as he made his way to the door and out into the village.

A few seconds later, his aunt and uncle came rushing out behind him. He was halfway to his horse when his uncle grabbed his arm and pulled him roughly to a stop.

"What is wrong with you?" he demanded.

"Speirr?" his aunt said in a gentler tone. "What is it?"

He looked back and forth between them, searching for

the words to make them understand what was in his heart. "I willna marry her."

"Oh aye, you will," his uncle said sternly. His dark eyes snapped fire at him. "Now march yourself back in there and finish this."

"*Nae,*" he said stubbornly. "I willna marry her while I love someone else."

"Who?" they asked in unison.

"Nynia."

They exchanged a deep frown.

"Who the blazes is Nynia?" his uncle asked.

"The fishmonger's daughter?" his aunt said.

The two questions came at him at once. Until his aunt's comment registered in his uncle's mind.

"The fishmonger's daughter?" he repeated.

His uncle moved to pop him on the back of his head, but Speirr caught his hand and glared at him. His days of being hit by his uncle were long over.

"Are you mad?" his uncle demanded, wrenching his arm free. "How do you even know her?"

Speirr tensed, expecting his uncle's condemnation. No doubt they would finally banish him from their clan just as they had done his mother.

None of that mattered.

Nynia was the only person who had ever really accepted him.

He would not fail her by marrying someone else while she had to go back to the misery of her life.

He refused to grow old without her.

"I know you don't understand and I know I should just go and marry the Gaul's daughter, but I can't." He looked at his aunt, hoping someone would understand his plight. "I love Nynia. I don't want to live without her."

"You are young and foolish," his uncle said. "Just like your mother, you let your heart rule you. If you fail to do this, you will never live down your mother's shame. You will be seen as nothing more than a ridiculed whoreson. Now get back in that hall and marry Deirdre. Now!"

"*Nae,*" he said firmly.

"So help me, Speirr, fail to do this and I will see you banished for it."

"Then banish me."

"*Nae,*" his aunt said, intruding on their argument.

She held that distant, faraway look that she got whenever she saw through the natural world into a higher level. "The gods are at work here, Idiag. Look into his eyes. Nynia is his soulmate. They are meant to be together."

His uncle cursed. "This would have been a great alliance for our clan," he muttered bitterly. "It would have ensured peace between our peoples and guaranteed that no one would have contested Speirr as my heir. But I won't argue with the will of the gods."

He patted Speirr on the arm. "Go, Speirr. Go claim your Nynia while I try and salvage what I can from this meeting and hopefully avert a war."

Speirr blinked in disbelief. It was the first time in his life that his uncle had ever been kind or merciful toward him. "Do you mean it?"

He narrowed his eyes at him. "Lad, you'd best be off before common sense returns to me."

Speirr shouted as he raced for his horse. Then he ran back and hugged his aunt, then his uncle. "Thank you. Thank you both."

As fast as he could, he ran to his horse and jumped up onto the back of it. He set his heels into its flanks and headed toward their own lands.

Speirr tore through the forest at a dead run. His black stallion flew through the tangled underbrush and weeds, kicking up dirt in their wake. The sunlight drifted through the trees, dappling his armor as he urged the horse faster.

He had to reach his Nynia . . .

Nynia sighed as her mother handed her the tattered old basket that held ten nasty-smelling fish. "Must I deliver this?" she asked her mother, her voice pleading for clemency.

"Your brother is off on an errand and they be wanting it. Now go, child. I'll brook no more arguments from you."

Nynia clenched her teeth as she took the basket. How she hated this. She would rather be beaten than travel to the smith's home where Eala would no doubt be waiting to take her delivery. Her own age, Eala was the smith's daughter but she acted as if she were descended from a line as noble as Speirr's.

The girl took great pleasure in humiliating her.

And today, Nynia was in no mood for it. Not while her heart was so sore from its loss.

By now her Speirr would be married to another. He would be lost to her forever.

Blinking back tears, she left the tiny hut she shared with her mother, father, and brother, and headed for the nicer side of the village where the rest of the people resided, upwind from the fishmonger, tanner, and butcher.

"Oh, Speirr," she whispered as she wiped away her tears. How could she make it through a single day without him? All her life she'd had him to see her through the misery of her work. She'd always looked forward to their meetings. Looked forward to sharing laughter and fun with him down by the loch.

Now those days were gone forever.

When he returned, it would be with a new wife.

One day, his queen would bear his children . . .

Pain assailed her even more. Nynia walked aimlessly through the village, her thoughts on the only man she would ever love and on the fact that she would never bear his children. Never be able to hold him again.

She drew near the smith's cottage and saw Eala wasn't alone today. She stood with a small group of friends, talking. She recognized three of the boys, and the girls would have been her friends, too, had she, as they so often reminded her, not smelled of fish.

"Oh bother," Eala said disgustedly. "It's the fish girl

with her fetid stench. Quick, everyone, hold your breath or you'll turn blue."

Nynia lifted her chin. They couldn't hurt her with their words. Not today. She was hurt enough.

She shoved the basket into Eala's hands.

Eala shrieked. "You're vile, Nynia!" she shouted, dropping the basket and dancing away from it. "No man will ever want so smelly a woman. Will he, Dearg?"

Dearg turned a speculative eye on Nynia. "I don't know. From what we saw her giving to Speirr the other day, I'd be willing to hold my nose."

Her face on fire, Nynia was horrified that someone had stumbled upon her and Speirr while they were making love in the woods.

"What say you, Aberth?" Dearg asked another handsome youth.

"Aye. She'd be good for a tup or two, especially since she's sheathed a strong sword, but you can marry her if you're like Speirr and common filth is to your taste. I'd rather not."

Their mean laughter rang in her ears.

Humiliated and embarrassed, Nynia had started away from them when she caught the sound of a horse approaching at a dead run.

Everyone in the village grew quiet at the sound. It was obvious the rider was in a dire hurry. His thick, deep voice could be heard urging the horse onward toward the village.

The instant Speirr came flying out of the woods, people scattered out of his way.

Nynia couldn't move as she watched him.

He had his head bent low, and both he and the horse were covered in sweat. United in power, beauty, and form, the two of them were a fierce and frightening sight to behold.

They flew as if the demons of Annwn were hot on their heels.

She expected him to keep riding past her, toward his home.

He didn't.

Instead, Speirr reined his horse in sharply before her, the fierce beast rearing and pawing at the air.

He jumped from his saddle and swept her up into his arms.

Her heart pounded with joy, but she was scared of this. Scared of what his disheveled appearance here meant.

"Fiù?" she asked hesitantly, using the proper term for *prince,* knowing that with so many witnesses, she could never call him by his given name. "What is it you would have of me?"

His amber eyes were shiny and bright and filled with his heart as he stared at her. "I would have you, my love," he breathed. "Every day for the rest of my life. I've come to marry you, Nyn. If you'll have me."

Tears filled her eyes. "Your uncle?"

"He wishes us well and will meet you when he returns."

Her hands shook as she held him tight.

"You are mine, precious Nyn," he whispered. "I want no other in my life."

"Even though I smell like a fish?"

He laughed at that. "And I smell like a sweaty horse. We're a perfect pair, you and I."

Only he would say such a thing.

Tears rolled down her face as she held him close and wept from happiness.

Her Speirr had come back to her and she would never let him go. They were meant to be together.

Forever . . .

Sunshine woke up with a feeling of warm serenity deep in her heart. She felt the weight of Talon behind her and smiled sleepily.

She didn't really remember her dream other than the fact that it had been about Talon.

And it had comforted her.

She checked her wristwatch and saw it was just after

noon. She should be at work by now, hawking her artwork in the square.

Yet she had no desire to get out of this futon.

Rolling over, she snuggled into Talon's body.

She laid her head on his shoulder and traced the tattoo on his chest. He was so warm and inviting.

"It's good to have you home, love." He whispered those words to her in a language she'd only heard once before when they had been making love last night, and yet she understood him.

She lifted herself up and realized he was still sound asleep. "Talon?"

He didn't budge.

"Speirr?" she asked, wondering why that name came to her mind, but somehow it seemed only right that she should call him that.

His eyes fluttered open. He frowned at her. "Do you need something?"

Sunshine shook her head.

He closed his eyes, rolled over and returned to sleep.

Oh, this was just too friggin' weird.

Why did she know that name and why did he respond to it?

Had it been part of her dream?

She tried to recall it, and for her life she couldn't.

As he lay there with his back to her, she saw something in her mind's eye. It was like a vague childhood memory.

She saw Talon as an adolescent youth, stretched out over a large stone table. There were other monolithic stones around them, forming something that vaguely reminded her of Stonehenge.

Talon was lying on his stomach, his arms under his head, as a tall, dark-haired man leaned over him. The man's black robes billowed as he beat Talon with a frayed whip.

Talon was looking straight at her, his eyes shining with unshed tears while he kept his jaw firmly locked.

Meet me later. He mouthed the words to her and she nodded.

Sunshine pulled back, alarmed.

Her dream rushing back to her, she scrambled from the bed and grabbed Talon's cell phone, then called her mother. She stepped outside the cabin's door so that Talon couldn't overhear her conversation.

"Sunshine?" her mother asked as soon as she recognized Sunshine's voice. "Where are you? Storm said you blew him off last night without calling."

"I'm sorry, Mom. You know me. I got distracted and forgot to call. Listen, I need to know something. Do you remember years ago when you and Grandma did that whole past-life regression thing on me?"

"Yes?"

"I remember you and Grandma telling me that I was an ancient Celt, right?"

"Yes."

"Do you remember anything more specific than that?"

"No, not really. I'd have to call Mom and see if she remembers. Knowing her, she might. Why? You sound panicked."

"I am panicked. I'm having some bizarre flashback kind of thing. I don't know what else to call it. It's just very, very weird."

"Are you with Steve?"

"Talon, Mom, his name is Talon. And yes, I am."

"You think you knew him in a previous life?"

Sunshine looked back at the door and swallowed. "Honestly, Mom, I'm thinking I was married to him."

Chapter 7

It was shortly after sunset when Acheron knocked on Zarek's door. He'd spent most of the day with Artemis, discussing what needed to be done since the human authorities were now looking for Zarek.

He could still see Artemis lying nonchalantly on her white-cushioned throne, her beautiful face completely disinterested. *"I already told you, Acheron, kill him. Only you are blind to the man's character. It's why I wanted him in New Orleans in the first place. I wanted you to see firsthand just how far gone he is."*

Ash refused to believe it. He, better than anyone, understood Zarek's nastiness. The need to strike the first blow before it struck you.

So he'd bargained with Artemis for more time for Zarek to prove to the goddess that he wasn't some rabid animal in need of a mercy killing.

But how Ash hated bargaining with her for anything. Still, he wasn't going to sign the order for Zarek's execution. Not yet. Not while there was still hope.

He knocked again. Harder. If Zarek was sleeping upstairs, he might not hear him.

The door swung open slowly.

Ash walked inside, his eyes instantly adjusting to the pitch-blackness. He closed the door with a mental push and reached out with his senses.

Zarek was in the sitting room on his left.

The ex-slave had neglected to turn on the heat so the house had a frigid chill to it. But then, Zarek was so used to the subzero temps in Alaska that he probably didn't even notice the more moderate cold of New Orleans in February.

Heading for the sitting room, Ash stopped as he caught sight of Zarek lying on the floor by the Victorian sofa. Dressed only in black sweatpants, Zarek appeared to be asleep, but Ash knew he wasn't.

Zarek's senses were as honed as his own and the ex-slave would never allow anyone to enter his sleeping area without being fully alert and ready to strike.

Ash let his gaze wander over Zarek's bare back. On the lower part of his spine was a highly stylized dragon. It was the only mark his back currently held, but Ash remembered a time when Zarek's flesh had been covered in scars so deep that Ash had actually flinched the first time he'd seen them.

A whipping boy for Valerius's family, Zarek had grown up paying the price every time Valerius or his brothers had crossed the line.

The scars hadn't been just on his back. They had been on his legs, chest, arms, and face. One facial scar over his blinded left eye had been so severe that Zarek had barely been able to open the eye. The scar on the cheek below that eye had given his face a twisted, misshapen look.

In his human lifetime, Zarek had walked with a pronounced limp and his right arm had barely functioned.

When he'd first crossed over and become a Dark-Hunter, Zarek hadn't even been able to meet Ash's gaze. He'd stared at the floor, cringing every time Ash moved.

Normally, Ash gave newly created Dark-Hunters a choice of keeping their physical scars or having them removed. In Zarek's case, he hadn't asked. Zarek's body had been so badly damaged that he had erased them immediately.

His second course of action had been to teach the man to fight back.

And fight back he'd done. By the time Ash had finished his training, Zarek had unleashed a fury so strong that it gave him incredible powers.

Unfortunately, it also made the man uncontrollable.

"You gonna keep staring at me, Great Acheron, or are you ready to chew me a new one?"

Ash sighed. Zarek still hadn't moved. He lay there with his back to him, his arm tucked under his head.

"What do you want me to say to you, Z? You knew better than to attack a cop. Never mind three of them."

"So what? I was supposed to let them handcuff me and take me to jail where I could wait for sunup in a cell?"

He ignored Zarek's rancor. "What happened?"

"They saw me kill the Daimons and tried to apprehend me. I merely protected myself."

"Protecting yourself doesn't require giving one a concussion, one a set of broken ribs, and another one a busted jaw."

Zarek rolled to his feet and glared at him. "What happened to them was their own fault. They should have backed off when I told them to."

Ash returned Zarek's glare even keel. Zarek possessed the ability to stir his anger even faster than Artemis did. "Dammit, Z, I'm tired of taking shit from Artemis because you can't behave."

"What's the matter, Highness? Can't take the criticism? I guess that's what happens when you grow up noble. You never have to worry about having your behavior censored. Everyone thinks you're perfect. Meanwhile you're free to frolic through your life. Tell me, what made you a Dark-Hunter? Someone scuff your boots and get away with it?"

Ash closed his eyes and counted to twenty. Slowly. He knew ten would never be enough to calm him.

Zarek raked him with that familiar sneer. The ex-slave had always hated him. But Ash didn't take it personally. Zarek hated everyone.

"I know what you think of me, O Great Acheron. I know how much you pity me and I don't need it. Do you honestly think I could ever forget the way you looked at me the first night we met? You stood there with horror in your eyes as you tried not to show it to me.

"Well, you achieved your good deed. You cleaned up your little foundling and made him all pretty and healthy. But don't even think that means I have to lick your boots or kiss your ass for it. My days of subjugation are over."

Ash growled low in his throat as he fought down the urge to splinter the man against the far wall. "Don't push me, Z. I'm the only thing standing between you and a deathly existence so bad it's beyond even your comprehension."

"Go ahead then. Kill me. Do you really think I give a damn?"

No, he didn't. Zarek had been born with a death wish. Both as a mortal man and as a Dark-Hunter. But Ash would never again kill a Dark-Hunter and send him into the agony of Shadedom. He knew firsthand the horrors of that existence.

"Shave your goatee, take the earring out, and keep your damn claws hidden. If you're smart, you'll stay away from the cops."

"Is that an order?"

Ash used his powers to lift Zarek from the floor and pin him roughly against the ceiling. "Stop pushing your luck, boy. I've had it with you."

Zarek actually laughed. "Have you ever thought of hiring yourself out to Disneyland? People would pay a fortune for this ride."

Ash growled louder, baring his fangs at the impudent ass.

It was seriously hard to intimidate a man who had nothing in life that meant anything to him. Dealing with Zarek made him feel like a parent with an out-of-control child.

Ash lowered him to the floor before he yielded to the temptation of strangling him.

Zarek narrowed his eyes as his feet connected with the floor. He walked nonchalantly to his duffel bag and pulled out a pack of cigarettes.

He knew better than to taunt the Atlantean. Acheron could extinguish him in a heartbeat if he chose to. But then, Acheron still held his humanity. He actually had compassion for other people, which was a weakness Zarek had never possessed. No one had ever given a damn about him so why should he care about anyone else?

He lit his cigarette as Acheron turned to leave.

"Talon will patrol around Canal, so I want you to take the area from Jackson Square to Esplanade."

Zarek exhaled the smoke. "Anything else?"

"Behave, Z. For the love of Zeus, behave."

Zarek took a long drag on his cigarette as Acheron opened the door without touching it and strode out of his house.

He held his cigarette between his teeth and raked his hands through his tousled black hair.

Behave.

He could almost laugh at the order.

It wasn't his fault that trouble always came looking for him. But he'd never been one to dodge anything either. He'd learned a long time ago to take his hits and his pain.

He clenched his teeth as he remembered last night. He'd seen the Daimons on the street as they headed to Sunshine's loft. Heard them talking about how they intended to damage her. So he'd followed them, until he had a chance to fight them without anyone seeing them.

The next thing he knew, he had four bullet wounds in his side and a cop screaming at him to freeze.

At first, he'd intended to let them arrest him and then call Nick to bail him out, but when one of the cops had hit him across the back with his nightstick, all good intentions had gone straight to hell.

His days as a whipping boy were over.

No one was ever going to touch him again.

Sunshine sat outside Talon's cabin, working on the paintings Cameron Scott had commissioned from her. While

Talon slept inside, she'd been out here for hours, trying to figure out why she was still here with him in his swamp.

Why she had come out here with him last night when she should have just gone over to her brother's.

Her revelation about their past life together had really freaked her out.

She had been his passive, June Cleaver wife . . .

Sunshine shivered. She didn't want to be anyone's wife. Not any more.

Marriage was a losing venture for a woman. Her ex-husband had taught her well that guys didn't want a wife so much as a maid who could provide them with sex on tap.

An artist like her, Jerry Gagne had seemed the perfect match. They had met in art school and she had fallen in love with the moody, mysterious goth chicness of him.

At that time in her life, she had loved him zealously and couldn't imagine a day without him in it.

She thought they were two comfortable peas who could carve out a pod that would last them for the rest of their lives. She'd assumed Jerry would understand her need to create and that he would respect her and give her the room she needed to grow as an artist.

What Jerry had wanted was for her to take care of him while *he* grew as an artist. Her needs and desires had always taken a backseat to his.

Their marriage had lasted two years, four months, and twenty-two days.

Not all of it had been bad. Part of her still loved him. She'd enjoyed having company and someone to share her life with, but she didn't want to go back to being the one who was responsible for where someone else put his socks—she could barely remember where she put her own socks. Dropping her projects and going to the store because someone forgot to get the eggs that he had to have for his homemade paints.

It was always her plans that changed. Her stuff that could wait.

Jerry had never made any kind of concession to her.

She didn't want to lose herself to a man again. She wanted her own life. Her own career.

Talon was a great guy, but he struck her as a creature like herself. A loner who valued his privacy. They had had a great time so far, but she was sure they weren't compatible.

She was someone who actually liked to get up and paint in the daylight. Talon stayed up all night long. She loved tofu and granola. He loved junk food and coffee.

She and Jerry had kept the same schedule, had all the same likes, and look what had happened. If they couldn't make a go of it, then it certainly didn't bode well for any kind of real relationship with Talon.

No, she needed to get back to her life.

As soon as he got up and they ate, she was going to tell him to take her home.

Talon sighed in his sleep. It had been a long time since he had last dreamt of his wife. He hadn't dared. Thoughts of Nynia had always had the ability to tear his heart out.

But today, she was there with him. There in his dreams where they could be together.

His throat tight, he watched her sitting before his hearth, her belly distended with his child while she sewed clothes for the baby. Even after five years of marriage and a lifetime of friendship, she was able to stir his blood and make his heart swell with love.

Growing up under his uncle's scornful eye and the disdain of the clan, he had only found her to give him comfort. She alone had made him feel loved.

He listened to her hum the same lullaby his mother had once sung to him when he was a very small child.

Gods, how he needed her. Now more than ever before. He was weary of fighting, weary of the demands his people had placed upon him since the death of his uncle.

Weary of hearing the whispers about his mother and father.

He was a young man, but tonight he felt ancient. And cold.

Until he looked at Nynia. She warmed him deep inside and made everything better.

How he loved her for it.

Moving forward, he sank down in front of her chair and placed his head in her lap. He wrapped his arms around her as he was wont to do and felt the baby kick his arm in protest.

"You've returned," she said gently, brushing her hand through his hair.

He didn't speak. He couldn't. Normally he would have bathed the blood from his armor and body before he sought her out, but the grief of the day was still too raw in his heart.

He needed to feel her gentle, soothing touch on his body, needed to know that for the moment she was safe and still with him.

Only she could ease the aching pain inside his heart.

His aunt was dead. Mutilated. He'd found the body when he'd gone to look for her after she didn't show up for the midday meal.

If he lived an eternity, he would never forget the grisly sight. It would live inside him along with the memory of his mother dying in his arms.

"It's the gods' curse," Parth had whispered earlier that evening, not knowing Talon was close enough to hear him speak to his brother. *"He is the whore's son. She lay with a Druid to beget a cursed lineage and now we'll all pay for it. The gods will punish us all."*

"Do you wish to challenge Speirr's sword for leadership?"

"Only a fool would challenge one such as he. Not even Cuchulainn could equal him."

"Then you'd best pray to the gods that he never hears you."

Talon clenched his eyes shut, trying to dampen the whispers that had haunted him all the days of his life.

"Speirr?" Nynia stroked his face. "Are they all slain?"

He nodded. After he had brought his aunt home, he had gathered his men and ridden after the Northern Gaul tribe. He'd found one of their daggers near her body and had known instantly they were responsible.

"I really am cursed, Nyn." The words stuck in his throat. After a lifetime of trying to prove to others that he wasn't cursed for his parents' actions, he was now cursed because of his own. "I should have listened to you when my uncle died. I should never have taken vengeance against the Northern clan. Now all I can do is fear what their gods will take from me next."

But in his heart, he already knew. There was nothing on earth more precious than the woman he held.

She was going to die.

Because of him.

It was *all* his fault. All of it.

He alone had brought the wrath of the Northern clan's gods down upon their heads.

There was no way to stop it. No way to keep her by his side.

The pain of it was more than he could bear. "I have offered up sacrifices to the Morrigán, but the Druids tell me it isn't enough. What more can I do?"

"Maybe this is the last. Maybe it will end now."

He hoped so. The alternative . . .

Nae, he couldn't lose his Nynia. Their gods could have anything but her . . .

Talon groaned as his dream shifted forward, into the future. He held his wife as she labored to bring their baby into the world.

They were both covered in sweat from the fire and hours of exertion. The midwife had opened a window and let in a cool breeze from the snow that was falling outside.

Nynia had always loved the snow, and the weather had

given them both hope that maybe everything would work out. Maybe the baby would be a new chance for all of them.

"Push!" the woman ordered.

Nynia's fingernails bit into his arms as she gripped him and screamed. Talon placed his cheek to hers, holding her close and whispering into her ear. "I've got you, my love. I'll never let you go."

She groaned deep and then relaxed as their son rushed out from inside her, into the hands of the midwife.

Nynia laughed as he kissed her cheek and hugged her tight.

But their joy was cut short as the child refused to respond to the old woman's attempts to wake him.

"The babe is dead." The woman's words rang in his head.

"Nae!" he snarled. "He sleeps. Rouse him."

"Nae, my *triath.* The child is stillborn. I'm truly sorry."

Nynia wept in his arms. "I am so sorry, Speirr, that I couldn't give you your son. I didn't mean to fail you."

"You didn't fail me, Nyn. You could never fail me."

Horrified and heartbroken, Talon held Nynia close as the midwife washed and dressed their son's small body.

He couldn't take his gaze from the babe.

His son had ten tiny fingers, ten perfect toes. A mop of thick, black hair. His face was beautiful and serene. Perfect.

Why did the child not live?

Why did he not breathe?

Grinding his teeth to stave off the pain, Talon willed the child to wake. Silently demanded his son to cry out and live.

How could something so perfect not breathe? Why couldn't the baby move and squall?

He was their son.

Their precious babe.

There was no reason why the child should not be alive and well. No reason other than the fact that Talon was a fool.

He had killed his own son.

Tears welled in his eyes. How many times had he held his hand over Nynia's stomach and felt the strength of his son's movements? Felt the loving pride of a father?

They had marked the days to the baby's birth. Had shared their hopes and dreams for him.

And now he would never know the boy who had already won his heart. Never see the child smile or grow.

"I am so sorry, Speirr," Nynia murmured over and over again, weeping.

He tightened his arms around her and whispered words of comfort. He had to be strong for her. She needed him now.

Kissing her cheek, Talon forced his tears away and offered her solace. "It's all right, my love. We'll have more children." But in his heart, he knew the truth. The god Camulus would never permit a child of his to live, and Talon would never again put Nynia through this. He loved her too much.

He was still holding her an hour later when all the color had faded from her face. When the last of his hopes had shattered and left him bereft of anything except resounding agony.

Nynia was dying from blood loss.

The midwife had done all she could, but in the end she had left them alone to say their goodbyes.

Nynia was leaving him.

He couldn't breathe.

He couldn't function.

She was dying.

Talon had picked Nynia up and cradled her against him. He was covered in her blood, but he didn't even notice. All he could think of was keeping her with him, making her well.

Live for me!

He willed his own life force into her body, but it wasn't enough.

Silently, he bargained with the gods to take anything

else—his life, his lands, his people. Anything. Just leave him his heart. He needed it too much to lose it like this.

"I love you, Speirr," she whispered softly.

He choked.

"You can't leave me, Nyn," he whispered as she shivered in his arms. "I don't know what to do without you."

"You will take care of Ceara as you promised your mother." She swallowed as she traced his lips with her cold hand. "My brave Speirr. Always strong and giving. I shall wait for you on the other side until Bran brings us together again."

He closed his eyes as tears seeped past his control. "I can't live without you, Nyn. I can't."

"You must, Speirr. Our people need you. Ceara needs you."

"And I need *you*."

She swallowed and looked up at him, her eyes full of fear. "I'm scared, Speirr. I don't want to die. I feel so cold. I've never gone anywhere without you before."

"I'll keep you warm." He pulled more furs over her and rubbed her arms. If he could just keep her warm, she would stay with him. He knew she would . . .

If he could just keep her warm.

"Why is it getting dark?" she asked, her voice trembling. "I don't want it to be dark yet. I just want to hold you for a little while longer."

"I'll hold you, Nyn. Don't worry, love. I have you."

She placed her hand against his cheek as a single tear fell. "I wish I had been the wife you deserved, Speirr. I wish I could have given you all the children you wanted."

Before he could speak, he felt it. The last expulsion of breath from her body before she went limp in his arms.

Enraged and heartsick, Talon threw his head back and gave his battle cry as pain tore through him. Tears fell down his face.

"Why!" he roared at the gods. "Damn you, Camulus. Why! Why couldn't you just kill *me* and have left her in peace?"

As expected, no one answered. The Morrigán had abandoned him, left him alone to face this pain.

"Why would the gods ever help a whoreson like you, boy? You're not fit for anything except licking the boots of your betters."

"Look at him, Idiag, he's pitiful and weak like his father before him. He'll never be anything. You might as well let us kill him now and spare the food to nurture a better child."

The voices of the past whipped through him, lacerating his aching heart.

"Are you a prince?" He heard Nynia's childhood voice from the day he had saved her from the rooster.

"I am nothing," he had answered.

"Nae, my lord, you are a prince. Only one so noble would brave the fearsome rooster to save a peasant."

She alone had ever made him feel noble or good.

She alone had made him want to live.

How could his precious Nynia be gone?

Sobbing, he held her and the baby for hours. Held them until the sun was shining bright outside on the snow and her family begged him to let them make preparations for the burials. But he didn't want to prepare them.

He didn't want to let them go.

Since the day they'd met, they'd never been apart for more than a few hours.

Her love and friendship had seen him through so much. Over the years, she had been his strength.

She was the best part of him.

"What am I to do, Nyn?" he whispered against her cold cheek as he rocked her. "What am I to do . . ."

Alone, he had sat there with her, lost. Cold. Aching.

The next day, he'd buried her out by the loch where the two of them had first started their childhood meetings. He could still see her waiting for him, her face bright with expectation. He could imagine her running across the snow, gathering up a handful to make a ball so that she could sneak up on him and drop it down his tunic.

He would have chased her then, and she would have run away, laughing.

She had adored the snow so much. Had always loved to tilt her head back and let the white, pure flakes fall onto her beautiful face and into her golden fair hair.

It seemed somehow wrong that she would have died on a day like this. A day that would have filled her with such happiness.

Wincing in pain, he wished that he lived somewhere where it never snowed. Someplace warm so that he would never again have to see this and be reminded of all he'd lost.

Oh gods, how could she be gone?

Talon growled from grief. He was on his hands and knees in the freezing snow, his heart bereft of anything except painful misery.

All he could focus on was Nynia lying in the ground, holding their baby to her breast. Of the fact that he wasn't there to protect her, to warm her. To take her by the hand and lead her wherever she was headed.

He felt a tiny hand on his shoulder.

Looking up, he saw the small face of his sister. Ceara had seen more than her fair share of tragedy.

"I'm still with you, Speirr. I won't leave you alone."

Talon wrapped his arms around her waist and drew her close. He held her as he wept. She was all he had left. And he would defy the gods themselves to keep her safe.

He hadn't been able to protect Nynia, but he would protect Ceara.

No one would harm her without dealing with him . . .

Talon came awake just before sunset with a sick feeling in his stomach.

He felt so alone.

His emotions were raw and tattered. He hadn't felt like this in centuries. Hadn't hurt like this since the night Acheron had taught him to bury his emotions.

Tonight, he truly felt the solitude of his life. The aching burn of it sliced through his chest, and he had to struggle to breathe.

Until he caught a whiff of something strange on his skin and in his bed.

Patchouli and turpentine.

Sunshine.

His heart instantly lightened as he thought of her and the way she stumbled through her vibrant life.

Inhaling her precious scent, he rolled over and found his bed empty.

Talon frowned. "Sunshine?"

He looked around and didn't see her anywhere.

"Would you leave me alone, you walking pair of boots!"

He cocked a brow at Sunshine's voice on the other side of his door. Before he could get up, the door swung open to show Sunshine fussing at Beth and the alligator hissing back in protest.

The two of them struggled in the doorway.

"Let go of my easel, you refugee from a luggage factory. If you need some wood for a toothpick, there's a bunch of it on the porch."

The side of his mouth quirked up at the sight of them battling it out, Sunshine inside his cabin and Beth on the porch.

"Beth," he snapped. "What are you doing?"

Beth opened her mouth, releasing the easel. Sunshine stumbled backward, into the cabin, with her easel in her hands. The gator hissed and snapped at him, swishing its tail and eyeballing Sunshine irritably.

"She says she was forcing you inside before it got dark and something decided to eat you," he told Sunshine.

"Tell Swamp Breath I was headed this way. Why was she . . ." Sunshine stopped and looked at him. "Oh jeez, am I really having a conversation with a gator?"

He grinned. "It's all right. I do it all the time."

"Yes, but no offense, you're kind of weird."

If that wasn't the pot calling the kettle black . . .

She shooed Beth out, slammed the door, then put her art supplies in the corner.

Talon watched her with interest, especially since the denim of her jeans cupped her rear rather nicely as she leaned over.

"How long have you been up?" he asked.

"A few hours. What about you?"

"I just woke up."

"You always sleep this late?" she asked.

"Since I stay up all night, yeah."

She smiled at him. "I think you've taken being a night owl to a whole new level."

She moved to sit on the futon beside him and rubbed her paint-stained hands against her thighs, drawing his attention to just how perfectly shaped they were and how much he would love to run his hand up the insides of them to the center of her body . . .

He hardened at the thought.

"Would you like me to make you some breakfast?" she asked. "There's not much in the kitchen that's not guaranteed to kill or rot you, but I think I could scrounge up an egg-white omelette."

He grimaced at the thought of what an egg-white omelette would taste like. It would probably be worse than the soy cheese.

Jeez, someone needed to introduce this woman to chocolate Reddi-wip shots. And on the heel of that thought came the question of what Sunshine would taste like covered in chocolate—he'd never gotten the chance to do that with her last night.

Oblivious to his thoughts, she continued her tirade. "Haven't you ever heard of bran flakes? Whole wheat?"

"No, I haven't." He trailed his hand up her arm to her neck where he could tease the softness of her skin with his fingertips. Hmmm, how he loved to touch her flesh.

She continued to lecture him. "You know, eating the way you do, you'll be lucky to live another thirty years. I swear there's more nutrition in Willy Wonka's Chocolate

Factory than anything I found in your kitchen."

Talon just smiled.

Why was he so fascinated by her? He listened to her voice as she lectured him, and instead of being irritated, he actually enjoyed it.

It was nice to have someone concerned enough about him that they would bother telling him what to eat.

"How about I just snack on you for a bit?" he asked.

Sunshine paused mid-sentence. Before she could think to respond, he pulled her across him and claimed her lips.

She moaned at how good he felt. How wonderful he tasted. She could feel his erection under her hip.

Her body melted against his.

The next thing she knew, he had her flat on her back on the futon and was leaning down over her, unbuttoning her sweater as her breasts tightened in expectation of his touch.

"You're very talented at distracting me," she said.

"Am I?" he asked, kissing the valley between her breasts.

"Um-hmmm," she breathed.

Chills shot the length of her body as he nibbled the skin just below her jaw. His hot breath scorched her while he cupped her breast with his hand and kneaded her gently with his fingers.

She ran her hands through his tousled hair, holding him close to her while his braids brushed against her skin, tickling and teasing her. Her body throbbed and burned, craving his blistering touch.

Talon closed his eyes and inhaled the sweet scent of her skin. She was so warm and soft. So womanly. He ran his hand over the bounty of her tanned skin while he teased her neck with his tongue and teeth.

Her hands slid over him.

Oh, he liked how this woman tasted. Loved how she felt under him.

He ran his hand over the black lace of her bra, cupping her gently. She hissed in pleasure, her legs sliding against his. He'd never cared for the sensation of denim on his body before, but when Sunshine was wearing it, he didn't mind at all.

He opened the catch on the front of her bra and released her breasts to his questing hand. He ran his palm over the hard nubs, back and forth, delighting in the way they felt.

He kissed his way down to them.

Sunshine held his head to her and she arched her back. He teased one breast with his tongue, flicking and sucking it until she wanted to scream from pleasure. It was as if he knew some secret way of wringing every bit of sensual ecstasy from the lightest touch.

And as he held her, something strange happened. She flashed back to a time long ago . . .

She saw Talon holding her just as he was doing now.

Only it was late spring and they were lying out in the woods, beside a quiet lake. She was fearful of being caught and, at the same time, she ached with longing for him.

His eyes were a deep amber and dark with passion as he braced himself above her on one arm and unlaced the top of her gown with his free hand.

"I've wanted you forever, Nyn." His whispered words tore through her as he dipped his head and sampled her freed breasts. She moaned in pleasure at the foreign sensation of a man kissing her there. She'd never allowed a man to touch her before. Never had allowed one to see her body.

Somewhat embarrassed, she still couldn't deny him this. Not when it gave him so much pleasure.

Her mother had told her long ago about the needs and wants of men. About the way they planted themselves inside a woman and took possession of her.

From that moment, she'd known she would never want any man but Speirr to take her that way. For him, she would do anything.

He lifted the hem of her dress up to her hips, baring her lower body to his warm, hungry gaze. She shivered as he nudged her legs apart so that he could look at the most private place of her body.

Her instinct was to lock her ankles together, but she forced herself to comply. She opened herself for him and held her breath as he stared at her with so much longing that it made her ache.

He traced his hand down her stomach, and outer thigh. Then ever so slowly, he ran his hand up her inner thigh, making her burn and shiver at the same time. She closed her eyes and moaned as his questing fingers touched the throbbing virgin flesh between her legs.

Her head swam at the strange feeling of him stroking and teasing her. He spread her legs wider, then slid his fingers inside her where he delved deep, making her body quiver.

She moaned as he moved his hand and placed his body between her legs. She felt his rigid shaft throb against her inner thigh.

"Look at me, Nynia."

She opened her eyes and looked up at him.

The love in his eyes scorched her. "It's not too late yet. Tell me you don't want me and I will go away without any damage being done."

"I want you, Speirr," she whispered. "I only want you."

He leaned down and kissed her tenderly, then slid himself inside her.

She tensed at the pain he caused as he tore through her maidenhead and filled her to capacity. She bit her lip and held him close as he slowly rocked himself against her.

"You feel so good beneath me," he breathed, his voice a deep half-groan. "Even better than I thought you would."

"How many women have you had beneath you, Speirr?" She was horrified by her words, but wanted to know and was too young to realize just how foolish her question was.

He stopped moving inside her and pulled back to stare down into her eyes. "Only you, Nyn. I'm as virgin as you are. I've had other women offer themselves to me, but you're the only one I dream of holding."

Her heart soared. Smiling, she wrapped her legs around his lean, naked hips. She cupped his face in her hands and pulled him down to her until their noses touched.

"Oh, Speirr," Sunshine whispered, holding him close.

Talon went rigid in her arms.

In the last thousand years, no one other than Ceara had ever used his real name. And only one woman had ever said his name the way Sunshine did just now.

It wasn't just what she said, it was the cadence of her voice when she'd said it. The shiver it had sent down his spine.

"What did you call me?"

Sunshine bit her lip as she realized her slip. Oh jeez, he probably thought she was calling him by another man's name. He would have no memory of his former life. Nor should she. She didn't know where these flashbacks were coming from.

All she knew was that they were freaking her out.

Her grandmother was really into past-life regression and had raised her with a devout respect for reincarnation. One thing Grandma Morgan had tutored her well on was that when you're reborn, you always forget your former life.

Why, then, did she remember him?

"I was clearing my throat," she said, hoping he would buy it. "What did you think I called you?"

Talon relaxed. Maybe he was hearing things. Maybe it was what this woman made him feel that was dredging up his long-forgotten memories. Or maybe it was the guilt he felt for wanting her the way he did.

Only Nynia had ever made him really burn like this.

Sunshine was so different. She made him feel even when he didn't want to. Even when he fought against it.

She buried her hands in his hair and pulled him down so that she could nibble his jaw. The feel of her hands on him, the warmth of her body under his . . .

He lowered himself over her, and buried his lips against her shoulder where he could taste the salt of her skin.

Talon sighed deeply. Contentedly.

Then, to his deepest aggravation, his phone rang.

Cursing, Talon answered it and found Acheron on the other end.

"I need you to guard the woman tonight. Keep her at your place."

Talon frowned. He wondered briefly how Ash knew Sunshine was with him, but the man's powers were nothing if not scary. "I thought you told me to stay away from her."

"Things have changed."

Talon bit back a moan as Sunshine nuzzled his nipple with her teeth. Keeping her here was far from a hardship. "Are you sure I'm not needed tonight?"

"Yes." Acheron hung up.

Talon tossed the phone aside and looked at Sunshine with a devilish grin. This night just got a whole lot better.

Chapter 8

It was near midnight when Ash left Club Runningwolf's.

Where the hell was Talon? He should be out on the streets, patrolling.

Ash had been trying to reach him for hours.

He called Nick again only to find out that Nick had neither seen nor heard from Talon either.

This was so unlike the Celt. He could sense that Talon was all right and not hurt, and if he wanted to, he could track Talon down. But Ash had never been that intrusive with his powers. Having been hunted and stalked, he couldn't bear to do that to anyone else. Not unless it was a dire emergency.

Free will was not something he would tamper with lightly.

As Ash returned the phone to his jacket, the hair on the back of his neck stood up.

"Look how helpless she is . . ."

"Yes, but she's strong enough to feed us all."

The voices whispered through his mind much like Spider-Man's spidey-sense . . .

And the wall-crawler thought he had super powers.

Pah-lease.

Ash closed his eyes and located the source of the voices. Four male and two female Daimons were in an alley off Royal Street. He started for his motorcycle, then stopped himself. There was no way he'd reach them in time by conventional means.

Glancing around, he made sure no one could see him, then he gathered the ions in the air around him. He let his body disintegrate into nothingness and used his powers to bend the physics of time and matter.

Unseen, he whispered through the city, straight to the alley where they had a woman cornered. She stood cringing, surrounded by the Daimons, her arms wrapped about her.

"Please don't hurt me," she begged. "Just take my purse and leave me alone."

The tallest Daimon raked his hand through her hair and smiled evilly. "Oh, this won't hurt. Not for long anyway."

Acheron solidified. He summoned a shield for the woman, to protect and confuse her. In her mind, she would see and remember an unknown figure scaring her attackers away.

In reality, he whistled.

The Daimons turned toward him in unison.

"Hi," he said nonchalantly as he walked toward them. "You Daimons wouldn't happen to be planning on sucking the soul of an innocent human, now would you?"

They looked at each other, then started to run.

"Oh, I don't think so," Ash said, throwing another shield up behind them to keep them from fleeing the alley. "No Daimon gets out of here alive."

They hit the invisible wall and rebounded off it.

"Man," Ash said, feigning a cringe. "It really makes you feel for the bug on a windshield, doesn't it?"

They scrambled to their feet.

The tallest of them, who was almost even in height to Ash, narrowed his eyes. "We're not afraid of you, Dark-Hunter."

"Good. It makes the fight more fair that way." Ash spread his hands out, creating a staff with his thoughts.

The male Daimons rushed him at once while the women backed away.

Acheron flipped the first Daimon to reach him over with his staff, then rammed the tip of it into the second. He embedded one end of the staff into the concrete and used it to balance as he jumped up and kicked at a third. He released the blade from the toe of his boot and sent it straight into the Daimon's chest. The Daimon disintegrated.

Ash landed gracefully on the street while the first two pushed themselves up and the other two backed off.

"Oh, come on, girls," he taunted them. "Don't be bashful. At least I give you a fighting chance, which is more than you give *your* victims."

"Look," the leader said, his voice shaking. "Let us go and we'll give you some important information."

Ash scoffed. "What information could you possibly have that would be worth me letting you go so that you could kill more humans?"

"It's worth it," another one said. "It's about—" His words broke off into a strangled cry.

Before Ash could move, all the Daimons disintegrated.

For the first time in centuries, he was too stunned to move.

What the hell just happened?

The human woman came flying up from her crouch and launched herself into his arms. "You saved me!"

Ash frowned. He couldn't figure out how she could see him until she kissed him passionately.

"Dammit, Artemis," he snarled, pushing her away. "Get off me."

She made an irritated noise low in her throat. Releasing him, she flashed from her blond human disguise into her fiery goddessness. Her auburn hair curled around her shoulders as she stood, hands on hips, and pouted at him. "How did you know it was me?"

"After eleven thousand years, don't you think I know what you taste like?"

Sulkily, she folded her arms over her chest. "If I'd been a real human, I bet you would have slept with me tonight."

He sighed disgustedly and allowed his staff to fade into

vapor. "I don't have time for your petty jealousy. You know, I do have other things to take care of."

She licked her lips and stepped to his side, then trailed her hand over his shoulders. She leaned to whisper in his ear. "I'm one of those things you need to take care of, love. Come home with me, Acheron. I'll make it well worth your while." She ran her tongue around his ear, raising chills over his body.

Ash shrugged her away. "I have a headache."

"You've had a headache for two hundred years!"

He looked at her dryly. "And you've had PMS for eleven thousand."

She laughed at that. "One day, my love, one day . . ."

Ash put a little more room between them. Enough so that she couldn't casually run her hands over his body. "Why are you here?"

She shrugged. "I wanted to see you fight. I just love the way you get all serious and lethal. The way your muscles ripple when you move. It really turns me up."

For once he didn't bother to correct her misuse of American slang. Instead, his vision turned dark that she would manipulate him like this. He hated the games she played, especially when they involved the lives of other people. "So you created Daimons out of nothing and then killed them?"

She closed the distance between them. "Oh no, they were real. And I'm not the one who zapped them. Believe me, I love the way your body moves when you attack. I would never give them in while you fought."

"You mean 'take them out'?"

"Mmm . . . in . . . out . . ." Artemis nipped at his shoulder while she ran her hands down his chest. "You keep talking like that and I *will* take you home with me."

His head was starting to pound. He removed her hand from his crotch where she cupped him. "Artie, could you stay focused for a minute? If you didn't zap them, who did?"

"I don't know."

He moved away from her. Again.

She stamped her foot like a child who just had her favorite toy taken away and glared at him. "I hate it when you mess up your hair, and what is this thing you have in your nose?"

Ash felt the stud vanish and the hole close. He clenched his teeth. No doubt his hair was blond again too. "Dammit, Artemis, you don't own me."

Her eyes flashed dangerously. "You belong to me, Acheron Parthenopaeus," she said, her voice full of rage and possession. "All of you. Mind, body, and soul. Don't you ever forget it."

He narrowed his eyes. "You have no real hold over me, Artie. We both know that. When all is said and done, my powers make a mockery of yours."

"Oh no, love. So long as your Dark-Hunter army and the humans they protect mean more to you than you do, I will always have power over you." She smiled coldly at him, then flashed out of the human realm.

Ash cursed and felt a childish impulse to send a lightning bolt slashing through the alley. No doubt she was trying to lure him back to her temple.

Like an idiot, he was going to go. He had to. He still didn't know who had zapped the Daimons, and if it wasn't Artemis, then there was someone else toying with him.

And woe to any other fool who dared to cross him. He tolerated Artemis because he had to,

He didn't have to put up with anyone else. And by Archon's thorny hammer, he'd tear the head off the next person who annoyed him.

"So," Sunshine said to Talon as she sat on his bed wearing nothing but a borrowed T-shirt, her legs tucked up under her. "Are you planning on keeping me here forever, or what?"

Lying on his side, he picked through the platter she had made for them until he found the M&M's he had insisted she include. "Depends. Do you plan to keep making me eat this healthy crap or can I have the leftover steak out of the fridge?"

She wrinkled her nose at him as she munched another strawberry. It still amazed her that she had found his small, secret stash of fresh fruit in the bottom drawer of his refrigerator. The man seemed to have an aversion to eating anything nontoxic.

"I don't see how you stay healthy eating the garbage you have in your cabinets. Did you know I counted five different kinds of potato chips?"

"Really? There should be six. Did I eat all the barbecue?"

"You are not funny." But she laughed anyway.

"Relax," he said, reaching for the banana chips she'd made. "Have a banana."

She gave him an arch look, then trailed her gaze impishly down his gorgeous naked body. "I already had your banana."

He smiled at her. "I think it would be more correct to say my banana had you."

Sunshine laughed again as she leaned over to feed him a strawberry. He held her hand to his lips while he ran his tongue over her fingers and gently nipped her skin before he let her withdraw.

He was unlike anyone she'd ever met before.

But unfortunately, it couldn't last.

Her heart sank as the reality of it hit her. She needed to get out of here before leaving him became even more difficult than it already was. She didn't want to hurt him or herself.

"You know, Talon," she said, picking through the strawberries. "It's been fun the last couple of days, but I really do need to get back home."

Talon swallowed his food and took a drink of water. That was easier said than done. He couldn't take her home, not if the Daimons were still after her and not if Ash wanted her protected.

Dereliction of duty wasn't something the Atlantean was forgiving about.

Dark-Hunters were protectors. Anyone who failed to uphold their code quickly found themselves spending eternity in painful torment.

Not that he needed that threat. The truth was, he didn't want to see Sunshine hurt. He liked her a lot more than he should.

Worst of all, he liked spending time with her. It had been so long since he'd just shared an evening with someone. And she was so easy to talk to. So funny and warm.

"Would you stay the night if I asked you to?"

He saw the sadness in her eyes. "I would like to, but what about tomorrow? You can't exactly take me home then, and if I use your boat, you won't have a way to leave your cabin."

"I could take you home tomorrow night."

She reached out and toyed with his small braids. Her smile was gentle and filled with regret. "No, Talon. As much as I would like to, I need to get back home. I have a job to do and I'm not independently wealthy. Every day I'm not in the Square, it's a day I'm not making money. I have to eat, you know. Wheat germ isn't cheap."

"If it's just the money—"

"It's not, Talon. I have to get back to my life."

He knew she was right. Sooner or later they would have to part company.

He would take her back as she wanted and then he could still protect her after dark, hidden in the shadows.

"Be a part of the world, but never in it."

He remembered the long-ago night Acheron had said those words to him.

"Because of what we do, we have to interact with people. But we must be unseen shadows who move among them.

"Never let anyone know you. Never give them a chance to realize you don't age. Move through the darkness ever watchful, ever alert. We are all that stands between the

humans and slavery. Without us, they all die and their souls are lost forever.

"Our responsibilities are great. Our battles numerous and legendary.

"But at the end of the night, you go home alone where no one knows what it is you have done to save the world that fears you. You can never bask in your glory. You can never know love or family.

"We are Dark-Hunters.

"We are forever powerful.

"We are forever *alone."*

Talon drew a deep breath. His time with her was over. "All right," he said. "I'll take you back."

He cupped her face in his hands and kissed her deeply. And as he tasted her, his thoughts drifted back into the past.

"Speirr?" his uncle's irate voice called from the other side of his door. "Can you please tear yourself away from your wife's embrace for one afternoon to actually attend business with me? My troth, the way you two carry on I can't imagine why you don't have five dozen children by now."

Nynia laughed from above him as she gently rode him. "You're in trouble again."

"Aye, but you're worth it, Nyn."

As she so often did, Nynia leaned over and rubbed noses with him before she kissed him passionately and slid off him. "You'd best be going or your uncle will have both our heads."

Talon winced at the memory and the pain it awoke inside him.

Sunshine pulled back and rubbed her nose against his just like Nynia had always done.

He went cold.

Something wasn't right. These memories, her actions . . .

The way she awoke his emotions.

He cupped Sunshine's cheek so that he could stare into her dark brown eyes. There was nothing about her features that reminded him of his wife, but her actions . . .

"Talon? What's wrong?"

He couldn't speak. He didn't dare tell her that she reminded him of a woman he had loved fifteen hundred years ago.

"Nothing," he said quietly. "You need to dress."

She got up.

"Speirr?"

Talon grabbed the blanket and covered himself as Ceara shimmered into his cabin.

"Is something wrong?" Sunshine asked as she noted his sudden discomfort.

He shook his head.

Ceara drew up short as she caught sight of Sunshine. Her eyes widened. "You have company?"

He didn't answer. He couldn't without clueing Sunshine into the fact that Ceara was with them.

"Is there a problem?" he asked.

"No," Sunshine said.

"Yes," Ceara responded. "Did you know Acheron is looking for you?"

Talon scowled. He grabbed his cell phone from the nightstand and dialed Acheron's number.

No one answered.

"Is his phone turned off?" he asked.

Sunshine's scowl matched his. "Whose phone?"

Ceara shook her head. "He's been trying to reach you all night."

His frown deepened. Looking down, he dialed Nick.

Again, no answer.

"This is weird," Talon said. "No one answers."

Sunshine shrugged the matter away. "Not really. It's almost two A.M. Maybe they're asleep."

"Trust me," he said, "these guys are wide awake right now." He turned back toward his sister. "Ceara, where's Acheron?"

"Ceara?" Sunshine asked. "Acheron? What are you talking about?"

Ceara ignored her interruption. "He's with Artemis at

the moment, but he's been worried about you."

"Why did you wait so long to come?" Talon asked.

"I couldn't get here any earlier. Something kept me blocked from you."

"Since when?"

"I don't know. Something has its power cocooned around you. Something dark and evil."

"Who are you talking to?" Sunshine asked.

"Sunshine, please, I'll explain in a minute. First, I need a few answers." He looked back at Ceara.

Ceara was staring at Sunshine curiously. She walked over to her and placed a hand on her shoulder.

Sunshine shivered. "What was that?"

Ceara jumped back as if the contact had shocked her. "Nynia," she breathed, looking up at him with a startled frown.

Something inside him screamed out a denial. This time when he spoke to Ceara, he spoke in their native Celt. "*Nae,* she's not. It's not possible."

"Possible or not, *bràthair,* it is her. She has Nynia's soul. Can you not feel it?"

Talon stared at Sunshine, his heart hammering.

Could it really be?

Wrapping the blanket around his hips, he moved over to where Sunshine stood and placed his hands on each side of her face. He tilted her head up so that he could look into her dark eyes.

In spite of his denials, he felt her. He had felt her the first moment he had looked at her under the lamplight.

From the deepest corner inside him, he'd known all along she was his Nynia. Known the first instant he had tasted her.

His hands shook from the truth of it.

"How can this be?" he asked.

But in his heart, he already knew. Camulus had sent her to him.

She was here to destroy him all over again.

His chest tightened to the point he couldn't breathe.

That was why he had been so attracted to her. Why he didn't want to leave her. Camulus wanted her to seduce him so that he would have to watch her die once again. In his arms.

Closing his eyes, Talon pulled Sunshine against him and held her tight, torn between wanting to fight heaven and earth to keep her and knowing in the end he would invariably lose.

No one ever defeated a god.

Sunshine struggled to breathe inside his crushing embrace. "Talon, you're scaring me. What's going on?"

"It's nothing. I just need to get you home."

Away from me before the gods realize that you're here and decide to punish you for it.

"Speirr?" Ceara asked, her voice sounding distant. "I can't stay here. I'm being pulled away again."

"Ceara?"

She was gone.

Talon clamped down hard on his emotions. He couldn't afford to have them right now. He had too many things to do and he needed all of his powers to face the challenge of keeping Sunshine safe.

Not to mention, he needed to find out what was interfering with Ceara's powers and Acheron's phone.

Sunshine's life was in his hands. This time, he wouldn't fail her.

Talon ground his teeth, wishing he could change history.

"Stay with me, Speirr, please don't ride out with vengeance in your heart."

Had he listened to Nynia the day his uncle was killed, his life would have taken an entirely different course.

But overwrought with grief and rage, he had denied Nynia's request and she hadn't argued the matter.

As always, Nynia had stepped aside and let him have his way. He'd gone straight to the northern Gaul tribe and had laid waste to them, never knowing that both he and the Gauls had been set up.

By the time he'd learned the truth, it had been too late to apologize.

The Gauls had been under the protection of the war god Camulus and under the leadership of Camulus's human son. The war god's wrath still resonated through Talon's life.

"I will exist only to see you suffer . . ."

It was a promise Camulus had delivered well on.

No, he couldn't fight Camulus and win. As a Dark-Hunter, he was strong and powerful, but not to the point he could kill a god.

Basically, he was screwed unless he got Sunshine back to her life and out of his, pronto.

Once they were dressed and Sunshine had her things, which she'd had to go back for three different times, Talon helped her into his boat and headed back toward New Orleans. The sooner he put distance between them, the safer she would be.

He would contact Acheron once they were in the city and see if maybe Acheron could call in another Dark-Hunter or Squire to watch over her until Mardi Gras. Someone whose presence wouldn't endanger her even more than the Daimons who were after her.

Once they reached his garage, Talon decided to leave his motorcycle behind and use the Viper tonight. He needed speed and had no desire to put Sunshine in any more jeopardy.

Breaking more speeding laws than he wanted to contemplate, Talon took her to her loft and then used her wall phone to call Acheron.

"What are you doing in the city?" Acheron demanded.

"I was told you were trying to reach me."

"Told by whom? I thought my directions were clear. You were to stay at your cabin with the woman."

Talon frowned. This was peculiar. Ceara had never been wrong before, nor had she ever lied to him. "You did, but then . . ." He paused as he tried to sort it out.

What was going on here?

"Yes?"

"Nothing, T-Rex. I guess I misunderstood."

"So why are you still on the phone with me?" Ash asked. "You need to get her back to the cabin. Now."

Talon didn't care for his haughty tone at all. Ash could be evasive and annoying, but he'd never before been an authoritative dick. "I can't, T-Rex. Something weird is going down. I have to leave her here."

"Why?"

Talon glanced around to make sure Sunshine couldn't overhear his conversation. She hadn't said a word to him the whole way back to her loft and now she was sitting on the sofa sketching and appeared completely oblivious to him.

He wanted to keep it that way.

Just to be safe, he lowered his voice. "She's my wife."

"Excuse me?"

Talon lowered his voice even more. "I think Sunshine is Nynia reincarnated."

"Well, isn't this interesting?"

"Yeah, and I can't protect her any more. I need someone else to watch her, okay?"

"Yes, I can see your dilemma."

Talon frowned. Dilemma? That wasn't an Acheron kind of word. "Is something wrong with you, T-Rex?"

"No. I'm just concerned about this situation. Are you leaving her now?"

"I need to."

"Perhaps you should wait until tomorrow night."

"What?"

"I can't get anyone there tonight. Why don't you continue to protect her until I can get someone else to take over? I don't really trust Zarek to watch her, do you?"

"Hell no. You're right. I definitely don't want to leave her here unprotected."

"Yes. It could be a problem. You spend the day there, and tomorrow I will take care of the matter."

The phone went dead.

Talon hung up with a weird feeling in his stomach. Something about that conversation just didn't seem right.

But as he looked across the room, his concerns were overshadowed by the vision of Sunshine.

She was still sitting on her sofa, sketching on her pad and humming a light tune.

It was Nynia's lullaby. The same song she used to sing while she worked.

Longing and pain tore through him so powerfully that he could barely move.

But it was the love he felt for her that overwhelmed him.

Against his will, he found himself approaching her. He knelt before her, laid his head in her lap and held her tight, grateful to have her with him, no matter how different she looked or acted.

His Nynia was back.

Sunshine was stunned by the familiarity of his actions. Instinctively, she ran her hand through the softness of his golden hair as she remembered even more about their past life together. He'd done this before. Many times.

"What is going on, Talon?"

"I wish I could tell you." He lifted his head up to look at her. The torment in those jet eyes reached out to her and made her heart pound for him.

Talon pulled back.

Now that he knew who she was, it made leaving her almost impossible.

But there was nothing else he could do. She would have to live out this life with someone else.

What choice did he have? He would never do anything to hurt her. Not again.

He'd killed her once, he wouldn't kill her again.

There was no way they could be together while the curse still bound him.

Styxx toyed with his cell phone as he thought over his conversation with Talon.

He smiled.

Oh, this was sweet. Talon already knew Sunshine was his dead wife reincarnated.

Perfect. Just perfect. He couldn't have hoped for better timing. Everything was going along according to their plans.

Zarek had swallowed the bait and allowed himself to be framed. Talon was now adequately distracted by his wife. Valerius was under the control of Dionysus.

And Acheron . . .

Well, he had something very special planned for that one.

As the Cajun French people of New Orleans would say, *Laissez les jeux commencer* . . . Let the games begin.

Chapter 9

"I guess you'll be leaving now," Sunshine said quietly even though part of her didn't want him to go. Her large loft suddenly seemed a bit desolate as she thought of him leaving.

They'd had a lot of fun at his cabin, creating their platter of food, making love to each other.

But now her sexcapade with him was over. It was time for them to go their separate ways.

Why, then, did it hurt so much to think of never seeing him again?

Talon nodded. "Yeah, I guess so."

He let go of her hand and started for the door. He could find someplace to sleep in the abandoned building next door to her. Find a floor that wasn't too far from this one so that he could keep watch over her until dawn. Then he could sleep in the building until tomorrow night.

It would be easier that way. Easier for both of them if he just broke off the relationship now.

There was no point in spending another day with her. Not when he knew he couldn't give her anything more of himself.

Not so long as he posed a danger to her.

Sunshine ached as he reached for her doorknob.

He was going.

It was over.

She couldn't breathe. A vicious pain stabbed her in the stomach at the thought of not seeing him anymore.

She couldn't just sit here and let him leave like this. "Talon?"

He paused and looked back at her.

"Why don't you stay the night? I know you can't get back home before sunup."

"No, I better not."

"But where will you go?"

He shrugged.

Let him go . . .

She couldn't. Not like this. It just didn't seem right. "C'mon. I'll be out of the loft early tomorrow morning and you'll have the place all to yourself while I work. No one will disturb you. I promise."

Talon hesitated.

Leave.

The command echoed in his head. He needed to.

He couldn't.

"You sure you don't mind?" he asked.

"Not at all."

Talon took a deep breath and headed back toward her.

His wife.

His ultimate salvation.

His ultimate destruction.

Nynia had been everything to him. He'd thought all these centuries that he was safe from his emotions. Safe from the pain that came with the memories of his wife.

Now it was all back. Even more painful than before.

"Is something wrong?" Sunshine asked.

"I'm just tired, I guess," he said, pulling his jacket off and setting it down.

Sunshine swallowed at the sight of his tight T-shirt that displayed his well-developed body. She was riveted by his impressive form. The man had the best butt leather had ever cupped. His legs were long, well shaped, and gorgeous, and all too well she remembered what they felt like when they were entangled with hers.

The feel of all his masculine power and beauty lying in her arms . . . thrusting between her legs . . .

She almost moaned aloud at imagining it.

But there was a wall between them now. As if he had closed part of himself off from her.

Gone was the tender man who had shared his body and laughter with her. Now she saw the powerful beast who had clobbered her attackers and sent them running in terror.

How she missed the gentler side of him.

"You've gone all stiff on me, haven't you?"

He arched a puzzled brow at her and looked baffled by her question. "Lady, I get stiff every time you come near me."

Heat rose in her cheeks and she scoffed. "I don't mean that kind of stiff. Though that kind of stiff is much better than the other one. At least with that one I know you like me."

Talon groaned as she glanced down at his pants where he was sure his erection was plainly visible. He felt his barriers crumbling. Felt a desire to be the man with her that he had always been with Nynia.

With Nynia he had been himself. She'd never expected that he be anything other than her friend.

Nyn had never seen the pathetic little boy who was spat upon and rejected. The one who had been made to clean up after his betters.

The one they had forced to grovel.

She had never seen the cold-hearted lad he had become because he was tired of being beaten and abused.

As a child, he had hardened his heart and learned to take their punches. He had learned to spit back and take down anyone who cast a jaundiced eye or who made a comment about either him, his mother, or his sister.

He'd told himself that he didn't need anyone's love or caring. And so he had learned to live like a feral animal, always ready to strike out when someone tried to touch him.

Until Nynia. She had tamed the beast in him. Had allowed him to be gentle with her. To be something other than hard and unyielding. Defensive and brutal.

With her he had just been Speirr. The boy/man who wanted someone to love him. Who wanted someone to love.

It had been so long since Talon had been himself with anyone.

His Dark-Hunter brethren turned to him for advice. Acheron depended on him for his strength, wisdom, and calm leadership.

None of them, not even Wulf, really knew him. He had never opened his heart up to anyone other than the woman who sat before him now.

A woman he didn't dare open himself up to in this lifetime.

"You are insatiable, aren't you?" she asked.

"Only with you," he whispered, moving closer to her as he tried to reconcile the woman she had been with the woman she was now. "I never could resist touching you. Being inside you. Feeling your breath on my skin. Your beautiful hands on my body."

Sunshine shivered at his words.

He approached her like some great stalking beast. His body was a symphony of movement.

His masculine, leather scent invaded her senses and made her mouth water.

Her head swam at his kiss, but she pushed him back, perplexed by his comments. "You say that as if you've known me for a long time. Why is that?"

"I feel like I've known you forever. Like I've held you in my heart for centuries."

She trembled at the words. This was the man who haunted her dreams. The Celtic poet and chieftain. The man she remembered riding out to battle, then riding home to love her.

But that couldn't be *this* man, could it?

And yet as she thought about it, she realized just how

weird her dreams really were. In them, she was blond and blue-eyed, but Talon . . .

Talon looked the same.

Right down to the tattoo on his body. The braids at his temple. He even wore the same torc. The only thing different was his eye color.

This couldn't be right. There was something strange about all this. Something that scared her on a level she'd never known existed.

Could he be the same man?

Could he?

It didn't seem possible, and yet living with her father and mother, she'd seen a lot of impossible things in her life. There were otherworldly powers at work in this world.

She pulled back from Talon's kiss and tilted his head so that she could see the skin just below his right ear.

There was a small scar there. A small scar that she, as Nynia, had once given to Speirr when they were fishing as children. She'd drawn back her rod to cast it and the hook had caught his ear.

The star-shaped scar was still there.

Just as it had always been.

Just as it was now.

No, it wasn't possible.

Was it?

She trembled in uncertainty.

His eyes were hooded as he stared hungrily at her. His breath fell gently against her face. She could feel his heart pounding under her hands, feel his strength and heat reaching out to her.

"I've missed you so much, Nyn . . . Nyn . . . neighbor."

Sunshine froze as he pulled back instantly. By his face, she could tell he was as surprised at what he'd said as she was.

"What did you call me?"

"Neighbor," he said quickly.

"Before that."

"Nothing."

Okay, this was too friggin' weird. And she wanted, no she *needed*, an explanation.

"Talon," she said, leaving the chair to stand before him. "Tell me what's going on. You know who Nynia is, don't you?"

His obsidian eyes flashed. "Do you?"

Oh God, it was true! He knew her. Somehow he remembered the past too.

He hadn't changed a bit. He couldn't be in daylight. He wasn't an American citizen and yet . . .

Oh, it didn't take a rocket scientist to figure this one out. Somehow, Talon was Speirr.

He *was* a vampire or an immortal or something. She knew it.

"How do you remember me?" she asked him.

"How could I ever forget you?"

She ducked his lips and pushed him back again. "Smooth, but that doesn't answer my question. There's something really odd about you, Talon. And it doesn't make sense that you are now as you were in my dreams. Not even I look the same. But you do. Why?"

Talon wanted to tell her, but couldn't find the words. *After you died I sold my soul for vengeance to a Greek goddess who now owns me so that I can spend eternity hunting down and killing vampires for her.* Even he had a hard time believing the truth of that statement and he'd been living the reality of it for fifteen hundred years.

She growled at him. "You're stiff again."

"Can't you just live for the moment? Accept me as I am?"

"Okay. But answer me one thing."

"What?"

"When did you graduate high school?"

He looked uncomfortable with her question. "I didn't."

"What year did you drop out then?"

Talon backed away from her. These were things he couldn't answer. Things he refused to answer.

The hurt in her eyes tugged at his heart.

"What's the deal, Talon? I'm not stupid. No one is so allergic to sunlight that they can't even walk in front of a window. And don't think it has escaped my notice that you never show your teeth. If I get too close to them when we kiss, you immediately pull away."

Talon wished he dared use his powers to make her forget him. To change this subject to something less volatile. "What? You want me to admit that I'm a vampire? That I howl at the moon when it's full?"

"Are you? Do you?" She stepped up to him and placed her hand against his chin as if ready to pry his mouth open. "Show me your teeth, Talon."

He stepped back. "I can't."

She gave him a mean glare. "You're Speirr, aren't you? Somehow it is you, *you,* I see when I dream. Isn't it?"

He looked away.

"I won't tell anyone," she insisted, softening her voice. "I just need to know."

"What difference would it make?" he snapped, growing tired of this conversation. "Would you throw me out?"

"No," she said breathily, sounding reconciled. "I don't think I could ever throw you out."

"Then why do you have to know?"

The fire returned to her eyes as she narrowed them on him. "Because I want you to be open and honest with me, to share your life."

Her words tore through him. Bitter longing swelled inside his heart as he remembered how hopeless having her had seemed as a mortal man. Back then only social standing and gossips had stood between them. Now the entire universe was united to keep them apart. "What makes you think I want to share my life? Maybe I'm just using you for sex."

Her face stricken, she backed away from him. "Are you?"

The pain in her eyes ripped him apart. He didn't want to hurt her.

"Are *you?*" he asked, turning the question back on her.

"Tell me what it is you want from me, Sunshine."

"I honestly don't know. Part of me is drawn to you and part of me is scared of you. There's something very dark inside your eyes. If I wanted to get to know you better, would you let me?"

"No," he said between clenched teeth, "we can't."

"Then you owe me a reason why we can't. You know I'm not some child in need of a father to make my decisions for me. I thought you respected me."

"I do."

"Then treat me like an adult. Tell me why it is you refuse to answer even the most basic question about yourself."

What she asked for was impossible. He could never tell her about his current life, not unless Acheron or Artemis released him from his oath.

"If I tell you who I am, your life will be in danger."

"I live in New Orleans over one of the most popular clubs in town and park my car in an alley where two men were murdered last night. My life is always in danger."

"Those weren't men last night and they weren't murdered." Talon didn't know why he let that escape.

"Then what were they?"

Tell her . . .

The command was so strong. Never once had he broken his Code of Silence. Never.

"The Daimons wanted to party with your girlfriend, Celt. Don't leave her unprotected."

She had a right to know what was out there gunning for her.

"Talon." She stepped into his arms and placed her hands on his face. Her touch was soothing and warm.

It almost succeeded in breaking him.

"Trust me. Whatever it is, I won't ever tell a soul."

"I can't, Sunshine. I can't."

"You won't, Talon. You won't." She expelled an irritated breath and dropped her hands. "Fine. Keep your secrets. Go ahead and blow me off. Live a happy life and do whatever it is you do."

She moved away from him.

Talon reached for her, but she bypassed his hand. "Sunshine . . ."

"Don't touch me. I'm mad at you."

"Please don't be mad at me."

She shook her head. "Oh, you're good with those puppy-dog eyes. That deep note in your voice. But I'm too far gone now to care. Just leave."

He winced at the pain in her voice and her command. It cut him all the way to his heart.

In that moment, he realized something. Zarek and Acheron were right. He was scared. Scared of leaving and scared of staying.

The last thing he wanted was to lose Nynia again and yet as he looked at Sunshine, it dawned on him that though she might have his wife's soul, she wasn't his wife.

She was someone else. Someone new and exasperating. Nynia would never have gotten mad at him. Not even when he deserved her anger. She'd always been timid and shy. Not bold and demanding like Sunshine.

If he said to leave a matter alone, Nynia would nod and drop the subject. She would never have kneed a Daimon or fought an alligator.

But even more astounding, he had to admit that he liked the fire in Sunshine. Her ability to stand up to him and the world around her.

"What?" she asked, blinking her eyes as if she couldn't believe what she saw. "You're still here? I thought I gave you an order."

He smiled in spite of himself. "I don't want to leave you, Sunshine. Can't you just accept me as I am?"

Sunshine looked away. "I like what little I know about you, Talon, but the problem is just how little I do know about you. You live in the swamp, seem to have a lot of money and no last name, and you like big, creepy gators and have a guy named Nick who runs errands. That's it.

That's the extent of my Talon knowledge and it's a really short list."

She met his gaze. "I refuse to have a relationship with a man who won't even trust me with his basic bio. Now if all you want is to get laid, there's the door. If you really want to stay, then tell me something about yourself. Something meaningful."

"Like what?"

"Tell me the name of your best friend."

"Wulf Tryggvason."

Shocked, she dropped her jaw. "Oh my God, you just answered a question. I think the world may end over it."

"You're not funny. So do I get to stay?"

She pursed her lips as she thought about it for a minute. "Fine, but only because I know you can't get back home before the sun rises."

Determined to keep distance between them until he answered her questions, Sunshine turned around and went to her bedroom. She grabbed a pillow and blanket from her bed, then returned to the living room and handed them to him.

He looked completely dumbfounded as he held her pink quilt and pillow. "What's this?"

"Until you come clean with me, you can take the sofa."

"You're kidding."

"Oh no. Not even a little. I'm not going to let you back into my bed until you let me inside your head."

Talon was completely stupefied as she walked over to the far wall and lowered her blinds.

"I told you about Wulf," he said.

She turned toward him, her look unamused. "You gave me a single name. Oooo. That tells me so much about you, doesn't it? Well, my best friends are Trina Devereaux and Selena Laurens. Now what does that tell you about me? Nada. Zilch. Nothing. It just means I have someone I can call when I get ticked off, and believe me, if it wasn't so late, I'd be dialing one of them like a madwoman."

Talon growled, but it didn't faze her in the least. The woman had entirely too much chutzpah.

"So tell me about Wulf," she said slowly, taking a step toward him. "What does he do for a living? Does he live here in New Orleans? Is he married? How long have you known him?"

"He lives in Minnesota and he's not married."

She looked pleased and yet at the same time managed to pull off a piqued look too. "How did you meet him?"

At Mardi Gras one hundred and two years ago when Wulf had been moved into the city for temporary duty— which was something he could never tell Sunshine.

Talon let out an aggravated breath. "I've known him a long time."

"Ooo," she breathed again. "Answers like that will get you voted into office, but they won't get you back into my bed. And they definitely won't let you near my body."

"You're being unreasonable."

"Hah!"

This was so unfair. He was trying to protect her and here she was asking him for something he couldn't give. Denying him her body because he didn't want to see her hurt.

How could she do this to him?

Angered by her continued insistence, he snapped, "I'm your husband."

She snorted and raked him with a bemused stare. "Not in this lifetime, buddy." She held up her left hand for his inspection. "I don't see no wedding ring on my finger, and the last time I checked, you didn't come charging into town on the back of your black warhorse, sweeping me off my feet and asking me to be yours."

Talon went cold at her words. "You remember that?"

Some of her anger seemed to fade as she nodded. "And I want to know how *you* remember it."

He tossed the blanket and pillow on the couch and lay down stiffly. "I told you, I can't tell you that."

"Then good night, sweetheart. Have pleasant dreams."

She came forward to kiss him on his forehead and walked to her room.

Royally ticked off, Talon watched as she made a grand show of pulling the drapes closed. That woman had a way of making him burn and this time it wasn't in a good way.

He was furious.

Especially when she switched on the light on the night-stand and he could see her body plainly through the thin fabric.

His heart pounded. He couldn't tear his gaze away from her as she peeled her clothes from her lush body and then climbed naked into her bed.

He could just imagine her lying there, the pink cotton sheets nestled between her warm, wet thighs. Her breasts pressed together as she lay on her side with her arm grazing and partially concealing the dark tip of her left breast. Her back naked and bare to his eager gaze and her hair fanned out around her head, just waiting for him to lie down behind her and pull her close to his body.

Then he would slide his hand up her thigh where he would cup her soft flesh and lift her leg, opening up her body so that he could slide himself deep inside her from behind.

Oh yeah, he could already feel her soft rear against his groin as he slid himself in and out of her hot body. Feel her head tucked under his chin as he buried his hand between her legs and stroked her with his fingers while he made the sweetest, tenderest love to her.

Her woodsy patchouli scent would surround him as she writhed to his touch and moaned in ecstasy.

Every hormone in his body snapped awake and his groin tightened, demanding her.

Nynia would never have done this to him. She'd never denied him access to her. Not once. All he had to do was crook a finger or cock an eyebrow and his wife had gladly stepped into his arms.

Right now, he missed her more than he ever had before.

"Sunshine?"

"No, Talon," she said firmly, turning off her light. "The answer is still no."

"I didn't ask you anything."

"I know that note in your voice when you said my name and I know what you want, and you know what I want. Guess which one of us is going to have to give in?" She paused, then added, "And for the record, it's not me."

He cursed under his breath. She was so damn stubborn in this lifetime. What had happened to his mild-mannered Nynia who gave him whatever he wanted, whenever he wanted it?

Fine, then, let her lie in there all unmolested and naked.

His body leapt at the word.

Groaning, he rolled over and faced the back of the couch so that he couldn't see her anymore.

He was a grown man, he could handle this. He could control himself.

Oh, bloody hell! No woman had turned him down before. This was excruciating and infuriating.

He plowed his fist into the pillow as he hardened even more. He was much too large for the couch and it was damned uncomfortable, but he would sleep here or die.

Sunshine listened to Talon moving around on the sofa. She almost felt sorry for him. Almost.

But she was tired of his secrets. Tired of his cryptic games. She'd done enough snooping around his house to learn that he probably wasn't a drug dealer, especially since he didn't even have a bottle of Tylenol, but he'd had all kinds of interesting electronic gadgets. Lots of leather, imported beer, and enough DVDs to sink a battleship. Not to mention the weird weapons she'd found. Some of them quite ancient in design.

There was something very odd about his life and until she knew what it was she wasn't going to let herself get any closer to him. She owed it to herself to know more about him before she let her goo-goo eyes lead her astray again.

She rolled over and forced herself to go to sleep. She needed to work tomorrow. Unlike him, she didn't have an endless supply of income.

"Well, look who's back."

Sunshine put down the book she was reading and smiled at Selena as Selena wheeled her small cart over to her. Dressed in a loose purple dress and black cape, Selena parked her cart to the right of Sunshine's stand of pottery and sketches, and started setting up her card table and psychic stuff.

"I know," Sunshine said wistfully as she bookmarked the page of her romance novel *Born in Sin* and set it aside. "I've been preoccupied the last few days. Sorry."

Selena spread a purple cloth over her card table. "So do I get to learn anything about this guy? Want me to do a reading for you?"

Sunshine sighed as she scooted off her stool to help Selena set up her signs. "I don't know much about him except he's a giant blond biker sex god who eats nothing but junk food, has a ton of money, lives in the swamp, and knows your brother-in-law, Kyrian . . . Oh, and he knows Grace's husband too."

Selena's face went pale. She looked up, startled. "Talon? You've been seeing Talon? More than once?"

Sunshine froze, torn between excitement and trepidation. Selena didn't look right. She looked rather sick at the news.

"You know him?" she asked incredulously.

Uncomfortable, Selena glanced around. "Oh Lord, please, please tell me he's not the sexual athlete who got hit with the Mardi Gras float. Please tell me that the guy I've been fantasizing about isn't Talon. I've had dinner with him, for goodness' sake."

"Okay, I won't tell you it's him, but . . . it's him. Ain't he great?"

Selena groaned. "Oh jeez. I'd heard rumors about him, but who knew they were really true? I can't believe this."

Sunshine was relieved. Finally, someone who could give her some answers, provided she pried them out of Selena. But Selena looked like she was going to be less than forthcoming.

"Lainie, you better spill what you know about him."

Selena opened her mouth, but by the set of her jaw, Sunshine knew what she was about to say.

"Don't you dare tell me you can't tell me anything," she said before Selena could. "I've heard enough of that from him."

Selena closed her mouth. "Well, he's a good guy for once. He's not your usual out-of-work biker and he does have a future. A really *long* future."

"And what else?"

Selena hedged.

Sunshine opened up Selena's folding chair that Selena used for her clients, then sat down beside her. "C'mon, Lainie. I really, *really* like this guy, and it's driving me crazy that he won't tell me anything, not even his birthday. So what do you know?"

"I'm not supposed to say anything, Sunny. I was sworn to secrecy."

"Sworn by whom?"

Selena set her tarot card box on the table. "I'm not supposed to say," she repeated.

"What is he, Mafia?"

"Oh no," she said, her voice thick with warning. "They make the Mafia look like Boy Scouts. These are guys no one crosses with impunity."

Someone worse than the Mafia?

"Who are they?"

"Look," Selena said. "Let's just say he's in Tabitha's line of work, okay?"

Sunshine frowned. "Ladies' lingerie? He hardly looks the type to sell that."

"No, goof-ball. What she does at night."

Sunshine formed a small O with her mouth as she understood. "He's a vampire slayer?"

"Yes, and a really good one too."

That explained how they had met in the alley. Sort of, except the people who had attacked her hadn't looked like vampires. They'd actually looked like yuppies.

"There's a lot more to it than that, isn't there?" Sunshine asked.

Selena nodded.

She smiled devilishly. "And you, my *best* friend on earth, my soul sister who shares Chunky Monkey scoops and beefcake e-mails at the drop of a hat, the woman who made me wear a frothy, ruffled lime-colored bridesmaid dress that added fifteen pounds to my hips, are going to spill your guts to me, aren't you?"

Selena stiffened. "No fair and the dress wasn't lime, it was mint."

"It was lime-icky green and I looked like a sick pistachio. But that's beside the point. You're going to spill everything because all's fair in love."

Sunshine wasn't sure which of them was most startled by the last part of that statement.

Selena turned to face her. "What? You're telling me you love Talon?"

Sunshine sat back as she tried to sort through her feelings for Talon. There was so much about him that she adored, so much about him that she craved, and at the same time she knew nothing about who and what he was *now*.

All she knew was how he made her feel whenever she looked at him. The way she wanted to go home right now and be with him.

"Honestly, Selena, I don't know. Every time I'm around him I feel so alive. So warm and protected—like nothing in the world can touch me or blight my happiness. He just fits with me. I know this sounds crazy . . ."

She paused as she glanced at Selena's psychic stand, which was filled with trinkets, rune stones, and tarot symbols. On second thought, crazy to Selena was par for the course.

Sunshine stared at her, trying to make her understand. "Talon and I were married in another life."

A dark light appeared in Selena's eyes. When she spoke, her voice was scarcely more than a whisper. "Does Talon know this?"

She nodded. "He even called me his wife last night when I made him sleep on the couch."

"Sleep on the couch?"

"Long story."

Selena turned one of her cards over. She looked at the Death card, then looked at Sunshine. "Did he say it was in *his* former life?"

"No. In fact, when I dream about him I look different, but he doesn't. He even has the same tattoos and that is weird beyond weird. I even recalled him getting those tattoos done. Now I'm not sure if I'm insane or what."

Selena covered Sunshine's hand with hers and gave a light, sympathetic squeeze. "No, hon. You're not a loon, at least not about this."

"Then what is going on?"

Selena looked around, then leaned closer and lowered her voice again as if fearful someone would overhear them. "Sunny, tell me truthfully, what are your intentions toward Talon?"

Sunshine was irritated by the question. "What are you? His mom? I promise I'll respect him in the morning."

Selena rolled her eyes. "This is really serious, Sunshine. Your current interest plays with some seriously bad things that wouldn't hesitate to kill either one of you if they thought you or he would betray them."

Sunshine winced at the deadly earnest tone of Selena's voice. This wasn't good. "He's a vampire, isn't he? I knew it!"

"Not exactly."

"That's what he said. So I'll ask you what I asked him— what is 'not exactly a vampire'?"

"A Dark-Hunter."

Sunshine was stunned that she finally had an answer. Of course, the answer made no sense whatsoever, but still it was a long-awaited start. "And that would be . . . ?"

"An immortal vampire slayer who sold his soul for an Act of Vengeance."

A chill went up her spine. "Sold his soul to who, the devil?"

"The goddess Artemis."

Sunshine scowled. Now that was the last thing she'd expected to hear. But then, given how weird this whole conversation was, she shouldn't be surprised by anything. "You're kidding, right?"

Slowly, Selena shook her head no.

"But that doesn't even make sense. I mean, there aren't that many vampires in the world, are there? Just how many Dark-Hunters could there be? Is he the only one?"

By Selena's expression she knew the answer wouldn't be pleasant. "There are thousands of Dark-Hunters and countless vampires. More correctly, they're called Daimons since they've been around a whole lot longer than the word *vampire*."

Sunshine sat there in a stupor as she tried to take it all in. "I don't get this. I mean, I always believed in vampires in theory, but not really in the flesh, and I'm having a hard time believing that there are so many out there that we have to have real slayers for them." She locked gazes with Selena. "No offense, but I always thought your sister Tabitha was a bit wacked."

Selena gave an odd half-laugh. "She is, but that's beside the point."

Sunshine tried to come to terms with what Selena was telling her. She still wasn't sure if she should believe it. Could Talon really be an immortal vampire slayer?

And yet, in a very odd sense, it explained a lot of things. A *lot* of things.

Oh Lord, he really was a vampire slayer!

She felt ill. "Where do the vampires come from?" she

asked Selena, "Are they demons or are they made from people, like in the movies?"

Selena paused, then spoke softly. "Okay, let me give you a short history lesson and see if that helps you make some sense of this. Aeons ago, two races were created—the human race and the Apollites. The Apollites were the children of the god Apollo. He wanted to create a super race that would outdo us in every shape, form, and fashion. They were beautiful, extremely tall, and they had massive psychic powers."

Sunshine swallowed as she recalled her attackers. That definitely sounded like them.

"But like many others who have such powers," Selena continued, "the Apollites abused them and started warring against humans, trying to subjugate mankind."

"The Apollites were vampires?"

"No," Selena said, "you're getting ahead of me. During the war between the Greeks and the Apollites, the Apollites killed Apollo's mistress and son. In anger over their murders, Apollo destroyed the Apollite homeland, Atlantis.

"For their betrayal, the Apollites were cursed so that they would have to drink each other's blood to survive, and they were forbidden to ever set foot under a single ray of daylight where Apollo could see them. Because his mistress was twenty-seven when they killed her, the Apollites were all condemned to die a horrible death on their twenty-seventh birthday."

"Die how?"

"They disintegrate and decay slowly over a twenty-four-hour period."

Sunshine gaped. "Oh, how horrible."

Selena agreed as she picked up her card and returned it to the deck. "They avoid that fate one of two ways. They either kill themselves the day before their birthday or they turn Daimon and start killing humans and gathering their souls into their own bodies to prolong their lives."

"How?"

Selena shrugged. "I'm not sure exactly. I just know that

they drain the blood out of us until we die, then they take our souls into their bodies. So long as the soul is alive, they can live longer. But the problem is, the human soul starts to die as soon as they capture it. So it's a constant quest to gather new souls to maintain their lives."

"And this gathering of souls is what makes them vampires?"

"Daimons, vampires, ghouls, whatever you want to call them. They suck your blood and your soul and leave you with nothing. Kind of like lawyers." Selena smiled. "Oh wait, I just insulted my husband."

Sunshine appreciated the attempt at humor, but she was still trying to digest all this. "And the Dark-Hunters? Where do they come from? Are they Apollites too?"

"No, they're ancient warriors. After Atlantis sank into the ocean, the Greek gods were angry that Apollo had created and then unleashed the Daimons on us, so his sister Artemis created an army to hunt and destroy them. The Dark-Hunters. Talon is one of her soldiers."

"She created them how?"

"I don't know. She does something to capture their souls and then returns the Hunter to life. Once they're brought back, the Hunters are given servants and money so they can concentrate on hunting and killing the Daimons. Their only job is to free the stolen souls before the souls die."

Sunshine breathed deeply as she absorbed all this information. It wasn't looking good for her or for Talon. "So Talon is sworn into Artemis's service forever, then." Sunshine let out a ragged breath. "Jeez, I can really pick them. Talk about a go-nowhere, hopeless relationship."

"Not necessarily."

Sunshine looked up and caught the sneaky look on Selena's face. "What?"

Selena shuffled her cards. "You know, Kyrian was once a Dark-Hunter . . ."

Sunshine's heart leapt at the words. "Really?"

Selena nodded. "They do come with an out clause. True

love can restore their souls to them and free them from Artemis's service."

"So there's hope?"

"Honey, there's always hope."

Chapter 10

After gleaning every juicy detail she could from Selena, Sunshine packed up her stand early and decided to go back to her loft. When she got there, Talon was still sleeping on the sofa.

Her lips twitched as she watched him. He looked so adorable and uncomfortable. He was really much too large for the pink and white couch, and his arms and legs dangled off into nothingness.

He'd pulled his shirt and jacket off and left them folded neatly on her coffee table, and his large Harley boots were on the floor underneath it.

His blond hair was tousled and his features relaxed while his sinfully long lashes were nestled against his cheeks. His two thin braids lay on the pillow as he breathed in blissful slumber.

He had one large, tanned masculine hand up by his face.

Looking at him now, she found it hard to believe he was an ancient immortal warrior whose very name was synonymous with death. But one who made her heart soften and her pulse race.

He was scrumptious.

Sunshine stared at the intricate tribal tattoo on his body. So, he really was a Celt. A real live, breathing, run-naked-through-the-heather-and-moors Celt.

Her grandmother would love it.

Closing her eyes, Sunshine let her memories as Nynia wash over her. But those memories weren't really *hers.* They were like memories of a movie she had once watched.

They were real to her and, at the same time, they weren't. She was no longer Nynia, and Talon . . .

He wasn't the same man he'd been then either.

Speirr had been full of fury and volatile emotions. Talon had bursts of emotion, but for the most part, he was calm and detached from his feelings.

Neither one of them was the same and yet she couldn't shake the feeling that they were somehow meant to be together.

But if what Selena had said was true, then he had a much higher calling than being her lover.

Not to mention that she was no longer Nynia. Parts of Nynia lived inside her, but she was a whole new and other person.

Did she love Talon because she was Sunshine or was it something left over from her previous life?

Would she ever know for sure?

"I will never love anyone but you, Nyn." His Celtic words echoed in her head.

Bit by bit, all her memories of their former life together were coming back to her. It was as if someone had opened a sealed door and the memories came pouring out.

She knew about his sister, his mother, his father. Even his uncle and aunt and bastard cousin.

She remembered the way he had looked as a young boy the first time the two of them had sneaked off together to play by the lake.

She remembered the way the clan had treated him. The scandal of his queenly mother being seduced by his Druid father. How Talon's parents had run off in the middle of the night to keep the clan from killing his father and beating his mother for their forbidden affair.

Everyone had hated Talon because of it. They had blamed him for his mother's weakness, for the fact that she had seduced their High Priest and left them without leadership.

They had blamed him for the fact that his mother had put her needs and wants above those of her people.

To atone for her actions, Talon had put everyone's needs and wants above his own.

Sunshine's throat tightened as she remembered everything he had suffered.

Nynia had been there that cold, snowy night when Talon had stumbled, frozen, into the hall, holding a screaming baby in his arms. His cloak had been wrapped around his sister to keep her warm. His shoes had been sold to buy Ceara milk that she had refused to drink.

Talon had stood defiantly before them all. His young body braced to take whatever malice they offered. Even now she could see the raw determination that had made his young amber eyes blaze.

"Your mother?" King Idiag had asked. "Where is she?"

"She has been dead almost two weeks now."

"And your father?"

"Six months past he was killed during an attack, protecting us from the Saxons." Talon had looked down at the screaming baby he held, then back up at his uncle. His face had softened and betrayed his fear. It was the only chink in his brave façade. *"Please, Your Majesty, please have mercy on my baby sister. Don't let her die too."*

Idiag had eyed him curiously. *"And what of you, boy? Do you ask for mercy for yourself?"*

Talon had shaken his head. *"No, Majesty. I ask nothing for me."*

His uncle had adopted Ceara as his daughter, but he had never really acknowledged Talon. He had scorned him just as everyone else did.

Idiag had never protected him from the clan's malice or blows.

Instead, he had told Talon to take it like a man because he deserved it and to never snivel.

And so Talon had.

Sunshine couldn't count the times she had found Talon by the lake practicing with his sword.

"I will make them accept me, Nyn. I will be the best warrior ever born and they'll never dare to speak to me with anything less than respect."

She had watched the angry, hurt boy grow into an embittered, fierce man. He had walked with a deadly swagger and a scowl so stern that even the stoutest of heart shrank at his approach.

He had fought his way into his uncle's heart. Fought until even the clan that hated him knew he was the only one capable of leading them against their enemies.

No one had dared meet Talon's gaze and only in fearful whispers did they dare to disparage his mother or him.

His uncle had had no choice but to accept him. It was either acknowledge Talon or lose his throne to him in war.

Talon had been invincible. Strong. Unyielding.

A man of power.

Until she was alone with him. Only then did his features soften.

Only then did he dare to laugh and smile.

And what haunted her most was the memory of Talon whispering his love to her as she died in his arms . . .

Her throat tight, Sunshine set her bag and thermos of coffee on the table, then knelt on the floor by his head. Tenderness flooded her.

She really did love this man.

She had changed in many ways.

In many ways, Talon had not.

He was still the same fierce warrior who walked alone. The same man who put others before him.

She traced the line of his brows with her fingertip. Then she leaned forward and kissed his cheek.

Startled, he jerked awake so fast, he actually fell off the couch.

Sunshine stifled her laughter. "I'm sorry."

Talon looked around groggily as he slid back on the couch, upright. It took him a few seconds to remember where he was. Clearing his throat, he frowned at Sunshine who was sitting back on her legs and watching him with an odd, weepy kind of look on her face.

"What were you doing?" he asked.

"I was kissing Sleeping Beauty awake."

He frowned at her words until he smelled something almost as enticing as her patchouli scent. "Coffee?"

She handed him the thermos from the coffee table. "And beignets. I thought you'd rather have those than my guava juice and cranberry muffins."

Talon looked at her suspiciously and wondered if a pod person had kidnapped her and was using her body. This couldn't be the same woman who had scavenged his cabin for hours looking for something "nontoxic" to eat. Nor the angry temptress who had banished him to a miserable day spent alone on her couch. "You're not mad at me anymore?"

"I want you to trust me, Talon. That hasn't changed."

Talon glanced away, unable to stand the pain in her eyes. He didn't want to hurt her, didn't want to keep anything from her. But he had no choice.

In so many ways she was his wife and in so many more she wasn't. He was having to learn her all over again.

But what surprised him most was how much he enjoyed getting to know her.

Sunshine was an incredibly sexy, entertaining and fun woman to be around.

She pulled a sugar-coated beignet out of the sack. "Hungry?"

Yes, he was, and not just for food. He was hungry for her body, hungry for her company.

Most of all, he was hungry for her eyes to laugh at him again and not be shadowed by hurt.

She lifted her hand toward his lips, offering him the pastry. He didn't take it from her hand. Instead, he leaned forward and took a bite of it, all the while watching her watch him.

Sunshine shivered as he nibbled the pastry, then he

moved to kiss her lips. She moaned at the sugary taste of him.

Sighing in contentment, she forced him to sit back on the couch so that she could straddle his hips.

"Mmm," he breathed. "I like waking up like this."

She set the beignet aside and carefully poured him a cup of coffee from the thermos.

He looked a bit nervous as he watched her. "Please don't spill that on me."

She gave him an arch look. "I'm forgetful, Talon, not clumsy."

Still, he took the cup from her hand as soon as he could, and drank the chicory-flavored coffee. She screwed the top back on the thermos and set it aside.

Sunshine ran her hand through his tousled hair while he drank, letting the golden waves wrap around her fingers. His muscles rippled with his movements, making her burn with desire. He really was a gorgeous, irresistible man.

"Just think how much nicer I would be if you told me something personal about yourself."

He clenched his teeth. "You are relentless."

She ran her finger down the line of his whiskered jaw and watched his eyes darken as he hardened underneath her. "Only when I see something I want."

Talon pulled another beignet from the sack and held it up for her to eat.

She pulled back with a grimace. "That stuff is hazardous to your health."

"Baby, life is hazardous to your health. Now take a little bite and I'll answer a question."

Skeptical, but willing to try, she took a bite, then groaned at how decadent and good it tasted. It reminded her a lot of Talon.

Talon smiled as he watched her savor her beignet. Until he noticed the sugar that had fallen from the pastry to her breasts. His body hardened even more.

She took another bite and more sugar fell over the tops of her breasts.

His throat went dry.

Before he could stop himself, he dipped his head and licked the powdered sugar from the flesh in the deep V of her sweater.

She moaned in pleasure as she cupped his head to her. She laid her head on his and spoke. "So, how long have you known Wulf?"

Distracted by her taste and scent, he answered without thinking. "A hundred years."

He went rigid as soon as the words registered. "I mean, I um . . ."

"It's okay," she whispered before licking his ear and sending chills over him. "I know you're a Dark-Hunter."

He pulled back and frowned. "How do you know that?"

"A friend told me."

"Who?"

"Does it matter?" She slid herself against him and placed her hands on his shoulders so that she could stare at him. Her dark brown eyes scorched him with sincerity. "I told you I would never betray you. I meant that."

"You're not supposed to know that term."

"I know."

Talon glanced away as he feared what would happen to her if anyone found out she knew about the Dark-Hunters and their world. "What else did your friend tell you?"

"That you're immortal. She didn't know how old you were, but said that you sold your soul for vengeance against your clan."

He narrowed his eyes. "Did she tell you why?"

"She didn't know why."

"What else did she say?"

"That true love could restore your soul to you and free you from your oath to Artemis."

It was true and yet in his case it didn't matter. Free or not, he could never have her. "Provided I want my freedom, you mean."

"Don't you?"

He looked down at the floor.

She cupped his chin in her hand and forced him to look at her. "Talon?"

He took her hands in his and kissed each one, then held them. How he wanted a lifetime with this woman. It was all he had *ever* wanted.

It was the one thing he could never have.

"It's not an easy question to answer, Sunshine. I took an oath and I always stand by my oaths."

"Do I mean anything to you at all?"

Talon flinched at her question. He would gladly sell his soul all over again for them to spend the rest of eternity together. "Yes, you do, but you have to admit that we barely know each other."

"I know and yet when I look at you, Talon, I do know you. I can feel you so deep in my heart that it aches. Do you not feel that too?"

Yes, he did. But he couldn't tell her that. He didn't dare. There was more than just feelings standing between them. There was the wrath of two ancient gods who would be extremely unhappy if he chose to be with her.

"I live a dangerous life, Sunshine. There's no guarantee whatsoever that Artemis will ever hand over my soul. There have been numerous cases in the past where she's refused Dark-Hunters that request, and even if she does give it up, there's still no guarantee you will pass her test and free me.

"Not to mention the small fact that I pissed off a major Celtic god centuries ago and every time I allow myself to love a human, he kills them. Why do you think I live alone in the swamp? Do you think I enjoy being a hermit? I would love nothing more than having a Squire or a human friend, but I don't dare."

That familiar steely look came into her eyes as if she had a plan. "Who did you tick off?"

"Camulus."

"What did you . . ." Her voice trailed off and she had a faraway look, as if she were remembering something. "You killed his son."

Talon closed his eyes. How he wished he could go back

and undo his actions that day. Had he just stayed home with Nynia and grieved for his uncle, none of this would have happened.

"Yes," he breathed. "I thought his son had led the attacking party that killed Idiag."

"Because you chose to marry me and not his daughter."

He nodded. "I was blinded by grief and didn't take time to learn that his daughter had married someone else." He swallowed as he remembered that day and the agony that still lived inside his heart.

"Nynia tried to stop me and I wouldn't listen. After I had slain their warriors and king, Camulus came to me on the battlefield and cursed me. I didn't learn until afterward that my uncle's attack had been staged by his illegitimate son, who was trying to get me and Ceara out of the way so that he could be king. Then it was too late. The die had been cast and all our fates sealed. The truth of it all didn't come out until my death."

He cupped her face in his hands as the agony of that day washed through him anew. "I'm so sorry for what I did to you. What I did to us. There hasn't been a day in my life when I haven't wished that I could go back and right that wrong."

"You didn't do it, Talon. You did what you thought was right." Sunshine held him close to her, trying to soothe his guilt and pain. "Surely there is some way to beat Camulus's curse. Isn't there?"

"No," he said. "You have no idea how powerful he is."

She pulled back to look at him. "But have you ever tried to appease him or talk to him about it?"

Before he could respond, her door crashed open.

Sunshine gasped, then scooted off Talon's lap. Her heart pounded as she saw a man coming slowly through her doorway, walking as if he had all the time in the world.

He wasn't nearly as tall as Talon, probably no more than six feet. He had long black hair that fell freely around his face and he was dressed in a pair of black leather jeans, a gray henley, and a black V-neck sweater.

He was startlingly handsome, but at the same time there was a dark, sinister aura around him. One that said he delighted in making other people suffer.

Talon got up, ready for battle.

The stranger gave a cocky, arrogant smile. "Hope you don't mind the intrusion, but my ears were burning. Naturally, I just had to come and see what the two of you were talking about."

Without being told, she knew this was Camulus.

Talon let out a curse, then the next thing she knew, two daggers came out from under Talon's coat on her coffee table and flew into Talon's hands.

He sprung the release with his thumb, ejecting the blades into a circle of three blades, then crouched into a menacing stance that said he was ready to engage the god.

"Wait!" she said, hoping to avert a fight that could cost Talon his life. She looked at Camulus. "Why are you here?"

Camulus laughed evilly. Coldly. "I'm here strictly to torture Speirr by killing you. Why else would I bother coming?"

Horrified, she stepped back.

So much for negotiating with this man. He was evil incarnate.

Talon leapt across the couch, straight for the god's throat.

Camulus pulled a sword out of thin air. "Oh Speirr, how I have missed you. No one ever fought like you."

Sunshine's eyes widened as they engaged each other. She'd never seen anything like it in her life. Forget Hollywood. It had nothing on the two of them. They fought with malice and with consummate skill.

Talon deflected Camulus's sword with the srads, then ducked the next swing. While the god prepared his next attack, Talon swung about and caught him on the arm with one dagger.

The god hissed as his blood flowed from the wound.

"I won't let you take her," Talon said from between clenched teeth. "I'll kill you first."

Camulus attacked even harder than before. Faster.

Talon met him stroke for stroke. Lethal assault for lethal assault.

"You never could learn your place, Speirr. You never knew when you should just lay down the sword and play nice."

Talon caught his sword between two blades. "I don't play nice with enemies. I execute them." He head-butted Camulus, who staggered back.

The god shook his head. "You've improved."

"I've had fifteen hundred years to perfect my skills."

As Talon lunged, six more men came through the door. Two of them shone bright flashlights into his eyes.

Talon cursed and ducked, covering his eyes as if the lights were searing to his senses.

"I really wish I had more time for this," Camulus said. "But I fear I'm bored now."

Talon turned toward Sunshine who grabbed the lamp from her end table and brought it down on the head of the first man who reached her.

"Damn you, Camulus!" he snarled.

"Och now, Speirr. It's you who are damned."

Talon tried to reach Sunshine, but one of the men opened fire on him. The bullets weren't lethal, but they were extremely painful as they lacerated his chest, back, and arms. He staggered and then fell.

Sunshine screamed as she saw Talon hit the floor. Terrified, she started for him and then felt a bullet rip into the back of her shoulder. All she could think of was saving Talon and herself. She didn't have a gun in her house, but she did have a baseball bat in her bedroom.

She had to get to it.

It was little protection against a god. Still, a slim chance was better than none at all.

As she ran for her bedroom, she realized it wasn't a bullet that had hit her.

It was a potent tranquilizer.

The room swam in front of her eyes as she struggled to

walk. Her legs were heavy, hard to move, and felt as if she were trying to walk through murky concrete.

It was too much effort to move.

The next thing she knew, everything went black.

Bleeding and hurt, Talon fought as best he could. Every time he got up, someone shone another light straight into his eyes and shot more bullets into his body. His eyes burned like fire and he could barely open them.

He struggled to reach Sunshine.

Camulus hit him with a god-bolt and slammed him against the far wall.

Talon stared at him, his body throbbing and aching as he bled.

Nonchalantly, Camulus picked Sunshine up in his arms and stared at her. "She's a pretty little thing, isn't she? Even more lovely than she was the first time." He looked back at Talon with a sinister grin twisting his lips. "You have no idea what I intend to do with her." He kissed her on the cheek. "But I promise you, you will find out."

Talon roared with the weight of his rage. "So help me, Camulus, I'll kill you if you harm her."

Camulus threw his head back and laughed, then strode casually from the room.

Talon could barely breathe from the pain as Camulus lowered him and he fell to his knees. He was covered in blood, which made it even harder to move across the now slippery hardwood floor. But it didn't stop him from trying.

Keeping Sunshine safe was all that mattered.

Someone started ripping the blinds down from the windows, spilling sunlight into the room.

Talon growled as the daylight singed his skin and he lunged for the door where Camulus had vanished.

Three men rushed him, knocking him back.

He kicked and punched his way through them and followed Camulus.

He ran after them to the back door of the club where they vanished into the alley.

Thinking only about saving her, Talon didn't realize he

was in the sunlight until he felt his skin catching fire. Cursing, he fell back into the club and watched helplessly as Camulus paused at the car and held Sunshine's head up so that Talon could see her face.

"Say goodbye to your wife, Speirr. Don't worry. I'll take really *good* care of her."

Camulus put her in a car and drove away.

"No!" Talon shouted. He wouldn't be the death of Sunshine.

Not again.

Chapter 11

It was close to four in the afternoon when Nick rounded the corner of the Pedestrian Mall and caught sight of Ash standing outside of the Corner Cafe, waiting for him. The Atlantean was leaning back against the red-brick wall with his arms folded over his chest and one leg bent and braced on the wall in a way that looked nonchalant, and yet Nick knew Ash could launch himself into action at the slightest provocation.

Dressed in black leather pants, a black T-shirt, and a long, pirate/Colonial style coat, Ash was watching the tourist crowd cut a wide berth around him.

A lethal, dark aura surrounded him. An aura like the one around a wild predator that was both graceful and attractive to behold, but one that let a person know that at any minute they could wind up as lunch.

No one was ever sure how to approach the oldest Dark-Hunter and so most people treated Ash like a visit to the dentist.

In all honesty Nick felt sorry for him. It must be hard to wield so much power and not have anyone to confide in. Ash kept a big distance between him and anyone who would get close to him—both physically and mentally.

Nick tried to treat him just like he would any other guy he hung with and he suspected Ash liked that.

At least he seemed more relaxed around Nick than he did the other Hunters or Squires.

"Look, Mommy, a giant!"

Nick turned to see a little girl around the age of five pointing up at Ash.

Her mother took one look at Ash, gathered her daughter into her arms, and hurried across the street toward the cathedral as fast as her legs would carry her.

Ash waved at the little girl who was still telling her mom to look at him. Poor guy.

Nick closed the distance between them. "You know, if you dressed a little less scary, people might not do that to you."

Pulling his sunglasses low on the bridge of his nose with his forefinger, Ash gave him a wry smile. "Trust me, Nick, it's not the clothes."

He was probably right. Ash had a way about him that was unnaturally intimidating and lethal—kind of like you knew something about Ash wasn't quite human.

Nick noticed Ash had changed hair color. Again. This morning when he'd been at Kyrian's, Ash's hair had been purple. "Back to being black-haired, eh?"

"Back to being annoying, eh?" he quipped.

Nick laughed.

Ash pushed himself away from the wall and picked his black backpack up from the ground. Nick had never known Ash to leave it behind and he'd always been curious about what it contained.

However, he wasn't suicidal enough to try to find out. Ash guarded that bag like a treasured jewel.

"So, how was your test?" Ash asked.

"It sucked. I could have used my microscopic two-way communicator with you. I'm taking Classical Greek civilization with Julian Alexander and he's kicking my ass. That man is one tough drill instructor."

"Yeah, he was never one for nepotism."

Nick inclined his head toward the restaurant, which was only about half full. "Do you mind if I eat while we have this meeting? I skipped lunch to study and now I'm starving."

"Sure," Ash said, then held the door open for him to enter first.

Now that Nick thought about it, Ash did that a lot. He never let anyone get behind him. He always stood with his back to something or kept the crowd in front of him.

His mother would call that a gunfighter's itch. That nervous twitch of someone who expected at any moment to face an unseen attack.

Nick sat at the far end of the bar counter while Ash straddled a stool and kept his back to the wall so that he could watch the diners and the door.

A burly, older bartender came over to them. "What can I get the two of you?" he asked in a deep, hoarse voice.

"Give me a Bud Light," Nick said.

The bartender nodded, then turned to Ash. "What about you?"

"Same."

The bartender narrowed his eyes and gave Ash a thorough once-over. Nick clenched his teeth to keep from smiling. He knew what was coming before the bartender spoke. "You got any ID on you, kid?" he asked Ash.

Nick laughed.

Ash kicked Nick's stool as he fished his mock ID out of his back pocket and handed it to the bartender who studied it very carefully.

"No offense," the bartender said at last, "but with those sunglasses on I can't tell if this is you or not. If you want a beer, kid, you'll have to take them off."

His jaw muscle ticcing, Ash removed his sunglasses.

The bartender cleared his throat as soon as he caught sight of the eerie silver color. "Man, I'm sorry. I didn't realize you were blind. Here's your ID."

Nick laughed even harder as the bartender took Ash's hand into his and put the state-issued ID card into it. Ash was the only Dark-Hunter who ever got carded.

As the bartender walked off, Nick couldn't resist teasing

Ash. "So, does this make you visibly challenged?"

"No," Ash said, putting his ID back into his pocket, "but if you don't lay off me, I'm going to make you breathing impaired."

Nick sobered. Slowly. "Sorry, it's just funny as hell to me. I love that ID Jamie made for you. Born 1980. Yeah, right. What year were you really born, anyway?"

Ash rubbed his forehead. "9548 B.C."

"Whoa," Nick breathed, impressed by the date. He'd known Ash was old, but this was the first time he'd been told the exact year. "You really are older than dirt."

The bartender returned with their beers. "Are you eating anything?" the bartender asked.

Nick ordered red beans and rice, then returned to their conversation as the bartender ambled off again. "How old does that make you?"

Ash took a drink of beer before answering. "Eleven thousand five hundred and fifty-one years old, and yes, I feel every day of it."

"Wow, I had no idea. Hell, I didn't even know we had people back then."

"Yeah, I was part of the original Bedrock crew who worked in the quarry on the back of dinosaurs and ran with the Flintstones. Barney Rubble was short, but he played a good game of stone-knuckle."

Nick snorted, then laughed. He really did like Ash even though the guy was extremely strange. "So, why am I here?"

"I wanted to talk to you in a place where I knew Kyrian couldn't overhear us."

"Okay, why?"

Before Ash could answer, a tall brunette knockout with long, shapely legs and wearing a very short black skirt walked up to the bar beside them. She glanced at Nick disinterestedly, then she placed an elegant, manicured hand against Ash's chest, stood on her tiptoes and whispered in Ash's ear.

He gave her a kind smile. "I appreciate it, love, but I'm involved with someone."

The brunette pouted and handed Ash a business card. "You change your mind, let me know. I promise, I don't bite."

"Yeah, but I do," Ash said under his breath as she walked off.

Nick wasn't sure he'd heard that so he chose to ignore Ash's hushed comment as the bartender brought his food.

"You know," he said to Ash, "that's so not fair. I don't understand how it is you dress like a freak and still women want to do you."

Ash turned his head and gave him an amused smirk. "When you got it, you got it."

"Yeah, but it's seriously annoying to those of us who want it. The least you could do is share." Nick took a bite of food. "Who are you involved with anyway?"

Ash didn't answer. He never did. "Back to our discussion. The reason you're here is that I need your help to break the news to Kyrian that Valerius is in New Orleans."

Nick choked on his bread. "Oh, like hell."

"Nick, this is serious. Sooner or later they will cross paths and I want both him and Julian prepared for it. If, Zeus forbid, one of them kills Val, Artemis will have free rein to go after them. I don't want to see either one of them suffer or die. They have wives and kids who need them."

Nick wiped his mouth and swallowed. "What do you want me to do?"

"I want you to back me up. Help me convince Kyrian that he doesn't need to extract revenge on Valerius."

Nick let out a tired breath as he raked his plastic fork through the beans. That was something that was much easier said than done. "You're asking a lot of me, Ash. Personally, I'd like to help him beat the crap out of that arrogant bastard."

"Nicholas Ambrosius Gautier, you watch your language!"

Nick jerked around at the sound of his mother's melodic

Cajun drawl. She stood behind him with the Nick-you're-in-trouble-buster scowl on her face. At forty, she looked a lot younger and had her long blond hair put up in a bun. Dressed in jeans and a blue sweater, she would have been very attractive if she weren't his mother.

Ash moved Nick's beer closer to him.

His mother clucked her tongue at Ash. "Now don't you be covering for him, Ash." She wagged her finger at Nick. "Are you driving?"

"No, Mom, I'm sitting."

"Don't get smart with me. You know what I mean."

He offered her his charming smile that usually worked to get his butt out of trouble. "It's my first, and I won't drive if I have any more."

She turned to Ash with the same motherly scowl that managed to be both peeved and loving. "What about you? Are you on that motorcycle of yours?"

"No, ma'am."

"Mom," Nick said, annoyed by her interruption, "what are you doing here?"

"I was walking to work and saw you two in here. I just wanted to stop in and say hi since I won't be home until late and you busted out of the house at dawn without so much as a goodbye to me." She gave him a hurt look. "Can't a mother spend five minutes a day with her son without it being a criminal offense?"

Now he felt like a total heel. "I'm sorry, Mom. I had to do a few things for work this morning and I wanted to get it done so I could have more study time."

She ruffled his hair. "It's okay, I understand."

Then she looked Ash up and down, opened his coat and sighed in concern. "I swear you're even thinner than you were the last time I saw you." She motioned the bartender over and ordered red beans and rice for Ash. "You want anything else?" she asked him.

"No, thank you."

She wagged her finger at Ash. "You're going to eat all of it, right?"

"Yes, ma'am."

Nick pressed his lips together to keep from laughing at Ash's Eddie Haskell impersonation and his mom trying to mother an eleven-thousand-year-old warrior. Only Cherise Gautier would have that kind of gall. "Mom, he doesn't need you to baby him."

She straightened the collar of Acheron's coat and smoothed it with her hand. "Trust me, Nick, he needs someone to watch out for him, just like you do. You boys just think you're all grown-up and ready to take on the world."

If she only knew . . .

"Now," she continued, "why don't you bring Ash over to Sanctuary tonight and let me make him some strawberry shortcake and Cajun hash browns to put some meat on those lean bones of his? You can study in the back room if you need to and keep me company while I work."

His mother would never accept the fact he was grown. To her, he would always be five years old and in need of her to watch out for him. Still, he loved his mother.

"Yeah, okay. If I don't have to work, I'll stop by."

"Good boy." She reached into her purse and pulled out two twenties, then handed them to Ash. "You can pay for the red beans and rice with that, and if you have another beer, you better take a cab home too. Got me?"

"Will do, Mrs. Gautier," Ash said as he took the money. "Thanks."

She smiled, then kissed Nick on the cheek and squeezed Ash's forearm. "You boys behave and try to stay out of trouble."

Nick nodded. "We will."

Once she was gone, Nick turned back to Ash. "Man, I'm sorry about that. Thanks for being so cool with her."

"Nick, never apologize for your mother. Just be damned grateful you have her." Ash handed him the forty dollars.

"Believe me, I am," Nick said as he pocketed it. He smiled at his mother's loving nature. She'd always had this insane need to mother the world, but then, she'd been thrown out of her father's house at age fifteen when they had learned she was pregnant with him. So, she tended to have an affinity for anyone she thought was another abandoned or neglected youth.

The bartender returned with Ash's red beans and rice.

Ash took one look at it and slid it over to Nick. "I hope you're hungry."

Nick was, but two orders was more than even he could handle. Suddenly, it dawned on him that he had never once seen Ash eat food. "Do you ever eat?"

"Yeah, but what I need isn't on the menu."

Not wanting to pursue that one, Nick frowned. "Now that I think about it, why are we meeting in daylight? How can you be out in the sun and not go up in flames?"

"I'm special."

"Ahhh, so we're back to the visibly challenged thing, huh?"

Ash shook his head.

As Ash reached for his beer, he noticed the TV out of the corner of his eye. Turning his head, he felt his body go numb in disbelief as he saw Zarek's picture on the early news.

A waiter turned the sound up.

". . . believed to be the same man who murdered a woman in the Warehouse District earlier last night . . ."

Nick cursed. "Is that who I think it is?"

Ash could only nod as he watched the webcam pictures that had captured Zarek's fight with the Daimons and the arrival of the police.

". . . the police department is offering a reward for any information on the suspect."

Nick and Ash cursed in unison as they showed a perfect sketch of Zarek's face.

"We're screwed," Nick breathed.

"Screwed blue and tattooed," Ash snarled. He pulled his cell phone from his coat and left the bar to call Zarek. The last thing he needed was for anyone to overhear this particular conversation.

Nick followed him outside. "What are we going to do?"

Ash hit the cancel button. "His phone is off. He must still be asleep."

"Are you ignoring my question or did you not hear it?"

"I heard you, Nick. I don't know. We have to keep him hidden. With those pictures, he's as good as convicted."

"Can you monkey with them?"

"I don't know. My powers are iffy at best with modern electronics. The best I can do is blow them . . ." His voice trailed off as he saw something even more gut-wrenching than Zarek's face on the news.

Ash let out a disgusted sigh and looked up at the darkening sky. "Are you bored up there, Artie, or what?"

"Huh? What's up?"

Ash inclined his head down Chartres Street to the two figures who were headed straight for them. Almost equal to him in height, the brothers moved like two dangerous predators, slowly, rhythmically. They looked to the left and right, scoping out everyone they passed as if sizing them up as an opponent, a conquest, or a victim.

Dressed in black, both of them wore long leather coats that swirled around their biker boots. They each had one hand tucked into the folds of the coat as if concealing a weapon.

Oh yeah, these were two of the most dangerous creatures Ash had ever known. More so because they would kill anyone who threatened them without a moment's hesitation.

"Who let the dogs out?" Ash snarled.

Nick frowned. "What?"

"We have two members of the Katagaria moving in," he explained to Nick.

Katagaria were animals who could take human form and pass through society to procure victims or anything else they craved. Like any other wild animal, they were extremely lethal and unpredictable.

"Oh God," Nick breathed, "don't tell me they're Slayers."

"That depends on who you ask."

"What do you mean?"

"The Arcadians would call them Slayers. But to their Katagaria brethren, they're Strati."

Nick frowned. "*Strati* means what?"

"It's the correct term for Katagaria soldiers. Slayers kill indiscriminately anyone and anything that crosses their paths. Strati kill mostly to protect themselves, their pack, and their territory."

"So, they belong here?"

Ash shook his head as the two wolves drew closer. They slowed as they caught sight of him.

"Acheron Parthenopaeus," Vane said, stopping in front of him. "It's been a while."

Ash nodded. It'd been at least a couple of hundred years since he had last seen them. They had been on the run then from the human Arcadians who hunted their unique species through time. The two brothers had been trying to find someplace safe to hide their sister from their enemies.

Vane was the older of the two brothers; he had shoulder-length dark brown hair with reddish highlights. His feral green eyes never missed anything. Fang was about an inch taller than Vane and had short black hair and hazel eyes. Either one was dangerous when alone—together, they were damn near invincible.

"Vane. Fang," Ash said, inclining his head to each in turn. "What brings you two to New Orleans?"

Vane cast a suspicious look to Nick, then must have decided something about Nick wasn't too threatening. "We're denning."

Ash grimaced at the term, which meant the Katagaria wolves had a pack here, and were planning on settling in New Orleans for a while. "That's a real bad idea. It's Mardi Gras and we have a lot of Daimons who tend to party then. You need to take your pack—"

"We can't," Vane said, cutting him off. "We have six females in our group about to give birth."

"And another one who gave birth this morning," Fang

added. "You know our laws. We're stuck here until the pups are old enough to travel."

This was getting better and better. Pregnant Katagaria were Daimon magnets due to the strength of their souls and the psychic powers their breed carried. Not to mention the fact that New Orleans was home to three groups of Arcadians who would love nothing more than to claim the skins of Vane and Fang.

"You do know there are three groups of Arcadian Sentinels here?" Ash asked.

Vane's eyes darkened threateningly. "Then you'd best tell them to back off. We have young, and if I catch them anywhere near our den, I will rip them to pieces."

Ash took a deep breath and would have laughed at the absurdity of what he faced had he not felt ill. This just wasn't his day.

He had a horny, pissed-off goddess to contend with. A Celt who was MIA. A Roman general in a city with three men who wanted to disembowel him. An uncontrollable Dark-Hunter the police wanted for murder. And now a Katagaria wolf pack that was popping out seven litters of pups right in the heart of their enemies.

Yes, it was good to be in charge . . .

Nick sniffed the air and looked around. "What is that? Do I smell gumbo?"

Vane and Fang stiffened as Nick moved closer to them.

In spite of the fact that Vane was growling under his breath, Nick pulled back a corner of Vane's coat to display a bright pink box that he had hidden in his left hand.

"What is that?" Nick asked.

"Gumbo," Vane said, his voice low and gravelly.

"Since when do werewolves eat gumbo?"

Ash cringed at Nick's question.

Fang lunged at Nick, but Ash caught him and forced him back before he could reach Nick's throat.

"We're not *were*wolves, cattle-boy," Fang snarled. "We are wolves. Period."

Nick looked bemused by the insult. "Cattle-boy?"

"Slang term," Ash supplied. "Stemming from the fact that they view humans as food."

Nick took a step back.

"Pink boxes, huh?" Ash asked, amused at the thought. No wonder they were hiding them.

Vane passed a menacing glare from Nick to him. "Anya had a craving for gumbo and chocolate. And she wanted it from the Flamingo Room and nowhere else."

Ash felt the corners of his lips twitch. "I can't believe you would run this errand for your sister."

Fang snorted. "Yeah well, remember, the term *bitch* was invented for our females."

Vane growled at him. "She's our littermate, Fang. Show her respect."

Fang's eyes flared, but he tilted his head down in submission to his older brother.

Vane handed the pink box to Fang, then pulled a pen from his pocket and wrote down a number. He handed it to Ash. "That's my cell. You need help with the Daimons, let me know. We have a dozen Strati in our pack and the last thing we want are Daimons sniffing around our females and pups."

Ash took the number and put it in his pocket. He'd barely concealed it when he noticed the rest of the Strati moving in.

They moved stealthily around the street corner like a herd of wild dogs. Fanned out and dressed in black, they looked very much like the lethal killers they were. Everyone on the street rushed away from them, and eyed them nervously.

So much for being low-key. But then, the Were-Hunters had never cared who or what knew they existed. If anyone gave them trouble, they ended up as lunch.

The Strati surrounded him and Nick.

"Dark-Hunter," Stefan growled. Standing even in height with Ash, he was the Strati leader and Vane's mortal enemy. The two of them fought together when they had to, but otherwise couldn't stand each other. "What are you doing with our *filos*?"

Ash noted the way Stefan's lips curled as he used the affectionate term for a male pack member. There was no love lost between Vane and Fang and their packmates. Still, Ash was an outsider and the pack always presented itself as a unified whole to any outsider.

"I was sharing information," he said.

Stefan narrowed his eyes on Vane. "Did you acquire our supplies?"

Vane snorted as he glanced at Nick. "It's a sad day when cattle can smell it and you can't."

Stefan started to attack, but the steely look on Vane's face set the older man back. Stefan was leader because of his age and experience. Vane was subordinate only because he had yet to challenge him. Should Vane ever choose to challenge Stefan for supremacy, there was no doubt who would win.

"Later," Stefan said to Ash before he led the bulk of the Strati away.

Vane and Fang stayed behind.

"Use the number if you need us, Ash," Vane said.

Ash nodded.

They joined the rest of their pack and mounted the motorcycles they had parked on the street behind them.

Ash didn't move until they were gone from his sight.

"Now that's a scary bunch of folks, ain't it?"

"No, Nick," Ash said slowly. "They're not folks. They're animals. They might walk in human form for a short time, but at the end of the day, they are all wolves."

His cell phone rang.

Ash answered it. It was Talon, his voice filled with pain and rage.

"I need your help, T-Rex. I'm at Club Runningwolf's. They took Sunshine."

"Who took Sunshine?"

"The Celtic god, Camulus. As soon as the sun sets I'm going after him."

Chapter 12

Talon was furious. He'd been calling for Ceara and she had yet to respond. He'd tried to spirit-walk and couldn't.

His unleashed emotions were restricting his powers and he had to get hold of them so that he could think straight.

But it was impossible.

He had to find Sunshine.

She was out there alone with no one to protect her. And if anything happened to her, he was going to find some way to make Camulus pay—god or no god, no one was ever going to hurt her again.

He paced the area inside the back door of Runningwolf's like a caged lion. Anger boiled through his veins. It was pungent and tangible. He wanted to rip something apart with his hands. Shred something with his fangs.

The darkest part of the Dark-Hunter was unleashed and, for the first time, he understood some of what Zarek felt.

It was a rage so raw, so powerful, that it controlled him completely.

He slammed his hand against the brick wall beside the door.

"I will get her back!" he growled.

His ravaged body throbbing and bleeding, he had no intention of going back upstairs to Sunshine's loft even though his injuries hurt so much that he felt the overwhelming need to sleep.

He was not going to lie down and tend his wounds.

He would stay awake if it killed him again.

Over and over in his mind, he kept seeing Nynia die in his arms, only now it was Sunshine's face he saw. Her sweet, Southern voice he heard calling out to him.

As soon as the sun set, he was heading out to find Sunshine and bring her home. No matter what it cost him.

God help anyone who was dumb enough to get in his way.

It was fifteen minutes to sunset when Acheron and Nick arrived at the back door and entered the dark hallway of the club. Talon stepped back, away from the fading sunlight that streamed in through the opening.

"What happened?" Ash asked as Nick closed the door.

Talon struggled with the fury and worry inside him. The emotions were so strong that if his powers hadn't been dampened, he was sure he would have been able to use nothing more than his thoughts to level this building to its foundation. "Camulus broke in with about half a dozen humans. They came loaded for Dark-Hunter and carrying halogen flashlights."

"Are you bleeding?" Nick asked as his eyes adjusted to the darkness. Looking pale and horrified, he squinted at Talon's wounds. "Jeez, you're bleeding like crazy."

Talon disregarded Nick's nervous tone. "They shot me."

"No, bud," Nick said. "They turned you into Swiss cheese. Ash, look at his back."

Ash growled when he saw it. "Are you all right?"

"I'm sore, but well enough to hunt and plenty able to kill."

"Jeez," Nick breathed. "I thought your powers included healing."

Talon looked at him drolly. "They do, but I heal by absorbing pain and injuries into *my* body. It's kind of hard to do that when I'm the one who's hurt."

"Nick," Ash ordered. "Go get Talon more clothes. Now."

Nick left immediately to carry out the order.

Ash gave Talon a hard stare with those eerie silver eyes. "You can't go out there covered in blood, with dozens of bullet holes riddling your flesh. I think people might get a little suspicious and wonder how it is you can stand upright and not be, say, *dead*. The last thing I need is for another Dark-Hunter to make the evening news."

Talon stood firm against the order. "I told you, T-Rex. I'm heading out as soon as that sun sets. Thirteen minutes and counting."

Ash glared at him. "Dammit, Celt. You better get a hold of yourself and think through this."

"I'm fine, Acheron. There's nothing wrong with me that killing a few people won't cure."

Ash's eyes narrowed even more. "Turn around and face the wall."

Unsure of what Ash intended, but trusting him completely, Talon obeyed.

He felt Ash splay his hand against the center of his back. His touch was hot and electrifying, and it radiated heat all the way through his body. Talon hissed as his injuries began to throb even more. Then in the span of a few heartbeats, the bullets worked themselves out of his skin and the bullet holes began knitting themselves shut.

Son of a bitch, he'd never known Ash had this kind of power. He was seriously impressed.

While his wounds were healing, Talon's cell phone rang.

Ash stepped away from him while he answered it.

"Missing her yet, Speirr?"

"Damn you, Camulus. Damn you!"

A laugh answered him. "Tell me, is it better to know love and have lost it or to have never known it at all?"

Talon saw red. "Where is she?"

"Talon?"

His stomach twisted violently at the sound of Sunshine's terrified voice. "Baby, are you okay?" he asked, his voice cracking.

"They haven't hurt me, but they want you to come to a warehouse on Commerce Street. I—"

"Sunshine!" Talon shouted, his heart pounding. "Sunshine, are you there?"

"Oh, she's here, Speirr. But she needs you. If you want her, be at 609 Commerce at seven o'clock sharp. Bring as many friends as you want and let's see who gets to take Sunshine home tonight and in how many pieces."

The phone went dead.

Blind, torrid rage pierced him. Oblivious to the threat of the sun, he headed for the door.

Ash caught him. "Talon, look at me."

He refused. All he could see was Sunshine dead.

"Talon!" Ash shouted. "Get a friggin' grip. If you go out there like this, you're dead."

"What the hell do you know about it?"

"Celt." Ash tightened his grip on him. "You're doing just what they want. You're about to run headlong into the last minutes of daylight. Think. Out of all the Dark-Hunters I have, you are the one I depend on to keep his head on straight. Don't let them do this to you."

Talon's breathing was ragged as he tried to tamp down his anger and fear. "I can't let her die."

"She won't if you control yourself. You have to leash your temper." Ash released him.

Talon clenched and unclenched his fists as he stared at the door.

"Think, Talon," Ash said, his voice strangely soothing. "Remember what I taught you. Remember that you became a Dark-Hunter because you couldn't control your rage. You have to find your peace. Your balance."

Talon took a deep breath and expelled his anger slowly. *Very* slowly. "All right. I'm mostly calm."

"Good. Because I don't want you to be mostly dead." Ash stepped away from him. "We'll wait on Nick to return with your clothes and then we'll go get her."

Talon nodded, his gut still knotted over having to wait. But Ash was right.

If he didn't do *exactly* what Camulus said, he would kill her just for spite.

Talon winced at the thought. "He's going to kill her now, isn't he?"

"I don't know, Talon. I hope not."

Talon paused for a moment as he remembered the address Camulus had given him. "Commerce Street. Isn't that almost right where that woman was murdered?"

Acheron looked puzzled. "What woman?"

"The one you called me over to see."

Ash stared at him blankly.

"You know," Talon insisted, "the woman you said you thought might have been murdered by Zarek."

Acheron scowled. "I didn't call you over to see a murdered woman and I damn sure never thought Zarek would kill a woman."

"Yes you did."

Acheron shook his head slowly. "No I didn't."

Talon duplicated his scowl. What the hell was wrong with the guy? Was Acheron finally going senile?

It wasn't like him to be so scattered.

That was Talon's job at the moment.

"T-Rex, I met you over there. Remember? You called me, and while I was with you, Zarek had his little party with the police. I know it was you. There's not another man on this earth your height who looks like you."

The color faded from Acheron's cheeks. If Talon didn't know better, he'd swear he saw real worry in Acheron's eyes.

Something was really wrong.

"What is it, Ash?"

Acheron stepped away from him. "There's something I need to do. Stay here and I'll be back in plenty of time to go after Sunshine."

Talon caught his arm as Acheron headed for the door. "You better fill me in on this. Now."

"I can't."

"Acheron, this is no time to play Oracle. If you know what's going on and what we're dealing with, you need to come clean."

To Talon's complete amazement, Acheron vanished.

· · ·

Ash couldn't breathe as he flashed himself into Katoteros, a small nether region between dimensions. This was his private domain where no one but he was ever supposed to tread.

Centuries ago, Hades had relegated him to this non-place. Or more correctly, Hades had incarcerated him here.

Since the day Artemis had freed him, Ash had used this place as a touchstone to remind him of what he was.

What he had been . . .

Now, Ash struggled for control. He had to have a few minutes to collect his thoughts. His emotions.

His stomach knotted, he felt ill as memories and pain took turns assailing him. The air around him sizzled and snapped in time to his volatile state.

He had to get a hold of himself. He couldn't afford to unleash his emotions.

No one would ever be able to stop him if he did.

Ash raked his hands through his long black hair and shouted his ancient battle cry. Lightning flashed and gray thunder clouds roiled across the eerie blue-black sky above him.

This couldn't be happening. Not now.

And yet there was no other explanation. Styxx was free. Somehow he had escaped from the Vanishing Isle and been turned loose in New Orleans.

How could it have happened?

Now Styxx was pretending to be him. He was mixing with Ash's men and talking to them . . .

Horror pierced his heart.

He had to stop him before Styxx revealed Ash's past to anyone. Ash couldn't bear the thought of anyone knowing about his human life. Knowing about what he'd been.

What he'd done . . .

"Acheron?"

He flinched at Artemis's voice. "This is my place, Artie. You promised me you would never come here."

She materialized before him. "I felt your pain."

"Like you care."

She reached out to touch his face, but he folded his arms over his chest, and moved away from her. She sighed and dropped her hand. "I do care, *akribos*. More than you know. But that isn't why I'm here. I have learned of Zarek."

Ash growled low in his throat. Of course, she would never come because he was hurt. She'd taught him long ago that his suffering meant nothing to her. "I'm handling it."

"Handling it how? He has been exposed and is now being sought by the human authorities. He jeopardizes everything. He must die."

"No." He snarled the word at her. "I will take care of it. I just need more time."

She had that familiar calculating look on her face. "And what will you give me for this time you request?"

"Dammit, Artemis, why must everything be a bargain with you? Can't you, just once, do something because I asked it of you?"

"Nothing is free," she said as she walked a circle around him. He cringed as she raked her hand over his back. "You of all people should know that. A favor requires a favor in turn."

He took a deep breath and prepared himself for what was to come. Like it or not, he would have to play supplicant to her to keep Zarek safe. "What do you want?"

She pulled his hair back from the nape of his neck and nuzzled him with her lips and nose. Against his will, his body broke out in chills and hardened.

When she spoke, her voice was low and husky. "You know what I want."

"Fine," he said resignedly. "You can have me, just don't send Thanatos in yet. Let me get Zarek back to Alaska."

"Mmm," she breathed against his neck. "See . . . it's so much better when you cooperate."

He stiffened as she licked his skin.

"Question?" he said coldly. "Did you free Styxx just so you could screw me?"

She pulled back sharply and stepped around him to give him a shocked stare. "What?"

Ash watched her carefully, wanting to know the truth. "Styxx is loose in New Orleans."

Artemis appeared flabbergasted. "I would never do that to you, Acheron. I had no idea he had escaped. Are you sure?"

In spite of himself, he was relieved to know she hadn't betrayed him. Again.

"Talon saw him and thought he was me."

Artemis pressed her hand to her lips. Her green eyes were terrified. "He'll be coming for you."

"He already is. I'm sure that little dance with Zarek outside of the club was a setup to get you to kill Zarek. No doubt, Styxx is trying to neutralize my men. Either to keep them from protecting me or to keep me distracted."

"I won't let him have you," she said emphatically.

"This is between me and my brother, Artie. I want you to stay out of it." Ash moved farther away from her. "I'll be back at dawn to fulfill our bargain. In the meantime, leave Zarek to me."

Vane was still in human form as he helped his sister eat her gumbo.

She was the only living creature he had ever allowed to see the tender side of him. To the rest of the world, he must always be ruthless and harsh lest their pack prey on Anya and Fang because of their mixed heritage.

Vane clenched his hand against Anya's thick, soft fur and fought down the pain inside him. She and Fang were all he really had in this world.

All that had ever meant anything to him.

On the day Anya had mated with the Strati warrior Orian, Vane had thrown a fit. He had always known her reckless and stupid mate would meet an early death.

A few weeks ago, the Fates had proven him right.

He could still hear the sound of her voice when she had learned of Orian's death and had told him that she was more than mated to Orian. She had allowed the wolfswain to bond her to him as well. With their life forces melded into one, Orian's death would normally have been hers, except for the fact that she carried Orian's young.

But as soon as the pups came into this world, she would join her mate on the other side of eternity.

His heart broken, Vane blinked back tears.

Anya looked up and licked his face.

"You like the gumbo, huh?" he asked, stroking her ears with both of his hands.

He heard her laughter in his head. *"Thank you for getting it."*

He nodded. For her, he would walk through the fires of hell to claim a simple drink of water.

She sank down beside him and rested her head on his lap. *"You should take wolf form before the others grow suspicious."*

He watched the way her fur cradled his fingers. How he was going to miss her when she was gone. She was the most beautiful wolfswan he'd ever seen, and he didn't mean her looks. It was her gentle heart he would miss most of all. The way she always worried after him.

"I will, Anya. I just want a few more minutes."

He sensed Fang coming up behind him in wolf form. His brother butted him in the back with his head, then nipped playfully at his shoulder.

A flash of light appeared to the right of them. Vane looked up to find Acheron standing in the swamp. The Atlantean glanced around to make sure they were alone, then spoke quietly. "Can I have a minute?"

Fang growled.

"It's all right, *adelfos,*" Vane said, pushing his brother back. "Watch over Anya."

Vane rose to his feet and walked Acheron into the woods, away from the den. If any of his pack learned he had brought a Dark-Hunter into it, his life was over.

"You should have called me, Ash."

"This couldn't wait. I have a problem and you're the only one I trust to help me."

Now that shocked him. Immensely. "*You* trust *me*?"

Ash gave him a wry look. "No, not really. But I have a renegade who is pretending to be me and threatening my Hunters."

"What's that got to do with me?"

"You owe me one, Vane, and I need you and Fang to act as backup. I need some muscle that they won't see coming."

"When?"

"Now."

Talon paced the floor of Sunshine's loft. He'd quickly showered the blood from his body and changed into the clothes Nick had brought. He was staying calm, but it was a real challenge.

"She is unharmed, Speirr," Ceara said. "I swear it."

He let out a long, weary breath in relief. He was grateful Ceara had managed to come to him this time, but it was a hard struggle for her to stay with him. The power that was blocking her was one they had never before encountered.

He only hoped Ceara could battle it a little longer and continue to help him protect and watch over Sunshine.

"Can you tell me where she is exactly?" he asked his sister.

"Oh jeez," Nick said from the breakfast counter where he sat, waiting for Ash to return. "You're not talking to the dead again, are you? I hate it when you do that."

"Shut up, Nick."

Nick curled his lip. " 'Shut up, Nick, heel, sit, fetch.' Love you too, Celt."

Talon glared at him. "Why don't you go scrounge up something to eat so that your mouth is occupied?"

"That I can do." Nick scooted off the bar stool and headed into the kitchen.

"*Nae*, I can't find her," Ceara said. "I can't pinpoint her exact location. I told you, something powerful protects her. Something that is beginning to feel like a god's power to me."

"Camulus?"

"I'm not sure. Part of it feels like it could be a Celtic god and yet there is something more."

"What?"

"It's more like powers are commingled. Like two gods are protecting themselves."

"Why?"

She shrugged.

Nick cursed. "There's no food in here. There's nothing but grass and tofu and shit. There's not even a Coke. Man, T, your girlfriend is whacked."

Nick pulled out the block of soy cheese and smelled it. "This looks kind of edible though. I mean, you can't really screw up cheese, right?"

"Yeah, Nick. Eat the cheese." He turned back to Ceara while Nick searched for a knife to slice it. "Will they free her?"

"I can't tell you the future, Speirr, you know the rules."

"I have to know she's going to live."

Ceara hesitated before she answered. "Today, she will."

"And tomorrow?"

Ceara looked away. "I can't tell you that."

Talon cursed.

Suddenly, a bright flash of light entered the room. Talon shielded his eyes from the glare and watched as Acheron and two men appeared just inside the doorway. He'd never seen the two men before, but one look told him they were Katagaria. The air around them was rife with animalistic, psychic power.

"Oh man," Nick snapped. "I hate that poofing shit. You scared me so bad, Ash, you made me eat this crappy cheese." He looked back at Talon. "What is this stuff anyway?"

"Soy cheese."

The Katagaria exchanged a disgusted look.

"So much for *my* dinner," the taller Katagaria said. "Now his whole system is polluted. Be at least a week before it leaves his cell tissue and he's edible again."

Nick paled considerably.

"You ready to go after Sunshine?" Acheron asked Talon.

Steeled with determination, Talon nodded. "Let's do it."

Acheron glanced to Nick in the kitchen. "Nick, I want you to head over to Zarek's and keep him out of sight for the time being. He's under house arrest, so if I catch him out and about, he's in deep shit and so are you."

Nick grimaced. "Okay, but for the record, I want you to know that if a woman's life wasn't on the line, I'd tell you to stuff that order."

Nick walked out the door, past the Katagaria, mumbling all the while. " 'Nick, fetch my car, fetch my clothes, sweep the chimney, make my bed, watch my psychopath, fetch my slippers.' Yeah, I'll fetch those slippers and stick them someplace real uncomfortable." Just when Talon thought he was through, he heard one last parting comment. "I swear, my mother should have named me Fido."

"Hey, I'll have you know my best friend is named Fido," the taller Katagaria said over his shoulder.

The other Katagaria shoved him lightly. "Would you stop?"

Acheron indicated the taller Katagaria with short black hair who had made the first comment. "Talon, meet Fang." He motioned to the one with longer hair and green eyes. "And his brother, Vane."

"Why are they here?" Talon asked Acheron.

"Let's just say that if the bad guys are armed with halogen lights again, they won't have the same effect on the Katagaria that they had on you."

"Yeah," Vane said, smiling evilly. "Lights just make us attack more."

Good, they had at least one surprise in their corner.

Now if he could just get his hands on Camulus.

"So, what's the plan, girls?" Fang asked.

"For none of us to get killed," Acheron said.

Vane led them out of the loft, downstairs to Talon's car. Talon saw the two black and gray Ninja motorcycles that must belong to the Katagaria. Since the were-animals had to move quickly to avoid their enemies, they tended to prefer racing bikes to running or walking, which depleted the strength they needed for fighting.

Talon checked his watch. It was twenty minutes to rendezvous. Part of him wished Ash would just poof them over to the warehouse, but he knew better than to ask.

Ash was capricious with that one power and got rather testy when asked to use it.

Talon got into the Viper while the other three started their bikes. He pulled out of the alley first, with the guys right behind him, and headed for Commerce Street.

They reached the Warehouse District a few minutes later.

The streets were bustling with activity, both tourist and local. This popular area was New Orleans' premier art district and was often referred to as the SoHo of the South.

It didn't take long for Talon to find the old abandoned warehouse that had been a popular art gallery during the 1980s. It had closed down in the early 1990s and been vacant ever since. The large-paned windows were dark, some partially boarded up and broken. The once red doors were now cracked and peeling, and held together by a thick chain and padlock.

There wasn't a single sound coming from inside as the men left their vehicles and gathered into a group.

"Uh, guys," Fang said slowly as he removed his helmet, "you do realize this is most likely a trap?"

"No, you think so?" Talon asked sarcastically.

Fang rolled his eyes.

Talon summoned his powers, letting them surge and feeling just how fragmented they were. This wasn't good.

He didn't know what was waiting inside that building, but he would fight his way through hell itself to keep Sunshine safe. Powers or no powers.

They headed for the building with Ash pulling up the rear.

"Ooo," Fang said as Talon worked the padlock. "Breaking and entering. Brings back fond memories, eh, Vane?"

"Shut up, Scooby," Vane said, using the derogatory wolf Katagaria term for a brainless, cowardly pup. "And watch your back."

Talon snapped open the lock and opened the door. It creaked loudly as the door fell off its hinges.

Talon cursed, then irritably shoved the door aside.

Entering the building one by one, they fanned out, and then paused inside the dark, empty room that was covered with at least a decade's worth of dust, spiderwebs, and grime.

Every so often, a car would go by outside, the headlights illuminating some of the dilapidated interior.

The place was totally silent except for a strange, rhythmic thumping coming from upstairs and the sound of rodents scurrying around the floor.

"Ewwww-eee-wwww," Fang sang in a voice reminiscent of some B-movie soundtrack. "Hey Ash, you vant to suck my blud?"

Ash gave him a droll, blank stare. "No, thanks. The last thing I want is to catch parvo from you, or some other freaky dog disease that makes me lift my leg around hydrants."

Vane smacked his brother on the back of the head. "Next time I'm leaving you home."

"Hey, that hurt," Fang said, rubbing his head.

"Yes, but not as much as this will." The disembodied voice came out of nowhere.

Talon heard something whirling through the air. He moved his head sharply to the left to avoid its trajectory and caught it as it started past his shoulder.

Arching a brow at the huge medieval throwing ax he held, he passed it over to Vane.

Vane curled his lip. The Katagari looked less than amused. "Hey dickhead, you should know something." Vane tested the edge of the blade with his thumb. "You attack my brother, you really piss me off."

Vane tossed the ax back at the one who'd thrown it.

Talon heard a groan an instant before searchlights pierced the darkness.

Talon and Ash hissed in pain, ducked low, and shielded their eyes.

In the next second, something crackled and the lights went out.

Ash tossed a lightning bolt into a corner where it must have hit its mark, since Talon heard someone shriek. The odor of burning flesh wafted through the room.

Then, Daimons came out of the darkness, attacking. Talon caught the first one to reach him, and flipped him to the floor. He toed the release for the blade in his boot, but before he could use it to kill the Daimon, another one caught him about the waist and shoved him back.

"Hot damn, Daimon food," Fang said with a laugh. "Hey Vane, you want the white meat or dark?"

Vane caught one of the Daimons in the chest with a knife, right in the heart. The Daimon disintegrated. He laughed at his brother who was slugging it out with another Daimon. "How about I grab one leg, you grab the other and we make a wish and pull?"

Talon rolled his eyes at them, then he spun around and used the toe of his boot to finish off the Daimon who had grabbed him.

He went after the first Daimon, who was making his way toward Fang's back. Talon caught him just before he reached the Katagari.

The Daimon turned on him with a hiss, and tried to stab him. Talon turned his wrist under and snapped the knife out of his hand.

"Bad move, inkblot," Talon said, slugging the vampire.

The demon staggered back. Talon used the knife to finish him off. The Daimon disintegrated as the stolen souls ran free of his body and drifted up toward the ceiling.

Something out of the corner of his eye caught Talon's attention. He turned his head to see Ash being mobbed by a group of Daimons.

Ash was fighting them off with his staff, but there were so many of them attacking that it was like trying to brush ants off while standing in the middle of an anthill.

Talon went to help.

Where had all the Daimons come from?

They usually congregated in New Orleans this time of year, but damn . . . it looked like half their world population was here in this room.

Working together, Talon, the Katagaria, and Ash finished them off.

"Thanks," Ash said as the last one disintegrated.

Talon nodded and folded up his srad into a single dagger, then returned it to his boot.

"Well," Fang said, mimicking a thick Southern drawl. "I have to say it's mighty nice of them Daimons to clean up after themselves when you kill them. It's much better than slaying an Arcadian." He held his hands up to them. "Look, Ma, no mess."

"Does Fang have an off switch?" Talon asked Vane.

Looking a bit apologetic, Vane shook his head no.

But Talon was no longer paying attention to them.

He had far more important things to focus on. "We have to find Sunshine," he said, heading for the stairs.

"Wait," Ash called. "You have no idea what's up there."

Talon didn't slow at all. "And I won't know until I get there."

With no thought except to save her, Talon followed the thumping noise to a door at the far end of the upper hallway. By the time he reached it, Vane, Fang, and Ash had caught up to him.

Talon flung open the door, ready for battle.

Instead of another group of Daimons, what they found

was Sunshine tied on a bed in a room that was lit by a small lantern. Moaning, she was writhing and twisting as if she were on fire.

Terrified something was wrong with her, Talon rushed to her side while Vane and Fang searched the room for more Daimons.

What had they done to her?

If they had touched or harmed her, he would hunt them down and tear them to pieces.

As soon as Talon released her from the bed she latched onto him with a viselike grip.

"Hi, baby," she breathed throatily, rubbing herself against him as she ran her hands through his hair and over his body. "I've been thinking about you, wanting you to come to me."

Oblivious to the others in the room, she kissed him feverishly and started trying to pull his clothes off. For a full minute, Talon was too stunned to move.

Then his hormones surged, wanting her as much as she wanted him.

She pushed him back on the bed, climbing up his body as if she were ready to do him on the spot.

His body instantly on fire, Talon had never seen anything like it. He had to literally struggle to keep his clothes on. Not that he would have objected had they been alone. But there was no way he was going to perform before an audience.

Acheron watched her, his eyes haunted.

There was something about Acheron's expression that reminded Talon of someone reliving a bad nightmare.

"Sunshine?" Talon said, trying to inspect her for damage. "Are you okay?"

"Umm-hmm," Sunshine groaned as she nibbled her way down his chin to his neck. His body was instantly hot and hard for her.

"C'mon, baby," she breathed in his ear. "I need you. Right now."

"Hey, Vane," Fang said. "I didn't know human females could go into heat, did you?"

Vane gave his brother a droll look.

It didn't curb Fang in the least. "You think she'll need a stand-in after she wears out Talon, like a Katagari female would? I don't normally do humans, but for a piece of that I might be tempted."

Talon saw red.

Vane clapped his hand over his brother's mouth and pulled him back. "Fang, I think you better stop or Talon might turn you into a wolf kabob."

Ash shook his head as if forcing himself to wake up from a trance. He pulled Sunshine back, away from Talon. Sunshine fought and hissed like a wildcat as she struggled for her release. Ash whispered something in a language Talon couldn't understand and Sunshine immediately went limp in his arms.

"What did you do to her?" Talon asked angrily.

"Nothing dangerous." He carefully placed Sunshine back in Talon's lap. "It's a small sleeping spell to keep her calm and let you get her home safely."

Ash lifted Sunshine's hand and sniffed her skin.

Talon had already caught a whiff of the strange spicy orange scent that seemed to permeate Sunshine's body.

Ash turned to Vane and Fang. "Would you guys mind waiting for us downstairs?"

Vane inclined his head. "We'll do another sweep of the building to make sure there aren't any more Daimons hiding out."

He led his brother from the room.

Talon cradled Sunshine against his chest, grateful to have her again, but concerned over what had been done to her. He had also noticed how strangely Ash was behaving; the man was much weirder than normal. "What's wrong with her?"

Ash let out a long, tired breath. "She's on a drug called *Eycharistisi.*" At Talon's frown, he defined the unfamiliar word. "Pleasure."

"Come again?"

"It's a very potent aphrodisiac. It floods the body with endorphins and destroys any and all inhibitions. One hit and all the user can think about is finding someone to stimulate them to orgasm."

Rage descended as Talon thought about why someone would give her such a thing. "You think Camulus had sex with her?"

"No, I think someone else did it as a message to me and a warning to you."

"How so?"

Ash's cheeks were mottled with red—something that only happened when the man became truly angry. In fifteen hundred years, Talon had only seen Ash's skin mottled three times.

"Pleasure was the drug du jour in Atlantis and hasn't been produced since the entire continent sank to the bottom of the Aegean."

A bad feeling settled in Talon's gut. This wasn't just about Sunshine and him.

He narrowed his eyes on Acheron. "What's going on, T-Rex? First someone is messing with me who looks like you but isn't you. And now someone has access to a drug that vanished eleven thousand years ago along with your homeland, and he's fed it to Sunshine who was kidnapped by Camulus. What's the deal?"

"Offhand, I would say Camulus has teamed up with someone else."

"Who?"

As expected, Acheron didn't answer. "I need you to stay out of this."

"It's rather hard for me to stay out of it when this person keeps dragging me into it. And I won't stay out of it so long as Sunshine is threatened."

"You'll do as I tell you, Talon."

"I'm not your boy, Ash. You better take another tone with me. Quick."

Ash's cheeks turned even redder. "Are you questioning my authority?"

"No, I'm questioning your judgment. I want you to come clean with me about who and what we're dealing with and why this man gave Sunshine this drug."

"I don't owe you an explanation, Celt. All you need to know is that I have an old enemy pretending to be me."

"Why?"

"Well, it obviously isn't to be nice to me and win over my friends, now is it?"

Talon growled at Acheron's inability to tell anyone jack about his past. Why was the man so damn secretive?

"Is he a shapeshifter or a demigod?"

"Last I checked, he was human."

"Then why does he look like you? Is he a relative?"

"I'm not going to play Twenty Questions with you, Talon. He's not your concern. He's mine."

"Will you at least explain to me how in the future I can tell you two apart?"

Acheron removed his sunglasses. "Our eyes. I'm the only human ever born with eyes like these. He won't have them and he won't remove his sunglasses for fear of revealing himself."

"Why is this guy after you?"

"He wants me dead."

"Why?"

Acheron stepped away from him. "Your orders are simple. Take her back to the swamp. I don't know how much of the drug they gave her, but I'm sure she'll still be feeling it when she wakes up. Trust me, when she does, she's going to put a really big smile on your face."

"Trust you," Talon repeated. "Funny how you keep saying that when you never trust anyone with even the most basic facts about yourself. Why is that, Ash?"

As expected, Ash didn't answer. And in that instant, Talon realized how Sunshine must feel when dealing with him.

It was a wonder she tolerated him at all.

"Hey Ash," Vane called from downstairs. "There's something down here you need to see."

Talon picked Sunshine up and carried her downstairs. Ash followed behind them.

Vane and Fang were in a small room off the main one. On the far wall someone had painted an eerie Greek symbol of three women and a flock of doves. Three notes were taped to it—one above each woman's head.

Talon saw that one was for him, one for Sunshine, and one for Ash.

Crossing the room, Acheron pulled the letters down, opened the one addressed to Talon and read it out loud. " 'You didn't listen to me, Celt. I warned you to keep her in your swamp where she would be safe.

" 'I'll bet it's now tearing you up that you don't know when, where, and how I'm going to kill her. But rest assured, I *am* going to kill her.' "

He opened Sunshine's next and read it out loud as well. " 'Talon, are you reading Sunshine's letters? What? Don't you trust your girlfriend?

" 'Don't worry. She hasn't been unfaithful to you. At least not yet, though it was hard. We had to tie her down to keep her from screwing every one of us.' "

Talon bellowed with rage. "So help me, I'm going to find that son of a bitch and rip his heart out."

Furious, Ash opened the last one, but this time he didn't read it out loud.

The note was addressed to him. The handwriting was different.

I know you, little brother. I know all you've done. I know how you live.

Most of all, I know the lies you tell yourself so that you can sleep.

Tell me, what would your Dark-Hunters think of you if they ever learned the truth about you?

Keep them out of my way or I'll see them all dead.

And you I'll be seeing on Mardi Gras.

Ash balled the note up in his fist and disintegrated it with his thoughts. Impotent rage rushed through him, setting fire to his blood. If Styxx wanted a war, then he'd better gather a whole lot more Daimons.

Styxx had no idea what he was playing against.

"What did that one say?" Talon asked.

"Nothing. Take Sunshine to your place and keep her there until the drug wears off, then call me." Ash rubbed his eyes as the Katagaria led them from the building.

Once outside, Talon placed Sunshine in the car while the others stood nearby.

Vane had his arms folded over his chest as he looked at Ash. "So, Ash, where does all this leave you?"

"Basically screwed. In the next twenty-four hours I have to find a way to get Zarek out of here before the cops find him, and unless I miss my guess, the next act of my nemesis will be to tell Kyrian and Julian who their new neighbor is."

Talon caught Acheron's gaze. "He wants your attention scattered and unfocused."

Ash nodded. "Yeah, and he's doing a really good job at it."

An idea occurred to Talon. "You know, I think we've all been forgetting something."

"And that is?"

Talon indicated the Katagaria to remind Acheron that the wolf patria wasn't the only group of Were-Hunters in town. "That your pal doesn't know about Sanctuary. I think we need to go put the bear clan on standby. I'm sure Papa Peltier and the boys would be more than happy to lend us a hand on Mardi Gras. They owe me a few favors, and if the Daimons come out like they did tonight, we'll be needing all the help we can get."

"True."

"And if I were you," Talon continued, "I'd go ahead and break the news to Kyrian about Valerius just like you were planning on doing. And keep Zarek on standby here in the city."

"What about the police?"

"Trust me, T-Rex, I know my city. The police will be so distracted on Mardi Gras that Zarek could introduce himself to them and they wouldn't realize it's him. But if I were you, I'd pretend that I was getting Z out of here just in case your 'friend' is watching. Call Mike and have him fly in and ride Eric out under the cover of darkness so that they'll think it's Z. And keep Zarek in hiding and bury Valerius until that night."

Acheron set his jaw. "It's risky."

"So's living in a swamp."

Vane moved forward. "I can set up sentries around Talon's place. If they make a move on him again, Fang and I can be there in a heartbeat."

"Why are you willing to help us?" Talon asked. "I thought it was your policy to let Dark-Hunters rot."

"It is. But I still owe Acheron a debt." He turned to Acheron. "After this is over, consider it paid in full."

Acheron nodded. "Done."

Talon said his goodbyes to the group, then got in the car and headed home.

As he drove away from the district, he reached over and took Sunshine's hand into his and held on to it tight. Her bones felt so fragile in his palm and yet he knew the strength this lady possessed. The grace and determination.

He'd been so afraid when Camulus had taken her.

He didn't like living with this fear. He didn't like feeling anything. He'd been without emotions for so long that having them now hurt even more.

How he missed his calm serenity. He was used to having complete control and yet every time he looked at her he felt his emotions spin out of control.

Sunshine touched him so deep in his heart that he knew he'd never be the same again. And it wasn't just because she was Nynia. It was because she was her.

Sunshine held strength, courage, and fire. She was her own person and he loved the challenge of her.

She was precious to him.

Talon loved her more now than he ever had as a man.

And the pain of that thought was enough to cripple him.

Talon got her back to his place and laid her carefully on his futon. He wasn't sure what Acheron had done to her, but she slept peacefully.

His phone rang.

He answered it to find Ash on the other end.

"Did you make it back with her?"

"Yeah, she's still asleep."

"Good. I was worried about you two."

He frowned. It was Acheron's voice but that wasn't something Acheron would normally admit to.

All his instincts went on full alert. This was definitely not Acheron. The voice and tone were the same, but now that he knew there were two of them, he could hear the difference in their personalities.

This was the imposter.

"So how long do you think it'll be before the drug leaves her system?" Talon asked.

"I don't know. One dose can keep you pumped anywhere from one to three days."

"Really? You seem to know a lot about it."

"Yeah, well, when I was mortal I was so addicted to it that I was willing to sell my soul for it."

"And who might you be?" Talon asked.

"Excuse me?"

"I know you're not Acheron."

A dark laugh sounded in his ear. "Very good, Dark-Hunter. Very good. For that, I shall let you and Sunshine live another day."

Talon snorted. "Boy, you've got a lot to learn about me if you think you could ever be a threat to me or mine. You come near her again and I'll make boots out of your hide."

"Oh, I don't think so. But I am impressed that this time you figured me out. I had begun to wonder if you would ever be able to tell us apart."

Talon tightened his grip on the phone. "Yeah well, if you're going to impersonate Acheron, you might try learning a little more about him."

"Trust me, Dark-Hunter," he said, his voice confident and evil. "I know Acheron a lot better than you do. I know things about him that would stun you into silence and make you hate him forever. He's not what you and the others think."

"I've known him for fifteen centuries. I think by now I know a thing or two about his character."

"Do you?" he asked sarcastically. "Did you know that he had a sister he let die? That she was only a few feet down the hall, screaming for his help. And while he lay in a drugged and drunken stupor, she was torn to pieces?"

Talon was horrified by what the man described. But he knew Acheron better than that. Acheron would never, drugged or not, be so far gone that he wouldn't render aid to a stranger. When it came to those who fell under his protection, Acheron would move heaven itself to keep them safe.

"I don't believe you."

"You will. Before I am through here, all of you will learn the truth of him." The imposter hung up the phone.

Talon tossed his phone to the nightstand and ran his hands over his face. This was a nightmare.

He was torn between his need to protect a friend he had known a thousand lifetimes and a woman whose soul meant more to him than his own life.

And he'd never felt more helpless. Not even when he had watched his uncle slain. At least then he'd held a weapon in his hand and had seen his attackers.

This time, there was nothing solid to grasp onto. There were two enemies out there. One pretending to be Acheron and the other a cowardly god with a vicious vendetta.

What was he going to do?

He turned around and looked at Sunshine.

Her black hair was a dark cloud on his pillow. Her face was relaxed and peaceful, her tanned skin a soothing sight against his sheets. Even now he could feel her in his arms, feel the heat of her body under his, the warmth of her touch on his skin.

How could he protect her?

"Trust in the Morrigán, Speirr. Never doubt her loyalty to you. Never question her actions. Just know that when she can, she will always help you." Those were the last words his father had ever spoken to him.

Closing his eyes, Talon could still see his father's face in the firelight that night. See the older man's pride and love shining at him as his father embraced him and sent him to bed.

He had held tight to those words, and no one had ever defeated him in battle. Not by ambush or by trickery.

In the end, it had been the enemy at home who had destroyed him. The last person he had suspected.

His cousin had wanted to be king so badly that he had known the only way to power would be to kill off both Talon and Ceara.

Talon had never suspected his cousin of setting up the death of his aunt and uncle.

Talon had learned of the man's treachery only after the Druids had slain him and Ceara.

The night Talon had shown up to take vengeance on his clan, his cousin had confessed everything, trying to get Talon to spare him.

It hadn't mattered. Young, angry, and hurt, Talon had taken his revenge against all of them, and then cast off his emotions and hardened his heart.

Hardened it until a fey beauty had looked up at him on a quiet street with large brown eyes that seared him.

He loved her. Her laughter, her wit.

She had made him feel again. Made him complete.

Without her, he didn't want to live at all.

But he refused to see her killed because of him.

"I have to let her go."

He had no choice.

Chapter 13

Zarek stood outside on the upper crosswalk of Jackson Brewery, looking down Wilkinson Street. He had his hands braced on the iron banister as he stared at the people below who were walking along Decatur Street, drifting in and out of shops, restaurants, and clubs.

Word had come down from Acheron that he was supposed to stay inside his townhouse until Mardi Gras. He probably should have listened, but taking orders wasn't exactly something he excelled at anymore.

Besides, the harsh February climate in Alaska kept him housebound entirely too much. He hated feeling trapped.

When he'd left Fairbanks, it had been fourteen below zero. It was currently fifty-seven degrees in New Orleans and even with the chill wind coming off the river, it was nothing like what he was used to.

This was a balmy summer night in comparison.

Though late June and July days in Fairbanks could get as high as the low nineties, by the time the sun set and he could go outside into the eerie twilight that never turned completely dark, he'd be damned lucky to feel a night as warm as this one.

And of course, in the dead of summer in Fairbanks, he'd be really fortunate if he could go outside for more than a few minutes before the sun rose again and forced him back indoors.

For nine hundred years, he'd been banished to that harsh, extreme terrain.

Now at long last, he had a reprieve.

Closing his eyes, Zarek inhaled the air, which was thick with life. He smelled the mixture of foods and river. Heard the sound of laughter and revelry.

He really liked this city. No wonder Talon and Kyrian had claimed it.

He only wished that he could stay here for a little while longer. Stay where there were others of his kind. Where there were people who would talk to him.

But he was used to wanting things he couldn't have.

The door on his right opened and a small boy stepped out. The runt was cute enough for an ankle-biter. He had short brown hair and was sobbing. The kid pulled up sharply at the sight of Zarek standing there.

Zarek ignored him.

"Hey, mister?" the boy said, his voice trembling. "Can you help me? I'm lost."

Zarek took a deep breath and pushed himself away from the railing.

He tucked his clawed hand into his pants pocket and turned around. "Believe me, kid. I know the feeling."

He offered the child his bare hand and was stunned at how small and trusting the boy was. He couldn't remember a time in his life he would have ever reached out to someone and trusted them not to hurt him. "So, who are we looking for? Your mom or your dad?"

"My mommy. She's really pretty and big."

Zarek nodded. "What's her name?"

"Mommy."

Now that was really helpful . . . not. "How old are you, kid?"

"I'm this many." He sniffed back his tears and held up four little fingers. "How old are you?"

"A lot more than four fingers."

The boy held up all ten. "This many?"

Zarek smiled in spite of himself. "C'mon," he said,

opening the door. "I'm sure there's someone inside who can help you find your mommy."

The boy wiped his face with his sleeve as Zarek led him into the Brewery. They hadn't gone far when he heard a woman gasp.

"What are you doing with my son?"

"Mommy!" The boy bolted toward the woman.

She grabbed the child up and the feral, suspicious look she cast Zarek let him know a hasty exit would be wise.

Some nights it didn't pay to appear dark and sinister.

"Security!" she shrieked.

Zarek cursed and ran back out the door. He leapt over the banister, to the stairs a story below, and quickly lost himself in the crowd.

Or so he thought.

As soon as he was halfway down Wilkinson, he saw Acheron waiting in the shadows.

This was just what he friggin' needed—Acheron to chew him out for locking Nick in the closet and leaving the house while he was under orders to stay put.

Zarek snarled. "Don't start on me, Ash."

Acheron cocked a brow at that. "Start on you for what?"

The hair on the back of his neck rose. Acheron was too relaxed and there was no tensing of his shoulders like Acheron always got when they came into contact with each other.

They had declared their mutual dislike for each other over two thousand years ago.

The man in front of him was acting as if Zarek were one of the Dark-Hunters Acheron was friendly with.

It sent a chill up his spine.

Hatred and anger he could take, a friendly Acheron made him nervous.

"Aren't you here to chew me out?" Zarek asked.

"Now, why would I do that?" He clapped him on the shoulder.

Zarek hissed as he moved away from him. "Who the hell are you?"

"What's wrong, Zarek?"

There was no way this was Acheron.

Zarek used his telekinesis to pull the sunglasses off the man's face. Instead of swirling mercury eyes, this man had blue ones.

The stranger narrowed his human eyes on him. "That was unwise."

The next thing Zarek knew, he was hit with a god-bolt.

Talon was strapped to his exercise bar, doing inverted sit-ups when Sunshine finally came awake

Hissing, she sat up in bed, slowly. Languidly. "It's so hot in here," she said, her voice low and throaty.

Talon relaxed his body as he watched her, letting himself hang upside down while his fingertips brushed the floor. "How are you feeling?"

She pulled her shirt off, over her head, and he instantly tensed at the sight of the black lace bra cupping her breasts.

"Hungry," she breathed, releasing the front catch on her bra. "And not for food."

He arched a brow at that, and at the way she trailed her hands over her breasts, down to her pants.

Oh, this was cruel.

She pulled her pants off slowly, sensually. "I need you, Talon."

"I think you need a cold shower."

She moved toward him like a stalking lioness.

Mesmerized, Talon didn't move until she reached him and ran her hand down his thighs. She bent her head to nuzzle and lick the back of his knees.

Talon moaned at how good she felt. His body hardened and throbbed as he pulled himself up, intending to unhook his boots from the bar. But he never got the chance. Sunshine waylaid his lips and kissed him passionately.

Sunshine couldn't think straight as she pulled back and stared into his midnight-black eyes. Her body was alive. On fire. All she could focus on was her throbbing need to have him inside her. A burning itch to have his hands on her body.

She'd never felt such potent lust. Such a hunger to taste and feel every tiny morsel of a man's body.

Oh, how she wanted him.

She took his hands and led them to her breasts. "Make love to me, Talon. Please."

Talon hesitated. "I don't know if we should do this while you're under the infl—" He stopped mid-sentence as she pushed his shorts up to his knees.

Possessed with a powerful lust she'd never known, Sunshine gently nibbled his sensitive hipbone. He moaned deep in his throat, spurring her on while she raked her hand through his short curls, letting them wrap around her fingers until she cupped him in her hand.

Talon couldn't move as wave after wave of pleasure racked him.

She ran her hand down his shaft, making him harden even more. "Hmm," she breathed. "What have we here?"

She took the tip of his shaft into her mouth, circling him with her tongue, drawing him deep into her moist heat. Reaching for her bare legs, he growled in pleasure and pulled her closer to him.

She sucked more of him into her mouth while her fingers stroked his sac, sending spikes of pleasure through his entire body.

It was a damned good thing he was hanging here. As good as she felt, had he been standing he would no doubt have been on the floor right now.

Closing his eyes, Talon savored the feel of her tongue and mouth caressing him, licking him, sucking him, of her hand spurring his ecstasy on to a dangerous level.

Talon encircled her waist with his arm and nibbled the tender spot of her hipbone. She moaned deep in her throat. The vibration of it reverberated through his entire body.

Sunshine shivered as Talon nudged her legs apart. She wrapped her arms around his waist, feasting on him while he stroked her tenderly with his fingers. She could feel his stomach muscles flex with his every move. The steeliness of them made her delirious, and when he took her into his mouth, she moaned aloud.

Her head reeling, she continued to tease him with her tongue and lips while he worked magic on her body with his mouth. She'd never felt anything like this mutual giving. The mutual need to touch each other and give each other pleasure.

His tongue slid over her core, caressing her, stoking her to such a height that her knees felt weak. She ran her hands down his back, to his shoulders, pressing him closer to her.

She rocked herself shamelessly against him, all the while licking and teasing him in return, tasting the saltiness of his body.

Her body quivered in bliss an instant before waves of pleasure tore through her. Crying out, she let her release wash over her.

Still he nibbled and teased until he had wrung the very last tremor from her body.

Only then did Sunshine pull back. He looked up at her and smiled. "I love the way you taste," he said, his voice hoarse.

She returned his smile. "You know, your face is *very* red."

He laughed as he pulled himself up and unhooked his feet from the bar. "And I have a headache from it, but I don't really care if my head explodes. You are more than worth it."

He started to pull his shorts up, but she stopped him.

Trailing her hands and lips down his steely abs, to his legs, she removed the shoes and shorts. "I'm going to lick you from head to toe."

He arched a brow.

She ran her fingers between his toes, sending chills all over him. "I am going to make you scream for mercy before I'm through with you."

Now there was a promise he wanted fulfilled. Talon closed his eyes and groaned as she licked his toes, one by one. Her tongue slid sensually between them, electrifying him and making his body even harder. Stiffer.

Then, she moved up his body, her nails scraping against his flesh. "You are mine to toy with," she said in a bad Slavic-style accent.

Talon hissed as she nibbled her way back up his legs. Her tongue and teeth teased the flesh of his legs, his inner thighs.

With a throaty laugh, she pulled back and smiled up at him.

Talon watched her heatedly as she cupped her breasts in her hands and wrapped them around his shaft. He fisted his hands while she rubbed herself up and down him.

"You like that?" she asked in an evil tone.

"Yes," he said, his voice deep and ragged.

"Then let's see what else I can find that you like."

Sunshine moved him to the futon and pushed him back into a reclining position, then she crawled slowly up his body, and straddled his hips.

She gasped as he slid his fingers inside her. She was so wet for him, so hot. She needed his touch.

He laid her back against the mattress, then knelt between her legs.

Her heart pounding, she stared up at him.

"Put your feet on the wall behind me."

She did as he asked.

He lifted her hips, then drove himself inside.

Sunshine cried out as he filled her with pleasure. He was so thick and full, his strokes masterful, as he rocked himself between her legs. From this position, he was able to penetrate her completely while she was able to lift her hips more and meet him stroke for stroke, driving him in ever deeper and harder.

Talon growled at how good she felt. He placed his hands on her hips, moving faster.

He braced himself over her with one arm on the mattress, and kissed her lips while he trailed his free hand down so that he could slide his fingers through the moist triangle of dark hair and stroke her cleft.

Her entire body quivered as he used his fingers to stroke her in time to his thrusts. He drove himself deep into her and then paused, savoring the feel of her moist heat. Oh, how he needed this woman. Needed this connection to her.

This wasn't just physical between them. It was so much more.

She moaned, then slowly started rocking herself against him.

"That's it, baby," he whispered in her ear. "Ride me all you want to."

And she did.

Closing his eyes, he ground his teeth to stave off his orgasm so that he could just feel her taking pleasure from him. He loved her like this. Wild and demanding. She was completely shameless in his arms.

How he had missed her and how damned grateful he was to have her again.

He wanted to possess her. To chain her to him for the rest of eternity.

If only he knew how.

Desperate with need, he sat back on his knees and took control again.

Sunshine growled with ecstasy as Talon slammed himself into her, even deeper than before. She met his strokes with a frenzied need.

And when she came again, she moaned his name.

She heard him laugh deep in her ear before he joined her.

She smiled as he pulled away from her and then lay down on the futon. Kissing him, she placed herself over him like a blanket.

"Mmm," she breathed. "This is what I wanted to do to you the first night we met."

"What? Screw my brains out?"

She punched playfully at his stomach. "That too, but no, I wanted to be your blanket."

He ran his hands through her hair, cupping her head. "Baby, you can be my blanket any time you feel the urge."

She definitely felt the urge. Smiling wickedly, she rubbed herself against him, then gave him a deep, passionate kiss.

"You do know I'm not through with you?" she said, using his words.

"No?"

She shook her head. "I'm just getting started."

By dawn, Talon was sweaty and exhausted. And he was sore in places he hadn't known a man could get sore.

He wasn't sure if he ever wanted to have sex again . . .

Talon laughed at the thought. Yeah, right. But he at least wanted a few hours of rest before they had another marathon.

He was still breathing heavily as Sunshine finally drifted off to sleep, lying by his side with her hand tangled in his hair and her leg draped over his bare thighs.

Jeez, Ash hadn't been kidding about her appetite. She had contorted his body into positions he hadn't known he was capable of. Right now, he had no energy whatsoever. In fact, he never wanted to leave this bed again, and if she had rolled over one more time and grabbed him, he might even have whimpered.

Groaning at the thought, he reached over to his nightstand, grabbed his phone, and called Acheron to check in. He only hoped that this time the phone actually worked.

It did.

As always, Acheron answered on the first ring.

"Hey, is it the good Ash or the bad Ash?"

"Good, bad, I'm the one with the gun."

Talon snorted at the answer. It was a quote from the campy movie *Army of Darkness* that Acheron adored. "Only the real Ash would be weird enough to pull that quote."

"Gee, thanks, Celt. So what's up? Has Sunshine come awake yet?"

"Yes, she did."

"And you're still able to walk and move?"

"Let's not go there."

Ash gave a short half-laugh. "Yeah, okay. So what do you need?"

"I got a call from the imposter not long after I got back here with Sunshine."

Total silence answered him. He couldn't even hear static on the cell line.

"Hey, T-Rex, you there?"

"I'm here. What did he say?"

"Mostly that he hates you. At first I thought it was you, but he said a couple of things I knew didn't sound right."

"Such as?"

"He said he—meaning *you*—had been addicted to this drug he fed Sunshine. Getting anything that personal out of you is like removing a tooth from a lion without a tranquilizer."

Again Acheron was totally silent.

"Hey, bud, you still with me?" Talon asked.

"Did he say anything else?"

"Yeah, he said you had a sister you let die. I called him a liar and we passed a few insults, then he hung up on me."

Talon heard Nick in the background calling for Ash while Zarek growled for Nick to let go of him. "Something wrong?"

"Nick just brought Zarek in. He's hurt. Let me let you go."

"Okay, but call back and let me know what's going on."

"Will do." The phone went dead.

Now that was weird too. Frowning, Talon set his phone down and returned to Sunshine.

Sunshine came awake screaming.

Talon grabbed her as she thrashed about on the futon.

"Shh," he breathed against her hair. "It's me, Talon. You're safe."

She was trembling against him. "I thought I was still . . ." She tightened her arms around him. "Oh God, Talon, I was so scared."

Anger pierced his heart. "I'm sorry I couldn't protect you. Did they hurt you?"

She shook her head. "They just scared me. Especially the one they called Styxx."

"Styxx? Like the Greek river?"

She nodded. "He had this crazy look to him. Spooky. His eyes were so full of hatred and he had a constant snarl. Camulus had to keep calming him down."

Talon ground his teeth. He fully intended to find both assholes and put a major hurt on them. "I'm sorry, baby. I promise you, they'll never get their hands on you again."

Sunshine tightened her arms around him. "I'm so glad you found me, but how did you know where I was?"

"Camulus called me."

The news stunned her. "Why?"

"I don't know. I think he just wants to play with my head. He's twisted that way."

She sat there, feeling sick to her stomach. "What did they give me?"

"Some kind of drug. An aphrodisiac. Did they use it with you?"

"No," she said. "They forced me to drink it, then left me alone. It was really nasty stuff. I still feel so light-headed and strange." She looked at him and smiled. "But I remember what I did with you."

"Yeah, so do I."

She laughed and her body protested the movement. "Are you as sore as I am?"

"Let's just say I'm in no hurry to get out of bed."

Sunshine traced his tattoo as she took comfort in being safe with him. It was so good to just feel him by her side again. To hear the sound of his voice. She remembered the gunshots they had fired into him and how terrified she had been that he would somehow die from the wounds.

Now there was no sign at all that he had ever been shot.

"I'm so glad they didn't kill you," she breathed.

"Believe me, I feel the same way about you."

She ran her hand over his nipple and then froze as she felt suddenly sick.

"Sunshine?"

She left the bed and rushed for the bathroom.

Talon followed after her and then held her while she unloaded the rest of the drug from her system.

Sunshine didn't know how long she was in there. It seemed like she would never stop heaving.

Talon stayed with her the entire time, holding her hair, washing her face with a cold, damp cloth.

"Are you okay?" he asked when she finally stopped.

"I don't know. I feel awful."

He kissed the top of her head. "I'll go get you a Coke and some crackers. It'll help you settle your stomach."

She thanked him, then went to the sink to brush her teeth while he went to get the Coke.

When she left the bathroom, she found Talon waiting in bed for her.

She sat down beside him and pulled the covers over her body. She was still shaky and queasy.

Talon handed her a cracker and a can of Coke.

"Hmm," she said, taking them from him. "You must like me a lot to let me eat crackers in your bed."

He brushed the hair back from her face. His eyes burned her with their intensity. "Yes, I do."

His words sent a chill over her. "Do you, Talon? Or is it Nynia you love? When you look at me, do you see Sunshine or your wife?"

"I see you both."

Sunshine cringed at his answer. That wasn't what she wanted to hear. All her life, she had struggled to be herself. Her parents accepted her, but the guys she'd dated had all wanted to change her.

Even Jerry.

The last guy she dated had only been interested in her because she reminded him of his ex-girlfriend.

Now she reminded Talon of his ex-wife.

She couldn't win for losing.

Why couldn't someone just love her for being Sunshine?

Would Talon be so tender and attentive now if she weren't his wife reincarnated?

"What do you like about me?" she asked, nibbling her cracker.

"I like your fire and I love your body."

"Gee, thanks. Does that mean if I were fat and hideous you'd run for the door?"

"Would you run for the door if I was?"

Touché. The man was quick with a comeback. "Probably so. No doubt, I'd break it down trying to escape you."

He laughed at that. "I'd run after you if you did."

"Would you?"

"Yes, I would."

But would he run after Sunshine or Nynia?

The question haunted her.

Sunshine leaned over and kissed his forehead. "You need to get some sleep. You look really tired." And he did.

It was almost noon and, unlike her, he wasn't used to staying up all day.

"Okay. Remember, Nick is four and a pound sign on the phone if you need anything. And don't go far. Camulus will be coming back, I just don't know when. At least here I know the gators will slow them down. So make sure you stay close enough that I can reach you if something happens."

She nodded. "If I'm not in the cabin, I'll be right outside the door painting. Promise."

"Okay." He nuzzled her cheek tenderly, then kissed her. "I'll see you in a few hours."

Sunshine tucked him into the bed, got dressed, turned out the lights, and quietly went outside to paint.

As the afternoon went by while she sat on the porch, she realized that Talon had lived out here for centuries and in all that time he had never once seen the beauty of the swamp during the light of day.

He'd never seen sunlight dappling the water. Never seen the vibrant green of the moss on the stump by his dock. At night the edge was taken off the colors.

It was such a shame that he had to live like that. Alone in a world without . . .

She cringed as the word *sunshine* popped into her head.

"Jeez," she muttered. "How cheesy is that?"

Still, it didn't stop her heart from aching for him.

He was loneliness.

Because of Camulus, Talon didn't dare let anyone close to him. How terrible it must be.

At dusk, she packed up her art supplies and headed inside with Beth eyeballing her from the dock. Sunshine wrinkled her nose at the bossy gator and tossed her the remains of her crackers.

Physically, Sunshine felt a lot better, but mentally she ached.

She watched Talon as he slept. He was a creature of the night. Literally. She couldn't change him. Ever.

He was immortal.

She was human.

There was no hope for them.

The thought made her want to cry.

"They do have an out clause."

But Talon would have to agree to it, and then what? Would she have to be his wife? Would he expect her to be as Nynia was?

She shivered at the thought. No offense, but as Nynia she had been a ninny.

Not that it was wrong to live to please your husband, but as Nynia she'd taken that to a whole new level. Nynia had never questioned him, never said anything back to him.

He said jump, she'd jumped and not even bothered to ask how high. Whatever he'd wanted, she'd done, regardless of her own thoughts or wants.

She had been a Stepford wife. Ew!

Sunshine didn't think she could behave that way if she had to. She was outspoken and stubborn. At times, she was even a little selfish.

She wanted a mutual partnership with a man. Someone who could handle her needs as an artist. Someone who could appreciate her while she appreciated him, faults and all.

She liked herself. Liked her life.

With Talon, she would never be quite sure if he loved her for being Sunshine or if he tolerated her because of Nynia.

How would she ever know the truth?

Talon woke up to the softness of a hand brushing through his hair. He didn't have to open his eyes to know who it was who touched him. He could feel her all the way to his heart.

Sunshine.

He blinked open his eyes to see her sitting beside him.

"Good morning," she said.

"Evening."

She handed him a cup of coffee. Talon took a drink, expecting to cringe, but it was actually good. *Very* good.

At his surprised look, she laughed. "My parents sell coffee at the bar. I may not drink the stuff, but I do know how to make it."

"You do it very well."

She beamed.

Talon sat back in bed to watch her. "What did you do while I slept?"

"Worked. I have to meet a client and show him some pieces he commissioned. If he really likes them, he's going to give me a contract to supply artwork and murals for his restaurant chain."

"Really?" he asked, impressed by the news.

Her eyes glowed with excitement, her cheeks pinkened. He could tell it meant a lot to her. "If I get the contract, no more stand at the square. I'll finally have enough money to open my own studio."

"You know, I could give you the money for that."

A sadness came over her. "So could my parents, but this is something I want to do on my own. I don't want anyone to hand me anything."

He well understood that. He'd spent most of his mortal life proving himself to others. "It never hurts to have help."

"I know. But it wouldn't be the same. Besides, I think it would be really neat to walk into a restaurant and see my stuff hanging there."

"Yeah, it would be. I hope you get the contract."

She smiled again. "What about you? What do you hope for?"

"I hope my cabin never blows apart in a hurricane during the daylight hours."

She laughed. "Seriously."

"I am serious. It could get ugly if it did."

She sat back on her heels. "You really don't have any plans for the future, do you?"

"There's nothing to plan for, Sunshine. I'm a Dark-Hunter."

"Do you ever think about quitting?"

"Never."

"Not even now?"

He fell silent as he thought about that. "If I could get past Camulus maybe. But . . ."

Sunshine nodded, understanding that stumbling block all too well. Camulus had laughed at her when she'd asked if he would/could ever forgive Talon.

"The earth will perish before I leave him in peace. So long as I live, he will pay for taking my son's life."

But she didn't tell Talon about that. She didn't want to upset him.

Somehow, she would find another way around Camulus.

"All right," she said. "I won't mention it again. Let's just enjoy what time we have."

"Sounds like a plan."

They spent the night quietly, playing games and talking. Sunshine scrounged through his kitchen and even found enough supplies to make edible body paint.

Talon introduced her to chocolate Reddi-Whip shots and delighted in the ecstasy on her face while she ate the decadent whipped cream.

And Talon finally got to douse her in chocolate and to lick it off her.

Who knew having an artist could be so much fun?

Talon had never in his life enjoyed anything more than this night. He'd never laughed so much. Felt so at ease and comfortable. There was no more hiding from her. She knew what he was, both as a Dark-Hunter and as a man.

She fell asleep not long after midnight and left him alone to think about them.

Talon went outside to sit on the porch. It was peaceful and cold outside. The fog on the swamp was thick and he could hear the water ripple all around him.

For centuries this had been his solitary existence.

He couldn't count the times he had sat here alone, just listening to the darkness.

And on the other side of the closed door he had heaven itself waiting for him.

If only he could keep her.

How did a man beat back a god? Was it even possible?

As a mortal man, the thought had never occurred to him, but now . . .

Now he wondered . . .

Talon went to bed a few hours after sunup. He'd only been asleep about an hour when he heard Sunshine rummaging around his desk.

"What are you doing?" he asked groggily.

"I'm looking for the keys to the boat."

"Why?"

"I told you, I have to go meet a client."

Talon rubbed his blurry eyes as he tried to focus on what she was saying. "What?"

"I told you about it last night, remember? I'm supposed to meet him at my stand at eleven. I promise I'll meet with him and then be back as soon as I can."

"You can't do that."

She paused and looked at him. "I told you how important this is to me. To my career."

"Sunshine, don't be stupid. This is your life we're talking about."

"Yes, it is." She went back to searching the desk. "And I'm not going to let some sick psycho screw up my one shot at what I want. Believe me, if that weirdo comes near me today, I'll make sure it's the last mistake he ever makes. I didn't know they were after me before. Now I do and I can take care of myself."

Angered that she would dare disregard him, Talon got up. "I'm not about to let you leave here."

"Don't tell me what to do, Talon. My own father doesn't order me around. I'm a grown woman, with my own thoughts, and I will not have anyone dictate my life to me."

"Dammit, Sunshine, be reasonable. I don't want you hurt."

"Why? Because you love me?"

"Yes, I do."

They both froze as he snarled the angry words.

Her heart fluttered. She wanted to believe that. Desperately. But was it true?

"Do you really?" she asked, her voice thick and heavy.

Talon watched as she opened the velvet-lined silver chest on his desk that held the torc that was identical to his, only smaller.

A woman's torc.

Nynia's torc.

She handed him the open box. "Or is it Nynia you love?"

Talon closed his eyes, unable to bear the sight of his wife's torc. He should have destroyed it centuries ago.

But he couldn't.

He'd shut it away and kept it out of sight.

It had never been out of his thoughts.

Sunshine closed the box and returned it to his desk. "I have to do this. *For me.* I won't live my life afraid. Camulus knows we're together. He can take or kill me here as easily as he can in town. He's a god, Talon. It's not like we can hide from him."

Talon winced as her words tore through him. In his mind, he saw his uncle cut down as he struggled to his side. Saw the killing blow that had sent his uncle to the ground before Talon could reach him.

Pain ripped through his chest. He well understood Sunshine's need to prove herself, to have something of her own. But he couldn't send her out there alone, unprotected.

Besides, he needed his full strength to fight and protect her, which meant he needed more rest. If he went out tonight while he was exhausted, he could get them both killed.

If he returned to bed while she was here, he had little doubt that she would sneak out of the cabin the minute he closed his eyes.

And if she took his boat, he'd be stranded out here until he could get Nick to bring him the other boat in the shed.

Dammit.

"Fine," he said irritably, reaching for his cell phone. There was only one person besides Ash who had the strength and powers to fight a god and possibly escape him. "You can go, but you're taking someone with you."

"Who?"

He held his hand up to silence her as Vane answered.

The Katagari didn't sound particularly happy to hear his voice. "I didn't give you permission to call me, Celt."

"Bite me, Wolf-boy. I need a favor."

"You'll owe me a favor for it."

He looked at Sunshine.

For her, anything.

"And I'm willing to pay it," he said to Vane.

"All right then, what do you need?"

"Can you take human form in daylight?"

Vane scoffed. "Obviously so. Ever tried to answer a phone without opposable thumbs? Not to mention the fact that I am speaking to you in English and not wolf."

Talon growled low at the sarcasm. "Yes, but can you hold and fight in human form during daylight?"

He snorted at that. "Oh yeah. Daylight doesn't bother me."

"Good. Sunshine needs to go to Jackson Square for a little while this morning."

"Did you okay this with Ash?"

"No."

Vane laughed. "Living on the edge. I love it. Okay, so what do you need me to do?"

"I want you to guard her until I can take over after nightfall."

"One guard dog coming up. Give me about half an hour to get there."

"All right, thanks."

"I would say anytime, Celt, but this is a one-shot-only deal."

"Yeah, I know."

Sunshine frowned as he hung up the phone. "Who was that?"

"That was Vane."

"Is he a Dark-Hunter too?"

"No, love. You're about to meet your werewolf."

Chapter 14

Vane wasn't just any werewolf, Sunshine discovered. He was *the* werewolf, judging by the tough, hard-edged aura he projected.

He entered the cabin wearing a pair of faded jeans and a white T-shirt with a weathered motorcycle jacket, black cowboy boots, and a body that would cause a traffic jam.

And when he removed his sunglasses, her breath caught in her throat.

Even in height with Talon, he was stunningly gorgeous. His startlingly green eyes were a perfect contrast for his hair which at first glance appeared an extremely dark chestnut, but on closer view seemed to be made up of every color known. There were traces of ash and gold, red and black. She'd never seen hair like that in her life.

At least not on a human . . .

He wore it long, hanging just below his collar. She could tell he didn't spend any time with it, just brushed his hands through it and went.

But what captivated her most was the raw, overt male sexuality he oozed. One that ranked right up there with Talon's sexiness. Vane moved with the fluid grace of a predator, with his head held low as if ready to attack.

Grrrr, but the man was a fetching beast.

"You're early," Talon said.

Vane shrugged, his body a symphony of movement. "It

didn't take as long to leave the pack as I thought it would."

The werewolf looked to her and gave her a knee-melting smile. "You really going to trust me with your female, Celt?"

"Yes, I am, because in this swamp, *I* rule."

Vane arched a skeptical brow. "That a threat?"

"It's a promise, Vane. I have my army camped on your doorstep to protect your family. I ask the same of you."

"I'll respect your trust, Celt. But only because I know how rarely you give it."

A look of mutual understanding passed between them.

Vane put his sunglasses back on. "You ready, baby?"

Sunshine stiffened at his offhand endearment. He might be cute, but she had no intention of letting him get away with that one. "You're not my boyfriend or my brother, so lay off the 'baby' thing, okay?"

He flashed a set of killer dimples. "Yes, ma'am." He held the door open until she walked past him. "See you after dark, Celt."

"Yes, you will."

Sunshine paused on the porch and looked about for their ride out of here. "Where's your boat?"

"I don't do the boat thing. It's loud and it takes too long."

"Then how are we going to get out of here?"

Vane smiled devilishly and held his hand out to her. "Trust me?"

Was he joking? "No, I don't even know you."

He laughed, a warm, rich sound that was seductive and charming, although strangely enough, it had no real effect on her. She could appreciate how appealing he was, but her heart and loyalty belonged to Talon.

"All right, then, Dorothy," he said. "Close your eyes, click your heels three times, and say, 'There's no place like home.' "

"What?"

Before she could blink, he took her hand and they flashed from the porch to a wooded area where a small trail broke through the trees. She had no idea where they were, but Talon's cabin was nowhere in sight.

Sunshine gasped. "What did you do?"

"I beamed you over."

"What are you, Scotty?"

He gave her a taunting look as if he were enjoying her discomfort. "It's correctly called a lateral time jump. I just moved you through horizontal time from Talon's porch, across the swamp to where my motorcycle is hidden. Simple."

"Horizontal time? I don't understand."

"Time flows in three directions," he explained. "Forward, backward, and laterally. If you do nothing at all, time always flows forward, but if you catch the Rytis just right, you can choose one of the other directions."

Totally confused, she frowned at him as she tried to comprehend what he was telling her. "What's the Rytis?"

"For lack of a better term, it's warp space."

When she continued to scowl, he pulled his jacket off. "Let me explain it this way." He held the shoulder of his jacket in his right hand and the end of the sleeve in his left. "Time is like this . . . If you want to get from here"—he moved his right hand—"to here," he said, moving his left, "you see how far you have to travel?"

She nodded as she noted the long length of his sleeve. The man had really long arms.

"The Rytis is essentially invisible waves that move around us all the time. Through everything on the planet. They echo and flow and sometimes they buckle. In essence, they do this." He compacted the sleeve between his hands so that his left and right hand were next to each other. "Now to travel from hand to hand, it takes a few seconds instead of several hours."

"Wow," she breathed as she understood. "So you can travel in any time direction? You can even go back in time?"

He nodded.

"And how do you do that? How do you catch this Rytis?"

He shrugged his jacket back on. "Baby, in this world, I'm the all-powerful Oz and there's not much I can't do."

Oh, this guy was getting irritating. "Stop calling me baby."

He inclined his head to her and moved to a tree. Two seconds later, a sleek dark gray motorcycle appeared out of nowhere.

"Okay, how did you do that?"

"In short, I'm a sorcerer. I can bend every law of physics known to mankind and a few not yet discovered."

She was impressed. "That's some serious talent."

Again that dark, deep laugh. "Baby, if you weren't with Talon, I would show you where my true talents lie."

She just bet he would too.

He handed her a helmet.

"You're calling me baby strictly to irritate me, aren't you?"

"My father always said I was born to be the barnacle up his nether regions. I guess I can't help it."

"Do me a favor. Try."

Flashing his dimples, he removed his sunglasses, put them in the inside pocket of his motorcycle jacket, and placed a helmet on his head.

"So tell me," she said. "If you can do all this magic stuff, why are we riding a bike into town? Couldn't you just time-jump us over to the square?"

He fastened his chin strap as he answered her. "I could. But as Acheron so often says, just because you can do something, it doesn't mean you should. Personally, I don't want to be some guy's lab experiment, so I try not to pop in and out of populated areas if I can help it."

That made sense to her. "Since you can time-travel, do you ever think about changing the past?"

"Yes."

"Have you ever done it?"

He shook his head and a dark earnestness came over his

face. "There are some powers in this world that are best left alone. Altering someone's destiny is definitely one of them. Believe me, the Fates have a nasty way of putting a hurt on anyone dumb enough to mess with their domain."

His ominous words rang in her ears. He sounded as if he had once made that mistake, and she wanted to ask if he had, but something inside told her to let it be.

Sunshine put her helmet on, then climbed on the back of the motorcycle and did her best to keep some distance between them. Vane was a handsome man, but something about him made her extremely nervous, and it wasn't the fact he was a werewolf or time-walker.

There was something about him she didn't trust.

At her request, he took her to the small art gallery where she kept her cart of artwork locked up and helped her wheel it to Jackson Square.

By the time they got there, it was a little after ten, and there was a huge crowd already gathered.

"I don't get it," Vane said as he wheeled her cart toward Selena's card stand. "Why are you setting up shop if you just want to meet a client?"

"Cameron said he wanted to see everything I sell. If I have to drag it all out for him, I might as well sell it to other people too."

She showed him where to set it up.

Vane did, but he didn't look too pleased about it.

Selena did a double take as she caught sight of them. "Someone new, Sunny?"

"No, he's just a—"

"Guard dog," he said, extending his hand out to her. "You're Selena Laurens, right? Amanda's older sister?"

Selena nodded as she shook his hand. "You know Amanda?"

"I know Kyrian."

"Is it just me or does everyone know Kyrian?" Sunshine asked.

Selena laughed, then turned back to Vane who was opening up Sunshine's card table where she usually placed her cheaper pottery pieces. "It's daylight so I know you're not a DH. Are you a Squire?"

He stiffened. "Don't insult me. I fetch for no one."

"He's not real friendly," Sunshine explained as she set up her stand. "I think he has rabies or something."

Vane gave her a half amused, half perturbed smile. "You know, Sunshine, I like your spirit."

Sunshine started to respond, but she felt someone watching her.

Scared and anxious, she looked around the crowd until she saw a bright, smiling face that was as familiar to her as her own.

Sunshine beamed.

Even though she wasn't very tall, the elderly woman stood out in the crowd and it wasn't just the insanely bright red shirt she wore. The older woman had an essence and presence that was as powerful and strong as Talon's or Vane's.

Her steel-gray hair was worn up in braids that were wrapped around her head. Her face was lined by a lifetime of happiness and smiles, and her dark brown eyes were bright and kind. The kind of eyes that drew people to the extremely wise woman.

"Grammy!" Sunshine said, as the older woman drew near. "What are you doing here? I thought you swore to never step foot in New Orleans again during Mardi Gras."

Her grandmother squeezed her tight, then pulled back to look at her. It'd been almost a year since they had last seen each other.

Oh, it was great to see her grandmother again!

Her grandmother ran her hand up and down her arm as if reassuring herself that Sunshine was healthy. "Well, that was my intention, but your mother called and told me that you were having all kinds of questions about being a Celt. So I thought I'd just pop in and surprise you."

"You certainly did. But I'm glad you're here."

Her grandmother arched a censuring brow as she caught sight of Vane. "And you are?"

"Vane Kattalakis."

She looked back at Sunshine. "Where's this Talon your mother told me about?"

"He'll be here later, Grammy."

She nodded, then pulled a small medallion out from under her shirt and placed it around Sunshine's neck.

"What's this?"

Her grandmother adjusted it so that it would be obvious to anyone who glanced at her. "Keep that close to your heart, little one. If that man comes after you again, you let him know who protects you."

"What man?" she asked, hoping her grandmother didn't know about her kidnapping.

She did.

"I know what happened, Sunny. You know I do."

Drat. Her grandmother had some eerie psychic talents.

"I don't think your necklace will scare him, Grammy."

"You'd be surprised. And if it doesn't, then he deserves what he gets." Her grandmother patted her on the shoulder and turned to Selena. "Have you been practicing those exercises I showed you, Ms. Laurens?"

"Yes, ma'am. I can feel my powers growing every day."

"Good. Now I better get back to Starla's. If that rank bastard comes near my baby—"

"Grandma!" Sunshine gasped. She'd never in her life heard her grandmother use such a word.

"Well, he is. Messing with my granddaughter. I'll boil his warts in oil and feed his head to the wolves."

Vane choked on that one. "You know, wolves don't really like to eat heads. Meat, yes, but heads are really hard on the jaws. Not to mention, the cranium gets caught between your teeth."

Her grandmother gave him a withering stare. "Are you being smart with me, boy?"

"Yes."

"Young man," her grandmother said in a haughty tone, "didn't your mother teach you any manners?"

"My mother only taught me one thing and, I promise you, it wasn't manners."

Her grandmother nodded. "I can see that. But you still have a very important lesson to learn in life."

"And that is?"

"One day you're going to have to let someone other than your brother and sister get close to you."

His face turned to stone and the look in his eyes was feral and fierce. "What do you know about my siblings?"

"More than you would care for. You have a hard road ahead of you, Vane Kattalakis. I wish I could ease it for you, but it's yours alone to travel. Just remember, you're a lot stronger than you think you are."

"Believe me, lady, my strength is the one thing I never doubt."

Her grandmother smiled at that. "It's amazing the lies we tell other people, isn't it?"

Her grandmother turned her back on him. "Selena, Sunshine. You two take care. And Sunshine, when tonight comes, follow your heart. Do as it commands, and it won't fail you."

"Okay, Grandma, I will."

Her grandmother kissed her cheek, then headed off toward St. Anne.

After she was out of sight, Sunshine turned back to see Vane looking agitated. "I'm sorry. She does that a lot to people. She tends to just say whatever pops into her head."

Vane didn't speak. Instead, he folded his arms over his chest and leaned back against the black iron fence that surrounded the square.

Sunshine finished setting up her stand, then checked her watch.

It was still a little while before Cameron was due, so she pulled out her sketchbook and started doodling.

Before she realized it, she'd drawn a picture of the man who had kidnapped her.

Vane looked at the sketch. "Damn good likeness."

Sunshine went cold. "You know this guy?"

"Well, yeah. Of course I do. So does Talon. Selena probably knows him too."

"Selena," Sunshine said, heading to her friend. "Do you know who this is?"

"Sure, it's Acheron."

"Who's Acheron?" she asked. Everyone kept mentioning his name around her, but she had no idea who or what he was.

"For lack of a better explanation," Vane said, "Talon's boss."

"Why would Talon's boss kidnap me? Do you think it's to keep me away from Talon?"

Vane laughed at that. "Not his style. If Ash wanted to keep you away from Talon, he'd just show up at your door and scare the crap out of you. Besides, he was the one leading the rescue party to you."

Well, that was nice to know.

But why did he look just like the guy who'd kidnapped her?

Her frown deepened. "He was there when Talon got me away from Camulus?"

"Yeah and I was too. Don't you remember?"

She shook her head. All she could remember was Talon. "How well do you know Talon and Acheron?" she asked Vane.

He shrugged. "I just met Talon, but I've crossed paths with Acheron a time or two over the centuries."

"Are you immortal too?"

He shook his head no. "My kind just lives a lot longer than humans."

"How long?"

"About a thousand years, give or take a century or two."

Wow. That was quite a while.

Sunshine couldn't imagine what it would be like to have that long to plan her future. But something inside told her that it might be as big a curse as a blessing to live that long, especially if you had to live it alone.

Sunshine watched Vane as he scanned the crowd around

them. Those hazel-green eyes seemed to take in everything.

"Why are you so open to talk about this while Talon refuses to tell me anything?"

He shrugged. "I didn't swear an oath of secrecy, and I figure you've seen enough spooky shit the last few days that knowing about me is the least of your problems. Besides, I dare you to tell anyone I'm really a wolf pretending to be human."

He paused and grinned devilishly at her. "I double *dog* dare you," he said slowly. "That, my friend, will get you locked inside a rubber room."

She had no doubt about that at all. And it explained why he felt so free to talk about his "differences." "Are you really a wolf?"

He nodded.

"Then how can you be human?"

"We're a different breed than your people. My race was created about nine thousand years ago when my great-grandfather decided to save the lives of his sons by magically splicing their DNA with a few choice animals. Thus we were born. One son made two half-blooded creatures. One that held a human heart and one that held an animal heart. I'm directly descended from the animal."

"So you have the heart of a wolf?"

Again, he nodded. "And the morals and the self-preservation instincts of one too."

"Do you ever wish you were human?"

"No, never. Why would I?"

And yet she sensed he was hiding something. There was a lot more to his feelings than he was willing to admit and it was obvious he didn't want her to delve into it.

So she changed the subject. "Does it hurt when you change forms? Is it like the movies where you get all hairy and bones crunch?"

He snorted at that. "No. That's strictly a Hollywood dramatization. Since we're born of magic, for the most part we wield it painlessly. I feel about as much pain transforming as you did when we bopped from Talon's cabin to my bike. All you get is a little electrical frizz going through you. It's actually kind of pleasurable if you do it right."

"It must be neat to be able to do all that." She tilted her head, squinted her eyes, and looked at him.

"What are you doing?"

"Trying to imagine what you would look like as a wolf."

"Pray you never find out."

She stepped back from him. "You know, I think you guys really get off on scaring people."

"Sometimes we do."

Not willing to investigate that any further, Sunshine continued to wait.

Unfortunately, Cameron didn't show.

Vane tried to get her to go back to Talon's but she refused. "Maybe he's just late. Maybe he had a meeting or something. I can't just leave."

Vane gave a low, very wolf-sounding growl at that and took up a seat behind her stand, leaning back against the black iron fence while she sat on her stool, hawking her wares and sketching.

The afternoon dragged on, but nothing happened.

Cameron still hadn't shown up.

Selena left at four for a brief break.

Vane was now sitting on the curb behind her. His long legs were stretched out on the street, and he had them crossed at the ankles. He was leaning back on his arms. The position pulled his cotton T-shirt tight over his impeccable body.

"You do this every day?" he asked.

"Pretty much."

"Man, this is boring as hell. What do you do to keep from going insane?"

"I usually sketch or paint, and before I know it, the day has passed and it's time to go home."

"Well, I don't get it."

People who weren't artists never did.

"Hi, Sunshine, you got anything new?"

Sunshine turned to see Bride McTierney approaching

her on the opposite side of the cart. A tall, plus-sized type of voluptuous, Bride had the face of one of Botticelli's angels. Her hair was so dark an auburn that it appeared black unless Bride was outside. Then it was a deep luminescent red. Bride usually wore it up in a clip with tendrils of it falling around her face.

A real sweetheart, Bride was one of her regular clients. She'd even taken some of Sunshine's paintings and used them in her boutique.

"No," Sunshine said, "sorry. I haven't been painting the fantasy or Jackson Square stuff lately. I've mostly been working on commissioned pieces."

"Rats, I just moved into a new apartment and was hoping you'd have something to make the drab walls tolerable."

Sunshine frowned. Bride had loved her place on Iberville. "Why did you move?"

"Taylor doesn't like coming all the way into the city at night so I thought it would be easier if I lived closer to where he works."

"But *you* work in the quarter."

"I know. It's one of the sacrifices we all have to make for love." She offered Sunshine a smile, but Sunshine could tell it was only a façade.

That was exactly what Sunshine was afraid of.

Why was it always the woman who had to sacrifice for love? Just once, couldn't a guy do it instead?

Bride sighed. "Give me a call if you paint anything new that I'd like, okay?"

"I will. By the way, you're looking really good. Have you lost weight?"

Bride beamed. "I'm down to a size sixteen. But I have to tell you that I am starving *all* the time."

"Yeah, but you're a knockout."

"Thanks. Taylor signed me up for an aerobics class at his club that meets four times a week and that helped to get a lot of the weight off."

"You don't sound like you enjoy it very much."

Pain darkened Bride's eyes as she averted her gaze. "I just hate having to put on sweats and then walk into a room filled with size-two women in leotards—like they really need those classes. It makes me want to head to Krispy Kreme even more than the diet does."

Sunshine laughed. "Tell me about it. I personally don't think they should make anything except gunny sacks for anyone under a size ten."

Bride smiled again. "Speaking of dress sizes and skinny women, I guess I better head back to the shop. You take care, okay?"

"You too."

Bride wandered off in the direction of her store.

"Who was that?" Vane was now standing up, staring after Bride with a hungry glint in his eyes.

How did he do that? The man, or rather wolf, moved with an eerie silence.

"Her name is Bride McTierney. She owns a boutique over on Iberville."

"She's . . . very nice."

Sunshine was amazed he thought so. Most guys were intimidated or just plain turned off by Bride's height and Rubenesque build.

Vane looked as if he had just seen a supermodel in the flesh.

Now this could be good . . .

He blinked and returned to sitting on the curb.

"You know, I could introduce the two of you."

He looked up at her, then glanced away. Still, she had glimpsed the regret in his green eyes.

"Wolves don't socialize with humans. You guys tend to freak out when you learn what we are. Not to mention, your females are rather frail. I don't like having to hold back for fear of bruising or killing my partner when I mate."

"And people think I speak my mind. Jeez. You will just say anything, won't you?"

"I told you, I'm not human. I don't share your inhibitions."

She supposed that was true enough. But it was a pity. Bride could use a man who accepted her as she was and didn't put her on strict diets and exercise regimes all the time.

"So," Vane said after a few minutes. "What's between you and the Celt? Are the two of you just casually carnal or is there something more?"

"Why are you asking?"

"Because you've asked me for a full bio. I figure turnabout is fair play."

Sunshine sat down next to him. "I don't know. When I'm with Talon it's like we fit. Like he's a part of me that I didn't know I was missing until I found him."

"Does he feel the same way?"

She sighed wistfully. "Who knows? With him it's hard to tell sometimes. I'm not really sure that *I* am the one he loves."

"True. Emotions don't appear to be his strong suit. Still, you must mean a lot to him for him to call me in."

"How do you figure?"

"Going against Acheron's orders isn't a smart thing for a Dark-Hunter to do. That man has life-and-death control over them. Secondly, Talon was willing to barter with me to keep you safe. Again, not a smart thing to do."

"Why, you're not going to hurt him, are you?"

"Not at the moment, but when you consider the danger my people live in, obligating yourself to a Katagari Slayer is one step away from blatant stupidity."

"A what Slayer?"

"The real term for what I am."

Sunshine frowned at him. "Okay, and what exactly is a Katagari Slayer?"

"Someone who kills without remorse."

A chill went down her spine and yet she found it hard to believe he could be capable of such a thing. He was feral, no doubt, but he didn't seem completely without a conscience in spite of what he said. "Would you really do that?"

"Baby, I would kill my own mother and not think twice."

She remembered what her grandmother had said about his siblings. "Yes, but would you kill your brother or your sister?"

He looked away.

She nudged his shoulder. "You're not as amoral as you pretend, Vane Kattalakis. I think there may be more human inside you than you think."

Sunshine returned to her cart and sat on her stool. She continued to scan the people around her, but as the sun set and Cameron didn't show, she saw no one who even remotely seemed threatening.

Well, no one other than her guard.

Talon was up and dressed before sundown. He was pacing the floor of his cabin, dying to leave and find Sunshine.

Anxious, he dialed Vane.

"She's still alive and unharmed," Vane said without greeting. "Sunshine," he called, "it's the Celt wanting a little reassurance that I haven't eaten you or anything."

Talon rubbed his head at Vane's odd humor as he waited for Sunshine to reach for the phone.

"Talon?"

"Hey, baby, you okay?" Talon asked, instantly relieved to hear her smooth Southern drawl in his ear.

It was the most blessed sound he'd ever known.

"I'm fine. Absolutely nothing has happened. It's been really boring today. Except for Vane. He's interesting in a very Cujoesque sort of way."

He smiled. His mood was instantly lighter just knowing she was okay. "I'll bet. You be careful and I'll be out there as soon as I can."

"Okay. See you soon."

His heart clenched as she made a kissing noise to him,

then handed the phone back to Vane. Gods, how he loved that woman.

"Ahh, Tally, me lub you too."

"Shut up, crotch-sniffer. You're not allowed to make lovey noises at me, only my honey is."

Vane snorted. "You know, I'm really going to make you pay one day."

"Yeah, I'll bring along a few extra kibbles for you."

Vane laughed good-naturedly. "For that, swamp rat, you owe me an extra nice plate of prime rib."

"You got it. How are you doing, by the way? You holding on to your human form without any problems?"

"I'm just peachy. Even managed to keep most of my clothes on and everything."

"Yeah, you do that. Don't want your scrawny body making my Sunshine go blind or anything."

"Trust me, if she hasn't gone blind looking at your fat, hairy ass, mine's not going to hurt her any."

"Hairy? Excuse me, but you definitely have me confused with your brother."

Vane laughed again.

"Seriously, though, the sun'll be down in about fifteen minutes. I'll head out immediately."

"I'm holding down the fort, Custer. Don't worry."

"Thanks, Bull. See you in a bit."

Talon hung up and waited until he could feel the tingling on his skin that always alerted him that the sun was gone and it was safe to leave.

It was about forty-five minutes after dark when Sunshine asked Vane to walk the short distance around the corner to the Coke stand and get her something to drink.

He balked, but she finally convinced him that she would still be in full sight and wouldn't wander off until he returned.

As soon as he got in line, she heard Selena's low whistle.

"Now that man looks scary with a capital *S*. He has serial killer written all over him."

Sunshine turned to see an extremely tall, dark-haired man rounding the corner. The horses that lined Decatur Street snorted and pranced uneasily as he passed by them.

It was as if they sensed something evil about him.

He looked so incredibly sinister that her stomach drew tight. "Should I call Vane back?"

"I don't know." Selena got up from her card table and moved to stand beside Sunshine. "If he makes a move on you, I'll grab him and you scream."

"Okay. Maybe he'll just keep on walking right past us."

He didn't.

He glanced at her cart as he came even with it, then paused.

Sunshine's gaze fell to the vicious-looking silver claws on his left hand.

He didn't speak a word as he approached her cart. She swallowed and instinctively moved closer to Selena. The man would be incredibly handsome if he didn't look so ferocious.

She exchanged nervous looks with Selena.

His dark, deadly gaze was focused on the bowls she had fashioned after a Greek design she'd seen in a museum catalog. With a gentleness she wouldn't have thought him capable of, he ran his hand over a red-figured bowl.

A flash of longing darkened his eyes, as if the design brought back some bittersweet memory for him. "You make these?"

She actually flinched as his intense black gaze met hers. He had a deep, provocative voice that was so heavily accented, it took her a minute to understand his question. "I do."

"Nice work."

She couldn't have been more stunned had he taken a gun out and shot her. "Thanks."

When he reached into his pocket, she braced herself to

scream for Vane until she realized he was just pulling out his wallet. "How much?"

"What are you doing here?"

She looked past the man to see Talon approaching. His long, angry predatorial strides brought him to her side. Fast.

"None of your friggin' business, Celt," the stranger growled.

"Get away from Sunshine, Zarek, or I swear I'll put you down."

Zarek tucked his wallet back in his pocket and turned to face Talon. "Try it, Celt, and I'll have your heart in my fist."

Talon lunged and shoved him back.

Zarek swung at him, but Talon ducked and shoved him again.

Vane came out of nowhere to break them apart. "Hey, hey, hey!" he snarled at Talon, forcing him away from Zarek. "What is this about?"

"I better not ever catch you around her, Zarek. I mean it."

Zarek flipped him off with his claw, then turned around and stalked angrily toward the Presbytere building.

Sunshine was terrified as she saw the wild look on Talon's face. He really looked like he could kill someone.

"Talon?"

"Stay back," Vane warned. "You okay, Celt?"

Talon couldn't respond. All he could feel was the rising fury inside him. The demanding, hot need he had to rip Zarek to pieces.

The moment he had seen Zarek, his mind had flashed back to Zarek in the alley with his victim.

God help the man if he *ever* attacked Sunshine that way.

He'd kill him regardless of the consequences.

Without comment, Talon pulled Sunshine against him and held her there. He fisted his hand in her hair, inhaled her warm patchouli scent, and just reveled in the peace he felt while holding her.

"You were supposed to be watching her, Vane," he snarled at the Were-Hunter.

"It was just Zarek, Celt. Calm down. He wasn't doing anything but looking at her dishes."

"He could have hurt her."

"But he didn't."

"Yeah, and you're damn lucky for that."

Zarek was still fuming as he made his way down Pirate's Alley.

When was he going to learn? Every time he had tried to help someone, it had always turned around and bit him on his ass.

He'd recognized the woman the minute he'd seen her and was wondering why Talon had left her unprotected.

He clenched his teeth. "Fine. Let her die."

What did he care anyway?

As he neared the end of the alley, he stopped. A foreign, cold sensation ran over him. It was one he hadn't felt since the night he'd crossed over from human to Dark-Hunter.

"Zarek."

He turned to see none other than Dionysus before him. The Greek god had his short brown hair impeccably combed. He wore a dark tweed jacket over a navy turtleneck and looked like some kind of high-paid corporate raider.

"If you're going to blast me, Dionysus, have at it."

Dionysus laughed. "Please call me Dion. Dionysus is just so passé."

Zarek stiffened as the god neared him. The power of the being was undeniable and it caused the air around him to sizzle. "Why are you speaking to me?"

Dionysus indicated the Pedestrian Mall with his thumb. "I overheard your little exchange with Talon. I was thinking we could make a deal, you and I."

Zarek scoffed at the very idea. "That would be like making a pact with Lucifer."

"Yes, but I don't smell like sulfur. And I happen to dress better. Luc always looks like a pimp." He offered Zarek a cigarette. "Go ahead, have one. It's even your brand."

Zarek took him up on it and eyed him suspiciously as he lit the cigarette. "So what's the pact?"

"Simple. I have a boy in town who is doing some favors for me. You ran into him last night. The one who looks like your boss."

"Yeah, I know the bastard. I owe him too."

"I know. It was unfortunate that the two of you met like that. But if you can put aside your anger, I think you'll like my deal a lot better."

"And that is?"

"My boy needs a few things. Now we could kill you, but I'm thinking a man of your 'special' abilities and skills would be better on our side than drifting through eternity as a disembodied Shade." Dionysus paused.

"Keep talking."

"All I need is for you to not hunt. Go home like Acheron wants and stay there until Mardi Gras. During my celebration, Styxx will be in touch. Help him with the final preparations and I will give you what you want most."

"And what do I want most?"

"An end to your suffering."

Zarek had to give the god credit, he knew what to offer, all right. "You're not trying to trick me, are you?"

"I swear by the river Styx that if you assist us, I will put you out of your pain. Completely. No tricks. No loopholes. One blast and you're beyond even death."

"And if I don't?"

Dionysus smiled evilly. "Hades has a nice corner of Tartarus waiting for you."

Zarek took a drag on his cigarette and laughed darkly. "Like that scares me. What's he going to do? Tear the flesh off my body? Break my bones? Better yet, why not hold me down and stomp on me until I bleed or make me shovel shit? Oh wait, been there, done that, and got the videotape."

Dionysus's green eyes blazed. "I can't believe Artemis lets you live."

"I can't believe you're a god with no better threat than that. But don't worry," he said as Dionysus looked like he was ready to strike. "I hate these assholes anyway and couldn't care less how many of them you turn into Shades."

The god calmed down instantly.

"I take it you know my cell number?" Zarek asked.

Dionysus nodded. "We'll be in touch."

"Fine. I'll see you Tuesday."

At Talon's insistence, Sunshine packed up her cart and let the men wheel it back toward her art gallery. But as they started away, she stopped them.

"What are you doing?" Talon asked as she opened up the small side door on her cart.

"Nothing."

He frowned at her as she pulled out the bowl Zarek had been looking at. She handed it to Vane. "Would you mind taking this to Zarek for me?"

Talon was aghast. "What are you, insane?"

"No, Talon. That man is in a lot of pain. I think he could use an act of kindness from someone."

Vane scoffed. "What he could use is a good butt-kicking."

"Vane, please." Sunshine urged him to take it.

He did, grudgingly. "Okay, but if he throws it at me, I'm going to want some compensation."

She kissed him on the cheek.

"Lame compensation, but in the presence of Talon, I'll settle for it."

Vane took the bowl and headed off down the street.

She turned back to Talon who was still frowning. "Zarek will slam it against a wall and break it the first chance he gets."

"I don't think so. Even if he does, I can always make another one."

He helped her lock up her cart and then led her back out to the street. "You have such a generous heart."

"That's what they tell me. So, shall we go hunt for Styxx?"

"Hell, no. I'm not going to chance you getting hurt."

She growled at him. "Listen, my grandmother said something to me this afternoon. She told me to follow my heart tonight. I don't know what she meant by that, but I trust her. She is an extraordinary psychic. Everything she has told me has come true."

"Look, Sunshine, I can't help what she said. I just know that I'm not willing to let anything happen to you. When Nynia died, I was so lost and cold, and I haven't been warm since. Not until I felt your hands on me. The only way I've been able to cope without you is to bury what I feel, but I can't seem to do that anymore. When I'm with you all I can do is feel and need."

"That's how I am too."

"So where does that leave us?"

"I don't know, Talon. I wish I did."

Talon put his arm over her shoulder as they walked back toward the square. He noticed other couples around them.

How he wished they could be a normal, happy couple with no worries other than a mortgage payment.

But it wasn't meant to be.

Camulus was playing with both of them and Sunshine was going to get hurt.

Talon only knew one real way to protect both of them.

"So where are we going?" Sunshine asked.

"We're going to see a god about a miracle."

Chapter 15

Ash ground his teeth as Artemis ran her hands through his long, blond hair. He shuttered his eyes as he watched her draw a lock of it between her fingers and flick the curl back and forth with her fingertip.

"I have to go," he said.

She pouted seductively, running her graceful hand down his bare chest, her fingernails gently scraping his skin. "I don't want you to go."

"Release me, Artie. I have to find Styxx before he hurts anyone else. He almost killed Zarek last night."

"Who cares? Zarek is better off dead."

"That can be said for most of us."

She painfully raked her nails down his arms, which were secured to her bedposts by a pair of soft golden cords. "I hate when you talk like that. You're so ungrateful after all I have done for you."

Oh yeah, she had done so much *for* him. More like *to* him and very little of it had been kind or enjoyable.

"Don't make me break your restraints, Artie." If he used his powers to untie her "special" cords, it would send a signal through Olympus alerting the other gods of his presence in her temple. Anytime he "visited" her, his powers were seriously restricted. He could do paltry parlor-type tricks such as open doors or dress and undress, but anything more than that would be picked up by the Olympian gods and would cause them to investigate the unknown source of power.

That was the only thing Artemis feared.

"You'd like that, wouldn't you? To have Zeus or one of the others find you in my bed?"

"Then let me go."

The golden cords unwrapped themselves from his wrists. Ash sighed as he moved his arms for the first time since dawn and let the circulation travel back into his hands.

A wave of exhaustion hit him, but he shook it off.

As usual, Artemis hadn't let him sleep at all while he'd been with her, and he'd now been awake for two days straight.

He was so tired, he wanted nothing more than to sleep.

"Oh, guess what I found out for you," Artemis said. "My worthless brother, Dion, has hooked up with yours and with the Gaulic war god, Camulus, in a bid for power. Is that a goof or what?"

Acheron froze. "What did you say?"

"Dion and Cam think they can retake their godhoods and they're using your brother as their ringleader. Can you say, rockball's chance?" She laughed. "Just imagine, a forgotten Gaulic war god, my brother, whose only claim to fame is sucking down wine and getting laid, and your brother, whose only good mark is he happens to look like you. And they think the cabbage can lead them to glory." She snorted, then laughed again. "I can't wait to see what these losers have planned."

Acheron stared at her. She might underestimate their abilities, but he had a sneaking suspicion of what they intended to do.

On Mardi Gras, the barrier between this world and the one where the Atlantean Destroyer was held would be thin.

There could be only one reason for them to have Styxx in on their plans . . .

They wanted to release the Destroyer and the only way to do that would be by killing Ash.

One way or another, Ash was going to make sure it didn't happen.

Come Mardi Gras, they all had a big surprise coming.

They had no idea who and what they were dealing with. The Destroyer was far beyond their ability to command or control. Once unleashed, she was the most merciless ancient god imaginable. One who had slain every member of her own family. Afterward, she would have destroyed the entire earth had she not been stopped and imprisoned.

If Camulus and Dionysus thought to bargain with her after they killed him, they were pathetically mistaken.

He almost smiled at the thought of them trying to reason with her. Mardi Gras night would be interesting, no doubt.

"By the way," Artemis said as she reclined naked on the bed and ran her bare foot up his spine in a long, cool caress, "your children have been very bad while you were here."

Ash stopped rubbing his wrist and looked at her. "What do you mean?"

"In direct disobedience to your orders, Zarek was out and about earlier this evening, and he and Talon got into a fight in the French Quarter."

Anger rushed through him. "What? When?"

"About two hours ago."

"Dammit, Artemis," he snarled. "Why didn't you tell me?"

She shrugged and ran her hand over her naked breasts in an effort to draw his attention to her. "I liked you where you were and I knew if I told you, you'd leave."

Ash glared at her. Her selfishness knew no bounds. Angry at her, he snapped his fingers and returned his clothes to his body. He made his hair black and grabbed his backpack up from the floor.

"I hate that hair color on you," she said petulantly, zapping his hair back to blond.

He stiffened. "Yeah, well, the only color I hate more than blond is auburn." He made his hair black again, then zapped hers to a matching shade.

Her furious shriek echoed through the temple as Ash mentally commanded himself back to New Orleans.

Sunshine felt an adrenaline rush as they approached the biker bar at 688 Ursulines Avenue. It was the best place in town to come meet friends, eat good food, and find all kinds of fun things to do.

"You didn't tell me we were going to Sanctuary."

Talon frowned. "You know about Sanctuary?"

"Honey, there's not a single woman in this town who doesn't know about Sanctuary, Land of the Bodacious Gods. Heck, me and my girlfriends want to get together and vote Mama Lo an award for her policy against hiring any man not seriously buff."

She noted the offended grimace on his face and couldn't help laughing. "Not that you're not buff. You can certainly hold your own against the Sanctuary Hotties. But face it, haven't you ever noticed that this place is like Hooters for women?"

"No. I can honestly say that I've never noticed how good-looking the men at Sanctuary are. Nor have I ever cared."

The outside of the club was a typical New Orleans building that had been constructed in 1801. The brick was a rust color and a huge sign swung over the old-fashioned saloon-type doors. It showed a full moon rising over a hill where a motorcycle was parked and proudly proclaimed this place as Sanctuary, Home of the Howlers—the Howlers being the house band for the club, and a mighty fine-looking group of men they were too.

The bar was open twenty-four hours a day, seven days a week, and was owned by the Peltier family. The owner, Mama Lo, had eleven studly sons who again warranted the woman an award for beautifying the city.

Each one of them was a prime male specimen guaranteed to make a woman pant.

Dev Peltier was at the door as they entered. A regular

bouncer, he was one in a set of identical quadruplets. Sunshine had never met a woman who didn't want to take one of the quads home. For that matter, they wanted to take them all home and use them as matching bookends in the bedroom. Only it wasn't books her friends wanted to sandwich between the quadruplets.

Dev had a pair of piercingly blue eyes and long, wavy blond hair that fell to the middle of his back. The only way she knew it was Dev as opposed to one of his brothers was the bow-and-arrow tattoo on his arm.

She paused as she realized it was identical to the brand on Talon's shoulder.

"Hey, man," Dev said in that shivery-hot, deep accent that was a cross between French and Cajun as he caught sight of Talon. The two of them did a high-five shake. "Where have you been?"

"Out and about. You?"

Dev gave him a wicked grin. "Mostly in and out."

Talon laughed. "I'm not going there."

Dev looked at her and winked. "Hey, little Sunshine, why you hanging out with this loser? You lose a bet or something?"

"Or something," she said with a smile.

"You know Dev?" Talon asked her, his body going rigid as if the thought made him jealous.

"Yeah," Dev answered before she could. "She comes in all the time. Her and Aimee play pool in the back."

"You come here alone?"

Sunshine shoved Talon playfully on the shoulder. "Would you stop? You're not my father and no one bothers me here thanks to Dev and his brothers."

"That's right, Talon, you know my policy. No one harasses a woman in Sanctuary unless she wants to be harassed."

"The exception being Aimee," Sunshine couldn't resist adding. The only daughter in the massive Peltier clan, Aimee couldn't get near a man without one of her brothers or her enormously tall, well-muscled father having a stroke.

"Double damn straight." Dev inclined his head to the coffin that was kept in the corner of the club right as you came in the door. "That's the last moron who asked my sister out."

Talon laughed again. "There's another place I don't want to go to. I'm looking for Eros, has he been in here yet?"

"Upstairs by the storeroom playing poker with Rudy, Justin, and Etienne."

"Thanks." Talon led her through the front half of the bar where tables and booths were set up for eating. The place was rather crowded tonight and the music from the Howlers was loud and thumping.

"Hey, Talon," Sunshine shouted in his ear. "Why do you and Dev have the same bow-and-arrow mark on your bodies?"

He glanced back to where Dev stood at the door. "Dev thinks it's funny that he bears the mark of a . . ." His voice trailed off, but she caught his unspoken meaning by the glint in his eyes.

The bow mark must be the signature sign of a Dark-Hunter. "Is he one too?"

"No, he's another *breed* entirely."

Understanding ripped through her. "A breed like Vane?"

He paused and lowered his head so that he could speak without being overheard. "Yes, and at the same time, no."

So he must be a were-beast of a different sort. "Does this mean his entire family is able to change . . ."—she shifted gears as a patron came too close—"their clothes to something entirely new?" she finished.

He nodded.

Wow! Who knew? An entire were-family ran one of the most popular places in town. Very chic.

Talon straightened and headed for the back where the pool tables were kept. There was an ornate pine staircase that led to the area above, where additional tables were set up for people to eat and watch the band as they played below.

Even the upstairs area was packed tonight.

Without stopping, Talon led her past the patrons and headed for the last table on the left, which was set in a corner.

Five people sat at it and four of them were playing poker. Etienne Peltier was leaner than his older brother Dev, but no less muscular. He had shoulder-length, straight blond hair and a face that could only be called angelic. But as Sunshine had learned on more than one occasion, the devil himself resided in that handsome body. No one wanted to cross Etienne.

Rudy St. Michel sat next to Etienne. Average in appearance, he looked like the typical New Orleans drifter with long black hair, and colorful tattoos covering every inch of visible flesh. He'd started working here about a year ago and was responsible for the arcade games downstairs.

Another bouncer, Justin Portakalian, had his back to the wall and one long, leather-encased leg stretched out over a wooden chair as he handed two cards over to Rudy. He was as gorgeous as any of the Peltiers, with medium-length, dark brown hair and hazel eyes that glittered with malice. At six feet six and with a bad attitude that redefined the term, he was someone Sunshine had always tried to avoid. He didn't talk much and had tossed her last boyfriend through the back door. Literally.

She'd also heard a rumor that Justin was fresh out of prison for murder, and something about his deadly demeanor added quite a bit of credibility to that speculation.

The other two people she didn't know. One was a blond biker who held a beautiful, barely dressed redhead on his lap. He looked up, saw Talon, and the smile faded from his lips. "What are you doing here, Celt?"

"I need to talk to you."

"Can't you see I'm winning?"

Talon looked at the poker chips by his elbow. "Yes, and I can also see that you're cheating."

"What?" The other men were suddenly animated.

"Talon, you dick!" The blond cleared his throat. "He's just kidding. Give me a minute, okay?"

Rudy snorted at Justin and Etienne as he adjusted the five cards in his hands. "I don't know why you guys are bitching. Both of you cheat too."

Etienne smiled that charming devil-may-care smile while Justin passed a less than amused glare at Rudy.

The blond biker started away from the table, then hurried back and grabbed up his cards.

"Just in case," he said to the others.

As soon as the blond stepped back to them, Talon introduced them. "Sunshine, meet Eros and Psyche."

Sunshine looked at them curiously. "They just think those names are cute, right? They're not really Eros and Psyche."

Eros gave her a peeved stare. "Why is she talking to me?"

"Cupid," Talon said, a warning note in his voice. "Play nice." He turned to Psyche. "Would you please do me a favor, Psyche, and keep Sunshine occupied while I deal with your husband?"

"Sure, hon." Psyche draped her arm over Sunshine's shoulders. "Come on, let's go see what kind of trouble we can get into downstairs."

Sunshine followed Psyche to the ornate staircase that led to the floor below, not far from the stage. The whole area was crammed with dancers and people who wanted to hear the Howlers sing, and with women who wanted to ogle the gorgeous band members.

She and Psyche went over to a pool table where a guy named Nick Gautier was playing a game with Wren, one of the Sanctuary busboys. Wren was a quiet, shy type who had an aura around him that said he would rather be invisible. Still, there was something dangerous about him. Kind of like he would gladly fight anyone dumb enough to disturb his introverted space.

His dark blond hair was long, and he wore it in a style that wasn't quite dreadlocks, but something not far from that either. His eyes were so pale a gray that they looked almost colorless.

As for Nick Gautier, Sunshine had met him here a few times. His mother was one of the cooks and he often came in for dinner and to play a quick game of pool with Wren.

"Hi, ladies," Nick said with his light Cajun drawl.

Psyche took the cue from his hand. "Rack your balls, Nick. We want to play."

Nick laughed. "Psych, one thing a woman should never tell a man to do is rack his balls."

Ignoring him, Psyche looked over to Wren. "You don't mind, do you?"

Wren shook his head no and handed his cue to Sunshine. Without a word, he quickly vanished into the crowd.

"I didn't mean to disturb you guys," Sunshine said to Nick.

"Ah, don't worry about it. Wren and I play a lot. He needed to get back to the kitchen anyway. You ladies want something to drink?"

"Beer," Psyche said.

"Water."

He nodded and left.

Sunshine watched as Nick navigated the crowd. She turned back to Psyche. "So you and Eros come here a lot?"

She nodded. "I've even seen you here a few times. You usually hang out with Aimee and some black-haired chick."

"Trina."

"That's her."

Psyche grabbed the cue ball and lined it up. "Yes," she said as she took her shot, sending six of the balls into pockets. "I'm a goddess and Eros is a god."

"How did you know—"

"I'm a goddess. I can hear every thought in your head." She smiled at Sunshine while she chalked her tip.

"That's a really uncomfortable fact to know."

"Isn't it, though?" Psyche blew across the tip, set the chalk aside, then knocked three more balls into the pockets. "And because I know what you're thinking, the answer is yes."

"The answer to what?"

"Whether or not Talon loves you."

Sunshine grimaced as Psyche sank the rest of balls on the table. "I don't know. There are times when I get the feeling he can't tell me from Nynia. I think he loves her more than me."

Psyche racked the balls again. "No offense, but that's stupid. You and Talon are soulmates. He will always love you no matter who or what you are. You, my friend, could come back as a humpback whale and he would love you. He can't help it. The two of you are destined for each other."

"Yeah, but—"

"There are no buts, Sunshine." She moved to stand in front of her. "I am the goddess of souls and soulmates. Unlike the other Olympian gods, I know when I see two people who were created for each other. If both you and Talon died tonight and were later reborn at polar ends of the earth, sooner or later the two of you would reunite. That's the schtick with soulmates. Alone you can survive, hell, you can even be with other people, but neither of you will ever be complete without the other." She glanced upstairs where they had left the guys. "You two can fight this all you want. But all you're going to do is make yourselves miserable."

She patted Sunshine's shoulder. "I know you don't believe me. I know it'll take time before you accept it. And that being said, the problem with your relationship isn't whether or not he loves you. It's that he can't afford to even think that thought."

"Why?"

"Because the minute he does, Camulus will kill you. Talon knows that. He will not let himself love you for fear of your dying again."

Sunshine swallowed at her words. Everything kept coming back to that one irritable and irritating Celtic god. "Is there any way to get around Camulus?"

"Maybe."

"Maybe? That's the best you can do?"

"Hey, it's better than no."

True, but still she wanted more hope than that.

"And what about Artemis?" Sunshine asked. "Even if we get past Camulus, what about her?"

Psyche twisted her cue in her hands as she thought about that never-to-be-forgotten fact. "She's tricky. With her you have to negotiate very carefully."

"So it's possible I could talk to her?"

"It's possible."

Sunshine's mind whirled at the thought. Could there really be hope for them?

Talon led Eros into the storeroom and shut the door. Quinn Peltier had soundproofed the room a few decades back to ensure that the Peltiers and other select friends could have emergency privacy if they needed it.

Originally, the room had been planned as a holding place in the event one of them accidentally turned into a bear while the club was occupied, but over time it had come to serve as a convenient place for one of the brothers to take a willing woman should they have an itch that wouldn't wait.

But that was another story.

Talon switched on the dim overhead light and faced Eros. "I need a favor."

"Favor, hell. Didn't you know that I'm supposed to vaporize any Dark-Hunter who gets near me?"

Talon looked at him drolly. "I'll remember that the next time you want to borrow poker money from me without Psyche knowing."

Eros smiled good-naturedly. "Good point. Okay, what can I do you to?"

Talon hesitated. Silently, he prayed Eros would give him an answer other than the one he feared.

"Do you know the Celtic god Camulus?"

Eros shrugged. "Not really. He runs with Ares, Kel, Ara, and those other war gods. Being the god of love and lust, I don't tend to associate with them. Why?"

"Because I was cursed by him and I wanted to know if

there is any way for me to break the curse."

"Honestly?"

"Yes."

"Most likely not. War gods as a rule aren't real forgiving. It kind of comes with the whole mass-destruction mentality. But it depends on what you did and what he used as a curse."

"I killed his son and he has forbidden me to ever love a human. When I do, he kills them."

"Ooo," Eros breathed. "Sorry, man, but something like that, you can hang up an out clause. Vengeance runs deep in the bones of the war gods. Now, if you had the blood of a god in you, you might have some leverage. Do you?"

"No. I'm fully human, blood-wise anyway."

"Then you're totally screwed."

Talon clenched his teeth at the truth, even though he wasn't surprised by it. He hadn't realized until then that he had started to see a future for him and Sunshine.

That in the back of his mind there really had been hope.

But it was futile.

"There's no way to keep Sunshine."

He hadn't realized he'd spoken aloud until Eros said, "If you love her, then I'm sure she'll pay for it."

Talon braced himself for what he had to do. Even though it tore his heart out and made him want to cry. He knew he had to do this.

It was the only way to protect her.

"Fine, then. I have one last request."

Eros gave him an understanding look. "You want me to shoot you guys with the lead arrow to kill your love."

He nodded.

Eros pulled his bow necklace from around his neck and made it larger.

Talon grabbed his hand as he aimed it at him. "Not yet. Okay? I just want a little more time with her. Can you wait until midnight?"

Shrinking the bow back to necklace size, Eros nodded and patted Talon on the shoulder. "Love bites, man. Believe me, I know."

Talon thought about Psyche and he felt a twinge of jealousy. "Yeah, but you got to keep your love."

"True. I'm damn lucky in that department." Eros shifted as if something had made him uncomfortable. "Where do you want me to shoot you?"

"Someplace that won't hurt."

Eros rolled his eyes.

Talon answered seriously. "The club Runningwolf's. I'll have her there at midnight."

Nodding, Eros took two steps away. "I'll see you at midnight."

"Thanks, Eros. I owe you."

"Yes, you do."

Talon inclined his head in mutual understanding. Now he was indebted to Vane and Eros. At the rate he was going, he was likely to lose a whole lot more than his soul before all was said and done.

He just prayed that in the end, Sunshine didn't lose her life.

But he wouldn't think about that now. All he had was a few more hours to spend with the woman he loved.

He wanted to enjoy what little time they had before she learned to hate him.

Talon left the room and stopped as he caught sight of Sunshine downstairs playing pool with Psyche.

She was so beautiful there. The stage lights played off her midnight-black hair. And her lush, sweet body . . . It was perfection.

Sunshine was everything to him.

Talon's thoughts scattered when he realized that a thin man of average height was talking to Sunshine and she didn't look happy about it.

Suddenly, their conversation escalated into a verbal fight. Sunshine was animated as she poked the man with her finger and pushed him back.

Psyche put her cue down and stepped between them.

Talon saw red.

Without thinking about the patrons or anything other

than Sunshine, he placed his hand on the banister and swung his legs over and dropped to the floor below.

The people downstairs gasped and scattered.

Pain shot up his leg and worsened as he took a step. Talon didn't care. The only thing he saw was Sunshine's distressed face. The only sound he heard was her angry voice.

"How could you do this, Jerry, you snake!"

"I told you before, Sunny, everything's fair in business."

"But he was *my* client. I sat out there all day today waiting on him to show."

"Yeah, well, you snooze, you lose."

"Here's another saying," Talon said, grabbing the guy and turning him to face him. "No one messes with my girl."

Sunshine froze at the look on Talon's face. It was truly scary. He stared at Jerry as if he were one inch away from making Jerry fillet.

"It's all right, Talon," she said, not wanting him to get into trouble or, worse, arrested for beating the slug.

She could tell by Jerry's expression that he was dying to say something snide, but the sheer size and ferocity of Talon kept his lips sealed.

She took Talon's arm. "C'mon, babe, let's go."

Talon really wanted to tear the guy apart. How dare he steal Sunshine's client from her? He knew how much it meant to her.

His anger snapped and hissed, straining against the control he was using to keep it leashed.

"Who is this dick?" Talon asked Sunshine.

"I used to be her husband, what about you?"

Talon's eyes flared. "Ditto."

Jerry couldn't have looked more shocked had Talon actually hit him.

Talon looked at Sunshine. A part of him felt extremely betrayed that she had dared marry someone else. It didn't matter that she'd had no idea about their past life together.

It still hurt.

Her eyes apologized to him. "I was going to tell you."

"When, Sunshine?"

She turned and glanced at Jerry. "You're such a jerk. I can't believe I was ever stupid enough to marry you."

She started through the now silent crowd.

"Hey, Sunny," Jerry called after her. "Make sure you go to Fallini's sometime and admire my work. Remember when you look at it that the best artist won."

Talon saw the tears in her eyes.

His temper exploded.

Rotating his shoulders, he turned and slugged Jerry so hard that he was knocked off his feet. He landed with a solid thump on the pool table, sending billiard balls rolling and bouncing.

Several members of the bear clan cursed as cameras flashed.

"Way to keep a low profile, Celt," Justin said snidely from beside him.

Talon ignored the panther. He took Sunshine's hand and led her through the crowd.

Nick met him and Sunshine at the door. "Man, Ash is going to flip when he finds out about this. I can't believe you pulled something like this with a Mardi Gras crowd to witness it. You're worse than Zarek."

"Just make sure you clean it up."

"Clean it up, hell. Do you know how many cameras just caught your stunt-jump from upstairs? My mom now thinks you're on the drugs she suspects Kyrian sells. We're screwed. My life is toast. I'm about to get lectured about working for drug dealers . . . again. My mom, bless her heart, is so goofy, she doesn't even realize she works for bears. I'm so screwed."

"Don't worry about it," Dev said as he joined them. "We have your back, Celt. Cleaning up indiscretions is our specialty. No human here will remember it tomorrow and we'll make sure none of the electronics show anything either. Everyone will be ticked off that all they got for a picture was a big black blob."

"What about me?" Nick asked. "I don't want any of your mind-meld stuff."

"I said humans, Nicky."

Nick looked extremely offended.

"Thanks," Talon said to Dev.

"Any time. I'll see you tomorrow for Mardi Gras."

Talon inclined his head to the bear and led Sunshine outside even though his entire leg felt as if it had been broken by the jump.

Once they were on the street, he confronted her. "You were married?"

"It was seven years ago, Talon. I was young and stupid."

"You were married," he repeated. "To *him*."

Sunshine took a deep breath and sighed. "Yes."

"I can't believe this."

"Oh, c'mon, Talon, give me a break. Don't hold something against me when I had no idea you even existed. If anyone has a right to be mad, I think it should be me."

"Excuse me?"

"Selena told me about you and your rep, bud. How you've pretty much laid every woman in New Orleans. You want to tell me about that?"

"That was different."

"Why? Because I'm a woman? You knew I wasn't a virgin, Talon. What did you expect?"

Talon didn't know. But then, it didn't really matter.

After tonight, she'd hate him anyway. The last thing he wanted was to spend the evening fighting with her.

This was all the time they would ever have.

"Okay, Sunshine. You're right. I'm sorry."

Sunshine was stunned. This was the first time she'd ever known a guy to cave so easily. "Are you really?"

"Yes," he said, his eyes sincere. "I don't want to fight, okay? Let's just forget about him and go eat."

She lifted his hand to her lips and kissed his knuckles. "Sounds good."

As they walked to a small café on Iberville, she noticed he had a slight limp. "Are you okay?"

"Yeah, I just twisted my leg when I jumped over the railing," he said. "Whenever I get mad, I tend to lose my Dark-Hunter powers, and without them, my body becomes human."

"Do you need a doctor?"

He shook his head. "As long as I stay calm, it should heal while we eat."

Talon kept her close to him the entire time it took them to reach the restaurant and be seated. He memorized everything about her. He would always remember her like this and those memories would live inside him right along with the ones of her as Nynia.

Or would he lose those memories when Eros shot him?

Would his mind somehow distort them so that he couldn't love her anymore?

His stomach knotted at the thought. What would it be like to not even have the comfort of his memories of Nynia and Sunshine?

To not remember the softness of her touch, the smell of her patchouli on his skin?

The way her eyes lit up every time she looked at him?

Grinding his teeth, he tried not to think about that, or to feel the pain in his heart.

This wasn't about him and what he stood to lose.

This was about her.

He had to do this for her.

She sat in the booth across from him, her head bent while she ate. The candlelight reflected the darkness of her hair, making her skin a creamy tan. A creamy tan that made his mouth water for a taste.

Talon watched the graceful gestures of her hands as she cut into her garbanzo bean salad and ate it. He loved those long, tapered fingers. Loved teasing them with his mouth, feeling them on his body.

"What made you want to be an artist?" he asked.

"I love working with my hands."

He reached across the table and took her left hand into his. He studied the delicate curve of it, the way it felt so dainty in his palm. "You have such beautiful hands."

She smiled and squeezed his with hers. "Thank you. They're the most valuable thing an artist can ever have. I used to have nightmares that something would happen to them, a severe scar or burn that would prevent me from ever using them for pottery or drawing again. Art is my life. I don't know what I'd do if I couldn't create."

Talon closed his eyes as agony washed over him. His emotions swirled, but he forced them down. He had to.

The clock was ticking for them.

Sunshine fed him a bite of her salad and he did his best not to cringe.

"Why aren't your eyes amber anymore?" she asked.

He swallowed his bite and took a drink of wine. "Part of the whole Dark-Hunter package. We're turned into predators so that we can track down and kill Daimons. Our eyes become black and dilate a lot more than human eyes so that we can see in darkness."

"And your fangs? Do you use them to suck blood?"

He shook his head. "No. Blood has never been to my taste. The fangs are just part of the package too."

"And do you like what you do?"

"There are times when it's fun and challenging and times when it's kind of boring. For the most part I don't mind."

She seemed to accept that.

She ate for a few minutes before she spoke again. "Talon, why did you give up your soul?"

He looked away. In his mind, he could see that day so clearly. He had been lying on the altar, his hands tied above his head, his chest bare and marked in blood with the sacrificial symbols. It had been a cool day, and every member of his clan had been there.

Dressed in black robes, the Druid priest had looked down upon him and smiled cruelly.

"Seize Ceara."

His cousin's words had rung in his head. It had taken a full minute before he understood what was going on. Horrified, Talon had watched his men grab his sister's arms.

"Speirr! Help me, bràthair, please!"

He had fought against the ropes until his wrists had bled and stung. He had screamed out for them to release her.

Like a caged animal, he had tried to reach her.

Over and over, she called out to him.

"It's the will of the gods that you both die for what your mother did."

His cousin had sunk his dagger deep into Ceara's heart.

She had looked to Talon, her eyes terrified and tear-filled as she struggled to breathe.

Worst of all, he had seen the disappointment in her eyes. She had believed in him, trusted him to protect her.

The men had released her and she had stumbled to the ground, landing on her hands and knees.

"Speirr?" Her voice had trembled as she reached a bloodied hand out toward him. *"I don't want to be dead,"* she whispered, her voice that of a child.

Before his eyes, she had died.

Panting in fury, he had let his battle cry roll out and then he had cursed them all. He had called down the wrath of the Morrigán and she had ignored him.

It was Artemis who had answered his cry for vengeance.

The last thing he'd seen was the Druid holding his head back and then making the savage cut across his throat.

Talon breathed deeply in and out and he sought to bury those memories. That was the past and now he had Sunshine to watch out for.

"It was youthful fury," he said with a calmness he didn't feel. "I had lost so much in such a short time—my aunt, my uncle, you, and our son. After I lost you, I walked around cloaked in grief. I struggled to make it through every minute of every day. The only thing that kept me going was knowing that the clan and Ceara needed me.

"When the Druids came to me and said that I would have to give up my life to the gods to protect the clan, it was actually a relief. I didn't think twice about allowing them to place me on the sacrificial altar."

Talon ground his teeth as he saw his sister in his mind again. The way she had looked that day. "Ceara was weeping, but she was trying to be strong. Everything was going as it should, until Murrdyd turned on her and told my clansmen to seize her. He said we both had to die to appease the gods."

"Was that the truth?"

"No. He wanted to be king. He needed both Ceara and me out of the way since we were legitimate heirs. I can understand his wanting me killed, but he didn't have to kill Ceara. It was the injustice of it that I couldn't stand."

She placed her hand over his. "Baby, I am so sorry."

He squeezed her hand as he blinked against the agony he felt. The only comfort he had ever known in his life was the touch of this woman. "So were they in the end."

"What did you do?"

Talon cleared his throat as he tried to squelch the memories of that night. The regrets. He had been like a single-minded monster raging through his village.

The only thought on his mind had been reaching his cousin.

Making the bastard pay.

"I went through the village killing every man who came between me and the ones who had killed Ceara. The women and children fled while I fought my way to Murrdyd. After I took my vengeance on him, I burned the entire village to the ground."

"And you've been serving Artemis ever since?"

He nodded.

"Have you ever met her?"

"Just the one time when she came to bargain with me for my soul. She met me in the nether region where a soul gets trapped after it leaves this world, but has yet to travel to the next."

"You haven't seen her since?"

He shook his head. "We're not allowed to have contact with the gods. They see us as an abomination."

"But what about Eros?"

He took a deep breath and felt a twinge of humor at the thought of the fun-loving, irreverent god of love. "He's a little different. For some reason, he likes hanging out with us."

Sunshine considered his words as they finished dinner. Poor Talon. He had been through so much pain. So much grief.

To some extent it bothered her that he was still confusing her with Nynia. They might share a soul, but ultimately, they were two entirely different people.

Not that it really mattered. So long as he was bound to Artemis and cursed by Camulus, he could never be free. He could never have a future.

While she'd talked to Psyche, the goddess had told her how to summon Artemis.

Sunshine really wanted to have a nice chitchat with that goddess and see if maybe Talon could earn his freedom again. If she accomplished that, then maybe they could do something to stop Camulus as well.

After they paid for dinner, they left the restaurant and headed for her father's club.

Sunshine didn't know why Talon wanted to take her home, but she snuck them in unnoticed so that they could have a little more time alone.

Talon led her to the dance floor.

Sunshine had never realized before just how hot a man could be when he danced. Personally, she'd always thought most men looked rather goofy.

But not Talon. He was the sexiest thing she'd ever seen in her life.

When the song ended, Talon urged her to introduce him to her father and brother. They were sitting nearby, going over paperwork and accounting stats for the club while Wayne helped them.

"Hi, Daddy, Storm, and Wayne."

They looked up and smiled until they saw Talon behind her.

"Sunshine, are you all right?" her father asked.

"I'm fine. I just wanted you to meet Talon. Talon, my father, Daniel Runningwolf."

Talon offered his hand, but her father declined.

"I'm a shaman and can't touch you."

Talon nodded at him with a look that said he understood. "Sorry, I wasn't thinking."

Wayne excused himself.

After he left, her father's dark brown eyes glittered

harshly as he swept his gaze to Sunshine. "Starla didn't tell me your boyfriend was soulless, kitten."

"She probably thought you'd flip out. Are you?"

"Yes."

Sunshine quickly sought to change the subject. "How's Mom, by the way?"

"She's fine. What about you?"

"I'm fine, Daddy. Don't worry."

"I'm your father, Sunshine. Worrying about you is my full-time occupation."

She smiled at him. "And you do it very well."

Still, he looked less than appeased.

Talon stepped forward. "Daniel, could I have a word with you?"

Sunshine frowned at the ominous note in Talon's voice. Her father's eyes narrowed even more before he nodded subtly. "Sunshine, stay with Storm."

She watched as the two of them drifted off and a wave of terror crashed over her. Something was definitely wrong.

Talon led her father to another corner of the bar. He glanced over to Sunshine and his heart wrenched.

"What is it you want with me?" Daniel asked.

"Look, I know you don't like me."

"Don't like you? You're a soulless killer. Granted, you do it protectively, but it doesn't change the basic fact that you are no longer human."

"I know that. It's why we're here. I'm going to release Sunshine into your protection tonight. There are some people who are out to harm her and I would really appreciate it if you watched out for her. I'll be staying nearby, out of sight, until after tomorrow night just in case the thing after her tries to take her again."

"From what my wife tells me, Sunshine won't let you leave her voluntarily."

"In another four minutes, she won't ever want to lay eyes on me again. I promise you."

He frowned. "What do you mean?"

Talon cleared his throat as he glanced to the large Budweiser clock on the wall over the bar.

Their time was almost up.

Damn you, Fates.

"Nothing," he said quietly. "Just take my word for it, your daughter is yours."

Daniel nodded.

As Talon walked back to Sunshine, his entire being ached. He couldn't stand the thought of what Eros was about to do. It cut him on a level so deep it was unfathomable.

But it had to be done.

They couldn't be together. It was foolish to think otherwise.

He had to do this to save her life.

From the corner of his eye, he saw Eros appearing in god-form. Invisible to humans, the god of love was easily discernible to Talon's Dark-Hunter senses.

"You sure?" Eros's voice echoed in his head.

Talon leaned over, kissed Sunshine gently on the lips, and then nodded.

He held her face in his hands, and stared at her brown eyes, waiting for the moment when they would turn dark with hatred. Waiting for her to stiffen and curse him.

Eros raised his bow up and shot it straight into Sunshine.

Talon swallowed as painful expectation tore through him.

Goodbye, my love.

She grimaced at him. "Ow! Talon, did you hit me?"

He shook his head and waited for the hatred to come into her eyes.

It didn't.

Seconds ticked by slowly as her frown deepened.

"I don't feel right." She rubbed her heart where Eros had shot her.

Then, amazingly, she looked up and focused her gaze on Eros. "Cupid?"

Eros looked around nervously. "You can see me?"

"Well, yeah," she said.

Eros shifted and looked a bit green.

Talon frowned as a bad feeling went through him. "What happened, Eros? Why doesn't she hate me?"

Eros looked even more uncomfortable. "You two wouldn't happen to be soulmates, would you?"

"Yes," Sunshine answered. "Psyche said we were."

Eros gave a sheepish grin. "Oops. I think I need to have a talk with my wife. Damn, she should have told me."

"Oops?" Talon repeated. "Eros, *oops* better not be in your vocabulary."

Eros cleared his throat. "No one told me you two were soulmates. See, this"—he held up his bow—"only works on lust and infatuation. Soulmates are a whole 'nother ball game. That kind of love, I can't kill. Nothing can."

Sunshine gaped as she understood what was going on. In that moment, she wanted to strangle Talon. "You tried to get him to make me hate you?"

Now Talon looked as sheepish as Eros. "Honey, I can explain."

She glared at him as rage rocked every particle of her body. "Oh, you're going to explain all right. How dare you try to monkey with my mind and heart? I don't appreciate your doing something so underhanded."

"Sunshine," her father said. "He's right. You can't have a future with him. He's not human."

"I don't care what he is. He and I have something together and I can't believe he'd do something like this."

"I forbid you to see him anymore." Her father's tone was stern.

She turned her anger toward her father. "And I'm not thirteen. I don't care what you forbid or not, Daddy. This is between me and him."

"I will not watch you die again," Talon said slowly, stressing each word.

"And I will not be manipulated. Nor will I just give you up."

Talon turned and stormed out of the club, his emotions churning. He couldn't do this. He couldn't.

He had to let her go.

It was for both their sakes.

Without looking back, he went to his motorcycle. He got on it, but before he could kick-start it, Sunshine grabbed his arm.

"You're not going to get rid of me like this."

He bared his fangs at her. "Do you not understand what I am?"

Sunshine swallowed. Suddenly everything Psyche had said made sense to her. He wasn't Speirr, the leader of his people. The frightened little boy who had turned his heart to stone in order to live. The man who had stolen Nynia's heart and then claimed her when no other would have.

This was Talon, the Dark-Hunter who spent eternity protecting strangers from the dark evil of the night.

She loved him even more.

He made her heart sing. Without him, she couldn't even imagine her future.

She didn't know how to conquer everything that stood between them, but he was worth fighting for.

"I know what you are, Talon. You are the man I was born to love. The *only* man I was born to love."

"I am not a man. Not anymore."

"You are mine and I will not let you go without a fight."

Talon didn't know what to do. The tone of her voice tore through him.

He wanted to crush her to him and hold on to her forever.

He wanted to push her away and curse. To make her hate him.

She stepped into his arms and kissed him deeply.

Talon groaned at the taste of her. Although he knew he shouldn't, he pulled her across his bike and started it, then headed off into traffic.

His love and anger roiling, he drove them out of the city, all the way to the edge of his swamp. The entire time the scent and feel of her permeated him, making his emotions even more volatile. Her body was pressed so close to him that it was all he could focus on.

Her warmth, her love.

He had to have her.

Unable to stand it, he pulled up into the woods and turned the engine off.

Sunshine was partially afraid of the feral look of him as he stared at her.

His eyes were blazing with fire and passion as he seized her and kissed her roughly.

His hunger tore through her, incited her. She wrapped her arms around his shoulders as he leaned her back over his gas tank.

She'd never seen him like this. It was as if all his emotions were out of control, as if he were living only to touch her. He kissed her neck and face as his hands loosened her blouse so that he could cup her breast in his hands.

He was wild and untamed and it seemed to her that he had more than two hands. It was as if he were touching her all over at once.

She wanted him desperately. Wanted him with the same need he had for her.

She kissed his lips, rubbing herself against his swollen groin as she pulled his T-shirt off, over his head. She ran her hands over the wide expanse of his chest, feeling his muscles bunch and flex.

He shoved her full skirt up over her hips.

"I need you, Talon," she whispered.

Talon wanted to possess her. Every part of him screamed out for it. He'd never in his entire life felt like this. He had to get inside her. Had to touch her. Had to feel her hands on his skin, her breath against his neck.

It was a need so powerful that it shook him.

She fumbled with his fly before she unzipped his pants, freeing his erection. He trembled as she sheathed him with her hands.

He choked at how wonderful her hands felt on him. "That's it, Sunshine," he breathed against her hair. "Bring me home."

She arched her back and gently guided him into the wet heat of her body. Talon growled ferociously at the feel of her.

Like an animal, he made love to her furiously.

Panting and weak from desire, Sunshine clutched him to her as he thrust himself against her until she was dizzy with pleasure. For the first time since they had met, he didn't hide his fangs from her. He let her see him as he really was.

Let her know the untamed beast that inhabited this man's body.

Their gazes locked, she watched the ecstasy on his face as he rocked himself between her thighs.

She cupped his face in her hands, mesmerized by the man and the predator he was.

All her life she'd heard tales of immortal beings, of vampires taking possession of their victims.

Tonight, she wanted to be his.

Talon was out of control with her. He knew it. His emotions surging, he couldn't think. He could only feel. She was his focal point. His everything.

Her scent permeated his head, covered his body, heightening his senses.

He heard the blood rushing through her veins, felt her heart pounding against his chest. The heat of her soft, feminine skin sliding against his.

Take her!

It was a feral command.

Primal.

Demanding.

Had he been in his right mind, he would have controlled himself. As it was, he couldn't.

Now, he was the beast that stalked the night. His only thought having her, he slid himself deep inside her and then he sank his fangs deep into her neck.

He felt her surprise for only an instant until complete sexual ecstasy tore through them both.

Their bodies and minds were united. Joined.

He felt every thought in her head. Every emotion. Every fear. Every joy.

He saw inside her heart down to her fear that he didn't love her as much as he loved Nynia. That he would never love her as much. He felt her hopelessness and her determination.

Most of all, he felt her love.

Growling fiercely, he let her essence wash over him. Let her seep into every corner of his being. There were no more secrets between them. No more places to hide.

She was as bare to him as he was to her.

And her love for him was the most incredible feeling he'd ever experienced.

Talon thrust himself in deep as his head and body exploded. Their orgasms were so fierce that he couldn't keep the motorcycle upright. Before he knew what had happened, they were lying on the ground, still entangled as his sense returned to him.

Sunshine stared up at him in the moonlight, her clothes disheveled and her face adoring.

In her mind, she could still hear his thoughts. His fear of losing her, his need to protect her.

She saw his guilt that he had allowed his sister to die. His need to right the wrong that had been done to Nynia.

The sadness and grief that lived inside him as constant companions.

Most of all, she saw his need to hold her. His need to not fail her.

She felt his power and strength, which were unlike anything she had imagined. He was a predator.

And he was the man she loved. One who loved her and one who was willing to do anything for her.

Even give up his own life.

"I love you, Talon," she breathed.

Talon couldn't believe what he had done as he brushed his hand against her neck and removed the telltale signs of blood. Her taste permeated his mind, his senses.

Zarek had been right, that was the most incredible high he'd ever known. And now that he'd seen inside her heart . . .

Gods, what had he done?

In one moment of careless passion, he had sown the seeds of both their destruction.

Chapter 16

Talon took her back to the cabin, but he didn't speak to her. He wasn't sure what to say.

She didn't seem to mind the fact that he'd bitten her, which was a very good thing.

But he couldn't get it out of his mind.

Her taste.

Her feelings.

Her love.

It would haunt him forever.

Sunshine went to the bathroom to freshen up while he turned on his desk lamp.

A few seconds later, someone knocked on the door.

Talon pulled his srad from his boot. Visitors didn't come often to his house.

"Who is it?"

"It's Ash, Celt. Don't have a coronary."

"Is it Acheron or Styxx?"

"It's T-Rex and I'm not wearing sunglasses."

Prepared for a trick, Talon opened the door carefully. It really was "old spooky eyes" and he didn't look pleased.

"What are you doing here?" Talon asked.

"Fighting Daimons. What about you?"

He caught the sarcasm and the condemnation in Ash's voice. "There were Daimons here? Where?"

"They attacked the Katagaria den and I went to help Vane and Fang."

Talon winced at the news. He should have been here to help fight. Damn, he'd screwed up royally. "Are they okay?"

"No. Their sister and her pups were killed in the fighting."

Talon's heart clenched at the news. That was one pain he knew all too well. The brothers would be devastated over her loss. "Man, I'm sorry."

"So, where were you?"

Before he could answer, Ash answered for him. "Wait, I know this one. You were at Sanctuary showing off your powers to a busload of Japanese tourists who were armed with digital cameras and camcorders. Congratulations, bud, we just went global."

Talon covered his face with his hand. "Oh jeez, are you serious?"

"Do I look like I'm kidding?"

No, he looked really pissed off.

"I can't believe this," Talon said.

"You? You can't believe this? I'm the one who has to go to Artemis to save your ass. She was freaking out over Zarek, now how the hell do I explain to her that Mr. Cool-Calm-and-Collected was doing his impression of Spider-Man in a bar loaded with tourists and ended up as the main feature on Tokyo news as what's wrong with American culture?

"Question. How many rules *did* you break in less than a minute?

"Worst of all, I now have Nick calling me up, wanting to know why he has to keep everything secret while you guys are running around exposing yourselves at random. The little prick even wants a raise because he can keep a secret while none of you can."

"I can explain."

"Okay, I'm waiting."

Talon tried to come up with a reason for what he'd done. There wasn't one.

"Okay, I can't explain. Give me a minute."

Ash narrowed his eyes. "I'm still waiting."

"I'm thinking about it."

Sunshine came out of the bathroom, then blanched as soon as she saw Acheron. She grabbed one of Talon's staves from the wall and went after him.

Acheron caught it in his hand as she swung it for his head. "Hey!"

Sunshine turned to Talon. "He's the one who kidnapped me!"

"I did not," Acheron said huffily as he tugged the staff from her grip.

"This is my boss, Sunshine. Acheron."

She formed a small O with her mouth. "Vane said you two looked alike. He wasn't kidding. Although now that I'm a bit calmer, you don't really look like him that much. He was scary, but you . . . you're *really* scary."

"If I had more time, I'd feel complimented." He handed the staff to Talon. "Outside, Celt, so we can finish our talk."

Talon didn't like being ordered about, but in this case he had no choice.

He had truly messed up and Ash had a right to vent.

Talon had put all of them in a very bad situation.

He went outside to stand on the dock where Ash was waiting with his hands on his hips.

Ash's face was mottled by fury. "You know, I've had a *really* wonderful night tonight. I got to tell Kyrian and Julian that Valerius is in town and spent, oh I don't know, three, four hours trying to keep them from going after the Roman. Then, just when I could relax and do my job, I find out there are Daimons in the swamp and no Talon to kill them. And why wasn't Talon here? Because Tarzan was swinging off a balcony to save Jane from Cheetah.

"Now all I can do is stand here and say, next fiasco, please, right this way."

Talon glared at him. "You don't have to be so sarcastic. I know I screwed up, okay?"

"No, *screwed up* is getting caught without your pants in

Sunshine's apartment. This is a little bigger than just screwing up."

"I'm not going to apologize for what I did."

A tic beat in his jaw as Ash glanced away. "There are a lot of things that are still up in the air about tomorrow night. A lot of unknown factors. What we *do* know isn't good.

"I have Julian and Kyrian, who want to put Val in a pine box. Val, who doesn't want to lift a finger to help anyone not descended from the Romans. Two pissed-off wolves who are going to want revenge over what happened tonight. Zarek, who is mental on his best day, and who is currently wanted by New Orleans' finest. Nick screaming that he's quitting because he's tired of cleaning up after psychos. An angry goddess who is going to want everyone's head over this. And the only Hunter I have who is reliable is you."

Ash paused and gave him a stern glare. "And buddy, no offense, but you haven't been reliable in days."

"I'm okay, T-Rex."

"No, Talon, you're not. You were swinging from the rafters and punching out innocent humans because of Sunshine. You risked not only yourself, but all of us and the Peltiers just to protect one woman from hurt feelings. Where was your head?"

Anger tore through him. "I'm not a child, Ash. I know how to prioritize."

"Normally, you do. But you're thinking with your heart, not your head, and that will get us all killed. We're Dark-Hunters, Talon, we don't *feel*."

Any other time, he would agree with that, but at the moment Talon was feeling a whole lot of frustrated rage. He didn't need this lecture. He knew the risks and the dangers even better than Ash did. He more than understood everything at stake.

"I've got it under control."

"Do you?" Ash asked. "Because from where I'm standing, you don't. You have directly disobeyed me when I told you to keep Sunshine here. You have made pacts with the Katagaria and with Eros, and that's not your place. You don't make those kinds of obligations, Talon. Have you *any* idea how that can play out?"

"I had to do it. I have to protect my wife. I don't care what it costs."

"Your wife?" Ash shook his head. "Talon, look at me." Talon did.

Ash stared at him intently, his gaze cold and unfeeling. "Your wife is *dead*. She died fifteen hundred years ago and was buried in your homeland. Sunshine isn't Nynia."

Talon roared with his anger and pain. It wasn't true. Sunshine was his wife. He felt it. He knew it. She was all that mattered to him.

All that mattered.

Before he could think twice, he attacked Acheron. He caught the Atlantean's throat between his hands and shook him, trying to make him understand.

"She's not dead!" he snarled. "Damn you, she's not dead."

Ash broke his hold and used his powers to immobilize him.

Talon hissed and snarled as he tried to break free, but it was useless.

And in that moment, he realized just how far gone he really was.

I've attacked Acheron.

The thought sobered him. Ash was right. If he didn't calm down and get a hold of himself, he could get them all killed.

All of them.

Ash took a deep breath and released him. "Talon, you have a decision to make. Dark-Hunters don't have wives. We don't have families. At the end of the day, we have no one but ourselves. Our responsibility, our *only* responsibility, is to the humans who can't protect themselves from the Daimons. You've got to get your head straight."

"I know." Talon breathed raggedly.

Ash nodded. Then his eyes turned a strange, deep silver.

"Tell me what you want to do. Do you want me to petition Artemis for your soul?"

Talon thought about it. Right now, he stood on a precipice that he had never thought to face. Not once in his entire Dark-Hunter existence had he ever dared to dream Nynia would be back.

That she would . . .

He closed his eyes and winced.

Nynia wasn't back. Acheron was right.

Nynia was dead.

The woman in his cabin right now wasn't his wife.

She was Sunshine. A vibrant, caring woman who had fire and spunk.

She might have his wife's soul, but she was someone else. Someone he didn't want to live without.

Someone he didn't dare keep.

He felt as if his heart were being shredded. Sunshine was human. In time, she could forget him and have another life. Someone else to love.

The thought pierced him, but he had to do this.

Either way, he would lose her. At least this way, she stood a chance for happiness that wouldn't kill her.

"No," Talon said quietly. "I don't want to reclaim my soul knowing that I'll lose Sunshine to Camulus's wrath. I don't want my freedom at that cost."

"You sure?"

He nodded, then shook his head no. "Honestly, T-Rex, I'm not sure about anything anymore." He looked at him. "Have you ever loved anyone?"

Acheron met his gaze stoically, and didn't respond to the question. "You know, the thing about life and love is that they are both ever-changing while people seldom are. If you know this woman and you really love her, isn't it worth the chance for freedom to have her?"

"But if I lose her . . ."

"That is an *if*, Celt. It seems to me the only certainty is if you don't at least try, then you will definitely lose her."

"But if I let her go, she'll at least be alive."

"The way you've lived since the day Nynia died?"

"That's not fair."

"I'm not paid to be fair. I'm paid to kick Daimon ass." Acheron let out a tired sigh. "You know, I met a wise man centuries ago in China who said to me, 'He who lets fear rule him, has fear for a master.' "

"Confucius?"

"No, Minh-Quan. He was a fisherman who used to sell what I'm told was the best *zong zi* ever made."

Talon scowled at the unexpected comment. That was the thing about Acheron, you never really knew what you were going to get out of him.

"You're a strange man, Acheron Parthenopaeus. Tell me, what you would do if you were me?"

Acheron folded his arms over his chest. "I would never presume to be anyone other than myself, Talon. I'm not the one who has to bear the consequences of your actions. That's for you, alone, to do."

Talon sighed. "Is it possible to fight a god and win?"

His eyes turned dull. Talon watched him curiously. There was something in Acheron's past that his question brushed on. Something deep and dark, judging by the look on Acheron's face.

"Celtic and Greek gods are very much like people. They make mistakes. And those mistakes are what will either make us or break us in the end."

"You're sounding like an Oracle now."

"Scary, isn't it?"

"Not scary, just irritating." Talon started away from him.

"Talon."

He stopped and turned back to face Acheron. "To answer your question. Yes, you can win battles with a god. But it's much easier to negotiate." Acheron's tone told him that he spoke with the voice of experience.

"How do you negotiate with a god who wants you to suffer for all of eternity?"

"Very carefully, little brother. *Very* carefully." Acheron

glanced away, into the swamp. "You know, I think you may be losing sight of something really important."

"And that is?"

"Very few of us are ever given a second chance to reclaim what we've lost. If Nynia came back to you, maybe there's a reason for it."

Acheron unfolded his arms. "You have my number, Celt. If you change your mind about the petition, let me know. But you need to make your decision fast. I need your mind clear by tomorrow night."

"Why are you giving me a choice when you didn't give Kyrian one? You petitioned Artemis and gave his soul to Amanda without his knowing it."

Acheron shrugged. "Kyrian didn't have a choice to make. Without a soul, Desiderius would have killed him. Your life isn't in danger if you don't get your soul back, Talon. Just your heart is. And as you well know, you can live without your heart. But do you really want to?"

There were times when he seriously wished Acheron was the twenty-one-year-old snot-nosed kid he appeared to be, and not an eleven-thousand-year-old wise man.

This was definitely one of those times.

"I'm going to take Sunshine back to town with me."

"No," Talon said automatically. "She stays here so I can protect her."

"It wasn't a question, Celt. You need time away from her to think. Time to clear your thoughts before tomorrow night."

He started to argue, then realized Ash was right.

He was going to have to let her go anyway. He might as well do it now.

It would be easier for both of them.

"Okay, I'll go get her."

Sunshine knew something was wrong the minute she saw Talon come through the door.

His face was haunted, his eyes dark.

"What happened?" she asked.

"Acheron's going to take you back to your loft." His voice was so dispassionate that it made her stomach tight.

"I see. And do you agree with him?"

"I do. I think it's for the best."

But she didn't want to go. The depth of how much she wanted to stay startled her. "I see."

Woodenly, she started gathering her things. But inside, inside she was dying.

Talon couldn't stand seeing her like this. He wanted to grab her and run away to a place where no one could find them. To hold her safe.

The only problem was, no one could hide from a god.

Sooner or later, Camulus would find them and then she would die.

He took her backpack as she reached for it. "I've got it."

She nodded, her eyes bright and shiny.

Neither one of them spoke as he led her outside to where Acheron was waiting. He handed her backpack to Ash.

"It's, uh . . . it's been fun, Talon," she said. "Will I see you again?"

He looked at Ash, who watched him with an arched brow as if he wanted an answer to that one himself.

"No," he said slowly.

She cleared her throat, but didn't speak. Instead, she walked over to Acheron. "I'm ready."

Ash stepped back and let her lead the way to the catamaran. "Celt," he said, "if you change your mind about our discussion, call me."

Talon nodded.

His heart breaking, he watched Sunshine strap herself in. Ash started the boat and then headed them out into the swamp.

It was over.

She was gone.

I am Darkness. I am Shadow.

I am the Ruler of the Night.

I, alone, stand between mankind and those who would see mankind destroyed. I am the Guardian.

The Soulless Keeper.

Neither Human, nor Apollite, I exist beyond the realm of the Living, beyond the realm of the Dead.

I am the Dark-Hunter.

And I am Eternal . . . unless I find that one pure heart who will never betray me. The one whose faith and courage can return my soul to me and bring me back into the light.

If not for Camulus . . .

"Not all of us are given a second chance to reclaim what we've lost. If Nynia came back to you, maybe there's a reason for it."

Aching, he turned his back on the sight of Sunshine leaving him and walked back into his cabin. He shut the door and looked about.

There was so much emptiness here now that Sunshine was gone. She had filled his home with happiness. Most of all, she had filled *him* with happiness.

His gaze fell to her pink cosmetics bag on his desk. She had forgotten it along with her hairbrush and hair ties.

Poor Sunshine, she was forever forgetting things.

"Speirr?"

He turned sharply to see Ceara beside him. "*Lurach*, are you here to judge me too?"

"*Nae,* my *bràthair*, I am here only to speak with you."

"About what?"

She reached out for him and then dropped her hand when she remembered they couldn't touch. "I just wanted to tell you before I leave that I have agreed with the god Bran to be reborn."

Talon's lungs seized.

He couldn't move.

He couldn't breathe.

Ceara gone?

Nae! The word tore through him.

She couldn't leave him. Not now. Not after all this time. She was the only solace he had left to him.

And at the same time, he couldn't bring himself to say that to her. To let her know how much he wanted her to stay.

How much he *needed* her to stay.

If he did, she would do as he asked and give up her future . . .

He could never be so selfish.

"What made you agree to it finally?" he asked, taking care to keep his voice level and smooth.

"It is time, Speirr. I want to live my life again. To find all the things I didn't have the last time. Love. Children. Even a job and a mortgage."

He couldn't smile at her attempt at humor, not while the pain inside him was so raw. So debilitating.

But he knew in his heart that she was right. It was time she had the things that had been denied her all those centuries before.

He wanted her to have all that and more. She deserved every happiness life could bring her. "I will miss you."

"And I shall miss you too, my *bràthair*."

He offered her a smile that he knew was hollow. "I wish you all the best, *lurach*. I send my heart with you."

"I know, Speirr. I love you too, but you have Nynia now. You won't be alone without me."

Yes, I will. Because I can't keep her either.

He nodded stoically. "I'll always remember you, Ceara."

Her eyes sad, she sighed regretfully. "I had best be going. Goodbye, Speirr."

Talon choked on his goodbye. He couldn't say the word. It hurt too much to say it. Saying it would make it real and he desperately didn't want this to be real.

He wanted this to be a bad dream he could wake up from.

But it wasn't. It was real. All of it.

Sunshine was gone.

Ceara was gone.

He had no one.

Feeling forsaken, he watched Ceara fade out of the room.

His heart shattered, he sank to the floor on his knees and

did something he hadn't done since the day Nynia had been buried.

He cried.

In his mind, he could see his father cut down by the Saxons while the boy, Speirr, had kept his mother and sisters safe from the murderous warriors.

He saw his mother and sister sick from a ravaging pox. Saw him working for Gara as hard as he could while the old woman took pleasure in making him suffer. At night, he'd cared for his sisters. And during those last few months of his mother's life when she'd been too ill to care for herself, he'd taken care of her too.

He saw Ceara as an infant who had been inconsolable as he tried everything to care for her. He remembered Gara turning them out into the dark night while they had no place to go.

It had been snowing that night too, and all he could think of was keeping his sister alive.

She was all he had.

And so he had carried her through the snowstorm while she screamed and howled. Through the leagues of frostbitten land until he had found his mother's people.

For his sister, he had begged and pleaded and allowed them to beat him until he couldn't stand.

He had never asked anything for himself.

Not until he found Nynia.

He had taken her and made her his, and by his own stupidity he had lost her.

They could never be together. Never.

I am solitude.

I am sorrow.

Talon bellowed in anger.

Suddenly, something to the right of him caught his attention. Talon frowned.

There was something sticking out from under his bed.

He moved toward it and pulled it out.

His heart stopped beating. Then it began pounding.

Sunshine had left them for him. There were three paintings of his cabin and dock and the view from his porch.

He stared at the vibrant, crisp colors that captured the scenery in the light of day.

They were beautiful, but nowhere near as beautiful as the woman who had given them to him.

A woman who had given him the greatest gifts of his life. He found a note sandwiched between two of the paintings. Opening it, he felt his stomach knot.

> *This is the swamp as I see it, but what I can't capture on canvas is you as I see you.*
>
> *No brush or paint will ever show the hero that you are. It will never be able to portray the sound of your voice when you whisper my name. The way my skin tingles when you touch me.*
>
> *The passion of you inside me.*
>
> *I love you, Talon. I know that I can't keep you. No one can ever tame a wild beast.*
>
> *You have a job to do and so do I. I only hope that when you think of me, it'll bring a smile to your face.*
>
> *Love always,*
> *Sunshine*

He reread the note four times.

For centuries, he'd loved Nynia. But what he felt for Sunshine was so much more.

"Yes, you can win battles with a god." Acheron's words hovered in his mind.

Talon drew a ragged breath.

Yes, he could win. He would go out tomorrow night and take care of Mardi Gras for Acheron.

But once it ended . . .

He was going to summon Camulus and end this once and for all.

By Wednesday's dawn, either he or Camulus would be dead.

Chapter 17

Sunshine wasn't sure what to make of Acheron as they entered her loft. He was lean and humongously tall, and those eyes of his . . .

She shivered.

Something about them made it seem like he could see straight through her. Like he could hear every thought she possessed.

She dropped her backpack beside the couch and watched him walk a circle around her loft, as if making sure no one was in here, and yet she sensed it was more habit than a real need he had to verify that they were alone.

He had such a deadly, graceful swagger. A predator's lope. There was something intrinsically sexual about Acheron. Something compelling, seductive. Just being near him made her want to reach out and touch him.

It was as if he were putting off powerful pheremones, and at the same time, she was scared of him. He was like a lethal, beautiful animal in the wild that part of you wanted to cuddle, even while the other part of you knew he was just as likely to rip your arm off as he was to cuddle back.

He was magnetic and fierce and he made her want to run for the door.

When he spoke, the powerful sound of his voice made her jump, but what struck her most was how erotic his voice was. It was so deep that it rumbled and every syllable he spoke went down her spine like a seductive caress. She'd never been around anyone whose entire body and character appeared to have been made for no other purpose than to entice women sexually.

Boy, did it ever work.

"Your brother, Storm, is below, cleaning up. You might want to have him spend the night with you."

"How do you know Storm is below?"

"I just do."

She frowned—he was even more eerie than her grandmother. "Why aren't you staying?"

"Do you want me to?"

No, not really. But she didn't want to offend him. "You probably have things you need to do."

He gave her a tight-lipped smile that seemed to indicate that he had heard her real response. "Then, good night, Sunshine."

He started for the door.

"Acheron, wait."

He paused and looked at her.

"Am I doing the right thing by letting Talon go?" she asked. "You need him, right?"

His mercury eyes seared her. "I think you need to listen to what your grandmother told you, Sunshine. Follow your heart."

"How did you know about that?"

He gave her a hint of a smile. "I know lots of things."

This was a very spooky man. She wondered if he was a missing member of the Addams family.

Acheron turned on his heel and walked out her door.

Sunshine stood there for several minutes, debating what she should do about Talon.

But in the end, she knew what her heart demanded she do . . .

She'd asked Psyche if it were possible to summon a goddess. She wasn't sure if Psyche had been honest, but there was only one way to find out.

"Artemis," she said out loud. "I summon you to human form."

Nothing happened.

There was no sound, no great flash of light.

Nothing.

Depressed, she started for her bedroom.

"Who are you? And why have you called for me?"

She froze at the sound of the peeved, thickly accented voice behind her.

Turning around, she saw an incredibly tall, beautiful woman standing by her sofa. Artemis had long, curly auburn hair that spiraled around the face of an angel and vibrant green eyes that didn't look happy to be here.

The goddess was dressed in a long, white sheathlike dress and stood with her hands on her hips.

"Are you Artemis?"

"Gee, let me think. Did you call for Artemis or for Peter Pan?"

Well, Artemis was definitely *not* a late-night person. She gave a whole new meaning to the word *cranky*. "I called for Artemis."

"Then since I'm not dressed in green and have the body of a woman and not some prepubescent boy, I guess I must be she."

"Are you always this irritable?"

"Are you always this stupid?" She crossed her arms over her chest and gave Sunshine a withering glare. "Look, little human, I have no patience for you. You're not one of my subjects and that medallion around your neck greatly offends me. So tell me what you want so I can tell you to go bugger off."

This was not looking good. Talon's boss-lady was a serious bitch. "I wanted to ask you if I could get Talon's soul back from you."

She cocked her head at the question. "You mean Speirr of the Morrigantes? The Celtic chieftain I snagged away from the Morrigán?"

"Yes."

"No."

"No?" Sunshine asked in disbelief.

"Is there an echo? No, human, his soul belongs to me and you can't have it."

"Why not?"

"Because I said so."

Sunshine was aghast. Furious at her too. Artemis would never be voted Miss Congeniality. The goddess needed some personal-relationship seminars. "Well, that just makes it official then, doesn't it?"

Artemis arched a haughty brow. "Little girl, have you any idea who or what you're dealing with?"

Sunshine took a deep breath and prayed for patience. She couldn't afford to lose her temper with the person who happened to own Talon's soul. Not if she wanted it back.

Not to mention the small fact that as a goddess, Artemis could probably wish her dead if she made her mad enough.

"I know, Artemis. I'm sorry. I don't mean to offend you. I am in love with Talon and I want us to have a future together. I would do anything to keep him with me. Can you not understand that?"

Artemis's face softened a degree, as if she could relate. "Yes, I understand."

"Then can I—"

"The answer is still no."

"Why?"

"Because nothing in this world is ever free. If you want his soul back you have to earn it or pay for it."

"How?"

Artemis shrugged. "*You* can't. You have nothing I want or value, therefore you have nothing to barter with."

"Oh, come on, are you serious?"

"Deadly." Artemis flashed into vapor and vanished.

Ugh! Sunshine wanted to throttle the woman. How could she be so selfish?

"Artemis!" she called out before she could stop herself. "You seriously suck!"

Closing her eyes, Sunshine sighed. What was she to do

now? There was no way that selfish heifer would ever let go of Talon's soul.

What were they going to do?

Amanda Devereaux-Hunter woke up at seven-thirty in the morning. She glanced absently at the clock and closed her eyes, then jerked to full alertness as the time dawned on her.

It was seven-thirty A.M. and her infant daughter, Marissa, hadn't awakened for her five o'clock feeding.

Not quite panicked, but definitely concerned about her baby, she got up and went to the nursery in the room beside hers.

As she neared the crib, her heart stopped.

It was empty.

At only three weeks of age, there was no chance Marissa had gotten up and walked away.

Oh God, it was Desiderius!

He'd come back for them!

Terror gripped her at the thought. Ever since she and Kyrian had defeated that monster, she'd had recurring nightmares of him returning from the dead for vengeance against them.

"Kyrian!" She raced back to the bed and woke her husband.

"What is it?" he asked grumpily.

"It's Marissa. She's gone."

Kyrian sat up, fully alert now. "Gone where?"

"She's not in her crib. I don't know where she is."

He sprang from bed and grabbed his pants from the floor. Without waiting for Kyrian, Amanda ran through the upstairs, her heart pounding.

Where could her baby be?

The thought of losing her child was her worst nightmare.

She dashed down the stairs to see if the front door was open. If maybe someone had come in and taken her.

As she started into the living room, Amanda pulled up

short. Shocked to the core of her being, she focused her gaze on the most unbelievable sight she'd ever beheld.

Acheron lay on the leather couch with Marissa cuddled contentedly on top of his muscular chest, up under his chin.

A pack of diapers was on the coffin-shaped coffee table along with an empty bottle of formula.

Relief and disbelief flooded her simultaneously.

When she had first met Acheron a little over a year ago, he had been the most terrifying thing she'd ever seen. A man possessed of incredible powers and contradictions, she had no doubt he could wish all of them into oblivion and yet there he lay with her infant daughter cradled tenderly in his huge hands.

"Is something . . ." Kyrian's voice trailed off as he, too, saw them.

She looked up at him over her shoulder. "I didn't know Ash liked babies."

"Neither did I. The uncomfortable way he's been behaving with Marissa in the house, I just assumed he had no use for them."

Kyrian was right. Ash had done nothing but avoid being around Marissa as much as possible. Every time she cried, he actually cringed and made a hasty exit. Amanda would never have guessed that he would actually tend her daughter.

Crossing the room, she reached for the baby.

Ash came awake with a look so feral and fierce that she stepped back with an audible gasp.

He sat up on the couch, but didn't move farther.

He blinked as he saw her and Kyrian.

"Sorry," Ash breathed. "I didn't realize it was you."

"I was just going to take her off you."

He glanced down at Marissa who was still sleeping within the shelter of his hands. "Oh. I must have fallen asleep while I was burping her."

He handed her to Amanda and the way he did it told her a lot. Acheron had an expertise that said he'd handled a baby more than just a few times.

"I hope I didn't scare you," he said apologetically. "She was crying when I came in and I went upstairs to make sure she was okay." He looked strangely pale, as if the thought of a baby crying was somehow painful for him. "Since the two of you were still sleeping and I was up, I figured I'd give you guys a break."

Amanda bent over and kissed him on the cheek. "You're a good man, Ash. Thanks."

A pain-filled look crossed his face as he pulled back from her. He got up from the couch and picked his backpack up from the floor. "I'll go on up to bed."

Kyrian stopped him as he started for the hallway. "You okay, Acheron? You look kind of shaken."

Ash laughed at that. "When have I ever been shaken?"

"Good point."

He clapped Kyrian on the shoulder. "I'm just tired."

"Yeah, I was wondering where you spent yesterday. You never came back here to sleep."

"I had something to take care of. Something that wouldn't wait."

Amanda sighed. "You know, Ash, one day you're going to have to learn to confide in someone."

"Good night, Amanda," Ash said. He inclined his head to Kyrian and headed for the stairs.

Amanda joined her husband as Acheron vanished upstairs. "I can't believe you've known him for twenty-one hundred years and you know so little about him that you can't even tell me his real hair color."

He shrugged. "Ash is so self-contained and -controlled that I doubt if anyone will ever know anything about him other than his name."

Sunshine lay in her bed long into the morning, remembering the sound of Talon's deep, even breaths while he slept.

She remembered the way he liked to keep his knee snuggled high between her thighs and his arm draped possessively over her chest with his left hand buried in her hair.

How she missed him.

Then, her thoughts drifted into the past. Far into her other life . . .

"Don't go, Speirr. There is evil in this. I know it."

Angry, he'd jerked his arm free of her grasp. "They murdered my uncle, Nynia. Cut him down before my eyes. I will not rest until I have vengeance."

As Nynia, she had been too afraid of losing him to press the matter. She'd always deferred to him in all things. He was her husband. But in her heart, she'd known he was about to set matters into motion that could never be reversed.

And she had been right.

Just as she knew somehow tonight would settle everything one way or another.

What if she lost Talon?

She couldn't bear the thought of it any more than she could bear the thought of living out her life without him.

She glanced around her loft, at all the familiar things.

Since the day she'd divorced Jerry, all she had wanted was her career, her art.

Now, alone with her stuff, it just didn't seem quite so important to her.

Her art didn't hold her at night. It didn't make her laugh or seduce her. It didn't make her body burn with desire or shiver with orgasms.

It didn't punch Jerry in the nose for being a jerk.

Only Talon did that.

Only Talon *could* do that.

Her eyes fell to the Snoopy dispenser as tears welled up. "I can't let him go."

If only she knew how to keep him.

Zarek sat in the darkened corner of the living room, listening to the city outside awaken. He should be sleeping, resting up for the night that was to come, but he couldn't seem to find the peace he needed.

Instead, he stared at Talon. "You almost look normal tonight. Are you going to stay that way?"

"I told you I could contain myself." So far, it was working.

Talon was at peace with the fact that come the dawn he'd be having it out with Camulus.

When Ash stepped forward to speak, it dawned on Talon that Zarek was nowhere to be seen.

Was he upstairs too?

"Where's Zarek?" he asked Ash.

"I have him guarding Sunshine."

Now that destroyed his calm.

"Like hell!" Talon roared.

"Trust me, Talon. I believe in Zarek to do the right thing."

Talon's response was emphatic. "I don't trust him. At all. And after this, I'm not sure if I trust you."

"Enough of the bickering," Ash said. "Just do as I told you and everything should work out."

"Should?" Talon asked.

When Ash spoke, there was an odd note in his voice that made Talon wonder how much more Ash knew than he was telling them. "We have predestinies, Talon, but human will can circumvent them. If everyone does as I've instructed, then things should work out the way they're meant to."

Talon clenched his teeth. "And if we don't?"

"We're all screwed."

"Gee, Ash," Nick said sarcastically, "you're just so damn comforting."

Ash gave him a wry look. "I try to be anyway."

Nick's answer was flat. "You fail admirably."

Talon was still stewing.

Ash spoke to all of them. "What I need everyone to know is that we have a truly sinister night ahead of us. It seems Dionysus and Camulus have combined their forces to try and get themselves reinstated to their full godhoods."

"How are they planning on doing that?" Valerius asked.

"The two of them aren't strong enough to do it on their own. They need the power of a third god to aid them."

"What god?" they all asked simultaneously.

"Apollymi."

"Who the hell is Apollymi?" Talon asked. "I've never even heard of her."

One corner of Ash's mouth turned up wryly. "She's an old god who dates back to my time. One who has powers over life, vengeance, and death. The Atlanteans affectionately referred to her as the Destroyer."

"Is she like Hades?" Valerius asked.

"Oh no," Ash said ominously, "this god makes Hades look like a Boy Scout. Apollymi finishes off her victims with an iron hammer and commands an army of malformed demons.

"The last time someone freed her, plagues and suffering permeated the world and she sent Atlantis straight to the bottom of the sea. She headed across Greece, laying waste to the entire country, and setting them back culturally thousands of years before she was finally returned to her holding cell. The Destroyer will unleash holy hell on this earth. Starting with New Orleans."

"Oh goodie," Nick said sarcastically. "I just love knowing about these things."

Ash ignored him.

"So how do they intend to free the Destroyer?" Talon asked.

Ash took a deep breath. "The only way to do that is with the blood of an Atlantean."

"Your blood," Talon said. It was a given, since Ash was the only Atlantean left alive.

Ash nodded. "At midnight, the threshold between this plane and the one where she lives will be thin enough to breach. If they unleash her . . ."

"Anyone else have an ulcer?" Nick asked.

Talon ignored his question. "How do we stop them?"

"With a lot of faith and by doing exactly what I tell you to do."

Nick snorted at that. "Does anyone other than me think that Ash is being just a little too vague about all this?"

Everyone except Ash raised their hands.

"You're not funny," Ash said to them.

Ash looked to Valerius. "I need you on the streets with the Peltiers. At eleven-thirty, Dionysus is planning to unleash his Daimons on the population in order to distract us. Slay any of them you find.

"Nick," Ash said, "I want you and Eric ready to mobilize if you're needed."

The Squires nodded.

Ash put his sunglasses on. "Talon, you stay with me. You and I are going after Dionysus and his crew."

"Just out of curiosity," Talon said, "how do you know all this?"

Ash ignored him.

"All right, children," Ash said, "head out and guard the streets."

"Just one question?" Eric asked him.

"Sure."

"Maybe I'm being dense but why are these guys after power now? Why didn't they do this last year or at some other time? Why wait?"

Ash's answer wasn't comforting in the least. "This isn't the first time they've tried to take their powers back. This is just the best shot they've had at succeeding."

"Okay," Eric said slowly. "So what happened to their powers to begin with?"

Talon answered for Ash. "When a god ceases to be worshiped, their powers diminish. If a god is defeated by another god, then a chunk of his powers is absorbed by the victor and he loses his ability to regain his former position."

Eric nodded. "Okay, one last thing. What happens if they do regain their powers?"

Ash looked away. "Let us hope we don't find out."

"Why?"

"Because according to Atlantean myth, the Destroyer is supposed to be the one who will bring about Telikos—the end of the world. No doubt Dionysus and Camulus are thinking that Apollymi will be so overcome with gratitude when they release her that she won't think twice about joining them and sharing her power with them.

"What they don't know is that there was a really good reason why Apollymi was imprisoned by the Atlantean gods. Even the other gods feared Apollymi's wrath, and in the end, she killed them all. Whatever we do, we can't ever let her escape. If they free her tonight, everything you know about this existence will change. *Everything*."

"Gotta love saving the world," Talon said. "Another day in the life."

Ash took a deep breath. "And on that note we have things to do."

Talon nodded, but in his heart, he wished he could see Sunshine one more time.

He didn't want to die without seeing her face again.

Duty, how it reeked.

Valerius headed out first.

Talon, Nick, and Eric went out through the back door with Ash pulling up the rear.

As Ash left the house, the back door slammed shut, catching the tail end of his long black coat.

Ash jerked to a stop and cursed.

Nick howled with laughter at the sight of Acheron trapped. "Don't it take the bad-ass right out of you?"

Ash arched a brow.

The door opened by itself, freeing his coat, then it slammed shut again.

Nick sobered instantly. "And that puts it right back in you."

Ash ruffled Nick's hair like an older brother. "Watch our backs and soothe Amanda's nerves until Kyrian returns."

"You got it."

Ash and Talon left the ornate courtyard and headed into the crowd of tourists and locals who were as thick as fog.

There were hundreds of people out. Hundreds who had

no idea that the very fate of the world rested in the hands of the two men dressed in black who were making their way slowly through them.

Two men who were tired tonight. Weary.

One because he had long ago ceased feeling anything except the heavy burden of his responsibilities.

Ash wanted nothing more than one single day to just lie down and rest. One day to find a moment's worth of comfort.

He'd spent eternity waiting for a second chance.

Waiting for an escape from the wreckage of his past and the damnation that made up his future.

Tonight, he had to face his brother for the first time in eleven thousand years.

The two of them had never been on equal footing. Styxx had hated him since the moment of his birth.

For Ash, this was going to be a long, long night.

Talon's thoughts were on Sunshine. On the gentle curve of her face. The beauty of her touch.

Was she in her loft painting?

Was she thinking of him?

"I love you." Her words tore through him.

Talon clenched his teeth, wishing he were touching her. Hoping that at the end of this night she would be safe from Camulus forever.

"Faith, Talon," Ash said as if he knew his thoughts.

"I'm trying."

Talon took a deep breath.

His death didn't concern him. It was Sunshine he couldn't allow to die. Right or wrong, he would see this through, and come morning she would be safe.

No matter what it took.

Chapter 18

Sunshine followed Zarek's directions to the Warehouse District, but getting there in the heavy traffic wasn't easy. They probably could have walked faster.

Normally the traffic wouldn't have bothered her; however, Zarek wasn't exactly friendly, and between his sour mood and the drunken revelers on the street who kept staggering out into the road, her nerves were pretty much fried.

She wasn't really sure why they had to go out tonight, but Zarek had assured her that Ash wanted her moved for safety's sake.

He'd promised her that Talon would be able to fight better knowing she was hidden away from Camulus and Styxx.

"So how long have you been a Dark-Hunter?" she asked, trying to do something to ease the tension between them.

"You don't care, so why do you ask?"

"Well, you're just Mr. Warm and Fuzzy, aren't you?"

He looked at her coldly. "When you kill things for a living, it tends to take the warm and fuzzy right out of you."

"Talon isn't like that."

"Well, bully for him."

She growled as she slammed on the brakes to avoid hitting a man dressed up like a bull. He pounded on the hood of her car and yelled, then dashed across the street.

Sunshine moved forward again, even more slowly,

through the bumper-to-bumper traffic. "You don't like Talon, do you?"

"Wish him dead every time I see him."

She frowned at Zarek's blasé tone. "I can't tell if you mean that or not."

"I mean it."

"Why?"

"He's an asshole and I've had enough assholes in my life."

"Do you hate Ash too?"

"Baby, I hate everyone."

"Even me?"

He didn't answer.

Sunshine didn't bother him after that. There really was something spooky about Zarek. Something cold and unreachable. It was as if he took pleasure in the fact that he shoved everyone away from him.

At least twenty minutes passed before Zarek shocked her by asking a question of his own. "You love the Celt, don't you?"

"Yes."

"Why? What is it about him that makes you care for him?"

She sensed Zarek was asking something much deeper than that. It was as if the concept of love were so alien to him that he was struggling to make sense of it.

"He's a good man who makes me laugh. He looks at me and I melt all over the floor. When I'm with him, I feel like I can fly."

Zarek turned his head away from her and watched the Mardi Gras crowd outside.

"Have you ever been in love?" she tried again.

Again, he didn't answer. Instead he directed her to a warehouse on St. Joseph Street.

The place was dark and forbidding. "Is this where we're supposed to be?" she asked.

He nodded.

She parked in an alley behind the building, and they left the car.

Zarek led her in through a back door and up a series of stairs. He opened a door at the end of the hallway and let her enter first.

Sunshine stepped inside. At first glance, she thought the tall blond man was Acheron with a new hair color. But when she saw Camulus standing by his side, she knew it wasn't.

It was Styxx who was standing between Camulus and a brunet man she didn't recognize.

Sunshine turned to run.

Zarek closed the door ominously and took up a blocking position before it. The look on his face told her that he had no intention of letting her pass through him.

"Come in, come in, said the spider to the fly," Camulus said.

Sunshine lifted her chin as she faced the men. Camulus was extremely handsome, but he had a smile that was pure evil.

Even more so than Zarek and that was hard to accomplish.

The man she didn't know was humongously tall with light brown hair and a goatee. He had an extremely refined, well-bred look to him.

"I'm going to take a wild guess that you are Dionysus," Sunshine said, remembering what Selena had once told her about the patron god of Mardi Gras.

He smiled as if flattered she knew him. "Guilty."

Camulus let out a long breath. "She's so bright. It's almost a shame to kill her. But . . . oh well."

"You can't hurt her," Zarek said from the door. "You promised me she wouldn't be harmed if I brought her here."

"So I lied," Dionysus said. "Sue me."

Zarek started for the god, but Sunshine stopped him. She wasn't really sure why she did that, it just seemed as if he were the closest thing to an ally she had in that room.

She turned back to Camulus, knowing exactly how he

planned to hurt Talon tonight. "I'm not going to let you kill me in front of Talon."

They all laughed. All except for Zarek.

"You can't stop us," Camulus said.

Zarek glanced down at her, then did a double take as his dark gaze fell to her necklace. "Uh, gods, I think you've forgotten something."

Dionysus curled his lip. "We forget nothing."

"Oh, okay," Zarek said sarcastically, "then you must already know that she wears a Marking Medallion."

They sobered instantly.

"What?" Camulus snarled.

Sunshine pulled her grandmother's necklace out of her shirt and held it up to them. She couldn't really believe it might help her, but hey, anything at this point was worth a try. "My grandmother said that the Morrigán would always protect me."

Camulus cursed. "Oh, this ain't right." He cursed again.

"This thing really works?" she whispered to Zarek.

"More than you know," he whispered back. "He can't kill you without making the Morrigán angry."

"Well, who knew?" she said, amazed by the knowledge. "Cool."

"Yup," Zarek concurred. "Better than a cross with Dracula."

She beamed. "Does it work against Dionysus too?"

He nodded.

Oh, this was good. Very, very good. "Okay, then, let's talk."

"Talk about what?" Dionysus hissed.

"Not you. Him." She indicated Camulus with a nod. "I want to talk about Talon's curse."

Camulus's eyes blazed at her. "What about it?"

"I want you to lift it."

"Never."

She held her medallion out to him. "Do it or . . ." She gave Zarek a sideways glance. "Does this have any power to hurt him?"

"Only if he hurts you first."

Damn. What kind of protection was that? She needed to have a talk with whoever came up with these things.

A calculating glint lightened Camulus's eyes. He sighed as if bored. "Oh well, since I can't kill you, I guess I'll have to content myself with killing Talon instead."

Terror consumed her. "What?"

Camulus shrugged nonchalantly. "It's rather pointless to let him live happily ever after with you when my intent was to make him suffer. Since you can't die, he'll have to."

Her hand shook as she held the medallion in her suddenly sweaty grip. "Won't Artemis be mad if you kill one of her soldiers?"

He looked at Dionysus, who burst out laughing. "Artemis, darling that she is, would most definitely care. However, she won't start a war with the Celtic pantheon over it. Unlike me, Cam is safe from her wrath."

"Doesn't it just reek?" Camulus asked. His happy smile belied his dire words.

Sunshine wanted to cry. This couldn't be happening.

By saving herself, she had condemned Talon to die.

No! She couldn't let this happen. "Okay, there has to be another way."

Camulus narrowed his eyes as if thinking about the matter. "Perhaps there is. Tell me, Sunshine. How much does Talon's happiness mean to you?"

"Everything," she said sincerely.

"Everything. Well, that certainly is a lot." His look turned steely cold, frightening. "Does it mean as much to you as your own soul?"

"Sunshine," Zarek said. "Don't."

"You, heel," Dionysus snarled.

Zarek cracked his knuckles. "Don't tell me what to do. I don't like it."

Sunshine ignored them. "What are you saying to me, Camulus?"

He tucked his hands into his pockets and acted as cool as someone chitchatting about the weather, not sealing the fate of her immortal destiny. "A simple trade. I lift his curse. You give me your soul."

Sunshine hesitated. "That seems easy."

"It is."

"So what are you going to do with my soul once you have it?"

"Nothing at all. I'll keep it with me, just like Artemis keeps Talon's."

"And my body?"

"A body doesn't need a soul to function."

Zarek put a hand on her shoulder. "Don't do it, Sunshine. You can't ever trust a god."

"Sure you can," Styxx said. "Trusting them is the best thing I ever did."

"I don't know," she breathed, searching her heart and mind, trying to decide what she should do.

Acheron and Talon stood on the crowded street. There were people everywhere, most of them drunk as they celebrated Mardi Gras.

Talon did a double-take as a man danced by him wearing a large diaper and a fake pair of gold wings. His long blond hair was tied back in a gold cord and he held a crossbow in one hand and a bottle of Jack Daniel's in the other. Drunk, the man was arbitrarily shooting his golden arrows at the people he passed by.

"Eros!" Talon snapped, grabbing the bow from him. "What are you doing?"

"I'm celebrating."

Acheron raked a less than amused stare over Eros's "costume." "What's with the get-up?"

Eros shrugged. "If you can't beat them, join them. They expect Cupid in a diaper, so here I am. Cute Cupid in a diaper." He threw an arm over Talon's shoulders. The god was so drunk he could barely stand on his own. "Hey, I found out something interesting. Dion has teamed up with another god for tonight's festivities. And would you believe, it's the same guy you were asking me about? What's his face, Camululu?"

Talon went cold at the name. "Camulus?"

"Yeah, *him*. I heard Dion saying they were going to party with your woman and that the psycho Hunter from Alaska was going to hand her over to them."

His blood boiling, Talon pushed Eros away and started back toward his car.

Acheron grabbed him. By the look on Ash's face, he could tell this was nothing Ash didn't already know. "Talon . . ."

"You knew!" Talon snarled at the betrayal. "How could you?"

Ash gave him a hard stare. "It's all right, Talon."

"Like hell it is." Rage gripped him hard. How could Acheron have betrayed him like this? How could he have turned Sunshine over into the hands of a man he knew was going to give her to the one god who wanted him punished?

"Damn you, damn you straight to hell!"

He punched Acheron in the jaw.

Ash took the hit without flinching, but when Talon moved to strike him again, he caught his hand. "This isn't accomplishing anything."

"It's making me feel better."

Ash grabbed him by the shoulder of his leather jacket and held him immobile. "Listen to me, Talon. The only way to save the two of you is to maintain your grip. Trust me."

"I'm tired of trusting you, Ash. Especially when you won't return it. Tell me what's going on here and why you sent Zarek to her knowing he was going to turn on her."

"It's the way things are meant to be."

Rage rolled over him. He wasn't some child to be lectured to about fate.

"Who the hell are you to say that? You're not a god, even though you pretend to be one with your vague-ass comments and spooky powers. You don't know the future any more than I do." Talon snarled at him. "If she dies, so help me, I'll kill you."

"Listen to me, Celt," he said sharply. "If you want to break Camulus's curse, the two of you have to confront him together tonight. This is the only shot you'll ever get to break free of him."

Talon didn't like any of this. Damn Ash for his secrecy. "Where are they?"

"They're in a warehouse. If you'll calm down, I'll take you to it.

"The night is far from over, Talon. Look inside you and find the peace you used to have. If you don't find it, you've lost even before you start to fight."

Talon did it, but it was hard. Nearly impossible. But he had no choice. He had to rein himself in or he would be useless to Sunshine.

When his head was clear, Acheron let him go.

"Maintain." The voice seemed to come from inside Talon's head.

Ash placed a hand on his shoulder.

One instant they were on Bourbon Street, the next they were outside a warehouse.

"What did you do?" Talon asked, wondering how many people had seen them vanish.

"I'm doing what I have to. Don't worry, no one saw us leave or arrive. I don't make those kinds of mistakes."

Talon hoped so.

Ash held the door open for him and Talon led the way into the building.

They were halfway through the main room when something akin to lightning flashed from upstairs. Screams rent the air.

Talon lost his calm as he sprinted for the stairs with Ash hot on his heels.

They rushed through a door and were almost run over by Zarek who was covered in blood and carrying Sunshine in his arms.

"What the hell?" Talon asked, terrified by the sight. "What happened to her?"

Before Zarek could answer, the door was blown from its frame.

"Run!" Zarek shouted.

No one had a chance. A swarm of hideous winged demons flew into the room. Talon cursed. He'd never seen anything like them. They were the color of rust and screeched like banshees as they flew at them.

They had three barbed tails that they wielded like whips.

Acheron held his hands up and blasted them with electrical energy. They recoiled, but kept coming.

"Get Sunshine out of here," Acheron ordered.

They headed back to the stairs only to find Daimons coming up from below.

Talon tossed two srads, taking out four of the creatures, but it didn't even slow them down. "We're surrounded."

Acheron spoke in a language Talon couldn't understand. The demons paused and flew around as if dazed by his order.

"It won't hold the demons for long," Ash shouted, his voice barely discernible over the ethereal flapping of wings and claps of thunder.

Ash threw his hands up and the Daimons ran into what appeared to be an invisible barrier between them.

Talon led Zarek down the hallway, hoping to find another way out of the building.

He shoved open a door to a smaller room.

"I think she's dying." Zarek's voice sent an electric chill through him.

"She's not dying."

"Talon, I think she's dying," he repeated.

The demons forgotten, Talon took her from Zarek's arms and laid her carefully on the floor.

Her face was so pale that it shook him.

"Sunshine?" he breathed, his heart pounding. "Baby, can you look at me?"

She did, but instead of the vibrancy he was used to seeing, he saw pain and deep regret.

"You're free, Talon," she whispered. "I made him break the curse."

"What?"

"She traded her soul to Camulus so that he would set you free." Zarek curled his lip at him. "I told her not to do it, that it was a trick. She didn't listen and as soon as she agreed, the bastard blasted her."

Talon choked. "No!" he roared at both of them. "Sunshine, why?"

"He said he would kill you. I thought he would just take my soul, Talon. I didn't know he would do this. I didn't know he couldn't take possession of my soul without killing me first."

Talon tore the medallion from Sunshine's neck. "Damn you, Morrigán," he shouted, throwing it against the wall. "How could you forsake her too?"

She pressed her cold hand to his lips, "Shh, baby. Don't say that. It's my fault."

"I told her there's always a catch. But she didn't ask the right questions."

Tears flowed down Talon's cheeks as he watched her struggle to breathe. Over and over in his mind he remembered every moment of their time together, both in this life and her previous one.

He saw Sunshine's bright, tender face the first time they had made love. Saw her wrestling for her easel with Beth.

Heard her singing "Puff the Magic Dragon" as she doodled.

He took her hands into his and kissed them, with their smell of paint, turpentine, and patchouli. Hands that created breathtaking works of art.

Hands that could tear him apart with a simple touch . . .

"I'm not going to lose you again," he breathed. "Not like this."

Zarek came forward. "What are you doing, Celt?"

"Get away from me."

Talon placed his hands over her chest wound and closed his eyes. He forced himself to calm down, forced his emotions to leave him, and then he summoned his Dark-Hunter powers, and let them wash through him. His immortal strength flowed, surged. It swelled up and moved from his hands into her body.

His arms burned as he, in turn, absorbed her injury into his own chest.

Normally, it would hurt when he did this. Tonight, the pain was crippling because this wound wasn't a small injury.

It was mortal.

Gasping from the wrenching agony of his heart being pierced, Talon fell back, away from her.

Sunshine lay still, waiting for the pain to return.

It didn't.

Afraid she was already dead, she reached up to touch her chest where Camulus's blast had struck her. There was no longer a wound there.

"Talon?" She sat up to see Zarek staring at him.

"Oh God, no!" she shrieked as she saw Talon lying on the floor, bleeding. She scrambled to his side and pulled him into her arms. "What have you done?"

"He took your injuries into his own body," Zarek explained. "Now, instead of you dying, he will."

"No, Talon, no! Please don't die," she begged.

"Shh," Talon said quietly. "It's okay."

Ash came running through the door, took one look at them and cursed. "What happened?"

"The Celt absorbed her injuries." Zarek's voice was scarcely more than a whisper and filled with disbelief.

Something struck the door. Hard.

"Don't worry," Ash said. "I have a shield on the room. The gods can't pop in here until they breach it."

"Yeah, but at the rate they're going, they'll have the door knocked down any second," Zarek said. He pushed Ash toward Talon. "Go, get him out of here. I've got your backs."

"You sure?" Ash asked.

Zarek nodded.

"So help me, Slave," Dionysus snarled from the other side of the door. "I'll see you obliterated for this."

Zarek laughed coldly. "Come get some."

Ash opened the door on the opposite side of the room.

Sunshine was terrified. She didn't know what was happening. She still couldn't believe Zarek had turned around and helped them. Nor could she think past the sight of Talon covered in blood.

Everything was happening so fast that she wanted to run away and hide. But she couldn't.

Talon needed her to be strong for him and she refused to fail him.

As she started away from Zarek, he called out to her. "Hey, Sunshine?"

She looked back at him.

"Thanks for the bowl." Then he turned around to wait for the gods to break through Ash's barrier and the door.

Amazed by his actions, Sunshine ran to help Ash carry Talon down the hallway and into the last room on the left.

Ash laid him carefully on the floor, then used his powers to seal the room.

Sunshine's hand shook as she knelt beside Talon. He was pale and trembling. His entire body was coated with sweat and blood. "Hold on, baby," she whispered, not sure if he could even hear her now.

"He's immortal, right?" she asked Ash. "He'll be fine."

Ash shook his head. "His heart is pierced. When it stops beating, he'll die. Again."

His face grim, Ash looked up at the ceiling. "Artemis!" he shouted. "Get your ass here, right now."

A flash of light almost blinded Sunshine as the goddess appeared beside her.

Artemis gave Acheron a furious glare. "What is your problem?"

"I need Talon's soul. Now."

She laughed incredulously at him. "Excuse me, Acheron, but you haven't paid the price for it."

"Dammit, Artie, he's dying. I don't have time to negotiate."

She shrugged. "Then heal him."

"I can't and you know it. It's a mortal god-bolt wound.
I'm not allowed to interfere with that."

Sunshine felt an electric ripple flow through the room.

Rage darkened her sight as she stared at the selfish goddess. Sunshine started to lunge at her, but Ash caught her
and pulled her back.

Sunshine trembled in fear and anger.

"Give it to me, *now*." Acheron's deep voice sounded like
thunder. "Do it and I'll give you a week of total submission."

A calculating gleam darkened Artemis's eyes. "Give me
two."

Sunshine saw the fury and resignation on Ash's face.
"Done."

Artemis held her hand out and a large maroon stone
appeared in her palm.

When Ash went to take it, Artemis pulled it out of his
reach. "You will come to me at dawn."

"I will, I swear it."

Artemis smiled in satisfaction, then handed the stone to
Ash. Ash returned to Talon. Then, he met Sunshine's gaze.
"Sunshine, you're going to have to take this into your hand
and hold it over the brand mark until his soul is released
back into his body."

She reached for it, but Talon caught her wrist. She
hadn't even known he was still conscious until she felt his
weakened grip on her arm.

"She can't, Ash."

"Talon!" she said, angered that he was stopping her.
"What are you doing?"

"No, Sunshine," Talon whispered, his voice strained. "If
you take that, it will scar your hand. It could leave you
unable to draw or paint ever again."

Her greatest fear.

She looked into Talon's pain-filled eyes.

Her greatest love.

There was no contest.

She grabbed the stone from Ash's hand, then cried out as it seared her flesh.

"Watch Talon's eyes." She heard Ash's voice inside her head. "And for Zeus's sake, please don't let go of his soul. Focus . . ." She did and the pain lessened, but still she could feel the fire of the stone searing her hand.

Time stood still as she stared into Talon's jet-black eyes. Memories of this life and of their former one merged in her mind. She flashed back to her own death, to Talon holding her close.

She leaned down and kissed him. "I'm with you, love."

Talon took his last breath and relaxed. Her own heart stopped beating as raw terror consumed her.

Please, please, let this work!

Ash placed her hand over Talon's bow-and-arrow brand mark. Slowly, the heat faded and the stone turned dull in color.

Still, her hand burned.

When it was completely cold, she dropped the stone and waited.

Talon didn't move.

He didn't breathe.

He lay there, completely still and unresponsive to her.

"Talon?" she asked, her entire body shaking with the fear that he was gone.

Just when she was sure he was dead, he drew a deep breath and opened his eyes.

Sunshine let out a joyful cry as she saw his amber eyes. She hugged him close as the door behind them flew open.

The Daimons, the demons, and the two gods spilled into the room. There was no sign of Zarek anywhere. She only hoped they hadn't killed him.

Talon jumped up and put himself between Sunshine and the others.

Ash rose to his feet, ready to fight.

"It's midnight," Dionysus said with a laugh. "Let the show begin."

The demons moved aside and out of their midst appeared Acheron's "twin."

"Hello, Acheron," Styxx said in a tone that was neither kind nor welcoming. "It's been a while, hasn't it? Eleven thousand years or so?"

Talon held his breath. He couldn't believe what he was seeing.

He had suspected as much, but now the reality of it came crashing down on him. Ash had had a twin brother all this time.

Why had he hidden it? And how could Styxx still be alive and not be a Dark-Hunter too? It didn't make sense.

Styxx approached Acheron.

"Stand down, Styxx," Ash said sternly. "I don't want to hurt you, but I will if I have to. I won't let you release her."

Styxx met Talon's gaze and laughed. "It's like some bad soap opera, isn't it? Good twin, bad twin."

His furious gaze returned to Acheron. "But then, we're not really twins, are we, Acheron? We just happened to have shared the same womb for a while."

Styxx moved to stand behind Ash who tensed noticeably. It wasn't like Ash to allow anyone to do that to him and yet he appeared to be frozen by some unseen force.

Styxx was so close to him that barely a hand separated them.

They didn't touch.

Styxx leaned forward to speak in a low tone near Ash's ear. "Shall we tell him who the good one is, Acheron? Should I tell him which of us lived his life with dignity? Which of us was respected by the Greeks and Atlanteans and who was laughed at?"

Styxx reached his hand around Ash's neck and placed it in the exact spot where Ash's scar often resided.

He pulled Ash back against him so that he could whisper in Ash's ear in a language Talon couldn't understand.

Ash panted as if in the throes of a nightmare.

His eyes were haunted and glazed, his breathing ragged. Still he didn't move to break Styxx's hold.

Talon watched, unsure of what he should do. Surely Ash could handle this. He'd never known of anything Ash couldn't handle.

"That's it, Acheron," Styxx said in English, between clenched teeth. "Remember the past. Remember what you were. I want you to relive it all. Relive every foul thing you ever did. Every tear you made my parents weep for you. Every moment I had to look at you and feel ashamed that you bore my face."

Talon watched as tears filled Ash's eyes and he trembled. He didn't know what secrets Ash hid, but they must be hideous to affect him like this.

Personally, he didn't care what Ash had done in his past. For fifteen hundred years, he had never known Ash to be anything but caring and decent.

Secrets or not, the two of them were friends.

"Let him go," Talon ordered.

Styxx cocked his head, but he refused to release Ash. He tightened his grip on Ash's throat. "Do you remember when Estes died, Acheron? The way my father and I found you? I have never been able to forget it. Every time I have ever thought of you, it's the image I have. You're repulsive. Disgusting."

"Kill him," Dionysus ordered, "and open the portal."

Styxx didn't seem to hear him, his attention was fixed on Ash.

Camulus started toward them with a dagger. Talon rushed him and they fought for the weapon.

The demons attacked as Styxx continued to taunt and insult Ash.

"Kill him, Styxx," Dionysus ordered again. "Or we'll miss the portal."

Styxx pulled a dagger out from underneath his coat.

His fight with Camulus forgotten, Talon tried to reach them.

But he couldn't make it.

Styxx raised his hand and sent the dagger straight into Ash's heart. He buried it all the way to its hilt.

Ash gasped and arched his back as if something had possessed him. The dagger shot through the air, bouncing off a wall above Dionysus's head. Light poured out of the wound, then seared it closed.

In the next instant a shock wave went through the room, knocking everyone off their feet. Styxx was hurled to a far corner while the gods were pinned to the ground.

Acheron rose from the floor, to hover spread-eagled several inches above it.

Unable to stand upright against the unseen force, Talon crawled to Sunshine and held her close so that he could protect her from whatever was happening.

No one could stand. Not even the gods.

Lightning bolts shot through Acheron's body, blowing out the windows and the lights. Electrical energy snapped and hissed all around. Acheron laid his head back as bolts of light pierced his eyes and mouth. They seemed to shoot through him and then out, into the room, emitting bright flashes of light.

The Daimons and the demons exploded in one bright flash.

A winged dragon seemed to come out from under Acheron's sleeve and wrap itself around him as if it were protecting him.

Or perhaps devouring him.

In all his life, Talon had never seen anything like this.

"What the hell is that?" Camulus asked. "Styxx, what did you do?"

"Nothing. Is this from the portal opening?"

"No," Dionysus said. "This is something else entirely. Something no one told me about." He looked up at the ceiling and shouted, "Artemis!"

Artemis appeared and was immediately pinned to the floor with the rest of them.

Talon tightened his grip on Sunshine, who clutched him fiercely as she trembled against him.

Artemis took one look at Acheron and her face went flush with anger. "Who's the idiot who pissed off Acheron?" she demanded.

The two gods pointed to Styxx.

"You fools!" she snarled. "What were you thinking?"

"We needed to kill an Atlantean to raise the Destroyer," Dionysus said. "Acheron's the only one left."

"Oh, you are so stupid!" Artemis snapped. "I knew your plan had to be a bad one. You can't just kill him with a dagger. In case you haven't noticed, he's not human. Where was your brain?"

Dionysus curled his lips at her. "How was I to know your pet was a god-killer? What kind of idiot ties herself down to one of his kind?"

"Well, gee, what was I supposed to do?" Artemis shot back. "Hook up with Mr. All-powerful God-killer or get myself a Mardi Gras float and hang out with him?" She pointed to Camulus, who looked extremely offended by her comment. "You're such a moron," she said to her brother. "No wonder you're the patron god of drunken frat boys."

"Excuse me," Talon snapped at them. "Could you gods focus for a sec? We have a bit of a situation here."

"Oh, shut up," Dionysus snapped. "I knew I should have backed up when I ran you over."

Talon's jaw went slack. "That was you who hit me with the float?"

"Yes."

"Damn, boy," Camulus said to Dionysus. "You've fallen a long way down. Yesterday Greek god . . . today incompetent float driver. Sheez, and I hooked up with you? What was I thinking? Artemis is right, what kind of idiot picks a float to mow a guy down so that he can go home with his dead wife? You're lucky you didn't kill him then and blow the entire plan."

"Hey, have you ever tried to drive one of those things? It's not exactly easy. Besides, he's a Dark-Hunter. I knew it wouldn't kill him. I just needed something that would hurt him enough to make her take him home. Need I remind you that it did work?"

Artemis growled at them. "You're so pathetic. I can't believe we share a common gene between us."

Shooting a nasty glare at her brother, Artemis struggled against the invisible force that held them down. Like the rest of them, she couldn't reach Ash.

"Acheron!" she called. "Can you hear me?"

Disembodied laughter filled the room.

Ash leaned his head forward and more lightning flowed through him. The dragonlike beast tightened its grip around him and hissed a fiery breath at the goddess.

Artemis tried to climb up his leg, but she was forced back, away from him.

"You know, folks," Camulus shouted. "The idea was to kill Acheron, free Apollymi, and reclaim our god status. Not piss him off and end the world. Personally, I don't want to be ruler of nothing. But if someone doesn't stop this guy, that chant he's making is going to undo life as we know it and un-create the world."

"What are we going to do?" Sunshine asked Talon.

Only one thing came to his mind.

He had to bring Acheron to his senses.

Talon kissed her lips, then moved away from her. He hadn't gone through death to get her back, only to lose her now.

He summoned his remaining powers and allowed them to cocoon him. He no longer had his Dark-Hunter immortality, but he did retain all the psychic powers that had been given to him.

Hopefully they would be enough.

He rose slowly to his feet.

A lightning bolt came at him.

Talon deflected it. He moved slowly through the maelstrom until he reached Ash's side. So long as he stayed calm, he seemed to be shielded from Ash's wrath.

"Let it go, T-Rex."

Ash spoke to him in a language he didn't understand.

"He says to back off or die," Styxx translated. "He's summoning the Destroyer."

"I can't let you do that," Talon said.

The laughter echoed again.

Wanting to distract Acheron from what he was chanting,

and not knowing anything else to try, Talon rushed him.

He caught Ash about the middle and knocked him to the floor. The dragon arched up, shrieking.

Talon ignored it as he slugged Ash.

Sunshine held her breath as she watched the two of them fighting. The entire building felt as if it were going to break apart.

The floor beneath her shook.

They were locked together like two great primal beasts and the fate of the world lay in who would win and who would lose.

She whispered a prayer as she watched them, awed by the morbid beauty and grace of their battle.

Zarek came through the door, bleeding, and was immediately thrown backward, against a wall.

Artemis tried again to reach Acheron and again he tossed her back while he fought with Talon.

"I'll give the boy credit," Camulus said. "He always was a fighter."

Talon stopped fighting as he heard those words.

"You never could learn your place, Speirr. You never knew when you should just lay down the sword and play nice."

Camulus had been right. Up until now, Talon had never known when to fight and when to withdraw.

Being calm was what had allowed him to reach Ash.

Then, he remembered what Acheron had said to him on the night he'd become a Dark-Hunter. *"I can show you how to bury that pain so deep inside you that it will prick you no more. But be warned that nothing is ever given freely and nothing lasts forever. One day something will come along to make you feel again and with it, it will bring the pain of the ages upon you. All you have hidden will come out and it could destroy not only you but anyone near you."*

He wondered now who those words had really been meant for. Him or Ash?

He looked up at Acheron and saw the fury of the man who was attacking him. This was what Ash had meant that night.

Both of them had kept such a leash on themselves for so long that their fury blinded them to reason. It made them attack when they needed to withdraw and rethink the line of battle.

Closing his eyes, Talon summoned the soothing calm, as Acheron had taught him.

Ash rushed him again.

This time, instead of fighting, Talon embraced him like a brother.

Possessed of a strength and power Talon had never known before, he cupped Ash's face in his hands and tried to make his old friend see him.

Ash's features were no longer handsome or human. They were those of a twisted demon. His eyes were blood-red and yellow, and there was no mercy in them. They were cold. Vicious.

The colors swirled and danced like fire.

Talon had never seen anything like this before.

Who knew Ash had this kind of power?

But he had to stop him.

One way or another.

"Acheron," he said calmly, slowly. "Enough."

At first he didn't think Ash had heard him. Not until Acheron turned his head to see Sunshine on the floor.

"Talon," he rasped hoarsely. Ash's eyes flickered, then he looked back at Talon.

Suddenly, another shock wave shot through the room, this one in the reverse direction from the first. It was as if the unleashed power were drawing back into Acheron.

The dragon shot up toward the ceiling, then vanished.

Ash's features transformed back into the face of the man Talon had known these centuries past.

Ash blinked his now silver eyes and looked around as if he were waking up from a nightmare.

Without a single comment, Ash stepped away from Talon, wrapped his arms around his chest, and walked across the room as if nothing had happened.

As he passed Artemis, she reached for him, but he dodged her touch and kept walking.

Artemis turned on her brother with a snarl. "Just you wait till Dad gets his hands on you."

"Me? He knew what I had planned tonight. Wait until I tell him about Acheron!"

Artemis curled her lip. "Oh, shut up, whiny boy." She held her hand out and zapped him out of the room.

Styxx shrank back as Artemis turned her gaze to him.

"You," she said, her tone thick with loathing.

Styxx gulped audibly. "How can you protect something like him? After I died, I was sent to the Elysian Fields while he was—"

"No concern of yours," she said, interrupting him. "You and your precious family, you turned your backs on him and condemned him for something that wasn't his fault."

"Not his fault? Please." Styxx tried to say something more, but his voice vanished.

"That's better," Artemis said. "Funny, the two of you sound alike and yet *you* whine. Thank Zeus, Acheron doesn't have that repugnant quality. But then, he was always a man and not a sniveling little child."

She backed Styxx against the wall. "I can't believe you. I gave you a perfect existence. Your own island, filled with everything you could ever desire, and what did you do? You've spent eternity hating Acheron, plotting ways to kill him. You don't deserve mercy."

"You can't kill me," Styxx squeaked out. "If you do, Acheron dies too."

"And I curse the day the Fates bound your life force to his." She narrowed her eyes at him as if she wanted nothing more than to splinter him where he stood. "You're right. I can't kill you, but I can make living a worse hell than anything you can imagine."

"What are you going to do to me?" Styxx asked.

She smiled evilly. "You'll see, little human, you'll see."

Styxx vanished.

Artemis turned to face them. She took a deep breath and seemed to calm down exponentially.

"Take care of your soul, Speirr," she said to Talon.

"Know that it was purchased for you at a very dear cost."
Then she too vanished.

That left them alone with Camulus.

"Well," Talon said to the Celtic god. "It appears your
friends have abandoned you."

Camulus sighed. "What a pity. Excess, War, and Destruction. Together, we would have had a high time on
earth. Oh well. I shall just have to content myself with
taking her from you again. After all, she gave me her soul
and now I wish to claim it. And of course, the fun thing
about souls, they can only be claimed from a dead body."

Camulus started for her.

Talon pulled his srads out ready to do battle.

Out of nowhere, a bright flash lit the room. It faded into
a form that was almost as dear to Sunshine as Talon's.

"Grammy?" Sunshine asked in disbelief.

Her grandmother stepped between them and Camulus.
She faced the Celtic god with a stern glower. " 'Fraid not,
hon. You don't own bupkis."

Camulus was aghast at her appearance. "Morrigán?
What are you doing here? This doesn't concern you."

"Oh yes, it does." Her grandmother transformed from a
little old lady into the beautiful war goddess Talon had met
in his days as a mortal man.

Talon went cold.

Sunshine sputtered. "Excuse me? What is this?"

Her grandmother looked at Sunshine apologetically. "I
didn't mean for you to find out this way, Little Bit, but
Acheron and I had to stop them from unleashing Apollymi.
And to get Talon free, we needed the two of you here to
face Camulus."

Talon gaped.

Ash had known all about this? Why hadn't he told him?

The Morrigán turned back to Camulus. "Sorry, Cam. For
once *you* forgot to read the fine print. You agreed with Bran
to let Nynia be reborn to mortal parents for your scheme.
You never specified that her grandparents be mortal too.

"Since I couldn't help Speirr escape your curse and his

bargain without declaring war on you and Artemis, I figured the least I could do was return his wife to him in the body of someone you couldn't touch. Nynia now reborn as Sunshine is flesh of my flesh, blood of my blood. When Speirr drank from her neck, he took my blood into him and now he, too, has my protection."

Camulus cursed.

Her grandmother wrinkled her nose. "It just reeks, doesn't it? You can't kill her or him unless you want to fight me."

Talon exchanged a stunned look with Sunshine.

"One day, Morrigán. One day . . ." Camulus flashed out of the room.

The Morrigán took a deep breath, then turned around to face them. "Congratulations, kids."

"I'm free?" Talon asked, still unable to believe it.

The Morrigán nodded. "With your Dark-Hunter powers intact."

Sunshine hesitated. "Is he still a Dark-Hunter?"

"No," her grandmother said. "Artemis released him from his vow when she gave up his soul. Once psychic powers are bestowed on someone, they remain with them forever."

Sunshine smiled. "So he can go out into daylight now?"

"Yes." The Morrigán looked suddenly uncomfortable. "By the way, there's something I need to tell you two."

"What?" they asked in unison, both of them afraid of what she might say.

"Because of the way our pantheon works, the two of you are . . ." She bit her lip and wrung her hands.

"We are what?" Talon prompted, terrified of what was coming next. When dealing with a god, one could never be too careful.

"You're immortal unless you renounce it."

Sunshine blinked. "What?"

Her grandmother cleared her throat. "You and your brothers were born immortal, sweetie. It's why you still look like a baby even though you're pushing thirty."

"Does that mean Mom's immortal too?" she asked.

"No. Since your father isn't, she decided that she would

give up her immortality to age with him. But since it was my blood that gave her immortality, it was passed on from her to you and then from you to Talon."

Joy ripped through Talon. "You mean I never have to watch her die again?"

"Never. Not unless you choose to."

"Oh hell no," Talon said, laughing.

"I figured as much." The Morrigán stepped back. "Well, I'm sure the two of you have a lot to do. Like plan a wedding. Go make lots of babies." She took their hands into hers and then pressed them together. "I expect a large number of great-grandkids from you two."

The Morrigán vanished, leaving them to stare at each other in wonderment.

Sunshine licked her lips as she stared up at him. She couldn't believe everything that had happened tonight.

Most of all, she couldn't believe she had Talon for her own. "So what's our first course of action?"

That familiar look came into his amber eyes. "Try to make a baby?"

She laughed at him. "Sounds good, but it'll probably take us the rest of the night to get back to your cabin."

"True, but your loft isn't that far away . . ."

Sunshine smiled. "No, it isn't."

He kissed her hand and then led her from the room.

They left the building and blended into the monstrous crowd of Mardi Gras celebrants who were heading home. Sunshine's heart was light as they walked hand in hand, until they reached the street.

Gasping, she pulled Talon back as a giant float narrowly missed him. Then she burst out laughing. "What is it with you and the Mardi Gras floats?"

"It's not the floats, love, it's you. Whenever you're around, everything else fades from my notice."

She bit her lip impishly. "You keep talking like that and I'll definitely take you home, lock you up, and throw away the key."

"That's fine with me, just make sure you're naked when you do it."

Chapter 19

Zarek watched as Talon and Sunshine vanished into the crowd. He was happy for Sunshine, but he couldn't understand what the two of them felt for one another.

He'd never known any kind of love.

"Fuck it," he snarled, limping away from the building. He needed to get back to his townhouse.

"Dionysus will be coming for you."

He paused at the sound of Acheron's voice behind him. "So?"

Ash sighed as he drew near. "Can we not have a truce?"

Zarek scoffed at the thought. "Why? Mutual disdain suits us so well."

"Z, I'm too tired for this. Give me something to use with Artemis. Something that will make her want to give you another chance."

Zarek laughed bitterly. "Yeah, right. After what I saw in there you don't honestly expect me to believe that she pulls your chain, do you? How stupid do I look?"

"Things aren't always what they seem."

Maybe, but Zarek wasn't willing to give on this. He'd screwed himself royally tonight. The moment he had turned on the gods, he'd known they would make him pay.

Not that he cared.

Let them come for him.

"Look," he said, turning his back to Acheron, "I'm tired

and hungry, and I just want to lie down until my injuries heal, okay?"

"Okay."

Zarek paused as a group of college students stumbled past, laughing and teasing each other. He watched them curiously.

They turned a corner and vanished.

He looked around at the drunken tourists and locals who were screaming and cheering. It was almost one A.M. now and still the city was alive and vibrant even though the crowd was being told to disperse.

"When do I go back?" Zarek asked, dreading the answer.

"Tomorrow. Nick'll be by to pick you up about two. He'll have a tinted van that can get you out to the airstrip without exposing you to daylight."

Zarek closed his eyes and winced as he thought about returning to Alaska. A few weeks more and spring would arrive.

He'd be housebound again.

A flash to his left caught his attention. Three seconds later, a Daimon came running through the crowd. The Daimon flashed his fangs and snarled at Zarek as if he had no idea who or what he was facing.

Zarek smiled evilly, anticipating what he was about to do.

"What are you?" the Daimon asked when he failed to scare or intimidate him.

Zarek quirked his lips. "Oh please, let me give you the job description. Me, Dark-Hunter. You, Daimon. I hit, you bleed. I kill, you die."

"Not this time." The Daimon attacked.

Acting on instinct, Zarek caught him in the throat and used his claw to kill him.

The Daimon evaporated as Valerius came running up through the crowd.

The Roman was breathing hard and had obviously been chasing after the Daimon for some distance. Valerius looked at Ash and inclined his head, then he glanced to Zarek and froze.

Zarek met his shocked gaze without flinching. As per Ash's orders, he had shaved his goatee off.

Recognition darkened Valerius's eyes as he stood there without blinking.

Zarek gave him a wry smile. "Surprise," he said quietly. "Bet you didn't see that one coming."

Without another word, he headed off into the crowd, leaving Valerius and Acheron to their own ends.

Epilogue

Brothers. The word hung in Valerius's heart as he stared at the marble bust in his foyer. It was the face of his father.

It was the face of his brother.

Zarek.

Pain racked him as he stood there trying to reconcile the past with the present. Why had he never seen the resemblance?

But he knew. He'd never really looked at Zarek before tonight.

A pathetic lowborn slave, Zarek had been so far beneath his notice that he had barely glanced at the boy.

There had only been one time in their lives when he had truly seen him.

He couldn't remember now what Zarek had been beaten for. For that matter, he couldn't even remember which of his brothers had committed the deed that had caused Zarek's punishment. It could just as well have been his misdeed as that of one of the others.

He only remembered that it was the first time he had recognized Zarek as a person.

Zarek had been lying on the cobbled floor, clutching his arms over his chest, his naked, scarred back bloody and torn.

What had struck Valerius most was the look on Zarek's

face. The boy's eyes had been hollow. Empty. Not a single tear was evident.

Valerius had wondered at the time why Zarek hadn't cried at such a harsh beating, but then it had dawned on him that Zarek never cried.

The wretched slave had never uttered a single word while they beat him. No matter what they said or did, the boy just took it like a man, with no sobs, no begging. Just hard, cold stoicism.

Valerius couldn't fathom such strength from someone who was younger than him.

Before he realized what he was doing, he'd reached out and touched one of the welts on Zarek's back. Raw and bleeding, it had looked so painful that he tried to imagine what it would feel like to have *one* such wound, much less an entire back full of them.

Zarek didn't move.

"Do you need . . ." Valerius had choked on the last of the sentence. He had wanted to help Zarek up, but knew they would both be punished if anyone saw him do such a thing.

"What are you doing?"

His father's angry voice caused him to jump. "I-I-I was l-l-looking at his back," he answered honestly.

His father had narrowed his eyes on him. "Why?"

"I was c-c-curious." Valerius hated how he always stuttered around his father.

"Why? Do you think it hurts him?"

Valerius had been too afraid to answer. His father had had that dead look that often came into his eyes. A look that meant the kind, loving father he knew was gone and the brutal military commander was there instead.

As much as he loved his father, he feared the military commander, who was capable of most any act of cold-blooded ruthlessness, even against his own sons.

"Answer me, boy. Do you think it hurts him?"

He nodded.

"Do you care if it hurts him?"

Valerius had blinked back his tears before they betrayed

him. The truth was he did care, but he knew his father would fly into a rage if he ever dared breathe that aloud. "N-n-no. I don't c-c-care."

"Then prove it."

Valerius blinked, suddenly afraid of what that meant. "Prove it?"

His father had retrieved the whip from the stand and handed it to him. "Give him ten more lashes, or I will see *you* given twenty."

Heartsick and with his hand shaking, Valerius had taken the whip and delivered the lashes.

Unused to wielding a whip, he had missed Zarek's back entirely. His lashes landed on Zarek's unscarred arms and legs. Virgin flesh that had never been beaten before.

For the first time Zarek had hissed and recoiled from the lashes. So much so that the last lash ended up cutting across Zarek's face, right below his brow.

Zarek had screamed, cupping his eye as blood poured from between his dirty fingers.

Valerius had wanted to vomit as he heard his father praise him for blinding the slave's eye.

His father had actually patted him on the back. "That's it, my son. Always strike where they're most vulnerable. You'll make a fine general one day."

Zarek had looked up at him then and the emptiness was gone. The right side of his face had been covered in blood, but with his left eye, Zarek had conveyed all the pain and anguish he felt. All the hatred that was directed both inward and out.

That look was seared inside Valerius to this day.

His father had beaten Zarek again for the insolence of that glare.

No wonder Zarek hated them all. The man was entitled to it. More so now that Valerius knew the truth of Zarek's parentage.

He wondered when Zarek had learned the truth. Why no one had ever told him.

Angry, Valerius gripped the stone bust of their father.

"Why?" he demanded, knowing he'd never have an answer now.

And right then he hated his father more than ever. Hated the blood that flowed through his veins.

But at the end of the day, he was Roman.

It was his heritage.

Right or wrong, he couldn't deny it.

Lifting his head high, he retreated from the foyer to his bedroom upstairs.

But as he ascended the steps, he lashed out one last time.

Turning around, he kicked his leg out, catching the pedestal.

The bust of his father toppled against the stone marble floor and shattered.

NEW ORLEANS, THAT AFTERNOON

Zarek leaned back as the helicopter took off. He was going home.

No doubt he would die there.

If Artemis didn't kill him, he was sure Dionysus would. Dionysus's threat rang in his ears. For Sunshine's happiness, he had crossed a god who was sure to make him suffer even worse horrors than those in his past.

Zarek still didn't know why he'd done it, other than the fact that pissing people off was the only thing that truly gave him pleasure.

His gaze fell to his backpack.

Before he knew what he was doing, he took the handmade bowl out and held it in his hands.

He ran his hands over the intricate designs that Sunshine had carved. She had probably spent hours on this bowl.

Caressed it with loving hands . . .

"They waste their time over a rag doll and it becomes very important to them; and if anybody takes it away from them, they cry . . ."

The passage from *The Little Prince* ran through his mind. Sunshine had wasted much of her time on this and given him her work. She probably had no idea just how much her simple gift had touched him.

"You really are pathetic," he breathed, clutching the bowl in his hand as he curled his lip in repugnance. "It meant nothing to her and for a worthless piece of clay you just consigned yourself to death."

Closing his eyes, he swallowed. It was true.

One more time, he was going to die for nothing.

"So what?"

Let him die. Maybe then he would find some kind of solace.

Angered at his own stupidity, Zarek splintered the bowl with his thoughts. Pulling out his MP3 player, he scrolled to Nazareth's *Hair of the Dog*, put his headphones on, and waited for Mike to lighten the windows of the helicopter and let the lethal sunlight in on him.

It was, after all, what Dionysus had paid the Squire to do.

TARTARUS

Screams surrounded Styxx, piercing the blackness. He tried his best to see something and saw only the strange pinpoint ghost-lights of eyes that were desperate to be of use.

This place was cold. Icy. He felt his way along a craggy rock only to learn he was encased in a small, six-by-six-foot cell. There wasn't even enough room for him to lie down comfortably.

Suddenly, a light appeared beside him. It faded to form a young, beautiful woman with dark red hair, fair skin, and the green, swirling eyes of a goddess. He knew her instantly.

She was Mnimi, the goddess of memory. He'd seen her likeness countless times in temples and on scrolls.

She held an old-fashioned oil lamp in her hand as she studied him closely.

"Where am I?" Styxx asked.

Her voice was faint and gentle, like a breeze whispering through crystal leaves. "You are in Tartarus."

Styxx swallowed his outrage. When he had died aeons ago in ancient Greece, he had been placed in the paradise of the Elysian Fields.

Tartarus was where Hades banished the evil souls he wished to torture.

"I don't belong here."

"Where *do* you belong?" she asked.

"I belong with my family."

Her eyes were tinged by sadness as she regarded him. "They have all been reborn. The only family you have left now is the brother you hate."

"He is not my brother. He was *never* my brother."

She cocked her head as if listening to something far away from them. "Strange. Acheron never felt that way about you. No matter the times you were cruel to him, he never hated *you*."

"I don't care what he feels."

"True," she said as if she knew his innermost thoughts, as if she knew him better than he knew himself.

"Honestly, I don't understand you, Styxx. For centuries, you were given the Vanishing Isle as your home. You had friends and every luxury known. It was as peaceful and beautiful there as the Elysian Fields, and yet all you did was plot more vengeance against Acheron. I gave you memories of your beautiful home and family, of your peaceful and happy childhood to comfort you and instead of gaining pleasure from them you used them to fuel your hatred."

"Do you blame me? He stole everything from me. Everything I ever hoped for or loved. Because of him my family is dead, my kingdom gone. Even my life ended because of *him*."

"No," she said softly. "You can lie to yourself, Styxx, but not to me. It was you who betrayed your brother. You and your father. You let your fear of him blind you. It was your own actions that condemned not only him, but yourself as well."

"What do you know of it? Acheron is evil. Unclean. He defiles everything he touches."

She danced her fingers through the lamp's flame, making it flicker eerily in the darkness of the small cell. All the while her eyes burned him with their intensity. "That is the beauty of memory, isn't it? Our reality is always clouded by our perceptions of truth. You remember events one way and so you judge your brother without knowledge of how things were to him."

Mnimi placed a hand on his shoulder. The heat of it seared his skin and when she spoke her low tone sounded evil, insidious. "I am about to give you the most precious of gifts, Styxx. At long last, you will have understanding."

Styxx tried to run, but couldn't.

Mnimi's fiery touch held him immobile.

His head spun as he rushed back in time.

He saw his beautiful mother lying on her gilded bed, her body covered in sweat, her face ashen, as an attendant brushed her damp, blond hair from her pale blue eyes. He'd never known his mother to appear more joy-filled than she did that day.

The room was crowded with court officials and his father, the king, stood to the side of the bed with his heads of state. The long, stained-glass windows were open, letting the fresh sea air offer relief to the heat of the late summer day.

"It is another beautiful boy," the midwife happily proclaimed, wrapping the newborn infant in a blanket.

"By sweet Apollymi's hand, Aara, you've done me proud!" his father said as a loud jubilant shout echoed through the room. "Twin boys to rule over our twin isles!"

Laughing, his mother watched as the midwife cleaned the firstborn.

It was then Styxx learned the true horror of Acheron's birth, learned the dark secret his father had hidden from him.

Acheron was the firstborn son. Not him.

Styxx, who was now in Acheron's infant body, struggled to breathe through his newborn lungs. He had finally taken a deep, clear breath when he heard a cry of alarm.

"Zeus have mercy, the eldest is malformed, Majesties."

His mother looked up, her brow creased by worry. "How so?"

The midwife carried him over to his mother, who held the second-born babe to her breast.

Scared, the baby wanted only to be comforted. He reached for the brother who had shared the womb with him these past months. If he could just touch his brother, all would be right. He knew it.

Instead, his mother pulled his brother away, out of his sight and reach. "It cannot be," his mother sobbed. "He is blind."

"Not blind, Majesty," the eldest wisewoman said as she stepped forward, through the crowd. Her white robes were heavily embroidered with gold threads, and she wore an ornate gold wreath over her faded gray hair. "He was sent to you by the gods."

The king narrowed his eyes angrily at the queen. "You were unfaithful?" he accused Aara.

"Nay, never."

"Then how is it he came from your loins? All of us here witnessed it."

The room as a whole looked to the wisewoman, who stared blankly at the tiny, helpless baby crying for someone to hold him and offer him solace. Warmth.

"He will be a destroyer, this child," she said, her ancient voice loud and ringing so that all could hear her proclamation. "His touch will bring death to many. Not even the gods themselves will be safe from his wrath."

"Then kill him now." The king ordered his guard to draw his sword and slay the baby.

"Nay!" the wisewoman said, halting the guard before he could carry out the king's will. "Kill this infant and your son dies as well, Majesty. Their life forces are combined. 'Tis the will of the gods that you should raise him to manhood."

The baby sobbed, not understanding the fear he sensed from those around him. All he wanted was to be held as his brother was being held. For someone to cuddle him and tell him that all would be fine.

"I will not raise a monster," the king said.

"You have no choice." The wisewoman took the baby from the midwife and offered it to the queen. "He was born of your body, Majesty. He is your son."

The baby squalled even louder, reaching again for his mother. She cringed away from him, clutching her second-born even tighter than before. "I will not suckle it. I will not touch it. Get it away from my sight."

The wisewoman took the child to his father. "And what of you, Majesty? Will you not acknowledge him?"

"Never. That child is no son of mine."

The wisewoman took a deep breath and presented the infant to the room. Her grip was loose, with no love or compassion evident in her touch.

"Then he will be called Acheron for the river of woe. Like the river of the underworld, his journey shall be dark, long, and enduring. He will be able to give life and to take it. He will walk through his life alone and abandoned— ever seeking kindness and ever finding cruelty."

The wisewoman looked down at the infant in her hands and uttered the simple truth that would haunt the boy for the rest of his existence. "May the gods have mercy on you, little one. No one else ever will."

MOUNT OLYMPUS

As Ash approached Artemis's sacred temple, he opened the oversized double doors with his thoughts.

With his head held high, he gripped the padded strap of his black suede backpack and forced himself to walk through the ornate, gilded doorway into Artemis's throne room where she sat listening to one of her women play a lute and sing.

Nine pairs of feminine eyes turned to stare at him curiously.

Without being told, her eight attendants gathered their things and rushed from the room as they always did at his appearance. They shut the door discreetly behind them and left him alone with Artemis.

Vaguely, Ash remembered the first time he'd been allowed inside Artemis's private domain on Olympus. As a young man he had been awed by the intricately carved marble columns that framed the throne room. They rose twenty feet from the marble and gold floor under his feet up to the domed gold roof that was intricately embossed with wildlife scenes. Three sides of this room had no walls. Instead, it looked out over the perfect sky where white, fluffy clouds floated by at eye level.

The throne itself wasn't as ornate as it was comfortable. More an oversized chaise longue that could easily double as a bed, it occupied the center of the open room and was covered with lush, decadent ivory pillows with gold tassels and trim.

Only two men had ever been allowed to set foot inside this temple. Artemis's twin brother Apollo and him.

It was an honor Ash would gladly have ceded.

Artemis was dressed in a sheer white peplos that left her lithe body all but bare to his gaze. The dark pink tips of her breasts were hard and puckered against the gauzy material, and the hem of it rose high on her legs, showing him a glimpse of the dark auburn triangle at the juncture of her thighs.

She smiled seductively at him, bringing his attention back to her perfect, beautiful face. Her long, auburn curls seemed as iridescent as her green eyes while she watched him with fascinated interest. She lay on her side, her arms folded over the high back of the chaise and her chin resting on the back of her hand.

Taking a deep breath, Ash closed the distance between them and stood before her.

Artemis cocked a finely arched brow as she gazed ravenously at his body. "Interesting. You look more defiant than ever, Acheron. I see no proof of the submission you promised me. Do I need to revoke Talon's soul?"

He wasn't sure she had the power to do such a thing, but then, he wasn't willing to chance it. He'd called her bluff before and had lived to regret it.

He shrugged his backpack off his shoulder and dropped it to the floor. Then he removed his leather jacket and draped it over the backpack. Falling to his knees, he placed his hands on his leather-clad thighs, ground his teeth and lowered his head.

Artemis unfolded herself from the chaise and approached him. "Thank you, Acheron," she said breathlessly as she moved to stand behind him. She ran her hand through his hair, turning it golden blond and freeing it from its braid so that it spilled over his shoulders and chest.

Artemis brushed the hair on the left side of his neck aside, exposing the flesh beneath it to her gaze. She dragged a long fingernail down his bared skin, raising chills over his arms and chest.

And then she did the one thing he hated most of all.

She blew her breath across the back of his neck.

He fought down the urge to cringe. She, alone, knew how and why he hated that sensation. It was a cruel thing she did to remind him of his place in her world.

"In spite of what you might think, Acheron, I derive no pleasure from making you bend to my will. I would much rather have you here by your own choice—the way you used to come to me."

Ash closed his eyes as he remembered those days. He had loved her so much then. Had ached any time he was forced to leave her side.

He had believed in her and had given her the one thing he had never given anyone else—his trust.

She had been his world. His sanctuary. At a time when no one would acknowledge him, she had welcomed him into her life and had shown him what it was like to be wanted.

Together, they had laughed and they had loved. He had

shared things with her that he had never shared with anyone before or since.

Then, when he had needed her most, she had coldly turned her back on him and left him to die painfully. Alone.

She had spurned his love that day and had proven to him that in the end, she was just as ashamed of him as his family had been.

He meant nothing to her.

He never would.

The truth of it had hurt, but after all this time he had come to terms with it. He would never be anything more to her than a curiosity. A defiant pet she kept around for her own amusement.

Again in a gesture she knew he hated, Artemis knelt at his back, her knees brushing gently against his hips. She ran her hand over his shoulder, and then down the intricate bird tattoo on his arm.

"Mmm," she purred as she nuzzled his hair with her face. "What is it about you that makes me want you so?"

"I don't know, but if you ever figure it out, let me know and I'll be sure to stop it."

She sank her fingernails deep into his tattoo. "My Acheron, ever defiant. Ever vexing."

She ripped open his T-shirt and removed it from his body.

Ash held his breath as she pulled his back to her front and hungrily skimmed her hands over his bare chest. As always, his body betrayed him and reacted to her touch. Chills ran over his skin and his gut drew tight as his groin hardened.

Her hot breath fell against his neck as she ran her tongue along his collarbone. He leaned his head to the right to give her more access to him while she unlaced his tight leather pants.

His breathing ragged, Ash clutched his hands against his thighs and waited for what was to come.

She freed his swollen shaft and sheathed it with her hands.

Her tongue teasing his neck, she ran her right hand upward to the tip of his manhood where she stroked him until he was so hard for her that he hurt. He moaned as she dipped her other hand down and cupped and stroked him from underneath while her right hand continued to tease him.

"You're so large and thick, Acheron," she whispered hoarsely as she used her fingers to coat him in his own wetness so that she could stroke him even faster. Harder. "I love the way you feel in my hands."

She took a deep breath in his hair. "The way you smell." She nuzzled his shoulder with her face. "The sound of your voice when you say my name." She ran her tongue across his shoulder blade back to his neck. "The way your cheeks mottle whenever you exert yourself."

She nibbled his ear. "The look on your face when you release yourself inside of me."

She brushed her breasts against his spine so that she could whisper her next words in his ear. "But most of all, I love the way you *taste*."

Ash tensed as she sank her long canine teeth into his neck. The momentary pain turned quickly to physical pleasure.

Reaching over his shoulder, he cradled her head to his neck and rocked himself against her hands as she stroked him even faster than before. He felt her and her powers flowing through him, uniting them even closer than the intimacy of sex.

His head swam until he could see nothing. All he could feel was Artemis. Her demanding hands on him, her hot, living breath against his throat, her heart pounding in time to his.

They were synchronized. Her pleasure was his and, for this moment in time, they were one creature with one heartbeat, bonded on a level that transcended human understanding.

He felt her desire for him. Her need to possess every part of his mind, body, and heart. He felt as if he were drowning. As if she were pulling him far away from himself, into a cold, dark cell where he would never again find his way back.

He heard her whispering to him in his mind. *"Come for me, Acheron. Give me your power. Your strength. Give me all that you are."*

He fought against her intrusion, and as always, he lost the battle.

In the end, he had no choice except to give her what she wanted.

Ash threw his head back and roared as his entire body shook in complete orgasmic ecstasy. Still she drank from him, taking his essence and powers into her own body.

He was hers. Regardless of what he might think, want, or feel, he would always belong to her.

Panting and weak from her possession, Ash leaned back against her and watched as a thin trail of blood ran down his chest . . .

Epilogue

Sunshine smiled as she carried her small box of oil paints into the living room. She'd been intending to take them to her new studio that overlooked Talon's swamp, but as soon as she had caught sight of her husband hanging her paintings of his old cabin up on the wall, she'd stopped.

He didn't seem to know she was there. He had the hammer hanging out of his back pocket as he lifted the framed landscape and placed it on the wall.

As soon as the two of them had emerged from her loft after Mardi Gras, Talon had decided to build them their own house.

Together, they had designed every detail. An extremely large computer room and a garage to accommodate his toys, and an open, airy studio for her art. They even had a game room with shelves that displayed his massive collection of Pez dispensers. Snoopy took a prime location in the center of the middle shelf.

But her favorite room was the small one that adjoined their master bedroom suite. The one that would hopefully be a nursery someday.

"Did I get it centered?" he asked, surprising her that he knew she was standing behind him.

"Looks good to me."

He glanced at her over his shoulder and caught her gazing at his nicely shaped rear.

"I was talking about the painting."

"And I was talking about your butt, but the painting looks all right too."

He laughed as he neared her and took the box out of her hands.

He brushed his hand though her hair and gave her a light kiss. Sunshine reached around his hips and gave a tight squeeze to his heinie.

"You keep doing that," Talon said throatily, "and we won't get any more unpacking done today."

She gave him a devilish grin. "That's okay. It's not like we don't have the rest of eternity to move in."

"Well, in that case . . ." He set the box down and scooped her up in his arms.

Sunshine laughed as he headed toward the indoor pool. "Where are you taking me?"

His look was purely sexual. "To the only room we haven't broken in yet."

"You are insatiable."

"I know. Evil to the core."

As they passed the dining room, she made him put her down long enough to grab a small, wrapped package.

Talon frowned, then he tossed her over his shoulder and sprinted with her to the back of the house.

Sunshine was still laughing when he laid her down gently next to the pool.

"What's this?" he asked after she handed him her gift.

"It's a housewarming present for you."

He opened it to find an Eddie Munster Pez dispenser.

A wide smile spread across his face. "I can't believe you found one."

Sunshine lifted his scarred right hand and kissed it. Then, she turned it over in her hands and studied the swirling design of the burn.

The first thing Talon had done when he had taken her

to her loft had been to remove the scar from her hand that she had received from holding the medallion.

Now that scar resided on his hand instead of hers.

"I love you, Talon," she whispered. "More than you will ever know."

He fingered her cheek with his left hand as his amber eyes scorched her with their sincere intensity. "I love you, too, Sunshine. Thank you for your strength and for giving up soy products."

She laughed at that, then kissed him passionately.

Talon stepped away from her as he caught sight of the box she'd brought in a few minutes ago. It held a collection of things they had packed up from his desk, including the box that held Nynia's torc.

"I've been meaning to do something." He removed the torc from around his neck and placed it with Nynia's.

Sunshine frowned as she watched him slide open the door to the back porch that looked out over the swamp.

"What are you doing?"

"I'm putting the past to rest. As much as I loved Nynia, I love you more and I never want you to doubt whose eyes I'm looking into when I make love to you."

He drew back to toss the torcs.

Sunshine grabbed his hand. She knew exactly what those torcs meant to him and what he was doing for her.

Kissing his lips, she took them from him. She pulled back with a smile. "I will never doubt you, Talon."

She took his torc and returned it to his neck.

He smiled tenderly, then placed the other one around hers.

Her skin tingled from the feel of his hands on her collarbone.

Staring into his eyes, she remembered the night she'd met him. The sight of the float running him over.

Even though she should hate Dionysus for all he had put them through, she couldn't.

After all, had the incompetent god backed up, her story would have had an entirely different ending.